FIFTEEN BILLION YEARS I

ALPHA AND OMEGA

"Lo, I am coming like a thief! Blessed is he who is awake, keeping his garments that he may not go naked and be seen exposed!" And they assembled them at the place which is called in Hebrew Armaged'don."

Revelation 16: 15-16 (RSV)
Holy Bible

By Rand McLester

InfusedMedia Co. LLC
www.infusedmedia.co
1-888-251-6088

To Mom and Dad, who made everything possible

ACKNOWLEDGEMENTS

I would like to thank Rozi and Amy for their assistance with editing and proofreading; and also express my appreciation for Rozi's work with the book's cover design. Finally, I'd like to thank the Infused Media team who put it all together.

PART I

CHAPTER ONE

It was mid-October...

...In the not too distant future —*bzzzz*: the alarm.

Conscious, and another day, waking. Swept away with waning drowsiness were fleeting images of the night's slumber, as reaching over he snuffed the irritating drone with a hand. Throwing back the comforter and sitting up he pivoted on the edge of the bed planting both feet firmly on the carpeted floor. Cooler room air swept in displacing the snuggly, warm-from-under-the-covers feeling; then sensing the chill in the soles of his feet: "Cold again today." Muttered words. Still groggy, rubbing his eyes and impersonally scratching he mused, *why do women yawn and stretch in the morning —stupid joke;* but he smiled anyway. Lethargically he stumbled out of bed, stubbed his toe on an errant boot, wend a course for the bathroom and hot shower; then two cups, black.

Lingering over his second cup of coffee, elbows propped on the breakfast nook table and gazing pensively out the bay window, he drew a slow breath. The steam felt good, the aroma delicious. Taking another sip then cradling the mug with both hands: a sigh. "Today..." his mood sober, the word spoken softly. Reflective, mahogany eyes blinked defining crow's feet that tracked from the corners toward graying temples over skin weathered by forty years of stress. Momentarily he considered, then decided, *today.*

Darting a glance at the wall clock he thought, *time to go.* A two-mile walk up Continental Drive to the Complex, not a granola thing, he walked to stay fit. Rising from the table and grabbing his coat he locked the door behind him —committed, beginning— setting a strong pace with a ground-eating stride. Two steps into the day his breath expelled as vapor clouds in the chilly morning air creating minute ice crystals on a dark mustache, so he walked quickly maintaining a constant gait knowing Reed would be waiting to join him along the way. And as he whisked along the bike path Doctor John Ames surveyed the city.

Butte, Montana: the copper industry's crown jewel for one hundred years, since the late eighteen-hundreds when mining magnates Marcus Daily and Augusta Hines influenced world commerce with corporate dominance of copper and metals mining from 'The Richest Hill on Earth'. Later mining was perpetuated by the Anaconda Company and Atlantic Richfield then experienced an inevitable decline; but not before their ambitions created the Berkley Pit, a crater chiseled into the earth sixteen hundred feet deep, seven thousand feet long, and fifty-six-hundred feet wide.

Underground was an unseen world of forty-degree temperature and stifling humidity with hundreds of miles of hardrock tunnels that tracked highgrade until the veins petered out: tunnels that were transformed to spiderwebs of pitch-blackness when the mining quit and the lights were turned off.

Below the city snaked seemingly endless ribbons of subterranean passages reaching from the old shafts and headframes, up the hill, uptown, to historic landmarks like the Dumas Hotel, Stockman's Bar, Finlen Hotel, Acoma Building, the old City Hall, and others —all the way to Chinatown. The mining tunnels; down-casts, up-casts, stopes, drifts and crosscuts; and the old steam tunnels and sewer system combined to create a world below the surface, a darker world of dank blackness… and the hope of a possible future.

Above was urban sprawl, a menagerie of old and new, not quite blended together, almost melded at the seam. Old Butte climbed with its steep inclined streets like a checkerboard concrete pour over a gray-tan landscape. On the west Excelsior, Montana and Main rose to Walkerville then abruptly halted at the Berkley Pit and North Ridge on the barren north boundary where Interstate Fifteen scaled

Woodville Hill on its way to Helena. Shaped solidly by granitic mountains the city rested in the shadow of the East Ridge embracing structural steel transmission towers on 'Exell Heights' and the Virgin Mary's ninety-foot statue, 'Our Lady of the Rockies', atop mountains rising another three thousand feet and looking down upon a cloistered metropolis.

In the valley lay the flats and 'Timber Butte' where residential homes filled the basin to capacity, and on the south, pushed against the towering Continental Divide until no more homes would fit, the newer part of town. Farther west, beyond the city, was more development extending along the valley contorted by nature's rock formations and reaching out until Butte and Anaconda almost combined as a single entity known as Commerce Valley, marshaled with three common denominators: microprocessors, environmental concerns, and money.

* * *

Moving quickly, wind in his face…

…Footfalls crunching on frozen ground, Ames blinked the cold away. As far as the eye could see green energy development and computer related industry filled the valley swallowing up Silver Bow Creek and all natural life forms, converting them to concrete and steel: at one end Anaconda's towering smokestack, a relic from her smelter times, and the other, the United States Scientific Research Complex, where the Berkley Pit once had been.

The Berkley Pit was an open pit mine excavated during the old times; then, when Arco turned the pumps off, abandoned and flooded with toxic water laden with heavy metals. Once an unnamed lake and the world's largest superfund site, now reclaimed and refilled, resurrected with high-level defense secrecy, only a select few privy to the extent of the Complex.

The Science Complex was a circular building two thousand feet across, a wheel with six connecting halls like spokes converging on a center hub, an auditorium two hundred feet in diameter. Two stories tall, it was constructed of granite, steel, and tinted plate glass. And the sunlight at five thousand feet, intense in the pristine atmosphere, sparkled on the immense structure and its secrets.

But everyone has heard the old axiom: 'All that glitters isn't gold'. And that was only the beginning, the first thread in a ball of twine and an unraveling of events and circumstance. There was more, much more...

...Beyond any imaginings.

* * *

On that cold October morning...

...In the not too distant future.

"Why is it, Doc, that every time this subject comes up we invariably seem to assume adversarial roles?" Reed was a young man recently graduated from 'Montana College of Technology', with sandy hair, green eyes and fair complexion, who spoke. His well-muscled frame was wrapped in a cobalt-blue pea coat, collar turned up to deflect the wind. Having met along the way they walked briskly toward the Science Complex.

"Probably 'cause your attitude is so predictably inflexible." Wide-awake from the cold Ames bowed his head slightly, chin into his coat; his stature, slender build, and salt-and-pepper hair complimented his confident demeanor and *'Marlboro man'* looks. Both men wore blue pea coats, gray western shirts, Levi-Strauss jeans and solid work boots, all graciously provided by 'the company'.

"I really don't think I'm that inflexible. We've pretty much proven the 'Big Bang' theory since the nucleus of the pulsar was deciphered, and the current study on dark matter and dark energy has corroborated a substantial part of the universe proportion concept."

"Reed..."

"Since the Hubble, the Hipparcos satellite, the Microwave Anisotropy Probe, the Youngstown, and the elliptical probe spectrometer —wherever that is by now..."

"—About nine trillion miles into deep space."

Facetiously: "Yeah, figures you'd know."

Ames grinned. "The Hubble gave us a first real view of deep space. Hipparcos and MAP determined with reasonable probability that the universe is about fourteen or fifteen billion years old. The Youngstown..."

"—I know Doc. And even with everyone else still debating the concept, I 'spose you've figured out the 'String Theory'."

"Not yet. Still working on that."

Reed shrugged. "All I'm saying is that it's like a puzzle, more and more the pieces have come together."

"Precisely my point," the other came back. "In all the known universe, isn't there a phenomenally exact order?"

"Agreed, there is a definite order; but it could be random chance, one in a billion. It doesn't necessarily mean there's a, God behind it all."

"Nor does it imply there isn't."

Offhand, changing the subject: "Doc, do you ever get the feeling of having done something before? You know... de'ja vu."

"I suppose from time to time everyone does; why?"

"Nothing really," shrugging the thought aside, "just wondering." Reed's question stirred a memory in the back of Ames' mind, something he couldn't quite put his finger on.

Still walking, both were silent a moment.

Dormant grass, meticulously trimmed before winter, lay a brown carpet below naked aspens, evenly spaced native junipers and Douglas fir. The grounds were impeccably maintained for appearances, as was the building —and they entered the Complex dwarfed by its enormity.

"Creative ingenuity," Reed observed extemporaneously as the tinted plate glass doors sealed automatically behind them.

"What is?"

"This Complex."

Ames commented solemnly, "More so than you'd think."

They continued across the expanse of carpeted lobby with its twenty-foot cathedral ceiling and mixture of accent and valance lighting intended to create the, *living room*, homespun effect. Located in the spacious foyer's center stood a million-dollar, circular, oak, reception area desk occupied by no less than six professionals, all absorbed with their work or engaged in subdued conversation with mixed company near the work station. The hall's periphery was a continuous face of wainscot and glass, ample offices set apart from one another with ceiling height divider walls and individual entrance doors. The oak veneer and 'Windex' sparkle proudly displayed busy suit-and-tie executives within the extravagant quarters, occupying their expensive time with unknown important business.

"Doctor Ames," a woman's voice from across the foyer redirecting the attention of both men toward the reception desk.

"Yes, Karen."

As she approached: "General Smith flew to Brazil last night concerning escalated guerrilla activity there. Your eleven o'clock meeting has been canceled." She was a pretty woman, short dark hair, mid-thirties.

"Thank you." He smiled, then added, "How's your daughter; she's two now, or three?"

"She's three, spunky as ever, and you're certainly welcome," her reciprocal smile a moment longer than customary. Reed grinned and Karen noticed turning away slightly embarrassed, leaving the men waiting for the elevator.

"Do you find something humorous about Smith being in Brazil this morning?" Ames inquired observant of his smirk.

"No, Doc."

The elevator arrived but the doors remained closed when the lobby indicator lighted. Each whisked a security pass through a scanner and the doors opened.

Entering the elevator Ames asked, "Then what's so amusing?"

"I think Karen likes you."

Shaking his head. "I wonder about you sometimes, you know it."

"I still think she likes you."

"I know."

The elevator descended: that, *going down*, feeling. When the doors opened they headed straight-away down a long corridor: neutral beige, the color of calm, the concrete texture of walls periodically interrupted by closed doors and following a double row of ceiling fluorescents to a vanishing point ahead.

Reed queried, "What did you mean by, 'more so than you'd think'?"

Ames glanced at the other as they walked, hesitated, then inquired: hushed words. "How many sub-levels are in this complex?"

"Four."

"No, there are six," he told him. Puzzled, Reed didn't speak. "And the construction workers who built it, can you tell me where any of them are now?"

Also lowering his voice, "Offhand? Not really," Reed answered, their footfalls creating hollow, empty echoes.

A glance: "You knew some of them, didn't you?"

"Yes."

"They're gone —all of them— three thousand military personnel."

"Military?"

"Army Corps of Engineers, not civilian construction workers; they were military, dispatched to South Africa for the Tembale Dam Project the day the Complex was completed." And matter-of-fact: "You recall the fiasco there when nearly everyone was killed by friendly fire?"

"Yeah."

"The project was scrapped, because it was never intended to be built, just contrived to eliminate everyone who worked on this project. And the few who did return have all died of natural causes, all in less than two years."

"How do you know that?"

Almost a whisper: "I could access the secure files until recently. Now the codes have been overwritten —and I'm sure General Smith had something to do with that."

"But you helped design the Complex," Reed said. "You know more about it than he does."

"Not what's on sub-levels five and six."

The young man asked, "How could two complete sub-levels be constructed without anyone even knowing?"

"Specialized engineers and Seal teams. They were built with caissons while the pit was still flooded, same as the others, standard underwater construction techniques. Build level six, backfill, drain some water. Build level five, backfill, drain more water —and so on." Ames paused, then continued, "Hell, no one even knew what the Complex was until the pit was back to grade and work began at ground level. Thirty years to dig it out, five to fill it in, quite an accomplishment really if you consider it. But there's more." Then more softly again: "I know there are six sub-levels; worked on it from inception to completion. Now blueprints, schematics, files—everything—has vanished. Seems peculiar."

"Smith?"

"I would suspect," he confirmed. "Five and six are similar to the other sub-levels, a six-spoke pattern from the central control hall, but with extensive reinforcement and no interconnecting corridors on the outer perimeter."

"Why make each corridor a dead end?"

"I'm not sure. They're also offset. They don't lie directly below the radiating corridors above them, but all six are spaced two hundred-forty feet apart in depth. That's consistent at all levels."

Reed thought while they continued walking, then intimated, "You do have a suspicion though, don't you?"

"Yes," the other confided, "I believe this complex was designed for military application; scientific research is only a contrivance." They stopped at a numbered door where a retinal scan allowed passage to the laboratory within. Before entering Ames turned. "Incidentally," he said, "Karen and I are close. Her husband Allan was one of the construction workers who didn't return from the Tembale Project."

The other side of the door: Level Three.

The expansive room appeared more like a warehouse than a laboratory, with a high ceiling and recessed fluorescent lighting. It was complete to a research engineer's wildest fantasy containing evenly spaced aisles of chrome-basket bins, storage compartments, and shelving cluttered with scientific paraphernalia and electronics —all the way to the far walls. An area was set aside for an office with plush furnishings, complete kitchenette, bath, and a sixty-inch, wall-mounted flat-screen television, as well as a separate work area with counters and cabinets and computer workstation that could sexually arouse any hacker.

Crossing the room without slowing down Ames picked up the remote clicking the power button waking the television, and still aiming he changed channels: 277-15-4-29. A blank section of the rear wall raised drawbridge-fashion revealing another room behind it. Not removing their coats both men crossed into the second laboratory. The wall section closed behind them, rumbling to a, *thud*. The television turned off.

Reed mused, "'Big Brother'[1]would have a cataclysmic contraction if they knew about the spare room, Doc."

Stoic: "When one designs a facility on the scale of this it doesn't hurt to include a few perks," and the smile. "That's one of the intrinsics of research and development."

"Well I can certainly appreciate your point of view," Reed quipped, "but secreting a complete lab is a considerable perk, don't you think?"

"Adequate comes to mind… justifiably adequate."

The second laboratory approximated the first in size but contained more equipment and twice the computing capacity. Every bit of available space was utilized, so much so it resembled a collectible dealer's back room. Counters, shelves and boxes, it was crammed to capacity with the exception of one darkened corner, a niche separate and unto itself.

"Justifiably adequate," the young man repeated stopping at a desk smothered with paperwork and a pile of electronics. He opened the bottom drawer, turned the handle one hundred-eighty degrees and a concealed side panel eased open revealing two weapons resembling hybrids from a 'Buck Rogers' fiction novel and short automatic rifles with silencers. Reed removed the weapons from the rack, cradling them, examining them almost reverently. "Brilliant comes to mind Doctor, justifiably brilliant." His muffled words faded in his breath as he examined each weapon, wiping a bit of foreign matter from one. "Frequency pulse laser." The tenor of his voice reflected pride. "One small step for man... one giant light-blast for mankind," he surmised, then a grin.

"What were you saying?" Ames asked, preoccupied at a computer.

"Just thinking," retrieving two belt knives from the open desk compartment, then before stepping away easing it closed with a knee.

"We ready?" without looking up from the monitor.

Reed answered abstractly, "Ready as we'll ever be."

Ames nodded, said, "Time to go," focusing his attention on another monitor.

Reed smiled.

"Computer... voice recognition code," Ames stated clearly.

"Access," a sultry, synthesized voice responded. The monitor blinked to life with a silhouetted 'Smiley Face': yellow on blue.

"Computer... is data transfer complete?"

"Yes, Doctor Ames. Compression transfer to IBM hard drive and micro disc complete."

Ames retrieved a two-inch disc from the CD port of the computer, slipped it into a gray antimagnetic envelope and put it in his shirt pocket. "Computer..." he hesitated, took breath, then: "Run program three, two, one, Philadelphia."

"Doctor Ames..." the machine responded.

"Yes?"

"The reliability of the IBM unit is ninety-nine point eighty-nine percent; mine is much greater."

"Yes computer; I am aware of that."

"Doctor Ames..."

"Yes computer."

"My logic chip has two-fold capacity of the IBM."

"I am also aware of that," Ames' voice was softer, almost sad, his attention focused on the smiley face, "but you can't go with us, only your data can."

'Smiley Face' frowned. "Yes, Doctor. I will miss you. Three, two, one, Philadelphia ready; press, 'enter'."

A single keystroke, almost regretfully, "I'll miss you too." Both watched silently as the computer deleted files, folders and directories, then scored and melted the hard drive rendering all information irrevocably lost.

"Three, two, one, Philadelphia complete, system INI deleted." The smiley face disappeared. The monitor went dark.

"See you when we get there," Ames whispered.

"It's almost spooky," Reed commented, "almost as if it were alive; you know, with feelings and emotions. You 'spose we've gone too far with technology?"

"Sometimes I wonder, Reed. Sometimes I wonder."

* * *

Without speaking...

...Ames walked to a wall switch near the unlit corner of the laboratory, swept a hand past a P.I.R. motion detector and the overhead fluorescents flickered then turned on illuminating a solitary object, a geodesic sphere twelve feet in diameter, geometrically beautiful and symmetrical, constructed of metal polyhedral lattice framework and translucent polycarbonate sections with metallic-flake embedded throughout: a giant shimmering ball from floor to ceiling.

Without fanfare Reed walked to the sphere. "Voice recognition, Reed," he said clearly, and after an inconspicuous red sensor in the structure wall turned green, sliding translucent panels whisked apart allowing access. Reed stepped up and inside and once more the light turned red.

At the portal he stopped. "Voice recognition, Ames." The light blinked to green again and he entered, and once inside: "Hatch closed." The door closed and disappeared.

Inside, the sphere was a circular control console with two upholstered captain's chairs locked on sliding tracks in the expanded-metal platform floor. From below the platform to the top of the domed ceiling the interior walls were overlaid with horizontal rows of magnetic coils, each row evenly spaced a couple of inches from the next, all of them perfectly aligned. The configuration allowed outside light to filter through the pellucid bullet-resistant polycarbonate and supplement the interior lighting causing the metallic-flake imbedded within the plastic panels to render a glitter effect. A second platform, below the first, was chock-full of neatly packed fuel cells sealed in black and yellow HazMat wrapping-plastic.

Seated, they checked instrumentation. "Fuel cells one hundred percent."

"Time travel, fact or fiction," Ames commented. "Engage."

Reed keyed the control panel and instantly a magnetic field whirled around them. Their hair stood straight out as if from electrocution, clothes puffed as though shot full of compressed air —or from an awful windstorm— skin stretched, teeth clenched —and the energy within the sphere soared.

"Light speed," Ames mouthed without words.

The exterior of the sphere glowed with rainbow hues, nearing transitional flux, the critical point of crossover, just a fraction beyond the speed of light.

—Then suddenly

Enveloped within shimmering trails of minutiae light, afterburn of subatomic particles, so incredibly beautiful... trillions of electrons, ions, protons and neutrons with energy trails of brilliant, resplendent sparkles —and the sphere was swallowed by their swirling radiance.

A dazzling magnetic cloud whirling around it, sparkling like fairy dust...

...A shrill whine —*pop*—it was gone.

***

Inside...

"...We did it!" Reed marveled at the same instant everything within the sphere turned shades of gray.

14

There was no color during time travel, color being an optical concept. Their clothes draped back to their bodies, their hair unwound and things seemed normal with the exception of their black and white state: like Lawrence Welk from a 1950's television set.

Ames asked, "How far?"

"Twenty... five years."

—And, *whoom!*

An explosion

—So incredible they were stunned.

Instant, brilliant white light from outside the sphere: blinding and penetrating. Intense heat, the next sensation —all around them— soaking in through the polycarbonate walls, then yellow light and what must have been flames. The heat was suffocating now, the plastic panels bowing and buckling; then red light and more heat, becoming unbearable.

Losing consciousness, "Accelerate," Ames coughed. "Accelerate."

Reed worked the keypad, steam and smoke wafting from the floor in wisps of gray-black fingers crawling with liquid motion, through the flexing walls, from everywhere it seemed. Both men now semiconscious, dizziness sweeping upon them, fading; and all around them incomprehensible fire and heat and light. Swimming images of confusion, light and fire —heat, opaque, and smoke— vertigo, liquid, and faint. Muddled... fading.

Finally, the world outside began to cool. And they continued through time.

* * *

The sphere cooled quickly...

...With the temperature drop awakening him suddenly, shaking himself back to awareness, Ames checked computer data. Reed, still groggy, momentarily slouched in his seat.

The cloud in his brain dissipating, to himself, Ames remarked in passing "Sixty-eight thousand years advance flux." Then he smiled, "Give or take."

One hand pushing himself up straight, one hand holding his head, "Not like the sudden stop after the fall that kills you with time travel," Reed finally muttered. And trying to press his frizzed hair back down, "It's that first step to neutral magnetism beyond light speed —what a rush."

"Sure enough. This is turning into an epic adventure," Ames half-joked.

Good-natured sarcasm: "Not yet, but it might."

Ames smiled. "Not yet?"

"Nope, not yet —but it might." Reed grinned. "Yes-siree-bob, it just might."

Both men proud, and now a little more relaxed, absorbed the satisfaction of their accomplishment. For a few minutes neither spoke, both wondering what was going on outside.

Eventually Ames decided, "Let's have a look at the future," then grinning, "and you can stop at a 'Seven-Eleven' and buy a comb."

"They'll probably be closed."

Ignoring that, "Coming up on ten million," Ames said clipping his sheath knife to his belt.

Reed considered: "December. Missed Easter."

Ames, adjusting the knife: Do you even know what Easter is about?

The other, not looking up, checking the panel: "Wasn't that when they crucified Christ and put him in the tomb, and after three days He rolled the stone away and stepped out into the sunshine, saw His shadow —then went back in for six more weeks of winter?" Ames leaned away, offering 'the look'. Reed looked back. "What?"

"You'll go to Hell for saying things like that, and I don't want to be too close —just in case you get struck by lightning."

Already wearing his knife Reed grinned and commented, "Let's see how it's evolved."

"You're incorrigible." Color blinked back on and both unsnapped their harnesses; then analytically, "Die-hard agnostic," Ames mused.

As they got up Reed reminded, "With all due respect, Doc, what about natural forces and evolution?"

Ames stepped to the door, turned and squared with his friend. "I believe in those too, but without faith in Someone or something more, humanity's existence is pointless." Reed said nothing but considered everything as Ames swept a hand past the sensor and the portal opened to an altered world.

CHAPTER TWO

"December twenty-fifth…"

…Ames' words were solemn. The sphere was on a prominence overlooking a world now barren, desolate and dark, a world of greylight.[2] Both quiet for a while, scanning, thinking, taking it all in. Below them lay a valley rising to another hill some distance beyond. Black sand with the glittery sparkle of obsidian covered the surface, as far as the horizon, interspersed with gray-brown tundra worn like a tattered mantle. There were no trees. A cold dry wind rattled the occasional scrub brush or ragweed. Nothing else grew here anymore.

The sky was empty, not a single cloud, the shade of twilight, glowing eerily, surrounding the sun, not yellow anymore, eclipsed by the moon, a strange color of red, fading away… dying. The entire world seemed to whisper foreboding with the wind; and they both felt it, like being alone and turning to look when you sense someone might be behind you… and no one is.

"Christmas in ten million years," Reed said to himself, "what have we done to our world?"

Ames thought aloud, "The true meaning of Christmas can be written on a brown paper bag." Reed looked at him. "Love," Ames whispered; then a sigh, "that's what Christmas was all about."

This time they agreed.

"Looks like mankind has about loved 'Mother Earth' to death."

Sadly: "It sure does." Ames continued to study the sky.

Reed knelt poking his hand in the black sandy soil, let it dribble between his fingers, scooped again working it in his palm, thinking. After a moment he stood.

"Doc," offering the sand to Ames. The man took the soil, surprised by its temperature, also manipulated it. "Kind of strange, isn't it?" The question was rhetorical. "Took me a minute. It's cold as ice, literally."

"And?"

"It's soft. Anything that cold should be frozen solid."

"Moisture." Ames looked at the sky again, still fondling the soil in his hand. "No clouds," thinking about it, "no precipitation, no water; just a dry, cold wind, and a dehydrated world."

"At least we still have the sun," Reed said. Then considering, changing the subject, "But fusion reactions don't diminish like a campfire burning down to embers; it should go white dwarf or supernova."

Ames agreed. "Deep space hasn't changed so fusion would be the same. Flare activity couldn't consume it, not enough time has passed. Ten million years isn't much in galactic time." He quit talking and thought.

Reed surveyed the horizon.

"Do you suppose," Ames finally began again, "the sun could be losing density; decreasing mass and temperature, but maintaining its volume?"

"Why, Doc?"

"Theoretically that effect could be caused by a black hole, or perhaps dark matter, or some anomaly we're unaware of."

"And that being the scenario," Reed prompted.

Half-jokingly, "Well, we might end up getting sucked into some parallel universe or the next 'Star Wars' sequel." Then more pensive: "I really don't have a clue."

"A world condemned to die," Reed muttered.

"Maybe."

"Are you considering other possibilities, Doc?"

Ames inhaled a deep breath. "There are always possibilities."

Reed grinned, encouraged by his friend. "The eternal optimist."
"Perhaps," Ames granted.

Eyes scanning the greylight landscape again, pointing to their left, Reed suggested, "Appears to be a city out there." Ames smiled, and the younger man knew. "Yeah," a lighter note in his voice, "well snug up your 'Hush Puppies', 'cause it looks like it's a long way." Reed slipped an arm through the sling on his weapon and waited.

Ames snugged the butt end of his into his armpit and nodded. "Just like walking to work." They commenced with a brisk pace.

* * *

Cold and constant: the wind...

...The city proved to be farther than it appeared and the ground-cold seeped quickly through to their feet. Distance can be deceiving over open terrain, the government-issue pea coats warm enough, but with the relentless wind, just barely. Fortunately, Levi-Strauss still made excellent blue jeans.

As they approached the outskirts of the city its most striking features glared starkly. The buildings were all square and without doors, windows, or roofs: four sandstone-type walls about twenty feet high rising from the ground. There were no streets or sidewalks; instead an elevated span of worn expanded-metal screen floor was set in place approximately halfway to the top of the structures. Roughly half the buildings were covered by red transparent domes anchored at each of the four corners and arched so the wall length was open.

The surrounding terrain, as far as possible to see, was black sand; but the ground the city was built on appeared to be a damp, multicolored mud similar to that in the geyser basins of Yellowstone Park in the past —a time long in the past. Around the perimeter of the city stairs led from the black sand to the platform, however, nowhere within the city was there access down to the mud floor.

Wary, alert, both scaled the stairs to the platform, their footfalls resonating with metallic tangs as they proceeded. The wind was their only companion, a constant one, incessantly nagging at their hair just above their collars. The city was quiet, seemed completely deserted. Looking around, they entered through what must have been a main artery, wider than most of the other walkways, perhaps one hundred feet across and stretching several miles before them to the opposite end of the city. Side by side they proceeded cautiously, observing, and not speaking for some time. No one was around.

Finally, "What do you think?" Reed asked, almost a whisper.

"Curious."

"What does that mean?"

"Means I don't know. What do you think?"

Lightly scratching his cheek, contemplating, Reed said, "Unusual construction by our standards, but undoubtedly serves a purpose here. No roofs, but without precipitation and with a constant climate, roofs might be unnecessary." Then considering, "But it is cold for dwellings open to the elements." Looking around: "Buildings appear to be made of sandstone, perhaps transported from another location. Don't see how though, haven't seen any type of machinery." Pointing: "Those dome bubbles could be solar collectors or moisture condensers. Only speculation at this point."

Glancing at the expanded-metal screen floor, "As far as these raised walkways, streets —whatever— the obvious assumption is they'd rather not be at ground level. The reasoning for that is a bit unclear though. Assuming wild animals would approach from the outskirts as we did would rule out its being for protection. If the inhabitants don't want to track through the mud down there, it seems, with all the empty countryside it would have been more logical to build a city somewhere else. It's not like this was the only location available.

Both continued without speaking for a couple minutes longer until at length Reed observed, "Where there's mud there's water, and they must need it, but..." he paused, considering again.

Ames nodded. "But... that's the part that doesn't quite figure."

Reed began to say something then stopped. "No, that doesn't make sense either," finally deciding, "have to think on it a while."

They turned from the central street toward one of the structures supporting a dome bubble, and circling behind it they found a ramp built into the rear wall and ascending to the top. They walked up, looked inside beneath the dome, and saw a massive array of glass tubing and hollow rods, each perhaps three inches in diameter. Inside the building the ramp descended ending at a platform near the bottom which was partially concealed by ground fog.

Followed by Reed Ames eased inside and down, carefully avoiding the glass menagerie. Half-crawling, he made his way to the center of the floor, and brushing the mist aside with a hand uncovered a small circular pond of clear liquid. He cupped a handful, smelled it, then tasted it.

He grinned. "It's water."

"Using condensers to collect it. Makes sense."

Rising, Ames asked, "Thirsty? It's good water, distilled."

Reed smiled. "Perhaps, Doctor, just a sip," and he knelt and drank, then followed Ames back to the top of the wall.

Continuing toward the city center, and after passing several of the buildings with no domes, they turned and approached one of the nondescript structures that rather resembled a stone box without a top. Circling it they found no ramp, instead, an incline of protruding spikes; so they climbed up and peered inside. The gagging stench of death —of a burned, ruptured corpse in an autopsy suite— reached out and smacked them in the face, an awful smell that soap can't wash off.

Reflexively jerking back, "Aww, kick the dog," Reed coughed out, trying to catch his breath, repulsed.

"Makes your eyes water," Ames admitted. "Wish we had some 'Vicks'."

Reed, blinking, trying to clear his head, said, "Whoa— I don't think even 'Vicks' would help."

They turned toward each other, took a deep breath, then looked inside again. There were six or seven visible humanoid skeletons, in various stages of decomposition cresting piles of raw flesh, entrails, and what must have been many more bodies heaped on the floor. Thick layers of fungi and mold partially concealed anything underneath and slimy, yellow-green fluid bubbled and oozed filling in lower places resembling split-pea soup depressions. With hoarding fingers, the mold had incessantly crept up the interior walls like black-webbed tentacles reaching to consume all the coagulated blood stains splattered and still visible above.

In the center of the room was a steadily glowing red spiral coil mounted on a raised, square, stone base —nothing else. The men moved back from the interior edge of the wall, both exhaling, then taking a breath.

Reed wondered aloud, "Do you suppose they're cannibals?"

"Well, now that you mention it..."

"—Don't say it, Doc. This is some serious shit here."

"And in there too," the other offered tipping his head toward the interior of the room.

"Doesn't anything spook you, Doc?"

Ames grinned. "Bloody Bones does, but he lives in garbage cans, not in places like this."

"What?" disbelief edged in his voice; "I'm being serious and you're doing imaginary childhood monsters that snatch up little kids when they take the garbage out at night."

"No I'm not, Reed." Ames paused, a crucial effect, then concluded ghostly, "Bloody Bones is *real.*"

"Get away from me." Reed didn't know if he should laugh or jump down from the wall; so they both just sat there for a minute surveying the surrounding area. Finally: "That does remind me of another monster, though," the younger man admitted.

"Oh really? Imagine that."

"Yeah, Flying Piggy. Hid in the back of our walk-in closet and rustled the clothes and made strange grunting noises every morning when we had to get ready for school. My little brother was afraid to go in the closet and get his clothes so he could get dressed —until he was about fourteen. 'Course, him being littler, we always hung his clothes *wa-ay* in the back, at the dark end of the closet too."

Ames smiled. Reed reminisced. "Yeah, mom would be yelling at him to hurry up and he'd be all crying and begging us to get his clothes for him…" He chuckled, "Good times."

Ames: "Being kids."

Reed, still looking around: "Yeah… being kids." Then he noticed the assembly of people and three giant crosses silhouetted on a hill beyond the far end of the city. "Over there."

Ames nodded. "Let's go."

* * *

Quietly, carefully...

...They bellied forward from the coulee to an observation point behind a tenacious ragweed destined to eventually be torn loose by the wind and undergo an instantaneous metamorphosis to a fabled, old Wild West tumbleweed. Until then, it would serve as camouflage.

A hundred yards away a multitude of people were assembled on the hill, most of them poorly clothed, wearing nothing more than sandals and tunics tied about the waist with pieces of rope. The women were plain, without makeup, and nearly indistinguishable from the men. All appeared unbathed, their faces and arms weathered with dirt and wind-blown dry, having long, shaggy hair, crusted and matted to tangles. None wore coats sufficiently warm to ward off the chill.

However, not all in the crowd wore rags. Scattered among the masses were a few dressed in black shirts and pants, well-groomed in appearance and having stylish haircuts. This privileged minority, all men, was well muscled and large. The crowd's attention was focused on a withered old man who resembled Moses, complete with beard and robe, both jostled by the wind. He chanted rhythmically and brandished a torch of wound straw, illuminating himself and intensifying the encompassing darkness.

The old man stood before the center cross. There were three, each seventy feet tall, constructed of wooden timbers, looming giant statues, seeming to disappear within the gloom of twilight-dark sky.

The ceremony continued for some time as the men quietly observed undetected by the locals. The old man chanted constantly forming arcs over his head with the torch, occasionally turning from the crowd to the crosses, then again back to the crowd. Eventually the people began to hum. As their mono-drone voice increased the old man's gestures quickened and the chanting intensified, more quickly and louder, finally culminating in near-frenzy when the old man pivoted throwing the torch at the base of the center cross. An accelerant pushed the flames up the massive wooden beam, spiraling around it, and when the flames were halfway to the top of the cross a burst of energy and liquid fingers of flame leapt from both sides, setting the other crosses afire: three boiling infernos of yellow-orange blaze.

Sixty feet above the ground, where the arms of the crosses reached out, pleading screams shrieked with terror. Three naked women were bound to the timbers by their hands and feet. For the first time they were illuminated and visible, crying out in horror and pain while the flames consumed them. And the wind and sky filled with the pungent taste of blistering flesh, the flames burning and roasting them, cooking them alive as they screamed struggling against their bonds. Then charring them and sudden-quiet… until their bodies boiled inside causing them to burst raining hot juice and sizzling scraps of meat onto those gathered, waiting below. Without fanfare the viscous odor of burning timbers quietly followed… and lingered.

The crowd hushed.

There was silence, except for the crackling of flames and random scattered thuds when chunks of burning flesh and wooden debris landed around the crosses as smoldering remnants of timber and life. No one moved. It seemed no one even breathed.

"Aw shit," Reed stammered with disbelief.

"Jesus," Ames mumbled. "What are they doing." It was a statement, not a question.

"Aw shit," Reed repeated.

Both were transfixed by the spectacle they'd just witnessed. Neither had any idea what it might have meant to the assembly of people, but the images and screams were not memories that either man would ever forget, indelible transcriptions in their mind's eye.

They lay mesmerized: watching, waiting.

The crosses burned with less intensity now, flames and black smoke billowing into a death sky, a crackling ocher of insatiable burn and raven winds twisting spirals into the dark. There were no more screams; only flame, smoke, and falling pieces of burnt debris. Then eventually the people began to disperse, slowly, reticently, moving again down the hill toward the city. But three remained on the hill.

"We'd better get out of here," Ames whispered.

"—Too late."

He heard Reed as a very large local wearing a black shirt and pants jerked him from the ground. Both had been seized and were being restrained. Reed struggled trying to free himself as an officer confiscated both men's weapons.

"We are visitors. Do you understand?" Ames asked them.

No response.

"We are not hostile," he insisted. Saying nothing, they showed no inclination they understood. Ames looked at his friend. "They don't talk much. What do you think?"

Held firmly, unable to free himself, Reed shrugged, then joked. "Darkmen?" Ames tried to turn but the officer picked him off his feet and threw him to the ground, onto his hands and knees. When he began to get back up the officer kicked him in the back of the head and he went down again, this time unconscious. "You ignorant dipshit," Reed snapped. Grinning a lecherous sneer, the officer pushed the pulse laser muzzle at his face and pulled the trigger. Nothing. Stymied, the officer was perplexed. "Won't work for you, Darkman," he snarled still struggling against the two holding him. And defiantly, "I'm going to kill you for what you just did to my friend."

The Darkman laughed wholeheartedly, flipped the weapon over, and smacked him squarely on the forehead. Reed's head snapped back —explosive— with white sparks in his vision; then everything went black. He thought someone might be dragging him by his feet and his head was going, *bumpity, bumpity, bump*... but he wasn't certain.

* * *

Strange music in his brain fading away...

...Reed gradually regained consciousness. At first his vision was blurred, little floaters kept getting in the way; but eventually it cleared and he became aware of his surroundings. He was lying face down on something slimy, cold and soft, exuding a fetid odor. Ames, still unconscious, lay a few feet from him. Then blinking things back into focus, he noticed something glowing a little farther away: a red, spiral coil mounted on a raised, square, stone base. Reed dragged himself to his friend, turned him over and prodded him.

"Doc," almost musically, gently shaking him, "come on, wake up."

"I'm awake," the incoherent reply.

"Okay then," he persisted, "wake up some more."

"Tinnitus," Ames mumbled.

"Only you would say something like that."

Ames raised his arms, covered his head with his hands, and took a deep breath. He coughed himself to awareness. "Shit, that smells terrible."

"Now you're awake. That sounds like something I would say."

"Where are we?"

"I think we're in one of those disgusting little buildings," Reed answered, using a finger, trying to clean out his ear.

"How'd we get here?"

"My guess is, they dragged us. Still haven't got all the dirt out of my hair and ears yet."

Slowly, Ames rolled onto his side, facing his companion. He shook his head, craned his neck and plugged his nose, blowing to clear the ringing in his ears. He studied the lump on Reed's forehead, blood trickling from the cut. "Edema, laceration and ichymosis on the frontal cranial lobe."

Reed nodded. "They're called goose eggs." He looked around. "At least this one's pretty much empty," meaning the interior of the building.

"Except for us?" Ames queried, looking at the top of the wall.

"Yeah."

"Well, so much for the diplomatic approach," Ames decided matter-of-fact. "They've got the pulse lasers?"

"Yeah. That's how I got the goose egg."

Ames' gaze traveled from the top of the wall back to his friend. Then he said, "They're not gonna keep them."

Reed smiled.

* * *

Several hours later...

...Both men moving about within the confines of their cell, Ames commented, "I can't identify any of these molds or fungi. They're different from any in the past."

"Maybe they're evolved," the understudy mused. He exhaled another breath toward the red spiral coil, studying it. His breath caused it to glow brightly, then after a moment it would diminish. "Assuming there's little vegetation to supply oxygen now, I think these people found a way to break down carbon dioxide molecules converting them back to carbon and oxygen." He breathed on the coil again, and again it glowed intensely. "There must be a chemical or molecular reaction occurring within the coil."

"Makes sense," the other agreed. "Likely they're not cannibals then, just really efficient at recycling."

Their conversation was interrupted by the sound of footsteps on the metal walkway outside the building, next voices, then a rumbling as an incline of the steel spikes emerged on an interior wall. Expected, they climbed to the top of the wall and down the other side where four officers were waiting for them.

"More Darkmen," Reed mumbled caustically, but not loudly enough for them to hear him.

They were led to a part of the city they had not yet seen, an open auditorium resembling a Roman amphitheater with stairstep tiers. With a capacity of several thousand it was spacious but not opulent, the entire structure made of the same tan stone as the other buildings in the city, and it was full of people. They were led through an archway into an arena, an expanse of screen floor similar to the streets and walkways. At the opposite side of the arena, on a raised circular platform the bearded Old Moses stood waiting.

"Suppose they've got any lions?" Reed mumbled.

Ames heard, but didn't reply.

The locals were apparently a simple people kept in submission and poverty, all dressed in rags and unkempt, understandably so with water at such a premium. But they were a curious lot. When Ames and Reed entered the arena some of them shuffled forward trying to get closer, but they were unmercifully shoved and beaten back by Darkmen who lined the perimeter. This civilization was not a democracy.

Reed whispered. "Too bad we don't have any beads to trade. I understand the Pilgrims got a pretty good deal on Manhattan Island."

Facing ahead: "Sometimes I wonder about you. Let me do the talking, all right?"

"Why not. You did just fine last time."

Ames smiled.

Approaching the platform both became serious. The old man was seated on an ornate wooden throne situated between two stone pillars, his wizened right hand holding what appeared to be a Viking war-ax. They didn't know if he could lift it though, it appeared to weigh almost as much as he did, a staff and their weapons lying beside him.

As the men were escorted before him, Old Moses picked up the staff with his left hand thumping it three times on the platform floor. Subserviently, the audience quieted. Darkmen pushed Ames and Reed to the steps of the platform, then retreated without speaking.

"Who are you?" the old man's most authoritative voice.

"We are visitors," Ames answered calmly, "not from another place, but from another time, in the past."

"Why are you here?"

"We've come to learn, to explore where people from our time have never been." Consciously recording he thought, *four Darkmen behind us.*

"How have you traveled here?"

"With a machine, a very complex machine," Ames answered, already anticipating the old man's next question.

"Where is this machine?"

"Knowing the machine's location serves no purpose; it will not work for you." A furtive glance to the right: *more along the wall; farther away, no immediate danger.* "I realize this world suffers, but attempting to escape to another time will not help. Every world has its problems, different perhaps, but none-the-less equally as difficult." To the left: *also along the wall.*

"You are intelligent beings," Old Moses observed.

A demure nod: "Very gracious of you," Ames returned, "and I'm sure you are also wise." The old man fidgeted. "You have accomplished great things," Ames flattered attempting to placate. "Your world is troubled, and still, you provide well for your people. Your city is impressive and provides safety, home for all these people," a sweeping motion with his arm toward the crowd, "a great accomplishment."

"Tell me of your world," Old Moses ordered deliberately changing the subject.

"He's leading you..." Reed voiced under his breath.

"I know," whispered back; then answering the old man. "Our world was so long ago, it is not relevant anymore."

"Did you have war?" Old Moses inquired.

"...Like a horse to water," Reed murmured.

Ames ignored him. "Yes, we had war. It seems war is inevitable in all worlds."

"And your weapons:" the old man broaching the subject.

"Our weapons will not work for you."

30

"Are they functional?" Old Moses interrogated.

Unruffled: "Your inquiry suggests that you already are aware the weapons won't operate." Ames cautiously smiled attempting to discount the old man's interest in the pulse lasers. Then, sensing the Darkmen easing closer from behind, he changed the subject again, this time turning so he could see them, yet maintaining his seemingly relaxed demeanor. "May I ask you the nature of your ceremony earlier on that hill?" indicating the three charred crosses, distant and just visible over the amphitheater. Reed was aware of his motives, both sensing impending, imminent conflict.

"Your intrusion was sacrilege, profane," Old Moses shouted, irritated that his conversational adversary could evade him with such eloquence.

"We deeply regret any intrusion. The purpose of our observation was to understand, to learn." Ames remained so cool that it nearly enraged the old man, now fidgeting noticeably.

The officers moved within striking distance. It was about to happen. Old Moses rose to his feet letting the staff fall, still grasping the handle of the war-ax. It would be four against two; the old man seemed so emaciated they didn't really consider him a threat.

"Enough of this trite dialogue," Old Moses bellowed, "show me your spacecraft."

Emphasizing, "It—is—not a spacecraft," Reed responded, speaking for the first time.

"I demand you show me."

Ames answered, "We must refuse," his voice cold.

"You will obey me," the old man yelled; "insolence will not be tolerated!"

"Neither will attitude," —and Reed sidestepped as two of the Darkmen came at him. The first, he sidekicked squarely in the sternum, a deflating, *oomph*, and the gristly snap of severing cartilage as the man went down. His next breath would be painful and paradoxical, indicative of flail chest. To the second he delivered a reverse roundhouse kick to the back of his neck. Inside the Darkman's head: the sound of boot heel splintering spine. The officer sprawled onto the expanded-metal floor, blood trickling from his mouth as he died. His neck was broken.

Ames seized the third officer's wrist, ducking and throwing him over his head. The man crashed to the floor —spread-eagle— a full body slam. Ames, now kneeling, turned to face the last of the four as the man reached down for him. Powerfully he hit him in the groin with his fist, full body weight into the blow. The Darkman's eyes blinked with disbelief as both his testicles ruptured. He didn't fall —but he didn't move anymore either. He was the same officer who had kicked Ames on the hill.

As other Darkmen were rushing in from the arena perimeter Old Moses hurled the ax at them and it struck only inches from Ames' knee, the blade slicing into the screened floor. Rising, Ames grabbed the handle and jerked it free.

"You lose, old man." With a strong arm and acrimony Ames flung the war-ax at Old Moses, the weapon hacking into him —squarely in the chest— carving through him, jerking him off the platform and hurtling him backward to the throne where the blade stuck in the high backrest. Dangling by the ax the old man hung there; eviscerated, his intestines bulging, draped like bulbous worms, blood gurgling from the leaking wound and his mouth. Even as he died, wheezing and blowing blood bubbles, he kept fidgeting and twitching.

A contorted face: "Ehew, nasty," Reed observed.

Leaping onto the platform Ames swept up both pulse lasers tossing one to Reed who grabbed it in mid-air. Spinning around Ames faced several of the Darkmen —closing— and aiming in front of them pulled the trigger...

—A shrill whine and bright flash

...Compressed sound waves pulsed by the laser flashed from the muzzle at the speed of light, the ripping blast peeling a twelve-foot hole in the expanded-metal floor hurtling chunks of shredded screen helter-skelter. The explosion catapulted several attacking officers while others hit and cut by shrapnel went down. Two plunged through the rip landing on the ground below, instantly smoldering and sizzling: the acids would dissolve them in less than sixty seconds.

They died screaming and writhing in the mud. Astonished by the weapon the others stopped, discretion being the better part of valor and not quite sure they wanted to engage the strangers now that Old Moses was hanging meat.

Ignoring them Reed focused only on the Darkman with the ruptured testicles, still teetering precariously from shock and pain. "Remember on the hill?" He didn't expect an answer. Vengeance in his voice, "I told you I was going to kill you." Reed raised his weapon, pressed it against the Darkman's chest. A small red LED on the trigger guard went out; a green LED lighted. "They won't work for you." A pause, his eyes narrowed. "They're signature encoded." The Darkman whimpering, his expression pathetic —payback. "Laugh now, tough guy." Reed squeezed the trigger.

Deafening —point-blank— there was a shrill whine and blast; the Darkman burst in half splattering in chunks and wind. Blood dripping syrup-thick and smaller pieces falling through the mesh floor, sizzled and dissolved below. The two largest leftover pieces of the Darkman lay quivering forty feet apart still somewhat coupled by stretched and torn entrails resembling gruesome white worms leaking fluid. Fragments of heart and liver were scattered and stuck to the expanded metal, the entire mess dripping onto the mud below.

With the still breath of death, the multitudes were silent,

Everyone watching,

Waiting…

Scanning, ready to fight Ames and Reed walked cautiously across the arena to the archway where they had entered. None of the officers tried to stop them. No one attacked. Two Darkmen stood at the entrance and the men, still moving toward them, slowed. When they were ten or twelve feet from the officers, they stopped. Everything within the coliseum was intensely quiet, except the wind.

"We're leaving now." Ames informed calmly. Neither officer spoke. Cautiously, one of them stepped forward to Ames then extended his hand. Wondering, Ames accepted the hand —and they shook.

"Thank you," the officer said solemnly; then stepping back he moved alongside the other Darkman allowing them passage... and the crowd began to cheer, jubilance they could not express before. The peasants continued their celebration of a new freedom, something that had been taken away and was given back by two strangers who they had never seen before and would never see again.

Silently, without fanfare, the men left the city and crossed a barren landscape toward the time machine. The wind was a constant companion; but it didn't feel quite so cold now, perhaps just a bit warmer than it had been before... or perhaps it was something else. Perhaps this world of Ten Million AD now possessed a glimmer of hope.

* * *

On a forgotten, deserted rise of black sand...

...In a desolate, forsaken land: wind-burned, cold, and shadows.

"Voice recognition, Ames."

"Voice recognition, Reed."

The access panels of the sphere parted and both men entered. "Hatch closed," Reed ordered over his shoulder. When the portal closed and disappeared for the second time on their journey, not even they could guess what the future held for them.

The geodesic sphere and a relentless wind whistling past on the barren rise of black sand tundra; the sphere seemed out of place, geometrically beautiful and symmetrical, the earth surrounding it ragged and worn.

Then... the sphere began to glow; a magnetic cloud of rainbow colors illuminating the surrounding area, coarse black sand reflecting the light: countless twinkling sparkles. And suddenly the sphere was entirely enveloped within shimmering trails of atomic particles, mesmerizing, so incredibly beautiful...

Then a shrill whine —pop— the sphere was gone.

All that remained was a barren world... and the Wind.[3]

CHAPTER THREE

This time...

...Expecting the unusual circumstances that accompanied the onset of time travel, prepared for the metamorphosis to black and white, they monitored terminals and transitional data until Reed finally spoke. Something was nagging him.

"Doc, what effect do you suppose the magnetic shield could have..." seemingly uneasy, "you know, on us?"

Without turning away from his monitor, Ames asked, "What do you mean?"

"Sure wish I would have brought a comb," mashing his frizzed hair down again.

"What?" Ames was puzzled.

"Seventy-two thousand flux... approximately," Reed recited still fussing with his hair; and each time he did it would spring right back, worse than before.

"I know our rate of advance flux," and next, inquiring, "what's bothering you? EMF has no effect inside the sphere. You know there's negligible risk of cancer —and for crying out loud, would you quit screwing around with your hair." Then it dawned on him. "I don't believe it." Amused: "You're worried it might cause you to go bald."

Reed, ego offended, retorted, "Well, you're old... older anyway. It wouldn't matter if you went bald." Shaking his head, Ames didn't respond. "I'm serious," he admitted, "male pattern baldness runs in my family Doc, and I really don't want to accelerate the process if I can avoid it."

Seriously: "I understand."

"Any thoughts?" Reed mashed his hair down again. "Any ideas?"

"Well, maybe…"

"What?"

"A baseball cap; you know, one of those ball caps with that little button on the top —to deflect the electromagnetic field. That should do it." It was all Ames could do to suppress a smirk.

Reed studied him; then said, "Eat shit."

Ames chuckles and bantered, "Good conversation and cheap wine, or is it the other way around?"

In spite of himself Reed grinned too; however, he had to slip in one more jab. "Just remember, you're old, and I'm not."

"At this point in time, the difference between our ages is inconsequential," Ames quipped.

"Touché," Reed threw back. They traveled on in their colorless world, until, "Twenty million coming up."

"All right."

Reed keyed the computer. "Locked. Should be just about... now." Color blinked back on inside the sphere. "July nineteenth. Looks like we just missed the Fourth of July."

"Let's take a look."

"Right behind you." Then to himself, Reed thought aloud, "Always enjoyed fireworks."

Ames heard but didn't comment.

* * *

The past ten million years had transformed Earth...

...Her insidious, inevitable demise waiting just a little longer. Now jutting rock formations, stark and eroded, stood like sentinels of the Badlands. No longer supporting any vegetation, any sign of life, it was empty, stripped to the bone; the near-darkness creating an eerie effect, a moonscape rather than anything resembling Earth, almost surreal.

Opaque and looming, rock formations seemed to elicit shades of gray, color difficult to distinguish with so little illumination from the sun. That too seemed to be dying, fading into the great vastness of space. A deeper red now but still in the sky, a smeared blot of rust on black canvas, the sun and full moon low on the horizon, plainly visible, together providing enough light to see, but barely enough… a strange alliance.

The Earth's temperature had declined another twenty degrees, the inevitable result of a world in a solar system with so little time remaining. It was cold now. Much had changed in the past ten million years, but one aspect was the same, the wind. It had waited and met them with indifference, and would again be their constant companion.

"A bit brisk," Ames observed snugging his collar around his neck and ears.

"Yep, it is." Reed huddled in his coat. A glistening layer of frost covered everything. "Lord, the Aurora Borealis is beautiful," he said watching, the northern lights floating above the horizon: electrical flames in the ionosphere, their colors enhanced by the darkness beyond. The borealis, stuff that Indian Legends were made of twenty million years ago, still as beautiful and mysterious to observe as it had been so long in the past. In Reed's mind the Aurora Borealis had always been the, 'Eighth Wonder of the World'. It would always fascinate him: blues, reds, greens, violets… lightshow in the sky.

"Air's thin," Ames remarked, his eyes still fixed on the light display overhead.

"Yeah. We'll have to take it a little slower this time; can't be much oxygen left." Reed scanned the horizon, unconsciously looking where the city had been before.

Ames noticed. "It couldn't be the same one, not after this long."

"No, it's not," Reed agreed. "It's a lot closer. I'll get the lanterns."
Moments later they headed in that direction.

* * *

The travelers entered the city, dwarfed by its magnitude…

...They were mere specks on a seemingly endless concrete floor. All around them were skyscrapers towering thousands of feet overhead: New York and Chicago combined and seeming to go on forever the way Los Angeles did, a sprawling megalopolis... and more.

This city could have accommodated thirty, perhaps fifty million people, and still had, 'For Rent' signs in some windows. It was immense. The summits of many of the taller buildings were indistinguishable from the ground; they were that tall.

However, the most impressive accomplishment of the city was not a single building, rather two gargantuan spirals that ascended thousands of feet, each crested with an enormous circular platform. The platforms shared the support of one mammoth glass pyramid spanning the space between the spirals.

First impressions of the city, its magnitude, detracted nothing from its complexity after more scrutiny. Intermingled among the skyscrapers were myriad lesser buildings, the entire aggregate of structures at one time having excluded the outside environment by means of interconnected glass transport tubes, some at ground level, others connecting buildings hundreds or thousands of feet overhead. Most intersected with perpendicular tubes resembling some futuristic byway, but others were express, nonstop to unknown destinations, enabling people to move from place to place like impulses zipping along neuro-pathways in the brain.

When there was life here this city was surely magnificent. Now it was dead, an empty shell of what it once had been. Many of the transport tubes were damaged, some severed completely. A number of buildings both large and small, were missing sections of concrete, several with huge holes that went completely through as if shot by missiles —in one side, out the other— a city charred and now deserted. The concrete floor lay gray and cold, littered with debris and scarred by craters, possibly the result of a war, another possibility, something altogether different.

The travelers stopped, inspecting one of the craters. It was fifty feet across and nearly a hundred feet deep. The concrete around the rim was broken, heaved up in great chunks and charred as though exposed to extreme heat for a length of time. Even more strange, the skyscrapers on either side of the crater were badly burned but otherwise intact.

"What kind of bomb could have caused it?" Reed wondered.

"I don't know."

"That makes two constants that I can think of, Doc, the wind, and war."

Ames studied the crater, then replied, "Perhaps you're right."

"Seems a shame. This must have been an incredible place to live."

"War has always been a waste," Ames contemplated aloud. "Why would God let mankind accomplish so much then wipe it all away with a war?"

Reed frowned, then sadly, "It wasn't God's idea to make war... it was man's." Despite his headstrong, somewhat reckless nature, the young man was perceptive.

A fleeting smile his only reply, Ames chewed his lip and continued studying the crater. Something about it seemed wrong, and that puzzled him. There wasn't enough debris around the perimeter for a blast to have been the cause. It seemed to have been sucked in... almost. He didn't mention it, but kept thinking about it; and it kept nagging at him.

It was cold and they moved on.

***

Quiet...

...Resembling two diminutive creatures crossing an endless landscape of dusty concrete overshadowed by an unworldly forest of looming colossuses of gray stone and steel. At one point as they walked silently past two towering buildings Ames peered down the darkened dead-end alleyway between them. And in the dim light, at the far end he saw a small leafless tree enclosed in a circular garden of dead grass that was protected by a short ornamental wrought iron fence. It stood all alone, withered and barren, branches mostly drifting to the left, quivering in the wind. This place was lonely... and empty.

Reed also noticed and glanced at his friend, but seeming unimportant at the time, neither said anything. And it was cold... so they moved on.

Eventually the two arrived at a five-story granite building fronted by Roman era pillars and concrete stairs a hundred feet wide, that a long time ago ushered people through the two-story arched glass doors. But now the glass was gray with dust, and the inside was dark. Lettering ten feet tall along its facade indicated it was a museum.

A fascination with him, Reed grinned. "Shall we?" For most kids it was candy stores, for him it was museums. Interested, Ames agreed.

As with most museums, inside it seemed larger than it did from the outside. Immense ornately engraved marble pillars rose stately and solid from a floor of similar stone and supported the domed ceiling fifty feet above. Towering silent and dark it boast unseen frescoes and art from a civilization long since passed, a Sistine Chapel from a different time. The sensation of emptiness was omnipresent: silent beyond sound, still beyond motion, even the cold did not stir. The slightest whisper seemed to intrude, interrupting the mood; and their hollow footfalls echoed through distant halls in the blackness: the feeling, *perhaps the night watchman will hear.*

All around them were millions of relics, a civilization lost, and sadly now, what might have been was a void. Remaining in the quiet was a treasure trove of knowledge and artifacts, ample exhibits and informational memorabilia to occupy an ardent individual for days, or weeks. Although there were countless objects deteriorated beyond recognition there was a like amount unaffected by the ravages of time.

The men moved from one exhibit to the next reading by lantern light, learning what was possible from the timeline displays, both trying to piece together a puzzle of years past from fragments of information that was there. They moved leisurely. There weren't any clusters of foreign tourists crowding them from behind, speaking gibberish they couldn't understand, making them feel uncomfortable for looking at a particular display for too long, rushing them when they might prefer to read a bit more.

There was no hurry. They were completely alone.

For several hours they meandered: fashions, household, music, agriculture, leisure, machinery, medical, architecture... on and on.

In one hall a chronicle of avionics history: replicas of every aircraft ever built, from the Wright Brothers' Kitty Hawk, to biplanes, 747's, space shuttles, to interstellar or exo-atmosphere space fighter jets... all hanging from the ceiling.

In the literature corridor Reed located the archives section: journals, books and scripts on many subjects, all hermetically sealed in glass display cases with two spring-loaded levers. Pull the right lever, the pages turned forward; the left, the pages turned back enabling one to read the entire text: pinball literature. He picked one at random and browsed, a journal that evidently was written about someone of importance, someone named Samuel something. He couldn't make out the last name.

"This must be a diary of some kind from early in the twenty-first century." He read, then commented, "Looks like they merged the Common Market into a Federation of Nations." The more Reed concentrated trying to make out the words, the more difficult it became, almost as if they were fading away. In the back of his mind the thought occurred: *something he should not read.* "So old I can't decipher much of it." He was enveloped with a peculiar sensation: subliminal, almost hypnotic. He blinked twice, gave up, and moved on.

Next was medical. Cancer research continued for years; progress was made, but never a cure. Reed mumbled, "Don't think they ever wanted to find a cure; just too much money in it. Big business."

Stem cell research was another matter. Great things came of it, and the entire world benefited with cures for more illnesses and injuries than anyone could ever have originally imagined. He read several pages then skipped back to cloning. Even bigger business. Reed didn't really approve of cloning, always thought of it as 'Frankenstein' shit.

Ames, browsing: "This one's on birth control." He chuckled. "Seems they had a few problems with overpopulation." Pausing while he read, then continuing, "Apparently they devised some efficient solution," but he didn't elaborate.

"They found a cure for the common cold," Reed said. "Let's see, medical researchers were working on a non-caloric body fuel and it was going to be credited to the department head, but the medical assistant actually made the process viable. He was pissed. Poisoned his supervisor's coffee —oh— and the chemical reaction with the chicory cured his boss's cold." Shaking his head as he deciphered the writing, "The med student confessed taking credit for curing the cold rather than the body fuel."

"Turned out all right then."

"Well, not exactly. He got his choice: life imprisonment or execution. He opted for the latter."

They left medical, ambled into science.

"An electron microscope," Reed recognized the smaller of three microscopes.

"The smallest one is," Ames read from the informational plaques, "but the second is a proton microscope and the largest is an ion microscope."

"Interesting," studying them, "wonder if they still work." Reed peered into the eyepiece. "Can't see a thing." He drew his head back looking for a switch, then realized, "No power."

"Let's go."

They wandered through many other sections, occasionally commenting but primarily observing, learning what had been accomplished over time. Space travel had become commonplace. Full-scale replicas of various crafts chronicled its history including models of several orbiting space stations, the lunar colony, and one on Mars. The plaques didn't mention whether or not those might still be operational, however that seemed extremely remote. There were also holographic and three hundred-sixty-degree surround theaters covering numerous subjects: botany, zoology, astronomy, anatomy, oceanography —too many to enumerate, but none functional— now dark empty quarters within a conglomeration of memories from a vanished civilization.

Finally, they arrived at the weapons corridor. It was larger than the others, but knowing man's nature that wasn't surprising. The displays began with Neanderthals' slings and arrows representing virtually every killing tool ever devised.

There were thousands of weapons: sticks, stones, axes, bows, rifles, pump, single shot, lever action, automatics, machine pistols, handguns, rockets, bombs, missiles, biological, chemical, neurological, nuclear, fusion and laser plasma. The aisles were crammed full, from the lowly South American blowpipe to the fastest seventh-generation jet fighter, an F-121B with low-level stealth capabilities, to scale model battleships, carriers and submarines. Mankind's destructive creativity had not stopped with terrestrial weapons. Space had become a second battleground, equally equipped and better financed. This corridor was truly amazing.

"Have you ever seen anything like it?" Ames finally whispered.

"Un-believable."

They separated moving along opposite sides of the great hall, viewing various sections leading from it individually. For a while each explored alone until Reed called from a section of antipersonnel devices. "You'd better take a look at this."

"What?"

A second time: "You'd better take a look." As Ames approached, he instantly recognized the frequency pulse laser neatly arranged in line among other similar looking weapons.

His reaction was, "Shit."

"It shouldn't be here," Reed commented, concern apparent in his voice. "We're the only two who ever knew about it, and it's unlikely it was replicated by accident." Ames agreed. "Well…" Reed paused, "like Alice said, 'curiouser and curiouser'." He shook his head, wondering, "What the hell, what next?"

The answer was less than a minute from arrival. At first it sounded like jet fighters swooping across the sky at high altitude, not a single formation but many, a squadron —more than that— and they just kept coming. Both listened with disbelief. Could it be others had survived here?

An instant later more passed, very close, a few hundred feet above. Roaring thunderously, sonic booms shaking the museum, piercing screams, deafening —entirely too close— it couldn't be aircraft.

Reflex reaction, the men dropped to the floor when the noise exploded around them. Startled wouldn't describe the flood of adrenaline-rush, momentarily too surprised to think neither moved. Then...

—Onto their feet: tense, rigid, coiled.

"Holy shit, what was that?"

Ames shouted, "Outside—"

Two cats on an asphalt roof in August, they ran, sprinting to the nearest exit and the presumed safety outside the trembling museum, but the expansive concrete floor offered just the opposite. In the open now, unprotected, the ground rumbling and violently quaking, everything was in an upheaval. Shuddering and shaking, titans were breaking apart, concrete and glass jitterbugging on the ground and raining down from above, bouncing at their feet, thundering, crashing and splattering everywhere.

They saw them at the same instant: fireballs roaring past overhead —hundreds of them— streaking with incredible force toward the sun. They soared thousands of miles per hour almost parallel to the horizon, like shooting stars all rushing in the same direction, stragglers randomly jerked from orbit and sucked to earth by gravity.

Meteors.

"—Incoming!" Reed's scream, drowned out by the roar.

A chunk of white-hot asteroid a hundred feet wide was approaching on a collision course with the city, its incredible speed dragging a tailflame ten miles long. Rotating, slicing through the atmosphere, blowing fire and vapor from pitted rock pores the meteor hurtled toward them. Its beauty was dazzling, a gigantic shooting star, blue-white flames and destruction almost close enough to reach out and touch. Dark sky was transformed to brilliant daylight in a fraction of a second as it screamed overhead, its blue-green vapor trail flame almost singeing them with its intense heat as the ambient temperature rose a hundred degrees and the frost layer melted more quickly than one could blink to avoid the blinding white light.

It seemed ridiculous even as the thought flashed through Ames' mind:

Make a wish...

—At that same instant, it struck

...Whoom!

Deafening noise. The ground vaulted and towering titans shook. The meteor hit the base of a skyscraper four miles beyond the museum, one entire wall disappearing within the explosion of fire and debris as the hurtling rock blew a crater into the earth below the structure burrowing a thousand feet deep in one-hundredth of a second. The entire skyscraper was vaulted ten stories into the air and hesitated — suspended there— before collapsing back to the earth. The meteorite's backdraft sucked the whole explosion into the crater and underground with an incredible, *whoosh.* Flames, explosion, debris —everything gone— for just the briefest hesitation of absolute silence with a hundred feet of empty space between the earth and skyscraper.

—Then, *whoom!*

From somewhere within the Earth's crust once it finally absorbed the meteorite's impact. Next, a guttural rumble and growling, a growing noise that mounted until abruptly, like multiple explosions detonating simultaneously the concrete floor erupted catapulting frozen earth and rock from the crater while the skyscraper still hovered above.

The explosion's shockwave flashed out —nickel-ferrite fire agate rupturing a still, frozen pond— the concrete floor ripping apart in ragged chunks, rising thirty feet with the incredible ripple, beginning to expand. Just as suddenly the skyscraper fell back to earth — crashing, exploding, crumbling— shattering with unbelievable force. It collapsed into the exploding crater causing the superheated ground to buckle and belch out a second shockwave. And fury blew a breath of flames that boiled up from below.

Expanding, destroying everything in their path, moving like two gargantuan submerged snakes tearing the floor and structures apart, mounting and building with increasingly relentless whipsaw motion, the shearwaves rushed. Skyscrapers collapsed, their foundations ripped apart and the structures above teetering then coming down. Five were hit, ten, a domino effect of unparalleled magnitude. Smaller buildings burst from the concrete floor spewn out by the erupting earth; even an earthquake wouldn't accomplish such absolute destruction. The structures were being thrown into the air, then falling back, shattered to bits within a thunderous roar of explosions with nothing remaining but piles of rubble and a pushing-rush of clouds and choking, pounding dust.

Reed yelled, "Bust me square!" as they bounced helplessly on the roiling concrete floor, watching the first shockwave as it approached. It resembled an unbelievable tsunami of rising earth, fracturing concrete, collapsing buildings and shattering glass rushing toward them.

Ames screamed, "Run!" his voice nearly drowned out by the crashing, explosive confusion that seemed to be everywhere now.

They ran, both sprinting as fast as they could, from certain death racing from behind. The rumbling concrete floor's motion either sprang them forward or interrupted their footfalls causing them to hesitate impeding their flight; but they didn't slow down —and it didn't feel cold anymore— sweat, adrenaline and fear will do that.

White-flash of detonation off to the right, another inbound meteor crashed: brain-rattling, thunderous, pulsing reverberations. More skyscrapers collapsed being absorbed within the extraordinary destruction, and the jolt threw both men airborne then onto the concrete. The pain would have been debilitating if there were time to think, but fear and adrenaline had complete control of them.

Reed, getting back onto his feet, glanced over his shoulder. The tidal wave of earth and fractured concrete was about to swallow them. Ames appeared injured and unable to get up, and with a powerful sweeping motion Reed grabbed him under the armpit and jerked him to his feet. Half dragging him, Reed carried his friend along with him, panic driven, fleeing frantically across a great expanse of open area, a sea of concrete with a fountain in its center.

"Fountain..." Ames managed to say.

Barely seconds until the shockwave would catch them, but it may be just enough time. Now, from under them —a thundering, splintering roar— the floor rising beneath them, rupturing at their heels, violently breaking into huge chunks that could easily crush them. The sensation of running uphill against an incredible tidal swell, the deafening noise of explosions and crackling cement pounding inside his head —with less than a second.

The fountain, was the single thought in Reed's mind —then somehow it was there. He dove headfirst jerking Ames along with him. There wasn't any water in it but even as they hit the cement bottom inside, it felt safe. It hurt to land, solid, jolting, abrasive, but surely no worse than being dead on the concrete floor outside. They could survive the pain.

An instant later the ripping shockwave captured them welling up from below and spewing the fountain onto the crest. The concrete floor beneath it fractured, splintering apart in monstrous chunks with pieces clinging to the fountain's base as it was pushed into the air —*rushing up*— explosions, confusion, rattling noise and gray dust. The fountain held together and crashed down on the backside of the swell then into the trough as the second wave rolled at them.

Again, the swell shoved the fountain up, and again the men were airborne in the cement lifeboat swallowed within billows of chalk cloud and splattering bits of concrete that careened everywhere. Pieces of it crumbled apart, splitting fingers of fracture appearing throughout, but for the second time —falling and a solid slam— the fountain held together when it landed.

The shockwaves had passed.

The broken ground still rolled unevenly mimicking floating ice, undulated, shifting irregularly, constantly in motion. It was like riding an earthen-wave that wouldn't subside as skyscrapers still collapsed, crashing down and engulfing smaller structures that were crushed and buried by the toppling behemoths, all of it vanishing within the devastation.

All the while the asteroids continued screeching past, skimming over the earth at incredible speeds toward a vanishing point somewhere in space beyond the sun. And despite the annihilation of a city on the planet far below, the Aurora Borealis continued to dance the mysterious fire dance high in the ionosphere: cold, majestic, and beautiful.

Reed finally rolled over, his chest a little less tight, able to breathe again, and saw his friend lying beside him, looking back at him. Both were covered with dirt and powdered concrete dust.

"You okay?" Ames asked.

"Yeah. Are you?"

"Shoulder hurts some. Might have a couple of cracked ribs, but other than that, I'm all right." Then he added, "Thanks."

Reed grinned. "You're welcome. What made you think the fountain would hold together?"

"Neoprene liners, same as mining companies used for settling ponds."

Painfully pushing themselves up onto forearms and elbows, both men looked out from the fountain peering cautiously over the rim. The meteor shower appeared to be moving away, sweeping a destructive path across the sprawling megalopolis. One struck a skyscraper about midway cutting it in half by blowing a tremendous section from its center. With distant sounds of crushing and crackling the top collapsed onto the bottom and it all disappeared into a saffron-gray cloud of flames and dust below.

Just then a very large meteor, even larger than the one that nearly killed the men, struck the base of one of the enormous spirals dispatching a pulse of thunderous, *boom,* and echoing rumbles. The tremendous impact sent debris and ejecta billowing miles into the sky and the spiral began to crumble and fall —then streaking in— a second meteor hit the glass pyramid shattering it into millions of shards. First swept and scattered in the violent winds, then shimmering like crystals, they glittered as they descended: sparkles of twinkling rain floating benignly into the obscurity of amber flames and slate-smoke below.

Ames looked from the city to the fountain's pedestal looming over them. On top was a bronze, a statue of a man who looked like a Quaker or Pilgrim. His arms were extended, apart, as though welcoming someone, and clutched in one hand was a book. Ames didn't recognize whom the bronze personified, but he seemed familiar.

The area surrounding them still rumbled and shifted unsteadily but the seismic activity was subsiding. It might be safe now to try for their machine.

Ames looked at Reed. "Ready?"

"Right behind you."

* * *

Outside the sphere...

...The men finally stopped to rest, and exhausted both collapsed onto the ground, leaning against it. They sat that way, side by side without speaking for quite some time. The meteors were gone now, with the exception of a stray periodically skimming the horizon, bursting into flame, then disappearing in the distant heavens in the direction of the sun. Unknown to them, millions of asteroids were being drawn past the sun, but without Earth's atmosphere to ignite them they remained dark chunks of rock in a pitch-black space.

The wasteland that was once a magnificent metropolis continued to burn in the distance issuing billowing columns of ascending smoke that loomed as massive, particulate-gray mushrooms over the ruins. Smoke drift slowly trailed off from the fires to somewhere beyond the limit of vision, but even the wind couldn't clear it all away. Relentless, cold, and constant... the Wind.

After a time, adrenaline levels normal again and fatigued; the men dozed, then slept soundly. Neither was sure how many hours they had been awake: one drawback of time travel, its effect much worse than jet lag. Neither did they know how long they had slept when the wind and cold brought them back.

"Shoot, it's as cold here as it is in Montana," Reed stuttered, blowing into his cupped hands to warm his fingers.

Ames huddled pulling his knees to his chest. "We are in Montana, at least technically."

Reed grinned. "Yeah, just two seasons: winter and August."

Ames smiled, then serious: "Never die in Montana during the winter."

"Why's that?"

"Because if you do," the man explained, "they don't bury you. They just sharpen your feet and pound you in the ground."

Chuckling, "You natives are a bit strange." And Reed continued, "Reminds me of a story..."

Interrupting, "Don't start on the sheep jokes," Ames warned. "Now you're confusing Montana with North Dakota."

They stood slowly, gently limbering stiffened joints and stretching sore muscles. Both moved around enough to loosen up, feel revitalized. Ames favored his left shoulder and ribs a little but decided it wasn't anything serious, pulled muscles, painful but not debilitating.

"You all right, Doc?"

"Yeah, just beat up some."

"Know what you mean," the other responded. Then he inquired, "Ready?"

"You bet. Voice recognition, Ames."

"Voice recognition, Reed."

The portal panels whisked open, and just as Reed was about to enter Ames laid a hand on his shoulder. "Oh— one more thing," he said sternly, "don't *ever* mention fireworks again." Reed was still laughing after they were both inside and the portal sealed shut.

Moments later the sphere was swallowed by the dazzling magnetic cloud, swirling around it, beautiful with its radiance, sparkling like fairy dust...

Then a shrill whine —pop— it was gone.

Neither could know this would be the last time. What they did know: they left behind an incredible city smoldering in ruin... and the Wind.

CHAPTER FOUR

Out there, time flicked away, an incongruent blur…

…Inside, a black and white world. Absorbed at the terminals they worked without interruption, both monitors blinking endless processions of data, graphs, charts and numerical columns that were meaningless except to a mathematician or analyst: projections, variations, probabilities, and so on. Deck officers on the 'Starship Enterprise', hair wildly frazzled from an old episode of the 'Twilight Zone'.

"All systems within parameters," Reed commented after turning from the monitor.

"Fuel cells?"

"Ninety-eight percent."

Ames typed a few keystrokes. "Advance flux just over one hundred-fifteen thousand." Pivoting, he turned to Reed who was trying to flatten his hair without success. "Will you please quit. You're making me crazy."

Reed looked at him, both hands on his head, holding his hair in place more or less and replied, "—A baseball cap, that was a good idea. I know you were joking, but a ball cap would be just the ticket."

Exasperated: "Why not shave your head? You've got a knife."

"Cute, Doc."

Ames grinned, then scanned the interior of the sphere. Without prologue, "Folks, we've got a really, really big show tonight."

"What?" Reed quizzed.

"Ed Sullivan," Ames answered, presuming his imitation should have been obvious.

"Who's Ed Sullivan?"

"Was, Reed. Ed Sullivan's dead."

"Well yeah, Doc," chiding, "but don't you suppose they're all dead by now?"

Ames threw back facetiously, "Really?" then asked, "didn't you ever watch any of the old TV shows, the black and white ones?"

"No."

"Why am I not surprised." Then he explained, "Time travel reminds me of being in a black and white TV program, like before color television."

Stymied, Reed asked, "You mean television hasn't always been in color?"

Now the older man was surprised. "No, of course not. When television was first broadcast the picture was black and white, there were one or two channels, and it was only on a few hours each evening."

Disbelief: "You're kidding."

Ames asked, "You've never heard of 'the Beaver' —Beaver Cleaver? Ozzie and Harriet, Red Skelton, Jack Benny, Captain Kangaroo?"

"No."

"What is this world coming to," mimicking rankle, "that *does* make me feel old."

Reed pondered. "I never really thought about it. I just assumed there'd always been six hundred channels of HDTV —and Doc," he added, "you *are* old."

Opening his mouth, Ames began to respond but didn't have time —slammed, a violent jolt, and outside a brilliant flash— what must have been a cataclysmic collision interrupted him. The explosion was deafening hurtling the sphere sideways as if launched into space. Only their shoulder harnesses prevented them from being thrown through the wall panels and into oblivion, and their movement through time prevented their incineration —but they were unaware of that.

In the blink of an eye the time machine was catapulted, spinning with gyroscopic precision on an uneven course. Whirling recklessly, centrifugal force holding them still, neither man could move.

The gravitational force was excruciating, facial skin stretching and folding over itself, grotesque as floppy rubber masks. They were unable to close their mouths, nor could they pull their arms in to their chests. Outstretched, they were stiff-chicken wings on featherless birds, blood pushed so forcefully to their extremities it felt as though their fingertips would pop: intense pressure, spinning too violently to even make a fist. From reflex and surprise both held their breath, an involuntary reaction that kept their lungs inflated and prevented a ripped aorta or collapsed heart.

—Inside a golf ball smacked on a four-hundred-yard drive

In a blur of momentum and light precious seconds passed and they were still alive, but moving so fast images that should have been sharp and clear were only smears of gray. Guts pushed to their throats, they clenched their teeth holding it back until the sphere's violent momentum gradually lessened and the whorl-revolutions only made them want to vomit, not hope that their eyes wouldn't be sucked out and burst.

Still, they couldn't move and were aware that the sphere was no longer stationary, now free-falling through space, time-skipping at an incredible speed, bounding over and over like the sensation of being inside a beach ball rolling on water with no inclination to remain upright. And still flowing directionally at an incredible speed —flashing through time—time passing so quickly it possibly was never even there. Rotational motion eventually decelerated and the men could move again, but the revolutions at a forty-degree angle gave the sensation of a carnival ride that just wouldn't end.

"Mix me—in a blender!" Reed yelled, terror in his voice and a death grip on the chair's armrests.

"I'm—gonna—be—sick," Ames sputtered.

"Oh shit, don't puke, Doc. It'll splatter all over us."

Ames almost did, but held it back. Seeing Reed's tense anticipation of being soiled with vomit at such a critical moment was so comical he had to laugh; a nervous, haughty laughter prodded by fear, uncertainty and frustration with their constant rotation.

"What's so funny?"

"We could die any second," he managed to spit out, "and you're worried about getting barfed on." The geodesic sphere whirling around them —brains whirling in their heads— their eyes scrambling to focus and sort it all out —dizzying, sickening— and he continued to laugh, a sputtering, broken laughter.

"Screw-it. How do we stop this thing? We'll be puking together pretty soon if we don't."

"Lean into the motion," Ames said.

They did, a number of times, and eventually the rolling subsided until finally they were upright and reasonably steady again, but still moving through time and space. Only from inside the sphere neither had any idea what had actually occurred out there, or where they were going, or how quickly they were getting there.

* * *

Several minutes...

...And millions of years had passed since they left behind a city destroyed by meteors from the solar system's asteroid belt. The asteroids had continued to escape from their orbits for those millions of years, and eventually larger bodies began abandoning their orbits as well. Moons, planets, and ultimately even the sun, slipping from where they had been for so long, all being pulled to a distant region, toward the edge of the universe.

The sun and planets of our solar system weren't the only bodies being drawn across the expanse of empty space. Other stars with their systems were following, or leading; millions —billions of stars— perhaps trillions of moons, planets and other objects were enroute as well.

* * *

Somewhere, a long time ago...

...An extraordinary implosion: beyond measure, indeterminate, beyond reckoning. A vast type 'O' star had evolved to white dwarf then collapsed upon itself shrinking to the size of a grain of sand, becoming so dense it was able to literally push a pinhole through the fabric of space. Even the emptiness of space couldn't manage so much weight concentrated with such incredible pressure, all at one place; and the result, a diminutive hole through space itself... to a new space beyond.

A gigantic imploding star had punctured the fabric of space. The pinhole had ripped... and the hole had opened, the horizon of infinity a rent wound of ragged shreds forming an astonishing, inconceivable whirlpool of reformation.

Conception, the portal: the boundless jaws of the mythical Lion.

A whirling void of mystery and dark, it was born out there in the realm of unknown... the unexplored, and unexplained. Incredible beyond comprehension, the doorway to forever wound and roared with absolute silence in the vast emptiness and supernatural realm of the space-time continuum. Swallowing everything from everywhere it was a spiraling anomaly and incomprehensible power: destruction, obliteration, and oblivion; an astonishing, inconceivable whirlpool of reformation...

...The vortex opened.

The imbalance between parallel existences set in motion a universal tug of war: positive and negative gravitational forces so intense, so monumental as to be beyond comprehension, gravitational pull so powerful it was capable of grasping everything... and drawing it in. That happened a long time ago, and now, time had caught up.

Now the immense gravitational pull of the black hole was claiming all matter from the old universe within tens-of-billions of light years distance, pulling it into a new and parallel space. So strong was the attraction that nothing could escape, not asteroids, moons, planets, stars, galaxies, nebulae or dark matter. Nothing escaped... not even light.

While the geodesic sphere streaked onward through time universal order was unraveling, the complicated predictability of existence itself coming apart in space. And it was occurring on an unprecedented scale. As with all things, there is one constant... change. Be it an evolutionary alteration of one universe or the creation of another, it was destined for change, the catalyst being a black hole at the farthest reaches, on the perimeter... where time and space collide.

At the juncture of time and space the black hole roared with absolute silence, a mythical Lion swallowing everything in existence. Stars warped from spherical masses of hydrogen and helium into tongues of fusion hundreds-of-millions, billions, —trillions of miles in length. Celestial bodies and planets and moons searing along the spiraling, flaming path to the other side, drawn by such an incredible force they were misshapen, then literally pulled apart, limitless fragments hurtling along, rushing to an unknown destination.

Finally, even entire galaxies couldn't withstand the immense force drawing them, one after another being stretched across space or folded over upon themselves creating stellar collisions by the billions, universal space itself becoming liquid with gaseous confusion, fusion in its purest form.

—All of it, swallowed from space and into the throat of the black hole

—Everything, disappearing to somewhere on the other side, a place that might be only a dream... a figment of the imagination.

Such was the destiny of Earth and two men in a geodesic sphere moving through time in transitional flux. They traveled so fast not even their shadow could catch them... but the black hole could.

When the object hurtling through space struck Earth no life existed to record the collision. Whether it was a sister planet or something from some distant region was not important. The collision occurred and Earth ceased to exist, shattered to oblivion and the sum of its debris scattered as cosmic dust, then drawn away by intangible energy, the grasp of gravitational invisibility and pitch. Absolute black. It was sucked away... following everything else into the black hole.

The geodesic sphere and its occupants arrived and departed as the collision occurred. They were there —and already gone.

The sphere, without Earth to carry it, went into free-fall in space, spinning, rolling and following everything else into the black hole. They slipped through time and space concurrently, jettisoned forward to where time warps and space folds, toward a matrix turbulence and holocaust pitch. Deeper and deeper into the gravitational draw they went, always staying an instant ahead of the winding apocalypse, colliding stars and debris exploding and burning everywhere within the void. It was a continuous stream of liquid light created by countless melted stars and galaxies poured into a funnel so black it was capable of absorbing everything. Nothing would escape… not even light.

And the black hole remained. It swallowed everything from everywhere… for millions, then billions of years.

When time warps and space folds they are no longer relative. Distance becomes meaningless. There is no space between the fold. A thousand light years will arc, fold back upon itself: it becomes a single step. Time warps and tomorrow becomes yesterday, or yesterday can leap billions of years to the future. Strange beyond fiction, where time can stand still, or —*tick*— it's forever.

Such was the destiny of the time travelers.

* * *

"Screw it, Doc! Something's messed up..."

...Reed's fingers flew furiously over the keyboard punching with surgical precision even though they hung strapped into their seats and dangling at a forty-degree angle at the control panel.

Ames didn't respond; his attention focused on the computer in front of him, blistering keystrokes, precision and accuracy under stress, gleaned from years of practice. Perspiration trickled into his eyes but he ignored it, no time to wipe it away; seconds were too precious. Acutely aware that chaos lurked just beyond the magnetic field propelling them and the sphere through time, he resolved to know what that chaos was. Eyes skipping furiously from each screen to the next as the monitor blinked and displayed them, the data seemingly wrong but the computer repeatedly spitting back the same information.

Slow down, he thought, frustration overtaking him, *not possible,* brain scrambling to sort it all out. But he couldn't find an error. Exasperated, "Dammit!" hands fisted, he hit the control panel.

"What, Doc?"

"It's impossible."

"What?"

"It's—just—impossible!"

Reed clicked two keys and pressed, 'enter', so swiftly it seemed a single motion. The date screen blinked on his monitor, those columns a blur, the accumulated total adding then subtracting, then climbing again—at an incredible rate.

Disbelieving, "Judas Priest," he mumbled. "Doc, bring up your date screen."

Ames duplicated Reed's keystrokes and instantaneously the overhead monitors displayed identical screens with identical numerical columns. They both watched the accumulated total rise while the flux-speed column climbed, halted, subtracted, climbed again; leaped millions, subtracted again, climbed, and so on. It made no sense.

Overhead the message flashed: *critical flux… approaching time shear.*[4]

Confused, nervous, "Approaching time shear?" Ames murmured, his words trailing off.

"That can't happen Doc. That entire concept is unsubstantiated —same as antimatter."

"Then what else can it be?"

"I don't know but time shear is only a theoretical phenomenon of transitional flux. It can't be real… can it?"

"Transitional flux was only theoretical yesterday, or whenever."

"Yeah, I know. So?"

—Subatomic particles of the magnetic field whirling around them

"An anomaly?" Ames finally said.

The overhead screen: *time shear event threshold... intercepting horizon in twelve, eleven, ten...*

Reed looked at the sphere walls, the spaces between the magnetic coils providing a translucent image of what was out there. Liquid light cascading past them, perpetual waterfall flashes: brilliant, dazzling, luminous flares all streaking the same direction... to a vanishing point somewhere ahead of them.

Armpits drenched, shirts sticking to their backs, both men watched, trying to be rational, awestruck.

"Bust—me—backwards..." Reed said softly, "they really exist." Ames said nothing as Reed surmised, "That's why the asteroids were coming in almost horizontally. They weren't falling to Earth; they were being pulled past Earth. And the sun wasn't burning out, it was being sucked away." Both watched... filled with wonder and amazement, nerves wound with tense weight in their chests. And resignation: "Only one place where time warps and space folds," he concluded. "The computers aren't screwed up. The data is relaying exactly what's going on out there." He swallowed... hard.

Ames thought, *a black hole.*

The computer: *five, four, three...*

The concepts of space-time continuum and cosmic order had just been skewered, scrambled within the disastrous ruin of chaos swirling through a vortex of matrix turbulence just beyond polycarbonate walls, barely more than arm's reach away. Transcending their imaginations and capacity to understand —not only their world, their solar system, their galaxy— everything, everywhere, being ripped apart at the seams. Apprehensive, overwhelmed, the men continued watching the magnificent light show. "But... they're still only theoretical."

"Not any more, Doc."

The computer: *event threshold... intercepting horizon.*

Everything instantly blurred and stretched, like distorted slow-motion.

Outside the time machine, countless planets and moons —entire worlds— were interspersed among the immense volume of gases, likened to beach sand in a rush of whitewater shooting through an obsidian funnel. Galactic volumes of white-hot gasses surged, an immense jetstream of stars, clusters of stars, nebulae —entire galaxies— rushing and pouring through the absolute black of incredible quiet and void. They watched with amazement, wonder, and fear. It wasn't the fear of death that gripped them, dying is easy. It was fear of the unknown, apprehension, not knowing what was coming from the other side... if it really existed. This was an unknown experience. Even theorists dared not speculate concerning the death of a universe and the birth of another.

His words slurred, "Fourteen—billion—years!" Reed yelled inside the machine.

Never before had any human being encountered such tremendous cataclysm: the confusion, destruction, and reformation. Stars exploding then imploding again and again... unending cycles.

Planets and moons rupturing from within, scattered to limitless specks then swirled together and recompressed forming new worlds. Entire galaxies pouring and spiraling onward in twisted veins of liquid light —time warped, space folded— the billions of stars rupturing again into space. And it continued over and over, space compressed into a fluid channel pouring at the speed of light through the blackest blackness possible to imagine. Brilliant light thundering without sound —exploding, imploding, millions of times— too many to comprehend it all...

"Fifteen billion years!" Reed screamed.

—And the Rush—

...An incomprehensible surging torrent of blinding cataclysm erupting from the other side —exploding trillions of planets, stars and galaxies all at the same instant— too much to envision, unimaginable, incredible beyond description...

The 'Big Bang'!

—And the black hole was gone

...An Entire Universe Was Born!

CHAPTER FIVE

The geodesic sphere rested fifteen degrees off level…

…Partially submerged in the soft humus soil, its interior a jumble of debris and broken polycarbonate panels with equipment scattered everywhere. The metal framework had partially collapsed tearing loose hundreds of the magnetic field coils and interconnecting printed-circuit-boards. Dangling wires and bits and pieces: it was damaged beyond repair, a total loss.

Unconscious, both men remained strapped in their seats, held fast by the harnesses. Ames was slumped forward, arms hanging limp, not stirring. Reed, whose chair had broken free of the floor track and was lying sideways against the console, moaned very faintly. Both monitors displayed date screens with identical accumulated totals, a little more than fifteen billion years.

Ames' left hand twitched; then he raised an arm ever so slowly and leaned back onto his chair. His head throbbed. *Opening your eyes will make it worse,* a voice inside whispered, but he had to anyway. The voice was right: it was worse now.

"Reed," he muttered. "Reed… you alive?" He tried to reach out to his friend but the shoulder straps held fast so he clasped the buckle —pulled— and the harness let go. He fell forward onto the console catching himself before going to the floor. Wavering, he stood and turned then looked at his friend again. "Reed, are you alive?" Head still muddled, Ames staggered on the uneven floor.

Weakly: "I must be; but I'm stuck."

Ames was relieved and the dizziness was finally subsiding —but his head sure hurt. "You're still buckled in."

Reed opened his eyes, awareness returning. "Okay, that makes sense then, but why am I sideways?"

"Let me give you a hand. You're tipped over."

"Oh, then that makes sense too."

Ames unbuckled the shoulder harness and Reed tumbled from the chair onto him, and both went down in a tangle of arms and legs, rummaged around on the tilting floor for a minute, then got their wits together. From the floor both surveyed the sphere: the machine's interior was a shamble.

"Looks as beat up as I feel," Reed decided.

"Yeah," Ames agreed kicking a polycarbonate panel aside with his foot. Then he grinned, "But at least your hair's not frizzed anymore."

"Really?" Reed put a hand on his head. His hair was lying down again. "Yours too, Doc. And you're in color, not black and white."

Both men looked at the collapsed ceiling. Above them, through missing panels they could see a vivid blue sky. Fumbling over Reed and picking his way through the clutter Ames began crawling across the slanted floor. "Let's go see where we are."

"Right behind you."

* * *

The world was no longer dark and barren...

...A bright yellow sun washed this tropical land with warmth and daylight. The sun was beautiful, promising... misleading. Ames crawled from the wrecked time machine.

Reed followed him kicking the dangling portal panel and knocking it all the way out. Once outside, he picked it up, threw it back inside the collapsed sphere, reached in, retrieved the pulse lasers, then backed away from the machine. Squinting until his eyes adjusted to the bright sunlight, he assessed the sphere: the damage was severe, likely the machine was beyond repair. Not needing their coats each took his off and tossed it into the sphere.

Both stretched loosening sore muscles and bruised bodies, taking time to look around. Most of the land was forested with gnarled trees that resembled Banyan or fig trees with tentacle roots. From the canopy, descending through the understory, thickly foliated vines called liana intertwined with the tree limbs and suspended to the forest floor, a hodgepodge of mosses and ferns. Blossoming flowers were a rarity.

They were in a clearing encompassed by a forest, a jungle without the gagging humidity. It was very warm. But a jungle should be alive with animal sounds and birds; here it was quiet. It was also green, a deep beautiful, chlorophyll green.

"God, it's good to be alive." Ames' words were soft, instilled by the silence surrounding them, the mood and feeling of being inside a church. Pensive, unobtrusively he walked to the edge of the clearing without saying anything more.

"Sure is," Reed agreed, and as he turned, he saw his friend standing alone beneath a tree, and realized he might be praying. Respectfully Reed didn't interrupt; and it seemed for a moment, he too might even have bowed his head.

* * *

A narrow path led from the clearing...

...Into the jungle, and the men were soon following it, not knowing where it might lead. It was time to explore this place, a Tarzan world without Cheeta's incessant chatter. After a few miles the jungle opened into a clearing of sulfuric pools and tar pits, and after noting their approximate location they continued until eventually arriving on a bluff. The descent was a steep grade and at the bottom was a pool, crystal clear and unpolluted, reflecting deep blue in the dappled sunlight.

Reed smiled. "Thirsty, Doc?"

On heels and butts they scooted down to the pool and Reed sat down Indian-fashion while Ames lay his weapon aside stretching out on his stomach to drink. He splashed water onto his face then scooped again and drank slowly from cupped hands savoring the cool water. Satiated, Ames looked into the pool, and as the riffles disappeared the water reflected the image of someone standing over him, legs spread, straddling him. Instantly rolling onto his back he found himself looking up at a woman, stunningly beautiful. Her black, thigh-length, leather skirt was wrapped snugly around a slender waist and barely concealed the union of long, graceful, beautifully tanned legs. From below, the black, cut-off leather top exposed full breasts: round, firm, with beautiful nipples just barely visible. Her skin was bronze, copper colored, soft, covering muscle; and the sunlight played upon her blonde flowing hair creating a halo that trailed it all the way down her back to her waist. Her expression was stern, her primitive spear held poised.

Beautiful, was all Ames could think; she was simply too beautiful to fear. His eyes traveled the length of her body again, every inch of it, absorbing the vision very slowly. Transfixed, he couldn't take his eyes from her.

Perhaps she could sense it, the connection, and was also aware there was no danger. She lowered her spear and stepped back allowing him to sit up. They were different, but not enemies… these strangers.

"That's twice," Reed simpered, distracting his companion. He was still sitting where he was before, the women having surrounded them; all in black leather, all with flaxen hair, and all motionless; some armed with spears, others with bows and arrows.

Darting his friend a glance Ames asked, "Where'd they come from?"

"I thought they were shadows," the other admitted. "Next thing I know, they're here." Then with a relaxed grin he added, "It's not like it's the first time—you know—that we've been captured. Truth be known, actually I think we kinda' suck at being furtive, 'cause we're sure not very good at it. And this time, I really don't mind." Then, under his breath: "Now I think we're talking 'epic adventure'."

Ames turned again to the woman standing before him and couldn't help saying it. "You're beautiful."

"Thank you."

Amazed: "You understand?"

"Yes," to Ames. "You are not captured," to Reed. Then she continued, "You are different. Where are you from?"

Reed quipped, "He's different all right."

Ames ignored him. "We've come from the past."

"Where is the past?"

"It's not a place; it's a time, long ago."

"You have come from a different time?"

"Yes."

"I understand," she said.

"You do?" Puzzled, Ames said nothing more as the woman stepped away and spoke briefly and quietly with another in the group. Exchanging wondering glances, the men waited to see what might happen next. And shortly the leader walked back to Ames.

"Do you wish to come with us?" she asked.

Her polite manner caught him unprepared. "May we leave if we wish?"

"Yes, if you wish."

Without hesitating, "We'll come," Reed volunteered, and the grin. Ames shrugged. A hand motion by the leader and the men's weapons were returned. *We didn't even have to take them back this time*, Reed thought smiling. *Two of us, all these women... there are definitely possibilities.*

"Follow." The leader commanded.

They took a trail into the jungle.

* * *

Reed was still grinning, making assessments...

...When the footpath widened and they entered a clearing with rows of small gray-tan stone dwellings along either side. The huts were modest, a single room, only large enough for one or possibly two individuals. In the entire population, there were no men: Reed noticed details like that. The leader escorted Ames to one of the dwellings as Reed continued to follow the others along the path that curved to the left. When she approached the dwelling, the bronze door quickly rose —*ssst*— and seemed to disappear. Ames noticed that the door didn't fold at the top of the dwelling, nor did it rise above it, however his attention was distracted when she turned and asked placidly, "Do you wish to enter?" Not expecting her invitation, momentarily he hesitated as she waited patiently; then accepting amenably, they went inside.

The room was clean but dark, with no windows and only minimal light, a flame in a sepulcher that rested on a tripod base with splayed supports. The woman passed her hand over the flame and it intensified until she repeated the motion; then pointing she indicated a low, concave stone couch draped with black leather, and compliantly Ames stepped around the sepulcher and sat down. Without speaking she seated herself beside him.

Bundled nerves and dying of curiosity, a million questions to ask, so he began. "What is your name?"

"Tian,"[5] she replied effeminately. "What is your name?"

"Ames, John Ames."

"John Ames is a good name."

"Tian is a beautiful name. You really are quite beautiful."

She smiled. "Thank you. You told me before, and I have not forgotten."

"Yes, I told you before." Changing the subject: *objective mode.* "How does that fire work," indicating the sepulcher, "and the door?"

"The same as the others,"

Prodding, "How is that?"

"I am not able to explain how," she informed plainly. "The flame does not go out and the entrance allows passage." Her manner was calm, interested, and polite. Tian seemed very at ease, almost as though the men's arrival was anticipated... expected.

"Tian, you said Reed and I may leave if we choose."

"Yes. Reed is your friend?" Her eyes sparkled of hazel innocence reflecting alizarin firelight.

"Yes."

"Reed is a good name as well. You may remain here or leave; you are not prisoners." She frowned inquiring, "Why do you ask? Do you wish to return to the jungle?"

"—No," then a breath with the pause, "it's just difficult to be comfortable if one feels restrained."

"How long will you stay with us?"

"How long will we be welcome here?"

"I believe the prophecy was true," she began, "'Strangers who are different, but not enemies'. You will always be welcome here."

"Prophecy?"

"Later you will learn of it," she told him. "Now it is time to rest."

"But Tian, we just got here," he protested politely. "There are so many things I wish to know and…"

"—That is true," she conceded, interrupting him, "but do you not have customs where you are from?"

"Yes, but…" He stopped mid-sentence, understanding.

"We also have customs. It is time to rest now." Taking his hand in hers, she smiled. "No more, please." Her smile possessed charm of which she was unaware.

Reluctantly, "No more," he agreed.

Tian lay on the stone couch, moved over making room for him, and gently coaxed him by the hand until he lay down beside her. He said nothing more, and although exhausted, he was restless, so he waited while she slept.

* * *

Later…

…Tian awoke and found him leaning over the sepulcher, examining it. "How long have you been studying the basin?"

Quickly turning: "Not long. I was only curious."

First she pouted; then she smiled. "Now come with me if you wish, and we will talk of things you wish to know." As she rose Tian passed her hand over the flame in the sepulcher and it diminished.

Both went outside.

Darkness had fallen over the world and they left the village walking leisurely, ambling along a winding path. Nervously Ames slipped an arm around her slender waist and she did not resist, moving closer. Without speaking she lay her head against him, words unnecessary, body language always universal. The meandering path threaded a trail through the jungle and ended in a clearing on a point at the summit of a vertical cliff. The two people walked to a mound at the brink of the precipice and sat down quietly together.

Far below the cliff a river wandered its course, seeming to divide this world in two parts. Although Ames couldn't see it in the darkness, across the river lay a barren region of arid plain and rolling hills layered in rock and sand, and sparsely sheltered with groves of gnarled ancient trees, scattered runs of rye grass and thorned mahogany. Directly before him, spanning the distant horizon, ragged mountains heaved up the landscape with jutting peaks and sheer granite faces concealing an irregular topography of valleys and plateaus. The other side of the river was a harsh, hostile place... Forsaken Land.

From their vantage point overlooking the river, to their immediate left was a descent of several hundred feet to the lowland: lush, forested bottomland bordering the river, an expanse of floodplain two hundred yards wide. The lowland ended where it abutted the ridges, stairstep rock formations of fractured small cliffs that transformed to sheer rock face, the escarpment. Behind and to their left, on top of this geologic fault, was the village from which they had come. To their right the escarpment narrowed to a whitewater canyon guiding the river's path for a mile, then downstream again widening to bottomland and oxbow bends where the flow settled moving more leisurely once more. The plateau overlooking the whitewater escarpment was absorbed in dense jungle interspersed with small clearings until the forest ended abruptly at another range of mountains, a different kind of mountains.

Neither of them spoke for a while.

Even this soon it seemed natural, they were comfortable being together, sharing each other's company, perhaps each believing that some things are meant to be. Ames hadn't felt that before, a new experience. His mind and heart were captured by Tian, her flowing hair fluttering softly with the cool evening breeze, moonbeams sparkling and dancing upon the golden strands. The moon cast their faint shadows across the ground, over the cliff, and let them escape in the darkness of the vast canyon below.

A yellow light blinked and hovered nearby. "Lightning bug... firefly," Ames murmured: "Lampyridae Photinus."

"We call them candleflies," Tian whispered. "Why do they light up in the darkness?"

Ames held her close, sighed, then answered. "They burn the chemical luciferin to luminesce." He paused, a stirring inside: *subjective.* Softly, more subdued, "I guess they light up because that's how it was meant to be." And his gaze drifted to the heavens. Glimmering pinpoints of starlight peering from the dark, the constellations puzzled him; from mythology and superstitions of old, now something more, something new, an enigma, the first piece of... *The Puzzle.*

"John, how did you come here, to our land?"

No one ever called him by his first name; but when Tian did, it seemed natural, felt good. "In a machine, a machine that could move through time."

She looked at him. "I have heard of machines. How does it move?"

"It doesn't anymore." Still studying the sky: "It broke as we arrived here."

"Before it broke, how did it bring you here?" Her voice was soft, warm. Their eyes met.

"It's complicated to explain, but if you wish, I'll try."

Blinking placidly: "Yes, please."

"It may be difficult to understand, but basically," he began, "light travels very fast, and everything —well, except tacagons— but that part gets sorta complicated, so we won't go into that. Anyway, everything is made of elements composed of particles called atoms that travel as fast as light does. Because we are also made of atoms our atoms move at the speed of light too. Reed and I discovered a way to make the atoms in our machine —and us— go just a little faster than the atoms in everything else, just beyond light speed. When we did that, we could move through time because time is also relative to the speed of light. So... we jumped ahead of the rest of the universe —everything else."

Inquisitively, "What is the universe, John?"

"The universe is everything, everywhere, all put together."

She nodded.

Ames didn't think she grasped the concept, but asked anyway. "Do you understand what I'm trying to explain?"

"I believe so," she answered thoughtfully. "You made your days shorter than everyone else's days."

Ames grinned. "Close enough."

"May I ask another question, John?"

A nod, and smile.

"You and Reed have strange weapons. What are they?"

He thought, then answered, "Frequency pulse lasers." And being a creature of habit, he explained, "The trigger strikes a tuning fork, which emits a sound, a controlled frequency —pitch. Sound vibrates and that vibration is pushed on a laser, a beam of light — well, actually six beams of light. Light travels a lot faster than sound so the light beams compress the sound waves creating a pulse. And when that pulse strikes something, the target absorbs the oscillation —vibration— and is ripped to pieces."

"They are very dangerous?" she asked.

"They will only work for us. The weapon scans and deciphers our fingerprints as we touch the trigger."

Curious: "Fingerprint?"

Ames took her hand, indicating, "There are ridges and grooves in our fingertips. We all have different patterns." *Her hand is warm, her skin soft.*

Amicably, "Thank you. Now you may ask questions," she said.

"What are your people called?"

"Renoloi."[6]

Ames nodded. "A race called Renoloi."

70

"There are two people," she informed, "the Renoloi and the Trog."

Interest piqued, shifting his weight on his buttocks, "Trog? Who are the Trogs?"

Tian was reluctant, as though many troublesome and unpleasant memories had just been dredged. She did not want to answer. Demurely, "They are our enemies," she finally said.

"Two races," Ames repeated, "possibly more."

"There are two," she affirmed, "the Renoloi and the Trog."

Leaning forward, a bit closer, "Why are they your enemies? Tell me about them."

Troubled: "They have always been our enemies, a part of the prophecy. The Trogs shall be our enemy until one of the people are destroyed and no longer live on this world." She was becoming uneasy. "I said I would tell you of things you wish to know, but please, can we speak of other things?"

Ames, still holding her hand, felt it trembling. "Yes. We won't talk about the Trogs again tonight," his assurance a comfort, she relaxed a little. Putting his arm around her and hugging her gently he added, "I'm sorry." She snuggled, finding security within his embrace. She'd never had someone to lean on before… it was a wonderful feeling.

For some time, they talked or sat quietly, and Ames began studying the constellations again. Pinpoint minutiae of white light, silence and mystery, the stars glimmered in the vastness of heaven. He pondered: *The galaxy couldn't have changed that much. If only I could put my finger on it; what's wrong. Capricorn, Scorpius, Pegasus, Cepheus, Sculptor, Cetus, Orion, Sagittarius… they're out of place, but there's something else… something else is wrong.* Contemplating he studied, and thought for a while, until it finally dawned on him. "—That's it; they're all backward," he said aloud.

"What, John?" Tian asked a bit startled.

"The constellations have been bothering me, but I know why now." Preoccupied before, it was only then that he realized that she had almost fallen asleep, and seemed weary; so he suggested they return to the village. She agreed with a smile. Pensive, more intrigued now, Ames looked at the constellations once more before they started back.

By the time the couple entered the village the Renoloi were asleep inside their modest homes, and the two proceeded without speaking to Tian's hut where they spent the rest of the night together.

But before Ames fell asleep, he thought about what had happened so far: the cities, one so plain, with a glimmer of hope; one so magnificent, entirely destroyed. What did it mean? And how he and Reed had ended up in a primitive, strange new world where the constellations were all backward and life was simple and uncomplicated, with the exception of the door and sepulcher. The Renoloi were all women, all young women and children. He wondered why. And he wondered who the Trogs were. But most, he wondered what the future held for himself and his friend, and why Tian, snuggled beside him, cradled within his arm, could make him feel so warm inside.

A brief while later he was sleeping soundly for the first time in fifteen billion years.

From small beginnings: *The Puzzle*.

* * *

The door rose with a, *ssst...*

...Tian and Ames stepped out onto the main path of the village. Rising, an aureate sun was on the horizon chasing away the night fog. A fresh, clean morning. Tian smiled serenely as she and Ames walked along the well-beaten path.

"Your world is very beautiful, Tian."

"It has always been this way," she replied warmly.

Ames knew it had not, but didn't comment. Just then he saw a small child squatting alongside the path, busily scraping what appeared to be a piece of leather.

"Hello," he said kneeling beside her.

She meekly blurted, "Hello," then bashfully covered her eyes, hiding within her hands.

"What is your name?" he asked amicably. Timid, the little girl kept her eyes covered and did not answer, refusing even to peek. "Don't be shy," he coaxed, but in spite of his effort she wouldn't look at him.

"Tarin."[7] Tian spoke firmly, and immediately the girl looked at her. "He asked your name and you will tell him."

"Yes, Tian," she said obediently. And next looking to Ames, "My name is Tarin."

He smiled, winning her confidence. "What are you doing?"

The little girl finally grinned, proud of her work. "I am making leather." She presented the skin for his examination. "It is Chiqua."

"Chiqua, what's that?" Tarin shrugged her shoulders —looked at Tian.

"A small animal," Tian explained. "We use the meat for food and the skin for leather, as clothing."

Interested, Ames inquired, "What does it taste like?"

"You shall find out. Come, it is time to eat."

The mention of food reminded him it had been a long time since he had eaten anything, but he wasn't certain precisely how long. As he rose, he picked up the little girl.

"Are you hungry?" he asked playfully. Eyes bright with childish enthusiasm she shook her head and smiled: guileless, a child's smile. "Well, you've gotta ride piggyback then."

"What is piggyback?"

"It's like this," Ames said, flinging her around his shoulder and catching her by the legs. She squealed, latching onto him with a leeching grip. "Not quite so tight," his words sounding constricted. The little girl loosened her hold. "That's better." The three continued down the path, Tian and Ames side by side and Tarin giggling happily as she rode upon his back.

Arriving at a large clearing surrounded by jungle at the edge of the village, they found the Renoloi gathered around an open-pit fire. Several of the children were busy tending chunks of roasting meat skewered on spits over the fire. Others were bringing in large leafy stalks from the jungle while another group cut the stalks into pieces and crushed them in stone mortars. The juice was drained from the mash and poured into clay vases. Altogether, there were nearly four hundred Renoloi gathered for the meal.

Observing the morning's activity Ames spied his friend standing beside one of the women, both overseeing the children. Putting Tarin down, "There's Reed," he said glancing at Tian; and walking toward him Ames yelled over the din, "—Reed." Looking around, the younger man located him.

Raising an arm in response, "Doc, just a minute." Reed took the hand of the woman beside him and made his way around the fire. She was exceptionally pretty, very effeminate, and appeared easy-going and playful. Her shoulder-length hair was the color of sand and her blue eyes sparkled in contrast to the black leather she wore.

Meeting, Ames teased, "You've been keeping busy."

"Hell, I looked all over for you this morning, Doc," a lighthearted defense. "Oh, let me introduce you to Seana."[8]He turned to the woman: a sweeping arm gesture, pompous, good-natured overkill, "Seana, this is Doctor Ames, my friend."

"My pleasure, Seana," Ames returned cordially.

"It is nice to meet you, Doctor Ames," she replied hesitantly; then somewhat puzzled she turned to Reed. "Where is Doc?"

Slipping an arm around her Reed laughed. "No, Seana," he said, "Doc is a nickname."

Still confused: "A nickname?"

"When people are good friends they sometimes shorten or change their names," he explained.

"Why?"

"Because it's convenient, less formal."

"Of course," Ames interjected, "that's why I call him Reed." Ames smiled, but Reed wasn't sure just exactly what that meant.

"We will eat now," Tian informed them pragmatically. She walked to the center of the circle and Seana moved into the crowd. Most of the people were sitting on felled logs arranged within the enclosure, while others perched atop large granite boulders around the clearing periphery.

Ames told Reed, "Her name is Tian," answering the question his curious glance had asked.

Reed observed, "She seems rather serious about everything."

"Has to be, she's their leader." Presently, a piece of meat and small cup of the extracted liquid was given to each Renoloi. The men received theirs last. "I'm starved," Ames admitted.

"Me too —stray dog hungry." Reed bit into the chunk of meat, chewed slowly and swallowed. "Sure doesn't taste like anything I've ever had before." He thought about it, then whispered, "Shit, this is terrible."

The entire village was staring at them and both noticed they were being watched. Ames looked at Tian with misgiving and her smile revealed understanding —that here, some things were new to them. She asked calmly, "Do you not bless your food?"

Caught off-guard, "Ex—cuse me?" Reed sputtered. Embarrassed, Ames said nothing.

The Renoloi bowed their heads and Ames followed their example. Reed stared in amazement, until Ames elbowed him in the ribs; then compliantly, he lowered his head too. When the brief blessing was finished everyone began eating.

After the meal Tian returned to the center of the circle. When she raised her arms, without exception —a hush— there was immediate silence. "We have strangers with us," she began. "They have come from a distant place. They are friends and shall be treated as our own." Voice firm, yet compassionate, "All will make them feel welcome as long as they choose to remain with us." Eyes scanning the crowd, her words definitive and clear, "We have customs that may be unfamiliar to them; accordingly, all will allow patience and tolerance. Is that understood?" Her demeanor staid, the candor and authority of her spoken word unquestioned, the Renoloi acknowledged her command. "Very well," she concluded. Leaving the circle, plainly she walked to the men.

"Thank you, Tian. That was very courteous of you," Reed commented.

"They like you," she replied addressing both of them. "It is the correct way." Seana was approaching and Reed, excusing himself, went to meet her.

Shortly Tian and Ames left the circle and walked back up the path. "Who are the Trogs?" he asked without prologue.

"Please, John," almost pleading, her expression serious.

He insisted, "It's just the way I am and I won't be satisfied until I find out." For a moment Tian said nothing, considering quietly; then as they passed a young woman sharpening her spear, she began...

"If you must know, I will tell you of the Trogs." Overhearing her leader's last word, the woman nearby immediately picked up her spear and hurried into her hut. Glancing over her shoulder Tian saw the woman go into the dwelling. Ames saw her too. "Now, John," she said turning back to him, "do you understand why I do not like to speak of our enemies?"

Convinced: "Yes."

"We are a peaceful people," she explained, "but the prophecy said the Trogs would be our enemy until one race was no more."

"Tell me, Tian... please."

"They are large," she said calmly, "very large."

"As tall as I am?" he asked quickly.

"More, much more," was her reply, "and they are different, just as you are different."

"Men?"

"No. You and Reed are men; that too was in the prophecy."

Puzzled: "What else can you tell me about them?"

She answered, "They tame great beasts to kill for them."

He deliberated, and at length, "May I ask one more question?"

"Yes," she was hesitant, "one more question."

"Where are the Trogs?"

She looked at him, concerned. "Why do you ask me that?"

"Where are they?" he repeated.

She turned to the distant mountains. "Beyond the cliffs where we were last night, far into the Forsaken Land."

Ames kissed her on the cheek, whispered, "Thank you." Quickly turning he hurried up the path, Tian following.

"Piggyback, piggyback," a childish voice called out. Tarin ran from her mother's hut to meet him.

He stopped and knelt with a cordial smile and his apology. "I can't piggyback right now, Tarin —but we will later, okay?"

"Yes," she replied beaming, and she watched as he and Tian continued.

Soon after rounding the curve in the path Ames located him. "Reed, wait a minute." The younger man, with Seana, stopped, waiting for his friend.

"What's up?" he asked in his usual, congenial tone.

"We're leaving for a few days."

"Where to?"

"I'll explain on the way. Get your weapon and meet me at Tian's hut."

Without reservation, "On my way." He hustled toward Seana's home with her following.

When Ames turned around Tian was standing there, worried. "Why, John?"

"It's something I need to do. I don't expect you to under…"

"—But you do not know the way," she objected.

"We'll find it."

"No," she said, then volunteered, "I will show you."

Direct, Ames asked, "Are you sure?" She nodded. Taking her hand in his and tendering a smile he assured, "I'd like that, and we'll be fine; we all will."

A reciprocal smile; next she turned and called two Renoloi, "Kimo,[9] Nitana…"[10] and as the women joined her Tian told them, "the men and I will be gone for several days. I leave the village in your care…" her words being absorbed in the commotion. Understanding, the women turned then left, and Tian went to her hut to get her spear.

* * *

Shortly...

...Renoloi sentries positioned high in the gnarled trees in the lowland bordering the river watched as Tian and the men approached with a small group of Renoloi. Tian signaled the sentries with a whistle —a solitary note— and a sentry concealed somewhere within the canopy returned the call.

A primitive world: in this land there were no birds.

The river separated the land of the Renoloi from the Forsaken Land, and remaining behind the group of Renoloi watched silently as Tian and the men waded through the chest-deep water flowing with a gentle current. Shortly they arrived on the other side and disappeared into a grove of trees beyond the opposite bank.

"Take care," Kimo whispered from the Renoloi side of the river. Then she and the others turned back toward the village.

CHAPTER SIX

Standing inside the treeline, dripping water...

...Tian paused with a fleeting glimpse back toward the opposite bank, then to both men, "Now the journey begins."

Reed, to Ames: "Doc, you haven't told me yet where we're going."

"There are other inhabitants on this world."

Considering that, "Okay."

By mid-afternoon it began to rain tiring the trio; and it kept on raining, for three more days. Out of a sky the color of slate constant torrential downpours hampered their progress. And the windswept nights thoroughly chilled them.

* * *

The fifth day...

...Reed woke before sunrise and rekindled the fire to warm his sleeping companions. He stepped quietly to the mouth of the cave and gazed down the mountainside into a dark abyss. *Whata bitch getting up here.* Then studying the high peak towering overhead, *looks almost impossible,* he thought, *but I guess we've gotta do it.* Just then the sun's first rays crept over distant summits scratching colorful etchings in an ostensibly limitless sky, the darkness below gradually blending to greylight. "Well," he sighed, "at least it isn't raining."

Ames' eyes opened just wide enough to see his friend silhouetted at the mouth of the cave. "Reed," he whispered. The man turned.

"Yeah, Doc?" His voice was subdued, but his smile was not.

"We should be going."

Stepping again into the cave, as Reed approached he noticed that Tian was still sleeping. "Why not let her rest a little more? She was exhausted last night, and she said it's just over this peak."

Ames looked at the woman, smiled, "Yeah, I suppose you're right."

Reed dug into his pocket retrieving a handful of brown berries as he kneeled. "Care for some breakfast?" offering Ames some.

"No, thanks." Disdainfully: "I don't think I'll ever be able to look at another one of those stupid berries again."

Tian woke and yawned, and cheerfully, "Good morning." She yawned again and stretched.

"—Morning," Ames replied.

Grinning, Reed addressed his friend. "You know why women yawn and stretch in the morning don't you?"

"Yes, you've told me before."

"Because they don't have any nuts to scratch."

Shaking his head and the smile away, Ames told him, "You need some serious help, you know it." Reed winked; and having no idea what they were talking about, Tian ignored them.

"I am hungry," she said frankly, rising to her feet.

"Well here, have some berries," Reed offered. She accepted, and a reciprocal smile.

Grinning, Ames shook his head. "You two and your berries."

"They're good, Doc. You ought'a have some."

"I've already eaten so many I'm shitin' little black seeds —and besides, they've been in your pocket all night. Hard telling what else has been in there."

Reed chuckled. "But you said yourself that it's better than going hungry."

"I'm not that hungry."

Changing the subject Tian observed, "We had better be going."

"Okay, breakfast is over," Reed agreed.

The men shouldered their weapons carrying them slung across their back, and the three left the cave resuming the climb, slowly, tediously; the rest of the way up the mountain's face. The next few hours they made consistent progress, then luck turned acutely. Building quickly a towering cumulonimbus front swept in, and within minutes the sun was completely veiled by coagulating clouds and shadow-darkness that absorbed them preempting a cold, hostile wind.

Unexpected— a clap of thunder so loud it felt as though the entire mountain trembled as wind-pulse flashed an invisible blow. Crooked wizard-finger lightning sizzled overhead —too close— striking the summit of an adjacent peak with a flare of blinding white-burn — shattering— a sudden, ear-splitting explosion that puffed their hair as it rattled past. Ripped from the mountaintop ragged chunks of granite were hurled into the air trailing dust and debris as the lightning's static-afterburn embers twirled then wafted away. Plummeting stones struck the nearby mountainside with tremendous crashes and rumbles tearing loose more rock, all of it cascading down sending echoes from below.

"It's only a couple-hundred feet more," Reed yelled to his companions following below. Tian stopped to call back but Ames nervously prodded, tapping her leg with his hand.

"Keep going. Don't stop until you've reached the top." He had reason for apprehension.

Within minutes the wind began to gust, intensely bitter, surging powerfully and unrelenting with frost whistling in its song. Stinging cold it whipped at the gray-tan mountain trying to tear the climbers loose with ice-crystal breath. The three, vigilant of every move they made, impeded by the storm, managed to continue, but now much more slowly. One mistake would be their last.

They were within a few feet of the peak when suddenly, streaking sideways, frigid rain poured torrentially from an amorphous cumulonimbus-black sky companioned with winds so gray and blinding that it was almost impossible to see. And within seconds the jagged, cold, rock faces transformed to waxen sheets of black ice.

Reed made one last attempt to keep his balance on the icy ledges, then with a resolute effort lunged for a jutting rock crag at the peak of the high plateau. Only will to live and powerful arms kept him from falling, as slowly he inched his way up. The freezing rain pelted his face and arms raising welts and little burning cuts; but he hung on to that outcrop.

"—Reed!" Tian screamed. Her hand was slipping and she dangled precariously from the side of the cliff, rain and wind congealing, freezing her eyelashes together making it difficult for her to see. "Please, help me," she entreated, her right hand reaching for him as her left hand slowly slid along the icy rock.

Instantly realizing her danger, that quickly, he lowered himself from the precipice. "Take hold of my boot." He stretched out as far as he could, and desperately she grabbed, her fingers clutching his foot and pant leg just as her left hand futilely trying to cling to the slick rock, gave way. Another heartbeat would have been her last.

Ice lacing her hair, arms and fingers numb, terrified, she looked down at Ames. "Climb over Reed and get to the top."

"I cannot climb anymore." *Wind screamed in her face—*

Desperate: "Yes you can..." *—and howled in his head—* "you must." *—a grappling vengeance, to claim them for dead.*

Cold was numbing them, the rain flushing away their strength. He knew very soon hypothermia would begin its insidious process: confusion, sleepiness, lowered core temperature, unconsciousness, then death. That couldn't happen. Determined: they wouldn't lose this fight; they wouldn't die here on an unnamed mountain ledge.

Lightning flashed razor-burn bright light. Thunder peeled.

They would survive. The elements would not beat them. Tempestuous, a roar of the wind sizzled stinging their ears. Lascivious, cold freezing-rain hit their faces. The storm was vengeful. And it screamed from charcoal thunderheads.

Unremitting, tenaciously, freezing, Tian slowly pulled herself up, climbed from Reed's legs, grabbed his belt, to his back, then his shoulders. Three lives depended on her. His wrists were clenched so stubbornly around the rock outcropping she could see blood squeezing from between his fingers then flicking away with the icy water and wind.

"Hurry, Tian..." he said weakly, "hurry." Gently from his shoulders, and she was on the peak, at the plateau.

Over the noise of the wind: "I am here."

Faltering words, Reed told her, "Sit here, where I'm holding on. Straddle this rock with your legs on either side of it... so I can... gotta get lower." His strength waning: "It will hurt, but it's the only way." Puzzled but not questioning, she did what he asked, and he took hold of her ankles lowering himself within Ames' reach. Blood trickling down his wrists, "Hurry, Doc," he managed to say. His grip was so tight it cut off the circulation in Tian's feet; but he wouldn't let go unless he passed out. Tian sat straddling the jutting rock, leaning forward, holding onto it with both arms —and freezing cold as she was, she wouldn't let go either.

The cold, wind, and freezing rain were relentless, blinding, absorbing. Seconds now would decide the outcome, whether three people struggling to save one another would survive. Determination and dependence bound them, either they all win, or they all lose. Desperately Ames grabbed one of Reed's legs and started climbing, holding onto the mountain whenever possible to lessen the strain on Reed and ultimately Tian. Stiff with cold, he still moved quickly, precisely and calculated; and within those precious seconds was on top with Tian.

Immediately Ames laid down beside her, and hanging over the edge reached for his friend. "Can't reach him..."

Tian put a hand on his back bracing herself and strained with all her might lifting Reed a couple of inches by bending her knees. It was enough and Ames grabbed his right wrist lifting with adrenaline-induced strength. By now Reed's fingers were ashen from cold and he was physically drained, beginning to fade, his strength lost with his core temperature. Still, his brain told his left hand to reach for Ames —so he did. Hanging there, Reed managed to look up at his friend: a fleeting, fading, glimpse of gratitude, for just an instant; then he lost consciousness.

Holding his breath, gritting his teeth, flexing muscle —a surge of strength— Ames lifted Reed up to the plateau enough so Tian was able to grab his belt and help pull him onto the level surface. Together they dragged him under a granite outcrop and out of the rain where she hastily rummaged through the rock crevices for dry grass and kindling. Beyond the reach of ice-crystal rain, exhausted, they built a fire and rested until the next morning.

* * *

The sun was high above the horizon...

...When his eyes opened, rolling gingerly onto his side, his head struck hard dry ground with a, *thud,* that only he heard. The rain had passed and with it the water: not evaporated, just gone. His body tight and sore, Ames rose to survey the surrounding landscape. It was barren except for scattered groves of huge trees shading ground that was parched and cracked as though baked by the sun's intense heat. Mindful there had not been enough time he wondered about this world: where had the water gone so quickly, without a trace, no indication of what occurred the previous afternoon. Kicking Reed's boot gently Ames woke him from a sound sleep.

"Ah, beat me up," he muttered, trying to sit up, "my back is sore."

Ames knelt beside Tian carefully squeezing her shoulder to wake her, and when she opened her eyes, she offered a weak smile. It was clearly apparent this journey was difficult for her. Almost regretfully, he returned the smile. Then darting a look to Reed, "You remember yesterday?"

"Yeah," rubbing his face with sore hands, almost stifling his words, "but I was trying to forget."

"Well, see if you can figure it out." He looked around as Ames helped Tian to her feet.

"Gone, weird," he said, then droll, "like it was sucked up by a horrendous soda straw."

Ames grinned at the analogy. "I hadn't considered that; but I guess..." flippant.

"Good morning," Tian addressed Reed pleasantly, but tired.

Turning, "Hmm... oh, good morning."

"Tian," Ames asked, "where did the water go?"

Shrugging her shoulders, "I do not know; no one does." Unaffected: "It comes and leaves the Forsaken Land very quickly."

"But this isn't natural,"

"Nope," Reed agreed, "it's weird."

"Come now," she coaxed taking Ames' hand, "forget the rain. It is only a little farther to the Trogs."

* * *

Carefully, silently...

...The three bellied forward to the brink of the cliff that surrounded an expansive natural quarry fifty feet below. To their right, carved into the vertical rock wall, were ramps and dozens of yellow stone dwellings with thick metal plates interwoven for support. The buildings had holes in them fashioned for windows and doors and looked unkempt. Many were in disrepair and crumbling.

To the left, on the opposite side of the quarry, were two enormous boulders across which lay an uprooted tree trunk. Hanging by her wrists a Renoloi was bound to the ponderous log, periodically raising her head drawing a labored breath; but it was obviously painful with her body suspended.

In the center of the quarry was a tall, rust and gray metallic structure: the color of corrosion. Near the summit were three platforms, one above and two below, where large winged reptiles perched chained to each platform. Observant yellow-red eyes, toothed, snout-shaped beaks and pointed prominent crowns formed their heads atop long, serpentine necks, massive bodies, clawed feet, and folded bat-like wings. Surveying, the Pterosaurs watched the activity below.

Not far from the captured Renoloi a Troglodyte was beating a Tyrannosaurus with a massive knotted club, the carnivore chained by the leg to a stake anchored in the rock floor. The Trog was huge; an enormous, hairy, genetically masculine and lumbering individual who wore a matted fur garment interwoven with the same metal used in the homes. It provided a crude form of armor.

The great beast roared rank breath and defiance as it lunged repeatedly at the Troglodyte, the giant standing his ground, pummeling the dinosaur's head and neck until finally knocking it down. The sound of violent blows and walnut-shell crunch of bone ricocheted from the cliff walls echoing back in a primitive instant replay. Again and again the Tyrannosaur attacked the Trog, screaming, salivating, gnashing its teeth and clanging the chain, each charge ending with defeat and an uncompromising, dominating counterattack of monstrous blows. Over and over, a bloodbath of wills and primitive prowess, dinosaur and behemoth squared off in unremitting savagery to establish unquestioned sovereignty. At last, the Tyrannosaurus retreated to the stake and milled aimlessly, blood oozing from numerous gashes on its neck, its head battered and swollen. It would not fight the Trog again.

Scattered throughout the quarry were residue mounds of yellow mud and clay that had hardened around bubbling acidic pools of a creamy, green-and-yellow sulfuric liquid. In all there were perhaps four hundred Trogs and a dozen dinosaurs comprising the populace. From the quarry rim the three people watched, Tian lying between the men.

"Troglodytes," Ames murmured.

"Just poke me through a donut hole..." Reed finally spit out with disbelief, "un-frickin'-believable."

"Well," Ames whispered across to him, "she said they were big."

"They're not big, they're frickin' *giants*," Reed admonished. He looked at Tian lying beside him. "Certainly can't accuse you of exaggerating." Then shaking his head: "Talk about a penchant for understatement."

"How would you describe them?" she asked defensively. "I said they were big."

"—Behemoth, giant; I could think of any number of adjectives," Reed answered.

"Those are nouns," Ames reminded.

"I was thinking behemoth sons-a-bitches, Doc."

"Oh," Ames replied, "I should have known."

The trio continued to observe the activity in the quarry below; and the longer they watched, the more Tian's attention returned to the captive Renoloi, her emotional nature gradually taking control over her rational nature. She was eminently mindful of the danger below, but it became more difficult with each passing moment to stand by and watch one of her people die. The men were also aware.

"You know her?" Reed whispered.

"Ronto." She almost choked. "She was captured just before you arrived."

"That means she's probably been there for several days," Ames guessed.

"What will happen to her?" Reed asked.

"She will hang there until she goes Beyond."

Wanting to be certain Ames inquired, "Until she dies?"

Sober: "Yes."

For a moment there was silence; then he touched her arm. "I'm going to get her."

Reed darted a glance over Tian to his friend, "Aw jeez, Doc..." he began to say. And as he did, in her expression he saw contempt for the Trogs and empathy for Ronto, and a tear in the corner of her eye. "Right behind you," he finished. He started to rise.

"Cover me," Ames told him reaching over Tian and placing a hand on his shoulder. Ames was up and gone.

Reed and Tian watched while the man moved around the rim of the cliff eventually arriving at the brink above the captive Renoloi. He signaled them from there. Reed pushed his arm through the rifle sling taking the weapon from his back: he was ready.

Tian: "I am worried about John."

"He can take care of himself," Reed assured. Then, *John,* he thought, *he never lets anyone call him that unless...*

Quietly Ames crawled down the vertical rock wall to where gravel and dirt had sloughed off forming an incline; then he jumped onto the closest boulder and laid his weapon down. Startled by the noise the young Renoloi looked up fearfully as the man darted toward her along the top of the tree trunk. Sitting down and straddling the huge log he leaned over so she could see him.

Whispering, "Don't scream," lifting his index finger to his lips indicating silence. "Tian is on the far cliff." Unsettled, she listened, then heartened, looked to the opposite quarry rim, eyes scanning, searching for her leader. "I'm a friend." Ames quickly cut the leather bonds and the captive dropped to the gravel below. As the young Renoloi staggered a step and turned looking up at him, terrified, she unexpectedly screamed. Ames, just rising and putting his knife back in its sheath, was unnerved. "What the hell—" confused, then realized her attention was focused behind him; and sensing danger looked over his shoulder. A Trog poised on the cliff wall with a club.

The brute swung as Ames leaped to the side of the cliff narrowly evading a powerful, splintering blow that gouged the tree trunk. The Trog bounded heavily onto the far boulder landing above the ragged tear he had just hacked in the log. Although the young woman was within reach, crouching frightened on the gravel nearby, the giant's attention was focused on Ames clinging to a jutting rock on the cliff wall.

Moving— dead run.

By now Reed and Tian were circling the rim of the quarry, running as fast as they could directly toward them. Closing the distance.

Ames glanced at his weapon as the lumbering giant began trodding across the tree trunk, nearing him. A second time the Trog grunted and swung shattering the protruding rock in a blizzard of scatter and white-particle dust, throwing the man onto the near boulder beside the laser. Teetering, Ames lost his balance, but before falling —reached— managed to grab it, and pushed himself backward. He landed on the sloughed gravel incline at the side of the cliff where he waited for the towering hulk.

Confidently, swaggering side to side, the Trog shuffled like an upright bear crossing the log, hoisting his club as Ames leveled the pulse laser on the massive chest. Assuming a simian crouch then an ungainly bound, the Trog pounced from the log as Ames squeezed…

—A piercing whine

—Bright flash

Pulse blazed from the muzzle slamming through the giant rupturing his chest, spewing chunks and blood as it exploded out his back. While the Trog's momentum carried him forward Ames could clearly see daylight through the two-foot hole the pulse shredded through him. Collapsing, the giant was dead in mid-air, blood and entrails splattering the quarry floor with plashing scatter-slop. Falling short of Ames, the behemoth crumpled face down on the incline with a gritty-solid, *thud,* then slid feetfirst past Ronto pushing a swollen deluge of gravel in front of him. Ames signaled the terrified Renoloi up the cliff and she scrambled toward the rim.

Looking from Ronto to the dead giant, then across the quarry, he saw a number of Trogs closing quickly, legs thumping with great lumbering strides. Incited by the commotion one Tyrannosaur was attacking, eyes fixed, jaws gnashing, dragging a giant along by its chained leg. The Trog had his wrist tangled in the dinosaur's chain and couldn't free himself, his massive body bumping and skidding over the rock floor —road rashed— then being torn apart one chunk at a time.

First, a leg ripped off when his foot caught in a fissure. Next, his head folded back, splattering when his huge rolling bulk compressed it into the quarry floor. Then, his flopping torso slammed into a boulder and the impact ripped away his entangled arm at the shoulder allowing what was left to skid to a tumbling, blood-smearing halt as the dinosaur continued charging. Loose dog on a chain.

Ames pivoted, saw Ronto: *almost to the rim, she's safe.* He swung around. The analysis: *too close, can't make it, have to fight,* flashed through his mind, and he raised his weapon to take down the nearest giant, who was almost upon him.

—*Swoosh, rrrip*

The spear flew from above with lethal accuracy taking the towering Trog through his throat, ripping out of his back through the shoulder blades. Falling forward he blinked once breaking the spear when he hit the ground.

Hate in her eyes, Tian stood at the rim glaring down upon the fallen Troglodyte. "John, hurry—"

Then Reed was there beside her. "Eat this —bitch!" he growled, lightning bolts of laser-blast flashing into the attacking Trogs. He fired repeatedly killing the approaching brutes as he screamed, a half-laugh, almost maniacally, light pulses ripping their huge bodies to pieces: heads, arms and legs spun like flying shrapnel, torsos detonated and splattered like popping, ruptured hogs. They were torn apart and scattered in whorls of red spray amid explosions vaulting from the quarry floor. Dust and blood, splintered rock and flesh were blasted to vapor-winds and confusion —everything going everywhere— then falling back down obliterated in carnage, a literal rain of death. Reed's finger worked the trigger so fast the whines became a steady drone culminating in an almost unending stream of brilliant white light. Amazed, Tian watched him. She was terrified and at the same time awestruck, the power of this weapon seemingly incomprehensible.

While Reed killed, Ames climbed. His fingers tore at fractured and crumbling stone, boot toes furiously punching into fissures of rock kicking debris aside with his ascent. He was almost to the top, but not quickly enough; the Tyrannosaur was there —powerful, gigantic, eyes glaring— it was going to kill him. One vicious bite would cut him in half and its massive jaws were opening, rank with the stench of carrion, teeth glistening with impaling incisors salivating viscous drool...

—Tian screamed

"...Die T-Rex, die!" Reed thundered sweeping the laser from the reptile's head downward, the dinosaur exploding in sequence. Detonating, its head splattered. Tearing, its neck split apart. Its body distended absorbing one—two—three blasts as it swelled and ballooned then suddenly exploded completely —just pieces— with a windswept fury of entrails and blood-cloud splashing wave. Both hind legs shot sideways and finally the blast that catapulted its tail —*whoomph,whoomph, whoomph*— like an enormous twirling baton, over the quarry floor. Sticky fluid-mist and pieces still spilling down, Reed stood on the rim of the cliff beaming. "Awesome," he proclaimed proudly.

Ames was at the top, reunited with his friends and out of harm's way.

Without a word the four ran straightaway from the quarry putting as much distance as possible between themselves and the Trogs; and it was almost an hour before they finally stopped running, exhausted, none of them could keep going any longer. Tasting blood from the alveoli in their lungs caused by hard breathing, they had to rest. A small grove of the twisted trees provided cover.

Bent over, hands clasping his knees and panting, "Are you all right?" Ames finally managed to ask Tian.

Disgusted: "He broke my spear."

Relief in her eyes, "Thank you, each of you," Ronto said, looking from one to the next.

Tian to Ronto: "Are you badly injured?" Ronto shook her head, *no,* and Tian touched her forehead with three fingers. This gesture completed Tian turned to the men. "We should go now. It is a long way home."

A side-glance and standing upright, Ames asked, "Won't the Trogs come after us?"

"No. We are too few."

"Doc..." Reed began.

Redirecting his attention, "Yeah?"

Hesitant, almost apologetic: "...uh, I didn't mean to seem overly zealous back there at the quarry."

"You didn't."

"You don't think I got carried away then?" a bit relieved. "I mean, you don't think I'm a psycho, do you?"

"Well..." his friend grinned, "sometimes I might wonder about you —just a little."

"Yeah," Reed admitted, "my mom used to tell me that too."

Ames smiled. "How many Trogs did you kill back there anyway, twelve, fifteen?"

Reed thought for a minute. "You know, actually, after the first couple... all I could see was bits and pieces."

"You did all right." Ames assured. "We're all alive."

"Your weapons," Tian considered aloud, eyeing Reed's pulse laser. She didn't know what to think.

"Yeah," he grinned proudly brandishing the weapon, "they're some mean little suckers, aren't they?" A sideways glance, he winked; then turning he and Ronto walked off together.

Innocently Tian looked at Ames. "Reed has a language all his own. He uses words I have never heard before."

"Do you think so?" Ames asked straight-faced. "I hadn't really noticed myself." Without saying anything more he walked after Reed and Ronto. Tian, not knowing if he was serious, wondering... just followed.

Unhurried, the four began their return journey across the Forsaken Land.

CHAPTER SEVEN

Three days later…

…A dwindling fire illuminated the small enclosure surrounded by craggy rock outcroppings on two sides and dense vegetation on the others. Backs to the rock walls, the four people faced the crackling flames. The other three were talking quietly as Ronto moved to the fire and tore a small piece of meat from the Chiqua on the spit. To the men, the animals resembled a cross between hybrid kangaroo rats and reptilian spring hares. The woman tasted it, shook her head, then scooted back with the others.

"Not yet," she told Reed.

Doubtful, he asked, "What do you want, ashes?"

"She knows what she's doing," Ames assured. Tian leaned against him. She felt secure with John, and something else, warm inside. She had never felt that way before, didn't know really what the feeling even was. But it felt good. She wanted to feel that way forever, with him. When he put his arm around her, touching her skin with his rough hands, it gave her goose bumps. She tingled inside, almost a craving, and she squeezed her folded arms more tightly against her body trying to capture the feelings stirring within her, to save them.

Tian understood her feelings for Kimo and her people; they were the same. Their struggle to survive was their bond, caring for each other, dependent upon one another; it kept them alive. But this was something completely different that she did not understand. Tian didn't know the concept of man-and-woman; she was a hermaphrodite. The Legends told that, the genetics. But inside her something was beginning, a feeling, something. Every time John looked in her eyes or touched her it blossomed a tiny bit more. She didn't know of this kind of love. It was completely new: that warm, secure sensation that made her feel complete, the bland emptiness washed away. It felt so very good. She wanted to keep it. Just then Reed's voice brought her back.

"Is it done yet?"

"Yes," Ronto answered, "I believe so."

Reed's face brightened. "Finally, I'm starved."

Ames scooted to the fire and cut pieces of meat for each of them. When he handed Tian hers, they made eye contact and he saw the distant gaze; then, that deeper look, from somewhere within her. He felt it, the warmth, for the first time in his life, and he knew what it was. It felt wonderful.

They ate quietly.

Occasionally Reed and Ronto would talk a little, but Tian and Ames were reticent. She pressed closer, never saying a word; it wasn't necessary. If he moved, even a bit, to shift his weight, she could feel that prosaic emptiness nipping at her somewhere inside, returning; so she would snuggle against him again. It felt very good.

Reed noticed too. Despite his youthful, somewhat reckless nature, he was acutely aware of his surroundings and people he cared about. Once, as Ronto was about to ask Tian a question he intentionally distracted her, turned the conversation back to him leaving his friend and the woman alone. *Time is precious,* he thought. Then he smiled. *There are always possibilities.*

Having finished eating Tian rose and walked to the edge of the clearing gazing over the terrain that still lay before them. She didn't look back when Reed asked, "How much farther?"

"Hopefully, two more days."

"Hopefully?"

Now Tian turned to the man. "Danger still lies ahead. The Forsaken Land transforms. It is an evil place. It never gives, only takes away." Again she turned scanning the near-dark countryside still before them. Ames sensed her apprehension, rose from the campfire, walked to her and slipped an arm around her waist. When he did, she looked up at him and coerced a smile, then leaned her head on his chest.

"Let's go for a walk," he suggested. With pensive eyes and a stirring heart, she smiled willingly and they ambled into the surrounding twilight.

Scrawling circles in the dirt with a stick Reed looked at Ronto still seated beside him. "Spooky shit," he whispered with mock sincerity. Then he explained, "I don't believe in spooky shit myself—well—except for Bloody Bones. He's real, you know."

"I did not know." She was interested.

"Oh, heck yes, Bloody Bones is real," Reed assured and elaborated, "he snatches up little kids when they take the garbage out at night. You know Bloody Bones lives in garbage cans..." then considering, he tossed the stick onto the fire and continued, "well, I guess you wouldn't know about garbage cans, would you?"

"No." Ronto admitted innocently.

Shaking his head, "'Course not— obviously you don't know about that sort of thing." Reed couldn't help grinning. "Well, let me tell you about Bloody Bones..." He was gifted when it came to scary stories.

* * *

Tian and Ames moved along slowly...

...Not really going anywhere, just walking together. This was the beginning of a feeling of unity: it was new for both. Without knowing why he felt as he did, Ames was comfortable with this woman. He knew he could trust her, discuss anything and be completely honest, without fear. The constraints of leadership controlled Tian more than she herself was aware. It was difficult to lead, to know the answers, always; but with this man she had latitude to become who and what she felt inside, not always decisive, ostensibly infallible, simply mortal. With him mistakes were acceptable, something she'd never had before, a companion.

"Why are there no men in your race?" Ames asked prefatorily.

"We are hermaphrodites," she explained. "The Renoloi is female-dominant externally, male-recessive internally. The Trog is male-dominant externally, female-recessive internally." Her words sounded mechanical, memorized, as much as her candor momentarily surprised him. "Our internal organs are functional but very minimal." The explanation seemed almost clinical.

"How do you know that?"

"The Legends," she answered. It must have been obvious to her, seemingly surprised he asked. "The Legends told of our reproductive organs." Without intimation, lifting her leather skirt she took his hand and placed it on her groin. "Feel me," with straightforward innocence, "female-dominant externally. Would you like to examine my organs?"

"—Jesus, Tian." Ames blushed withdrawing a little, but still touching her. He wanted to touch her, his fingers moving ever so slightly, massaging her pubic mound.

Not at all bashful, she reached to his blue jeans feeling him. "You are definitely male-dominant externally; but I did not know the organ could be so rigid." The clinical Tian was fading; something was stirring within her and she was not certain what it was. She had never known these feelings before. She was innocent, intent. "It makes me feel very strange inside, John, when you touch me... there."

"I know," he whispered.

Ronto's scream startled them.

Both were instantly moving, running to help, and quickly they sprang into camp. Ronto was laughing, sitting beside Reed who was lying flat on his back, legs spread wide and a dumbstruck look on his face.

"What happened?" Ames demanded, breathless.

"Over there," Ronto explained, pointing and laughing so hard she brought tears to her eyes. At the opposite side of the clearing crouched a Compsognathus, a little dinosaur, perhaps two feet tall. It hopped once then darted back into the underbrush.

"What?" Ames was confused.

Reed, still clasping his hands on his chest but now laughing himself, explained, "I was telling Ronto a story when that little sucker ran right across my lap and bounced off my chest. 'Bout gave me a heart attack."

"He was telling me about Bloody Bones and garbage cans," Ronto volunteered.

Putting it together Ames chuckled. "Reed—you—gomer. Serves you right. Hope it scared the shit out'a you."

He admitted, "Took ten years off my life, at least."

"Bloody Bones?" Tian asked Ames.

"He was telling Ronto a scary story and it didn't turn out quite as he expected; it backfired." Tian smiled amused with nature's design in poetic justice, and they joined the others at the fire. Together the four talked and laughed for a while as the rest of the night slipped away serenely.

* * *

It was mid-morning: a bright blue sky and yellow-globe sun...

...The four people entered a clearing in one of the widely scattered groves of the dryland. In the uppermost reaches of a large twisted tree there was an enormous nest. Reed, first to notice the tangle of interwoven branches and dried mud, commented, "Look at the size of it."

"Similar to an osprey nest," Ames observed as they approached the tree, "structurally anyway." Arriving at the mammoth trunk Ames took hold of a lower branch and dug the toe of his boot into the coarse bark, starting to climb.

"Where you going, Doc?"

"Up there," indicating the nest overhead, "I want to see what's in it."

Reed seemed nervous. "What if mother bird comes back?"

Ames grinned. "I'll just be a minute. You stay here and cover me."

"Yeah, right." Skillfully Ames climbed to the higher limbs, as watching from below, Reed admitted reluctantly, "Climbs remarkably well for someone his age." Neither Renoloi understood nor acknowledged the crack.

Eventually arriving directly beneath the nest Ames was struck by the odor of decay and coppery scent of blood. Muscles tensed, he leaped and pulled himself up onto the edge of the nest as the three below looked on until he finally managed to drag himself into it by weaseling through the jabbing, scratching, mishmash of nest material.

Dirty gray and about the size of footballs, two eggs lay center stage. Examining them, Ames found them to be surprisingly heavy and their shells tough and leathery. He carefully carried an egg to the edge of the nest to show the trio waiting below. "Scrambled, poached, or fried," he quipped.

"Reed, what is he doing?" Tian asked nervously. "What does he intend to do with that egg?"

"Omelet maybe." Then disdainfully, "Why are you asking me? I don't know." And quickly he yelled up, "Put it back and get down here." Waving him off Ames disappeared into the middle of the nest.

Another minute passed.

"Tian, look!" Ronto said, alarmed, pointing to the sky. Darting looks where she pointed Tian and Reed immediately understood her concern.

"Aww—shit. 'Big Bird'," Reed worried out loud. Majestically a Pterosaur was soaring toward them. Reed called to his friend, "Doc, better get your ass out'a there —pdq."

Ames didn't appear.

Tian and Ronto joined Reed, yelling, but there was still no response from above. Absorbed, Ames was leaning over the eggs concentrating so intently that he heard none of the shouts from below, until finally Tian's voice caught his attention; so in a half-crouch he made his way to the edge of the nest and peered down.

A shadow eclipsed him and suddenly he became aware of a heavy flapping sound —and as Reed raised his weapon Ames realized what it was. Premonition directed his attention overhead: that queasy, *think I'll have a bowel movement,* feeling conveying the realization of being in the wrong place at a particularly inopportune time.

Looking up he saw the Pterodactyl hovering directly above him, and, *aww shit.* Pumping, gray-brown bat wings spanning thirty-six feet of sky conveyed taloned feet with eight-inch claws, a slender neck supporting the crested head and ramphotheca-layered pointed beak set between focused, angry reptilian eyes. Startled, Ames could do nothing but fall to the nest as the Pterosaur swooped down upon him striking the back of his head and neck.

Reed fired from below.

The blast grazed the nest rim shredding the edge in an explosion of wood splinters, splattering dried mud-dust and a chalky feces cloud, and continued on toward the Pterosaur's wing, blowing cleanly through. Wings spread wide, the reptile was momentarily bewildered and stunned by the tearing force; craning its ungainly head it saw the hole, then got mad.

With dexterity and speed induced by fear, Ames rolled onto his back, slipped his head free of the laser sling and triggered the weapon all in a single fluid motion. The ripping force creased the Pterosaur's body, slicing open its breast and blowing out the wing below the shoulder lifting the reptile off the nest. Now enraged, incensed by pain the Pterodactyl screamed wildly dropping on the man again.

It pounded him.

Clutching him by the waist its thick talons dug deep, opening gashes that instantly bled as it securely pinned him to the nest. Ames tried to target the head as the leathery bat wings pummeled beating him, flapping in powerful sweeping arcs effectively immobilizing him, preventing him from aiming and firing.

He could clearly see the pointed tongue and internally set rows of angled teeth as it chopped hollow clacks missing his face by inches, trying to tear him to pieces. The Pterodactyl's wild yellow-red eyes blinked slowly, its pupils expanding beneath closed eyelids, then opening, contracting horizontally again adjusting to the daylight, its sultry breath as rank and disgusting as a carrion fed dog.

Clutching Ames in its foot the Pterosaur began to rise, clearing the nest, when unexpectedly its head exploded disappearing in a flash of light that came from below. Still hovering and hemorrhaging, the wings continued flapping for a few more heartbeats, and with each pumping beat the reptile's neck squirted blood resembling a severed snake as it revolved and twisted aimlessly, nowhere to go.

Dead in mid-air it released its grip and dropped the man onto the rim of the nest as the Pterosaur went down. Ames landed hard and rolled over the edge, but with one last, resolute effort dropped his weapon, reached for a branch and clung to it. With blood and perspiration burning his eyes he saw the Pterodactyl fold and spiral, descending out of sight. Then everything began to fade, his grip loosened, and darkness overcame him.

Horrified Tian watched Ames drop, plummeting limply into the limbs of the tree jostling a verdant wave as he disappeared splashing into the leaves; then ensuing cracks echoing when the peripheral branches, too weak to bear his weight gave way. Reappearing, his body rolled off them and plunged toward the ground, but his fall was cushioned as he landed on the carcass of the Pterosaur then slid from it onto the dirt. He lay flaccid and motionless and his companions rushed to him, saw the blood soaking through his torn shirt, and Reed lifted his head studiously gently slapping him back to consciousness, the same way he had seen it done in the movies. Stunned, Ames stared blankly as he slowly regained his senses.

"I told you not to climb up there," Reed grumbled, "but would you listen... *nooo*," relieved his friend wasn't dead.

***

A while later...

...Beneath the tree, Tian and Ronto were finishing bandaging his ribs with strips of cloth that had previously been his shirt. Ames moaned just a little.

"Can you walk?" Tian asked tenderly.

"Yeah," slowly rising to his feet.

100

Reed, handing him his weapon: "That was dumb."

Ames drew a painful breath. "Yeah, yeah, I know," then he asked, "but didn't you ever fall out of a tree when you were a kid?"

"I 'spose, a couple of times."

"Did you get up and walk away?"

"Yes," Reed said, remembering.

"Then I can too," Ames whispered, determination in his voice.

"Doc, you're not a kid. You're old…er," Reed argued.

Ames chuckled, then winced. "—*Ouch,* don't make me laugh. It hurts."

"Serves you right," Reed threw back. Then more or less to no one in particular, "For crying out loud, if you'd gotten yourself killed how could we bury you?" And shaking his head disapprovingly, "Heck, we don't even have a shovel." His way of saying, *glad you're all right.*

Worrying over him Tian said, "The dressing should keep until we arrive home." Looking back up at the nest, Ames smiled. "What, John?" she asked curiously.

"It looks a lot higher from up there."

* * *

The four continued their homeward journey...

...Their progress only slightly hindered by Ames' injury; and Tian stayed close to him, the maternal instinct. With Reed and Ronto leading, they made their way through another wooded grove arriving at a rye grass meadow. In the clearing, perhaps fifty yards away, grazed a horned, armored dinosaur vaguely resembling a rhinoceros with its four-ton body trodding on short elephantine legs. Reed and Ronto stopped, crouched observing the animal, allowing Ames and Tian time to atch up.

"Triceratops," Reed said, then changed his mind. "No, Styracosaurus." Ames and Tian slipped in from behind them. "There weren't any dinosaurs here before. Where did they come from?" Reed asked, not really expecting an answer.

"They came with the rain," Tian replied. To him that explanation seemed less than plausible, but he didn't say so. The four watched for a few minutes as the animal ambled and grazed.

"What do you think, Doc?"

Viewing the placid reptile, "Possibly evolution gone full circle," Ames said quietly. "Keep to the woods," backing away. "Come on, we'll go around."

"Evolution? I thought you didn't believe in evolution." But Ames was already moving away, and didn't look back.

Not far from where they saw the Styracosaurus the woods ended abruptly and they were confronted with a large open marsh margined on the opposite side by a rim of high cliffs. To the left and near the center of this wetland another prehistoric creature lumbered, a savage four-legged carnivore with a pronounced dorsal sail. It was indifferently scraping the flesh from the flanks of a creature that was held fast in a weed-overgrown, partially concealed tar pit, black muck with the consistency of raw tree sap. The prey roared and struggled furiously, but to no avail; oozing, its precious life leaking out with each new wound the predator inflicted.

"Dimetrodon," Ames said.

Reed agreed, then added, "For crying out loud, we're in 'Jurassic Park'." Uneasy, Ronto edged a bit closer to him.

Watching the animal, "No," Tian corrected, "it is 'Vanishing Valley'."

Ames: "'Vanishing Valley'?"

"Yes, when it rains the valley rises. When there is no rain, the valley vanishes."

Now even more skeptical Reed opened his mouth, then paused, but finally had to say, "It figures; it really does."

Tian paid no attention; instead, she looked beyond the dinosaur, imagined beyond the cliffs, knowing what was waiting. Apprehensively she took Ames' arm pressing against him. "We cannot make our way from this land safely."

"Why not?" He felt her trembling, could sense her fear.

"I know. Within me, a voice: in this land one of us..." words cut short; she was truly frightened.

Trying to allay her concern, his expression earnest, penetrating beyond the sparkling hazel of her eyes. "Tian," he said solemnly, "you can do anything you believe you can." She listened. "If you believe in yourself... there are always possibilities."

Looking at him, she wanted to believe, but it was very difficult. Tian was a Renoloi... and the Renoloi possessed a gift.

"Stay low. Let's see if we can get across without being noticed..." Reed whispered, and he just had to add, "—or eaten."

They abandoned the cover of the treeline and headed across the open bog moving quickly and low, mostly concealed by the swamp grass. Their luck held until they neared the middle of the wetland marsh where the rhythm of their footfalls, sucking sloshes, gave them away. The predator noticed them, watched them; then began to follow.

It pursued slowly at first, gradually increasing its clumsy bounding strides, heaving its bulk from one side to the other as it moved. Ronto and Reed led the way through the high weeds with Tian and Ames close behind as the Dimetrodon began to close the distance between them. Knowing now they were being chased the four ran all out, weaving through, jumping over and flailing the marsh grass aside as they fled, running as quickly as possible, headed for the safety of the cliff at the far end of the marsh. With each bounding step the dinosaur was gaining. It would be close.

Suddenly disappearing into the soggy undergrowth Tian screamed, Ames and the others instantly aborting their flight to help, the Dimetrodon now loping at full speed. She was trapped, sunken to her thighs and stuck in one of the obsidian tar pits. Decisively Ames ran back and dropped to his knees reaching for her outstretched hand.

Reed reeled bringing his weapon to bear on the dinosaur. The Dimetrodon was almost upon them, the pair within six bounding strides and only seconds remaining as it attacked plowing through the brittle swamp grass, sucking up splattering globs of mud in its wake. The dinosaur's dorsal fin sweeping from side to side as it moved

—closer— a dark predatory boat vaulting over a lake of mire. Its long tail slashing through the high reed grass cutting uneven swaths and scattering it away —too close— massive feet punching holes in the sodden marsh as liquefied blobs heaved from beneath its belly.

It charged. Reed squeezed.

  —A piercing whine,

   —Bright flash

The Dimetrodon took the laser blast in its muscled shoulder, stumbling, knocking it down two steps short of Ames and the trapped woman, crushing swamp grass and plunging headlong, furrowing mud and stagnant water into a wave of muck. The viscous wall rose as a dark breaker, a deluge of sludge swept in a sheet and splattering as slop as mud drenched them burying them with fetid black soup.

Almost instantly the Dimetrodon reared its head, folded the dorsal fin flat and rolled over sideways; then back onto its feet reinflating the sail. Dinosaur dog doing tricks. It shook flinging mud as Ames and Tian cowered soaked in the camouflage of mire. Then bellowing a vicious curdling roar, ripping incisors bared leaking drool of saliva, the reptile searched for its prey as Reed fired again.

With the blast creasing its backbone the Dimetrodon's dorsal fin ripped apart tearing hide and flesh spewing blood in the air. Another blast. Pain driving it wild, it turned and charged the young man, blood spraying from arterial wounds and snorting mucus from its flared nostrils. Although seriously wounded the Dimetrodon was intent and bloodthirsty, bounding toward the two with untamed savagery, relentless, plowing a trench through the swamp.

"What does it take to put you down?" Reed muttered, standing his ground, aiming again at the charging predator.

Ronto looked behind them for an escape, only to see another dinosaur coming from their rear. It was different than the Dimetrodon, a Stegosaurus, moving considerably faster, already upon them.

"—Reed!" she screamed.

As he turned the animal slammed into him knocking him out of its path and headlong into the mud, continuing its charge, focused on the Dimetrodon. Terrified he'd been killed Ronto ran to the prostrate man, jerked him over and almost cried with relief when he blinked with white eyes and spit mud from a pink mouth. The rest of him was black.

Both animals crashed together in furious combat, a territorial violation. They maneuvered attacking one another, crushing and ripping out huge wads of swamp grass, kicking and plashing sheets of mud, throwing globs in massive slops. They fought: ramming, stumbling and falling, rising and charging, crashing together, slipping and going down again. Olive drab and furious the beak-nosed Stegosaurus rushed forward, a slamming broadside head-butt into the Dimetrodon. The carnivore burst a pain-filled deflated roar going down sideways from the impact, being squeezed under the larger reptile's bulk into the swamp mud.

The Stegosaurus overran the Dimetrodon viciously stomping and trampling it underfoot until it was nearly submerged. But when the Stegosaurus turned the Dimetrodon flashed a ruthless bite into its belly tearing it wide with an eruption of bowels. Screaming, the Stegosaurus reeled traipsing intestines from the wound, its bulging white entrails trailing out, dragging and mixing with the mire and matted grass. Untamed eyes glared from one to the other, both dinosaurs wild with pain, and angry, each determined to prevail.

As the Dimetrodon flailed freeing itself from the black cratered hole, the Stegosaurus powerfully whipped its spiked tail impaling the Dimetrodon's neck. The tail snatched back jerking the dinosaur's head and opening the spike wounds with puncture holes going all the way through the carnivore's neck, letting blood from both sides and pumping crimson onto its breast. The Dimetrodon retaliated, lunging onto the larger dinosaur's back, savagely sinking its teeth into the spinal plates then ripping them apart, leaving nothing more than ragged shreds of leathery hide. Blood poured over the Stegosaurus' shoulders and down its flanks mixing with the mud in a smear of murky violet.

Preoccupied with their rival, neither reptile noticed the two desperate people, Ames struggling feverishly and finally succeeding in pulling Tian free of the tar pit. Airborne: more sheets of water and whirling scatter-globs of mud. Still unnoticed, both quickly crawled beyond reach of the thunderous colliding animals' heavy trampling feet, thick crushing bodies and dangerous sweeping tails. Once clear they rose and ran to rejoin Ronto and Reed.

* * *

A short while later both Renoloi and the battered men hobbled along the safety of a ledge on the high ridge. From there they observed the conclusion of the furious battle in the marsh. Catching their breath, they watched as the Stegosaurus repeatedly slammed its weight against the Dimetrodon until the carnivore went down onto its side, beaten to the ground. Preparing for a final attack the larger dinosaur raised its head in a victory roar exposing its neck. Vulnerable, that suddenly the Dimetrodon rolled in the mud lunging at the other, in one decisive movement tearing out its throat in a bloody eruption that exposed its trachea and soft tissue.

The mortally wounded Stegosaurus reared its head thrashing wildly as blood gushed scarlet from the wound; then plunging forward it collapsed. Lying where it fell its breathing was heavy and labored spawning bubbles of mud, and finally ceased with a rasping groan of anguish and terminal puff. The Dimetrodon remained momentarily; loomed, roaring defiantly over its fallen rival, a victory in passing. Then exhausted, it lumbered toward the trees surrounding the marsh where it too could find a cool, shady place to die.

Ames, favoring his injured side, asked Tian. "Are you all right?"

"Yes, only frightened," she said trying to wipe the black ooze from her legs and hips.

Ames turned to his friend. "Thanks."

"No need; we're in this together, Doc."

"Are you hurt, Reed?" Ronto asked, her concern apparent.

"No, not really," picking dried bits of mud from his cheeks and forehead, "I've felt worse. It's about like getting run over by a frickin' Greyhound bus." He grinned, part of his resilient nature. "Did I ever tell you about that?"

"No, you did not, only Bloody Bones," she answered. "What is a Greyhound bus?"

"—Reed," Ames interjected.

"No really, Doc. This is a true story."

* * *

From the summit of the cliffs...

...The four surveyed the final obstacle between them and land of the Renoloi, the expansive darkness of 'Black Water'.

"Is that it?" Ames asked Tian. Reed and the other woman standing alongside, listened.

"Yes," she replied apprehensively shrinking at the thought of the mysterious terrain before them.

Frightened, Ronto insisted, "We must go around."

Eyeing the landscape Reed observed, "Just looks like a giant swamp to me."

Ames asked, "How many miles does it cover?"

"No one knows." Tian looked at him. "Are you angry that we fear this place?"

"No," he assured. "It's only a swamp. We can do this."

The travelers descended to the swamp, and stepping lightly, entered the stagnant water. It was chest-deep on the men, the women barely able to keep their heads above the surface, clutching the men's hands as they were absorbed within the gloomy abyss. Moving cautiously, quietly, ever-expanding ripples before them, they went deeper within. Progress was slow.

The swamp enfolded them with its tentacled arms of thick twisted trees wearing pulpy rough-textured bark and aberrant limbs reaching from the darkness. Clinging green mosses appeared ashen-gray in the shadows and seemed to watch them with wrinkled eyes. All around them were spiderwebs of lichen trailing matted strings, dragging across their faces and shoulders when they passed. In the dark there were dangling vines —or possibly water moccasins— they all looked the same in here. The odor of plant decay was subtly carried along on unseen breezes that wafted over the murky water they pushed before them. This was truly a dismal waterworld... out of place.

Darkness enveloped them like so many layers of fog, their procession meandering around massive tree trunks and submerged objects. And as they were absorbed within this opaque world, the canopy effectively blocking virtually all sunlight created an eerie shrouded darkness. Pushing forward, they could hear the water ripple and an occasional, *kerplunk,* when some unseen reptile or amphibian plopped from a log back into its murky aquatic realm. They proceeded slowly and cautiously, imagination giving rise to illusion, could be an enemy in the darkness. This was an unworldly place... it should not be here.

Only the four people moving through the water made any sound and finally Ames suggested, "It's getting pretty dark in here."

A match burst into flame reflecting off Reed's face, then flickering, illuminated the immediate area. "Find something for torches," he said. The women watched the match burn with wonder. Matches were new to them. Ames cut liana from overhead and wrapped them with moss.

"Where'd you get the matches?"

"Waterproof GI matchbox," he almost bragged. "Forgot all about them 'til just now."

"You do have your moments," Ames complimented; and he lit the torches.

"Thank you, Mr. Walker," Reed whispered breathing a sigh of relief.

"Who?"

"John Walker, an Englishman, Doc. He made the first friction matches in 1827. Made them with antimony trisulfide. As I recall, they were called lucifers."

They continued on.

Ames inquired, "Lucifers huh," artificially impressed, then, "where did you learn so much about matches?" striking up a conversation: distraction.

Trying to see beyond the torchlight, into the darkness, "Beneath this crass exterior dwells an individual of substantial intellect," Reed whispered half-joking. And he continued, "Later yellow phosphorous was substituted for the antimony, but it proved to be poisonous so it was replaced by non-poisonous phosphorous trisulfide." Watchful, searching the shadows: "They all worked about the same —you know— friction on a red phosphorous surface, oxidant materials ignited by friction when the striking surface is converted to white phosphorous residue, and so forth." Taking a breath, "But do you know where the first safety match was invented?" uneasy, his eyes constantly scanning their surroundings.

"England?" Ames guessed.

"Nope, Sweden. Fooled me too. The book match was an American invention."

"Fascinating," Ames commented. A grin.

Ronto observed, "Reed, you talk a lot."

"He's just nervous," Ames told her.

"Don't make fun of me, Doc," he warned. "It seems you'd appreciate having matches at a time like this."

"I do. Why?"

Reed, still looking around, answered, "Because it's not so spooky in here with a light."

They proceeded quietly for awhile.

"Why didn't we return the same way we came," Ames asked Tian, finally interrupting the silence.

"This is the way we came."

"This is the way we came? Before it was rocky dry ground with a few scattered wooded groves."

"It rained."

He agreed, "I know but..." snipping his response he asked, "do you mean four days of rain can change this land this much?"

"Yes. There are droughts and the land is barren with no life. When it rains all the water flows here and life returns." She reached underwater to her thigh, squeezed a leech and pried it loose, then tossed it away, *kerplunk*.

Darting her a side-glance, still skeptical and now willing to tell her so, Reed challenged, "That seems unlikely, in fact quite preposterous actually." Tian looked, acknowledging; but she didn't argue. Then reconsidering he concluded, "Well fuckit—so do giants and dinosaurs." Reed leading the way, they continued slowly.

On one occasion, when he moved too near a darker area of water Tian warned, "Reed, be careful of that place; it is black water."

Noticing the darker-shade area in the murky water he avoided it, glancing back and asking, "What's black water?"

"I do not know, but if you stepped there it would pull you under."

Reed, to Ames: "Quicksand?"

Ames looked up. "Probably."

Tian, still clinging to his hand, asked, "What is quicksand?"

He tried to offer a simple explanation. "Quicksand is a suspension, muck, formed by pressurized water under a layer of sand or similar substance. The water pushes the solid particles apart so they're less dense, not packed tightly enough to hold weight, and anything heavy tends to sink into it."

"It sounds like black water," she granted.

Minutes turned to hours with little conversation as the people tediously waded through seemingly endless murk, making their way through the dismal, duckweed swamp. Each replacing the moss as it burned, their torches afforded just enough light to penetrate the darkness and created imaginary, shadowy figures all around them with obscurity lurking just beyond. It seemed to take forever: weaving between tree trunks, detouring clear of the pools with black water, and avoiding the tangled maze of liana overhead. The dank humidity of the swamp gradually faded, blending to misty waves of cooler air slowly, unobtrusively creeping in.

"It must be night," Ames commented.

"Seems like we've been in here for a week." Reed rubbed his shoulders to warm up. He squeezed Ronto's hand. "Are you tired?"

"A little."

"Cold?"

"A little."

"Look on the bright side," Ames told them helping Tian around a submerged pool of black water, "at least now the water feels warm."

"The eternal optimist," Reed conceded.

Ames: "And not even a single snake… so far."

"Oh, now that's not even funny, Doc." Reed hated snakes.

For several hours more they continued their meandering travel; skirting obstacles, pushing through the dreary blend of mire and floating duckweed, stealing forward. Fatigue overtook them slowly, inexorably; and misjudgment, its inseparable companion, lurked dangerously closer until the inevitable happened. As Ames extended his hand to help Tian around another of the black water pools his foot slipped and he disappeared, sucked into the mire.

Clinging desperately to his hand, being dragged under Tian screamed, *"—Reed!"*

Immediately grasping the situation, the clear-thinking man reached for a limb of the nearest tree pushing Ronto, who was already holding his other hand toward Tian. Ronto clasped Tian's free hand forming a human chain —and that quickly— Tian also, was half-submerged in the deadly black water. Brown foam spewed up as turbid clouds of sediment stirred whirling around them in a life and death tug of war, the muck below sucking them down, Reed's strength pulling them out.

Straining pectorals and biceps his chest and arms bulged and flexed, his wet gray shirt clinging like a second layer of skin. The arteries in his neck throbbed with an adrenaline-push that forced his blood faster pumping oxygen for strength. Heart pounding furiously, he pulled, his grip on the limb so fierce that the bark squeezed out between his clenched fingers, bark slivers cutting into his hand. Dripping wet, beads of sweat formed on his forehead intermingling with the muddy water on his face.

Pull dammit, pull—squinting and clenching his teeth, veins defining thoroughfares on his athletic arms and chest. With tremendous exertion and a surge of power...

—Spl-oosh

...An uprising mound of froth and blast of bubbles where his friend had gone under, and an instant later the surface exploded in boil and spray as Ames gasped for a breath of air floating free of the black water. The wave washed past and after his companions had pulled him to safety, he slumped against the tree panting. With a grateful smile he re-centered the laser across his back by adjusting the sling across his chest; then as he pushed matted hair from his forehead he joked, "I slipped."

Reed felt around the bottom with his foot, located his weapon and went under to get it, surfaced and slung it across his back. "Don't do that again, Doc," he scolded. "Next time we'll leave you down there."

"I was beginning to wonder this time," Ames bantered, still catching his breath. He asked Tian, "How do you feel?"

"My back is sore." She frowned.

"Ronto?"

"My arms are sore," also frowning.

"Reed?"

"I'm sore all over."

Ames changed the subject. "Where are the torches?"

"We do not need them anymore," Ronto told him, pointing ahead of them. Dawn had arrived and in the distance light was visible under the canopy. Relieved, "We are almost out," she declared.

* * *

With renewed hope...

...Four weary people finally waded beneath a warm rising sun, once more visible through scattered broken clouds. And they surveyed the expansive lake that extended from the swamp to the distant rolling hills; it was a beautiful morning.

Turning toward the sun Reed warmed his face. "There's only one thing that could make me happier than that sun." Looking around he swished his arms through the chest-deep water and said, "Dry land."

"Once we cross the lake and are over those hills, we will be home," Tian told them, happiness shining in her eyes.

"And safe again," a relieved Ronto added.

The four made their way across the lake, more talkative now with the prospect of getting home, the shore appearing closer with each buoyant step. Walking was easier, the bottom being solid not mud and providing better footing even with buoyancy working against them.

Nearing the opposite bank, perhaps still fifty yards away, Reed commented, "The bottom feels like rock," walking backward, facing the others.

Following his friend, the women beside him, Ames observed, "Comparable to our own Mesozoic Era on Earth, which lasted about a hundred-eighty-million years."

"I'm aware of the duration of the Mesozoic," Reed said. "What do you mean by, 'our own'?" But there wasn't time for a reply. Just then he bumped into something submerged, something big, something very big, and kicked at it underwater trying to figure out what it was. Raising a hand to the others, "Wait, there's something here."

What had appeared to be floating driftwood, emerged —a giant snake— upward, out of the water. Surging boil heaved a six-foot wave as a monstrous reptile vaguely resembling a Brachiosaur with jutting jaws, that had been dozing lying on its side, lifted its eighty-foot length upright in a tremendous roll casting a shadow over the four in the water below. As the viper-shaped head and slender neck majestically rose the disturbed reptile saw the people, and with a serpentine movement attacked. The dinosaur opened its jaws, water and saliva pouring from its mouth; its attention focused on Reed, a bobbing cork in its body's massive wake.

Reed had barely enough time to unsling his weapon when the grinding jaws were upon him, and shielding himself he rammed the laser sideways into the dinosaur's mouth —crunched into worthless metal as water-slime spouted from the creature's bulging nostrils. Dwarfed by the towering behemoth the man was petrified but still managed to hang on to the mangled weapon, his only defense against its powerful teeth. The dinosaur raised its head carrying Reed along, that, *going up,* feeling; and as he dangled animatedly high above the titan shook its head and opened its jaws catapulting him seventy feet.

As he splashed into the lake the dinosaur's tail emerged from beneath him hurtling him back into the air.

Ames finally had a clear shot, targeting the head, the blast ripping through its throat tearing a large chunk of flesh with blood-pulse squirting from the open wound. Letting a tremendous scream, the enraged dinosaur turned on Ames, and as it did, its incredible body heaved another overpowering wave submerging him and the women.

—Water and bubbles, distorted noise

Ames surfaced swiping water from his face, ready to fire again. Looming the dinosaur lowering its head, jaws opening —the strike— coming in; then a shrill whine —the blast— and the skull shattering, blowing away its tiny brain. The colossus floundered then collapsed into the lake causing a roiling tsunami that pounded over them knocking Ames and the women to the lakebed's bottom. The concussion stunned Ames and he lost his weapon somewhere underwater as the fifteen-foot swell surged with its crushing-sweep of pressure from above, then rolled past.

For a moment the only sound was the scattering-sprinkle of water droplets falling back onto the lake. Then, as the chopping water surface finally began to settle, Reed's head popped up, and Ronto, and Ames —but not Tian. Each consciously counting others, the three immediately began searching for the Renoloi; and amidst the texture of undulating surface Reed first saw the expanding pool of blood-brown water percolating bubbles encircling the dinosaur's half-submerged head, then noticed a figure drifting beyond it, behind Ames and Ronto.

"Over there!" pointing toward the woman's body.

Ames spun around —choked, "No—" desperately swimming toward her.

Tian was floating face down.

With urgent, powerful strokes, Ames swiftly crossed the distance, and reaching her turned her, raising her head from the water. Without a word, Reed helped get her to the nearby shore where Ames lifted her limp, dripping body in his arms and hurried, carrying her to a grassy knoll beneath an old twisted tree. There he laid her down and they began CPR.

One thousand one, one thousand two, one thousand three...

One minute passed, then two minutes. "There's no pulse, no respirations, Doc." Ames refused to quit. He wouldn't stop. Three minutes passed, then four. "There's no pulse, no respirations, Doc." Reed choked on his words; but he knew.

One thousand one, one thousand two, one thousand three...

Ames refused to quit. He could feel the anguish of desperation creeping closer, the shadow of despair looking over his shoulder, the ghost of sorrow standing behind him somewhere, the specter of death lurking impatiently in an invisible doorway. Five minutes passed. Six minutes passed; seven.

Ames still refused to quit; but he knew.

"I'm so sorry," Reed whispered. He rose from Tian's body, lead Ronto away, trying to comfort her.

Ames did not move. He remained there, kneeling over Tian's body. For a moment he couldn't move, paralyzed with pain and emptiness. For the first time in his life, he felt completely lost.

Her words murmured softly, echoes inside his head: *'I know. Within me, a voice: in this land one of us...'*

His world was drifting away, and he wouldn't let her go. Sitting down in the grass, ever so gently he picked up her body cradling her in his arms, her head to his chest. Holding her to him he viewed the most precious soul he had ever known. Beautiful and silent, she made not a sound: motionless and limp, not seeming to be real, a damp, cool marionette without her strings. Inanimate and lifeless, a shell without the flame, her wet hair was matted, clinging to her face instead of flowing wistfully, beautifully, with the gentlest of breezes.

There was no movement within her torpid chest. The rhythmical expansion of her breathing was absent, gone with the beguiling smile and laughter... and the ember of love they had created, an ember that never had time to mature to the flame. It seemed as though the seed of a beautiful flower had germinated with hope, sprouted, peered from the ground and reached for the sky for the very first time: a simple quest for life and love snuffed without warning by the reckless footstep of a passerby not paying attention. The circumstances of life can be like that: uncaring, cruel, and detached. But this was a new world, and perhaps he'd dared risk the hope of expecting just a bit more.

He began to cry, softly at first...

...Then he broke down completely and sobbed. Tears dampened his face, trails of sorrow tracking wet lines to his chin, weathered and tired, worn down by life. His tears fell onto Tian's cheeks, almost as though she would cry too; then they glided in liquid paths toward her ear and slipped quietly away. Silently she lay there, her eyes closed, her expression calm with the reflective absence of the life from Beyond... the unknown experience that eventually captures us all.

"Why, God?" His voice was hoarse, pained. "Why did this have to be? Did she have to die?" and he sobbed, tears streaming down his face, not understanding, feeling more pain than he believed it possible to endure. The torment burned with a fire unlike that any injury could inflict; this pain was deep inside. This pain was bleeding that wouldn't heal; a churning, twisting, hollow knife blade of void. The darkness within a whirlpool spiraling into the aching chamber of loss... somewhere deep within his soul.

Holding her limp body to his breast he violently rocked back and forth and sobbed. The shirt she had so carefully, tenderly, used to bandage his ribs was now the woman's pillow. With his arms around her he pressed her head gently to his quivering chest, heaving with sobs of anguish... and a dark burning fire that could never be consoled.

"Why?" he pleaded, not understanding. "Fifteen billion years to find her... and now You've taken her away. If someone must die, why not me? Please don't do this." Clutching Tian, he continued to rock back and forth, holding her, never wanting to let her go. It made no sense to the man... preparation for the journey.

He wrapped her tightly within his arms, perhaps a futile attempt to capture the essence of who she really was, still a mystery, but now an inseparable part of him. He had tried, but they had not enough time to really know one another. "She didn't deserve this," he sobbed. "We didn't have time." He continued to rock back and forth, tears running down his face, clutching the only woman he had ever loved... suffering a pain that twisted inside and would never let go.

"Take me," he choked. "Please let her live. I need her." He cried... and rocked back and forth. "I believe in You... please, believe in me." He continued to rock back and forth, sobbing uncontrollably, and the pain, the torment, would not go away. Tian's soul was still and quiet as the vast emptiness of space; her skin ashen, the hue of death, eyes closed... her spirit wandering blissfully near the realm of Beyond.

Cradling her within his arms Ames tenderly kissed her forehead, tears dripping onto her cheek. With gentle fingertips he gingerly brushed matted hair from her face, a gesture of devotion. His eyes were blurred with tears and reddened with pain. His body trembled with torment. Within him the emptiness. He was so desperately alone. He cried... and he rocked back and forth.

Cold, aching-numb flashed inside causing his arms and legs to tingle then lose all sensation, a protective layer for his heart, to suppress the pain. But his pain was still there, the whirlwind of confusion stirring inside his brain, dizzying denial of reality... and Tian motionless within his embrace.

He sobbed... and he rocked back and forth. "Please," he murmured. "God, I need her." In a strange new world he could not understand, he cradled her to his breast. He was so desperately alone. He cried... and he rocked back and forth.

With shade of mystery traversing the sky, a billowing cloud concealed the sun...

"Please, God," the man pleaded painfully. He rocked back and forth.

A deep blue sky,

...And one billowing cloud.

Pictures clicked in his mind. A pristine pool at the base of a bluff and riffles of water smoothing away, she was standing over him, her expression stern. The bronze door and her hut when they entered for the first time, she was patient and innocent. The moon casting their shadows to the canyon from the cliff, like an insatiable thirst she wanted to learn, to know. Tarin along the path and the Renoloi at the meeting circle, she was firm in her leadership, and a heart laced with compassion. Their struggle to survive the icy rock faces of the mountainside. Then the quarry, the Trogs. She possessed sincerity and determination. Reed at the campfire sprawled out as the Compsognathus darted away, he could hear her laughter and see her smile: beautiful, enchanting, emanating joy and a wonder of life. All that and more absorbed within the vision of sparkling hazel eyes... the snare that captured his heart.

Fatigued, spent, he pressed his face against hers holding her to his heart and soul to ward off the encroaching, overwhelming awareness, the loss drawing him to an abyss of meaningless void. The shadow of death lingering somewhere nearby, just a few steps away, impatiently waiting to harvest his most precious possession.

Two halves of the whole, inseparable spirits: only once in a lifetime. His anguished words whispered into her ear, "I love you, Tian. I always will." Tears streamed down his face as he sobbed... and he rocked back and forth. Finally, he was too exhausted to cry, so he rocked back and forth. All alone... he rocked back and forth...

Very quiet. All alone.

...Tian coughed, spitting out water onto his bare chest, then moved, snuggled and curled within his arms. And as the man looked down and gazed into her hazel eyes with amazement, she smiled, a beautiful smile. "Why are you crying?" she asked weakly.

"Oh, God..." he stammered trembling. And he clutched her to his chest. "Oh, God..." was all he could manage to say.

He looked up to Heaven...

...Where the cloud had taken on a deep golden hue, and saffron flames of light crept through. Strangely illuminated, the area surrounding them almost glowed. And beneath an old twisted tree he cried again, this time with happiness, faith, and wonder. Cradling the Renoloi lovingly, with tears in his eyes...

And something warm inside,
     Ames gently rocked back and forth.
          ..."Thank You," he whispered gratefully. "Thank You."

* * *

Watching...
     From somewhere beyond the limitless reaches of infinity
          ...He knew John Ames was ready.

CHAPTER EIGHT

A lemon glow of calm reprieve...

...The sun shone warmly over the valley that stretched out before the river, the four travelers chatting with anticipation. The grove of trees lining the river separating them from the land of the Renoloi was in sight, growing larger as they were getting closer.

"We are almost home," Tian sighed, relief and joy in her words, her pace quickening until she was running.

Ronto and Reed joined her, Ronto grasping Reed's hand and urging him along as she called to Ames over a shoulder, "Hurry, we are home." Soon the three disappeared into the grove.

Ames followed, not trying to keep up, taking his time, considering their journey and what they had been through. His wounded side, still wrapped tightly with his old shirt, didn't seem to hurt so much anymore. Perhaps it was only his imagination, but it almost did seem like being home. Making his way through the trees he could hear the others splashing and playing in the water, and as he emerged from the grove he stopped on the stretch of beach, watching them.

Tian called to him smiling as she splashed water in his direction and gliding backward, a smooth graceful motion, her eyes sparkling with happiness, flaxen hair floating with liquid rhythm. Ames waded into the chest-deep water, picked her up by the waist and playfully threw her backward into the river; and as soon as she surfaced wiping water from her face with both hands, he rose from beneath her lifting her upon his shoulders. Reed cupped his hands for Ronto and the woman placed her foot in them —up, out of the river— but as he hoisted her she teetered uncertainly grabbing his forehead and they tumbled and went under. They tried again, successfully, and a moment later the two couples were facing each other in the middle of the wide river that seemed to divide this world in two parts.

As the two teams approached, playfully the tug of war began. Frolicsome, the women dodged and pulled at one another as Reed and Ames bumped back and forth raising bubble-foam waves. Tian leaned forward catching Ronto's leg with Ronto seizing Tian's arm, and when Ames veered away her awkward position pulled her off balance spinning them halfway around before they went under. When they bobbed into view Reed and Ronto were still laughing. Then Reed grabbed Ronto's feet and tried to dump her, but she clung to his forehead and dragged him down with her.

It was then Tian noticed several people on the opposite bank and called to them. "Kimo, Nitana, Nemuk."[11] The four left the water and were greeted warmly by those waiting onshore, eager conversation immediately ensuing. Reed walked away from the small gathering looking for Seana who stood by one of the large trees that lined the river.

"Seana," warmth and welcome, opening his arms. She ran to him with a smile playing about her lips. "What, did you think I'd forgotten you?" Picking her up he whirled her in the air, set her lightly on the ground and hugged her. They joined the others.

As Reed and Seana approached Tian was speaking. "Has anything happened in our absence, Kimo?"

"We will talk of everything after you have eaten and rested," her second replied. "Come now and we will celebrate this occasion." They crossed the lowland, climbed the ridges and followed a trail up the escarpment, then walked briskly to the village where a Renoloi throng lined the path welcoming their homecoming. "Your places are prepared for you," Kimo advised as they entered the village.

"Thank you," Tian said, smiling. "It is good to be home." Kimo nodded, and upon reaching Tian's home left with Nitana and the other villagers. Ames was waiting at the door, and as she entered the man followed pulling her close to him. The door whisked down. She was radiant. "I am so happy, John." He kissed her, withdrew, then kissed her again, passionately. "Is that one of your customs?" She was warmly receptive.

Softly: "Yes. It's called a kiss."

"It is pleasurable," she murmured effeminately, "please, kiss me again." Almost carefully, exploring, they did.

Bodies touching, moving rhythmically in unison, not separating, they slowly undressed one another, time temporarily suspended in the dim flickering light of the sepulcher. The two held each other, exploring their bodies as they rotated: slow-motion dance by candlelight, turning around and around, ever so close. They lightly touched the couch and lay down together.

Tian was unsure what this was all about, but she could feel, was aware of the hunger awakening inside her. Something wonderful was happening. Her dual sexuality had secreted her longing for physical pleasure somewhere deep inside her soul long ago... but hadn't taken it away. It had always been there, dormant, a chrysalis, now reemerging as the butterfly.

His touch aroused every nerve in her, trembling fingers exploring her body, caressing her tenderly, everywhere, ever so gently, such rough hands that could be so gentle. His face and lips were warm and soft yet firm and scratching, so irritating and foreign, an enigma —and she craved it. There was never enough. It filled her with desire she had never known before. His lips kissing her nipples, teeth so sharp, a twinge of pain —and still exciting her. Hands fondling her breasts, her nipples firm, wanting more as the spasms raced into her chest and abdomen.

She trembled loving the pleasure and excitement of this custom, holding his head gently in her hands, running her fingers through his hair. He moved lower kissing her abdomen and sides. His rough hands massaging her waist and hips, thumb and fingers alternately working her flesh caused her heartbeat to quicken. She perspired, loved the warmth they created, the glistening layer of liquid trickling down his shoulders and following the curvature of his spine. She became aware that her hair was matted against her own face and could feel droplets creeping down her back when she arched her shoulders. Perspiration was puddling between her breasts.

Her legs spread almost involuntarily when he kissed her inner thighs, holding his head gently, lovingly —and she wanted him. Even then she was not certain what it was, but now the hunger was guiding her, an instinct reawakened like a lost memory. She didn't need to understand anymore. It was natural and she knew it: the man-woman concept.

Just then his tongue traced across her thigh, between her labia, and she moaned with pleasure, couldn't help herself… knew he wanted to please her. He did. The exquisite sensation made her tremble quivering with excitement, and she breathed with passion. A knot in her abdomen sent electric waves through her body: passion, a new experience. She was wet and it was natural. His tongue continued, slowly at first then quicker and quicker until she couldn't lie still, trembling, arching her back, rigid, grasping his head pulling his face into her thighs, then flexing, calling his name and moaning.

Suddenly he stopped, looked up at her… and she knew. Warm and perspiring he slid upon her body, very slowly, experiencing every sensation. They were completely alive. She, spreading her legs, felt him enter, pushing deeply inside. It hurt just the smallest bit at first but the pleasure washed the pain away the second time he moved and she could feel herself sealing around him. It was how it was supposed to be, and felt like nothing she had ever known —yet intrinsic— as natural as breathing fresh air. She loved what she was becoming and wanted everything about him.

They moved in rhythm, in unison, touching, kissing, pressed together and joined together. Their harmony and cadence increased, perspiration intermingling, embracing, kissing: blood pounding inside, waves of electric pleasure pulsing through them. Tian gasped, moaning again and again each time he thrust into her; she could not be quiet anymore. So fervent a sensation she had never experienced before, she loved it, craved the closeness, the feelings all welling up from somewhere deep inside. Such intense intimacy and pleasure she had never known before, the pleasure of a man inside her. It surrounded her with dizzying ecstasy, overwhelmed her entire body: thirsting and craving, the hunger and completeness of making love. It was building inside her, growing, the feeling so intense —and finally she screamed: orgasm.

They had climaxed together.

* * *

A while later...

...They lay quietly, Tian cradled in his arms, facing one another, their faces barely inches apart, each still radiating body warmth.

"I love you, John," she whispered.

"I love you too. I always will."

* * *

Flames of the sepulcher...

...In Seana's home also burned with soft illumination, the dwellings all very similar within. Seana was seated on the stone couch, and Reed, having removed his wet clothes, lay quietly on the black leather cover, hands clasped behind his head.

"What happened in the Forsaken Land?" she asked, her gaze fixed upon the opposite wall.

"It's not important. I'd rather think about us right now."

Seana seemed puzzled. "Why, Reed? Did you not return with Ronto?"

Then realizing she was jealous, "Yes, but Ronto was a prisoner. We freed her and she returned with us." And reassuring, "She's a friend, Seana. You are much more than that."

Somewhat relieved yet not moving her stare from the wall, she persisted, "But in the river, you played as though you care for her?"

Reaching, stroking the back of her neck and shoulder with a hand, "I do care for her," he explained gently. "The four of us were dependent upon one another more than once just to stay alive. We were happy to be home, Seana. The Forsaken Land is dangerous and a difficult place to survive."

"I have not been there." She turned, facing him, looked into his eyes. "Tell me of the Forsaken Land. What is it like?"

Reluctantly: "Let's not talk about it," *something, somewhere... the back of his mind*, a peculiar sensation, subliminal, almost hypnotic.

"Please," she persuaded.

Relenting: "It's a harsh place." His words were hushed, pensive. "Not just that, but something more; it seems to be, feels, something almost malevolent there." Unable to decipher the foreboding: "I don't know. I can't explain it."

"What?" she insisted, "please tell me," her eyes wide, captured with his words.

Shaking his head, pushing, *it*, farther away, "Nothing, Seana... nothing." Then looking into her eyes again, "It is not a place I'd ever want to return to."

"That is not true." She smiled coyly. "You love adventure, Reed. You thrive on it."

His mood changing, "Not me." Then half-joking he said, "Seana, the Forsaken Land is an awful place. I'd die before I'd go there again."

She playfully slapped him on the chest and laughed sweetly, "Reed, you are so..."

"—Content," he interrupted, "to be here with you. This is home for me." He extended his hand to her. "Please, lay here with me. Hold me."

Willingly she complied, nestling into his arms. "What shall we do now?"

Reed —playful, opportunist— grinned, "Would you like hear the story of Uncle Remus? It's about Br'er Bear, Br'er Fox, Br'er Rabbit and the Tar Baby." His voice changed: the mischievous tone.

"Yes. I would like that." She smiled congenially.

As he began unraveling the tale of Br'er Rabbit, Reed's hand massaged Seana's thigh and buttock. Her toned body felt very supple, enticing, desirable —and they never made it to the part about the Tar Baby.

Both were unaware: woven within the fabric of their conversation... prophetic words.

* * *

Later that evening...

...Tian and Ames awoke, kissed tenderly, and as she rose from the couch preparing to tend his wounded side, he picked up the torn, bloodstained shirt from the floor digging into the pocket, and retrieved an anti-magnetic envelope containing a two-inch disc. He offered it to Tian.

"What is it, John?"

"Something very important. Is there a place you can safely keep it?"

"Yes." Taking the envelope she stepped to the far wall, knelt, and slid it into a crack along the upright wall and adjoining floor.

"No one must ever find it."

She understood.

* * *

As the door rose...

...Tian and Ames stepped out into the clean freshness of the night, she wearing a new black leather skirt and top and he a slipover leather shirt and his blue jeans. They ambled through the village along the path, the ambience comfortable, relaxed. The Renoloi were content; their leader had returned safely. Things seemed well.

"Where are we going?" Ames inquired observing that all the villagers were walking the same direction.

"To the ceremony."

Upon reaching the edge of the village they entered the meeting circle where the people were waiting. On this occasion the logs had been arranged forming a center ring or arena, and the Renoloi were gathered around them.

"I see we're late," he commented.

Tian replied unassumingly, "That is a privilege I maintain for myself alone."

"Well that hasn't changed over the years." He grinned. Reed and Seana, seated among a group of children off to one side, waved acknowledging their arrival as Tian led Ames to a high flat boulder where they sat down together. Quickly one of the children approached and presented each with a magnificently engraved flask. Ames thanked the child tendering a smile, then hesitated, turned to Tian.

She also smiled. He was learning. "No one must ever touch the goblet to her lips," she told him; "it was inscribed in the Legends."

Nodding, "The Legends," he repeated, then thought, *whatever they are.*

She dipped a finger into the flask, put it in her mouth, then did it again. "This way." Ames followed her example as Tian turned her attention to the center of the enclosure.

"What are the Legends, Tian?"

A finger to her lips —*shhh*— "The ceremony." He said no more and the ceremony began.

Earlier, within the circle four large poles had been set into the ground forming two "X's". As the villagers waited silently, four women carried a pole in on their shoulders, with what appeared to be a large luminous rock suspended from it, secured with liana. They placed the pole across the "X's", then without speaking left the circle. Two children followed carrying a weathered, wooden chest between them. It was placed below Tian and Ames.

Strangely, the wooden chest drew Ames' attention. It was just an old wooden chest like those commonly found on pirate ships long ago, and he knew he'd never seen it before... but somehow, it seemed familiar. Once the chest was in place the children opened its lid and left quietly.

Now, three young Renoloi entered the arena and approached the leader. Two women wore the traditional black leather skirts and tops, the other, a white leather skirt and top and white leather trailing robe. The Renoloi on the left carried a black metal staff four feet long, one end sharpened to a fine point. The woman in white removed the robe handing it to the Renoloi on the right and the other gave the White Renoloi the staff. Then the two in black stepped aside but did not leave the circle.

Without speaking the White Renoloi turned, slowly forcing the sharpened staff into the luminous rock, and a moment later as she withdrew it, the staff luminesced like the rock. The villagers were silent, Reed and Ames observing closely, the children moving back from the edge of the circle.

From the opened chest below Tian and Ames a man-sized reptile slithered out: half snake, half salamander. The White Renoloi assumed a warrior's stance as it glided toward her, then coiled and struck. She repelled it, but missed trying to impale its head. Recoiling —a twisted blur of speed— it struck again viciously digging needle-sharp fangs into her thigh and raking her with its clawed feet. Her expression revealed neither fear nor alarm, only excruciating pain.

Glaring eyes and flicking tongue, the serpent began treacherously coiling around the White Warrior's legs and hips, and she thrust at its head a second time. Again she missed. A heavy length of the serpent's body whipped encircling her arm and neck and it began to tighten its grip.

Reed started to get up but Seana stopped him with her hand. Ames saw her. He didn't move.

Squeezing and sliding, shifting forward and back, the creature's scaled hide scraped then sliced into the White Warrior's skin drawing blood with its intense crushing grip. Wheezing, gasping for air, the staff slipped from her hands as she ripped at the coil clutching her throat constricting her breath.

The serpent's suffocating chokehold slackened as it wound slithering lower, preparing to crush her, its raking clawed feet tearing her flesh in crooked lacerations. Venomous, it bit her savagely piercing hooked puncture wounds in her shoulder, bringing her to her knees.

Coughing convulsively she forced her fingers into its mouth, its teeth slicing her fingers and hands, dripping scarlet as she seized the creature's hideous head. Claws tearing through her clothes, exposed skin smeared with blood, breasts heaving violently she gasped for each breath against the serpent's crushing coils.

Choking she fell to her stomach, and as she went down awareness brought the White Warrior's senses back. She let go of the serpent's head reaching for her staff, first touching it, then clutching it desperately. The Renoloi watched the life-and-death struggle in breathless silence, each imagining herself in the desperate position of the warrior. As the woman tried to rise from the ground the weight of the creature prevented it, squeezing, holding her down. It seemed the lascivious serpent would prevail.

Rasping, almost wheezing, when at length she feigned giving up for a moment's rest, the creature loosened its grip on her body. And it was then, exerting one last determined effort for her life, pushing up she struggled to her knees. Quickly the anacondan coils constricted again and its head appeared between her torn, bleeding thighs. The White Warrior struck fiercely with a desperate stab, the staff slicing through the flat viper head. Hate and a nefarious blink of surprise glared in the creature's eyes; mouth open, tongue hanging out, it coughed slurping drool. Twisting, its head pinned to the ground, fangs grating with clicks and snaps, claws ripping, furrowing rage in the dirt, the serpent flailed in a crocodile's death roll; but with all her might she held it fast.

After a moment its momentum unwound, struggling subsiding, then finally still. Its eyes glazed over and the coils loosened around the White Warrior. Her breath returned giving her renewed strength and she pushed harder forcing the luminescent staff deeper into the ground, securing the serpent's head. When at last she was certain of the creature's death she collapsed falling onto the blunt end of the weapon.

No one moved.

The onlookers watched... as fading, evaporating, the serpent vanished. It turned to dust... and was gone. Still the people waited. At length the White Warrior stirred. Forcing herself up she rose slowly to her knees and pulled the staff from the ground. Nearly naked, she staggered before Tian, and sobbing with each painfilled breath, she uttered, "The Magnotite has gone Beyond."

Spellbound, the people watched as the White Warrior turned the staff to her own breast and slowly pressed it inward penetrating her heart. Horrified, now Ames began to rise but Tian quickly lay a hand on his knee stopping him, shaking her head, *no*. Eyes wide with disbelief, Ames watched.

Still standing where they were before, both motionless, the two black-clad warriors in the circle faded, evaporating, vanishing, turning to dust as minute swirling particles within wisps of filigree wind... and were gone. The White Warrior staggered back and fell, and like the serpent and two Renoloi she faded, turned to dust... and was gone.

The suspended luminescent rock diminished, returning to a natural state. The staff now blackened and bloodstained, remained stark, impaled in the ground.

Dumbstruck, Reed looked at Ames.

Ames was stunned, staring at the circle, perhaps expecting the warrior to reappear; but she did not. He watched as remnant glittery particles floated within evanescent wisps of wind, then drifted down ever so slowly... settling. Unnerved, finally he asked, "What happened to her?"

"Gone Beyond," Tian replied calmly, seemingly refreshed by the ceremony.

Not quite sure, Ames cautiously slid from the boulder and peered into the ancient chest where he observed a small green box with multiple lenses in one corner, and nothing else. Silently he stepped to the staff and knelt down; then with his fingertips picked up a pinch of the White Warrior's dust —to be certain. His eyes pleading, his voice wavering, "Tian... I don't understand."

"No one does." She explained, "The Legends said a hologram."

"A hologram..." he repeated; then rubbing his fingertips together, said, "...but the dust is real."

"I know, John." And she said no more.

* * *

Later...

...Ames and Reed were at the cliffs beneath a half moon that illuminated the clearing at the precipice. The night was still, their souls were not. Sitting together on the ground, they had not talked seriously in a while, and it was time.

"Doc, what do you suppose that ceremony was about?" picking up a small stick, manipulating it between his fingers.

"Don't know. What do you think?"

Reed shrugged. "Not sure. Could represent the struggle of good and evil, but a white warrior and serpent seems to connote some religious meaning. Do you suppose it could have been theological in some sense?" He continued without expecting a reply, as though simply considering possibilities. "The people seemed spiritually uplifted by the ceremony; did you notice their expressions afterward, so serene." Not a question, merely observation. "It was like a cleansing of some kind." And as he contemplated Reed began scrawling circles in the dirt with the stick.

For everything... there is a reason: *The Puzzle.*

Ames shrugged and said, "Likely we'll never know for sure." He took a breath, then continued, "It had to be a hologram, a miniature multi-lens projector was in that old box."

"Yeah Doc, but the serpent emerged from *within* the box. It was too big to fit in there; so where did it come from, and for that matter, where did that technology come from? We haven't seen anything here indicative of that." Reflecting: "We've encountered dinosaurs and cavemen —and that's not high tech."

Ames shifted his weight finding a more comfortable position as they leaned against a large boulder. He fingered the soil in his hand letting it trickle out slowly as he considered. "Need to learn more." Then he grinned and turned to his friend. "Cavemen?" he queried. "I thought they were behemoth sons-a-bitches?"

Reed smirked. "Well, fuckit—same thing." Ames chuckled and they were quiet again for awhile. "Doc..." Reed finally broke the silence.

"Yeah?"

"You never did tell me what you meant by that comment you made when we were in the lake."

Ames allowed his friend a glance, then again looked away. "What comment? I don't recall saying anything about Dinosaurus Enormicus."

"Dinosaurus—what?" Reed asked; then without interruption, "—No, not the dinosaur, when you said, 'Our own Mesozoic Era on Earth'."

Ames nodded recalling the statement. "Take a look at the stars." He did, studying them for a few minutes. "Where's Ursa Major?"

"In the north," Reed answered scanning for the constellation, "well, usually..."

"It's over there," Ames told him pointing to the southwestern sky. "The stars Mizar and Alcor, in the handle, appear as a binary star because of the angle." And he continued, "Cassiopeia and Cepheus are virtually inverted, upside-down. Polaris isn't the star the pointers of Ursa locate anymore, it's the bend of Draco's tail. Sagittarius should be facing Scorpius, and Orion and Sagittarius should be on different horizons, but they almost overlap now... seem to be opposing one another. Taurus is behind Perseus and Cancer isn't visible anymore." They continued to study the star formations a little longer.

Using the stick for a pointer, singling out each constellation in turn: "They have changed," Reed granted, "and... they're backward."

"Exactly," Ames mused. "So, consider then; when a world produces a mutant, does the world adjust to the mutant, or does the mutant adjust?"

"The mutant, obviously," still studying the sky.

"Uh huh," Ames agreed, then proposed, "and if all the stars and constellations are in different positions in space, would that suggest that we've remained stationary and they have moved, or that we have moved and they've remained pretty much the same?"

Reed grasped the implication, thought about it, then turning to his friend responded, "It's more than just Earth."

"What do you mean?"

Looking back at the sky Reed shuffled, sitting up. Interest piqued, he nibbled the end of the stick, then said, "Assuming the 'Big Bang' is accurate, even in fifteen billion years the stars couldn't have changed positions this much because the universe and its galaxies—everything—expands at a rate relative to what it always has. The constellations would spread apart, perhaps appear larger in the sky than before, but still maintain the same general configuration."

"Yes," Ames agreed.

"The stars are backward; and some of those stars that we see are entire galaxies, Doc. That means we're on the opposite side of the universe."

"Shoot, I hadn't considered that, but you almost have to be right," Ames allowed.

"Almost?" turning again to his friend.

"Well, you're very likely correct," he admitted.

Reed thought, then continued again saying, "That could explain the meteor shower too." He hesitated, tapping his nose with the stick. "Well, no I guess it wouldn't. That still doesn't make sense, even to me. Fuckit."

Ames interrupted. "Never mind that for now. There's still another problem."

"As if we really need another one; okay."

"Even at the speed of light, fifteen billion years isn't enough time to cross the entire universe."

Reed shook his head, aggravated and a bit confused, but aware that his friend was correct. He also realized there had to be an explanation, but figuring it out may take a while. "Well, the only other scenario that could possibly fit would be if the entire universe was rearranged and the star constellations appear to us to resemble what they once did simply because that's what we're familiar with —and are intentionally looking for."

"We would have to consider that as a possibility," Ames conceded bouncing a bit of dirt in his palm. "Our sun was a dying star, but here we have a full sun." Flipping the dirt away: "A lot may have happened in all that time."

"Well then, where are we... and furthermore, how did we get here?" Reed puzzled.

"A black hole," Tian answered from behind them. She, Kimo and Seana had approached unnoticed.

Startled, both men spun around beside the boulder. "Twist me crooked—" Reed gasped, "Tian, don't sneak up on a guy like that. You'll give me the big one."

Immediately Ames inquired, "Where did you hear of a black hole?"

"The Legends."

"The Legends?" he asked —to be sure— then said, "but black holes are only theoretical."

Listening, Reed was considering as they spoke.

"John, remember when I told you, 'Strangers who are different, but not enemies'? It was in the prophecies of the Legends." She and the others sat down.

"Well, yes but…"

"The Legends told of everything," Tian said calmly.

"And you said you would tell me later," he reminded. "Will you tell me of the Legends now?"

She smiled warmly. "Yes."

Seana volunteered, "I will build a fire." She set about doing so and Tian nodded a, *thank you.*

Tian sighed, then asked, "Where shall I begin?"

"At the beginning."

"That is not so easy as it may seem." She pondered and smiled recalling past memories, then began, "The Legends came with the birth of our world —even before that— with the birth of everything that is. So you may understand, I must first explain that only those chosen to lead the Renoloi people and their progeny were ever allowed to enter the Sacred Temple and study the Legends. The other leaders and I…"

"—Others?" Ames asked.

"Yes," she apprised patiently. "There are three other villages that we Renoloi know of. Tondra, Lita,[12] and Denen each lead their own people. The Legends spoke of twelve tribes, but the others must lie beyond the lands we know. Perhaps someday we shall find them."

She continued, "We would go with our mothers to the Sacred Temple and study the Legends, to learn all that we could, of all that had ever been or was to be." Remembering: "That seems so long ago. We were only children then. We studied often, until one night during a great storm there were violent explosions within Legend Mountain and it collapsed into the ground that held it for so long. Now Legend Range and most of the temple are gone."

"Earthquake," Reed speculated.

"According to the Legends, at the very beginning of time, the Spirit opened space with a hole, a black hole, and poured out all that you see, everywhere." Her eyes scanning as she spoke, "The stars were scattered forever, and worlds and moons to accompany them, all throughout the emptiness that was before."

Turning back to the men: "The Spirit sent the Legends to wait for the Renoloi, and they must have been here for a very long time because they were ancient long before the generations of Renoloi ever lived."

"Our world came to be when two dark bodies collided in space and were thrown from the black hole, burning with great fires that molded them together creating one world. It was at first a world of molten rock, but after a long time it cooled and the vapors formed great bodies of water and air to breathe."

"Eventually life began here, very small and simple in the beginning, but gradually becoming larger and more complex. So it continued until now. Now the Renoloi and the Trog are here, and shall be until one is destroyed by the other." She paused, thinking, remembering. For a while she remained silent, lost in thought, recalling herself with her mother a long time ago.

"Tian..." Ames coaxed softly.

She blinked with placid eyes. "Yes. I will continue."

Snuggling closer she leaned against him and stared into the small campfire Seana had built. Ames wrapped an arm around her and listened. "The Legends told of the beginning, and of something else, something I did not understand... 'Strangers who are different, but not enemies'. The strangers would come from Beyond when the black hole spilled out the stars as far as forever, but would not appear for many generations. Finally, they would arrive in a sphere of sparkling light that no one would ever see." She paused a moment, then said, "That part of the Legends did not make sense. I could not understand it."

"Our machine was a geodesic sphere," Ames explained. "The magnetic shield that allowed us to travel through time, from the exterior would look like a sphere of sparkling light."

"Then it would make sense. Now, I understand the rest of the 'Prophecy of the Strangers', John."

His concentration fixed upon her: "What else did the prophecy tell you?"

She returned his gaze. "That prophecy ended... and they would change our world." She could feel him tremble.

Reed, scrawling a circle in the dirt with the stick —stopped. "Oh Jesus..." he whispered, "what's that supposed to mean?"

"It can't be us, Reed; we're just two men."

"It *is* us, Doc; you know it as well as I do." No one spoke for a minute until, at length Reed continued. "It is... about us. It all fits."

"The sun wasn't dying, it was being drawn away, into space. The meteors weren't falling to earth, they were going past, being sucked away; and Earth's gravity was only capturing some of them. The collision that knocked us into free-fall: another body collided with Earth and we went into the black hole. That accounts for the flashes of light outside the sphere and transitional flux going berserk. The computers *were* accurate. It *was* a time warp."

"And now we're here, in a world created by the collision of two others, in a new universe. That explains the constellations all being backward —because they are. And we are on the opposite side of that new universe." Reed paused then concluded, "What was it Captain Kirk used to say: 'To boldly go where no man has gone before', or something like that." He chuckled. "Ain't that the truth —*shiiit!*"

"You are the strangers from Beyond," Kimo said. Seana nodded; she agreed.

"But we're only two men," Ames insisted; now he pulled Tian closer, she becoming his security, "we can't change a world."

In the flickering campfire light Reed looked at this friend detecting uneasiness in his expression. "It's been done before, Doc." Considering, he drew a final circle in the dirt, then tossed the stick into the flames and told him, "On November 24th, 1859, a man named John Murray published an article for a friend. It was one long argument based on three facts and two deductions. Fact: All living things vary. Fact: All living groups tend to increase in geometric ratio. Fact: The numbers of species tend nevertheless to remain fairly constant. Deduction: There is a struggle for existence. Deduction: In that struggle the fittest survive." He grinned. "Herbert Spencer termed it, 'Survival of the Fittest'. The article was, 'On the Origin of Species,' and Charles Darwin wrote it. And it certainly changed a world."

"Science versus religion," Ames recalled, "Evolution versus Creation: the debate that never ended."

"Yeah, that's the one." Then he added, "And you know what; it never will end, because there never was a beginning, and never will be an end."

"Perhaps this time we agree," Ames said softly. "Whoever, or whatever God is conceived to be, He always has been. And things will always change. There will always be evolution... changes with the new cycles. And God and the universe and evolution, will go on forever."

"Who is God?" Tian asked, almost a whisper. "I have heard of God."

Turning from Reed to her: "God is the One you call the Spirit who poured out the stars to fill the emptiness. He is love, knowledge, understanding, and so much more. He is everything good and beautiful. God made the rainbow, so we would wonder."

Very quiet for a moment, thinking, until she finally asked, "Then why did God create the Trogs?" words so subdued they barely escaped her lips.

Ames looked at her, uncertain. "I don't know," he said. "I really don't know. But there is a reason. For everything that happens... there is a reason."

"I do not know either, John, but I wish it were different."

"Two worlds merged into one," Ames murmured, his gaze drawn to the fire. "It's almost as if life is beginning over again in a new universe. All things eventually return to that from which they have come—ashes to ashes, dust to dust—a cycle with a duration of fifteen billion years... then beginning again."

"It was in the Legends," Tian said intently.

"The Legends," turning to her again. "They are the key, and you said now they are gone."

"Yes. Only the Sacred Temple remains."

"Can we see the Sacred Temple?"

"Yes; we will go tomorrow." Finally, she smiled.

With that, the five people rose and Reed stamped out the small fire filling the air with the acrid scent of wood smoke. Preparing to return to the village they milled around for a moment, each with their own thoughts, a beautiful star encrusted sky above them.

Still thinking about their discussion, "You know what's the spookiest part," Reed contemplated. "If we *are* the strangers in the prophecy, *someone* had to know ahead of time... that we were coming."

No one commented.

As they walked reticently along the trail through the undergrowth, mystery and darkness bade them goodnight.

Pieces: *The Puzzle.*

* * *

Early the next morning...

...Tian, Ames, Reed, Seana and Kimo set out for the Sacred Temple following the trail to the cliffs overlooking the river then meandering along the escarpment for a short distance, arriving at a bluff. At the bottom of the bluff was a small pool that looked familiar to the men. A little farther past the bluff the five entered a sheltered clearing with the wreckage of the geodesic sphere.

"Well hell," Reed said, "we walked for hours and were this close all the time."

Ames looked at Tian.

"Scouts observed from soon after your arrival: you traveled several miles through the jungle —in a circle," she explained, and smiled knowingly. "The jungle can be deceiving."

Reed critiqued, "So much for our wilderness skills."

"We could call it a circular pattern search," Ames offered, himself feeling a bit foolish. "Not lost, a reconnaissance."

Kimo and Seana snickered and Tian teasing, "We have all done it. It takes time to learn the jungle." Then she tugged him on. "This way; it is not far." Again they followed the trail along the cliffs until the jungle ended abruptly about a mile from the village.

They walked onto the rimrock, a plateau of ridges a hundred yards wide. Before them lay an expansive crater several miles in diameter, margined by a mountain range that appeared to have collapsed. Within the crater was a lone peak resembling a stone temple that had at one time been on top of one of the mountains and was now at ground level. It looked as though a gigantic, unworldly hand had reached down and pushed the entire mountain range underground leaving only the Sacred Temple untouched. It was enormous.

Moving quickly but carefully the people crossed the craggy rock face of the crater, and as they approached the men could see openings around the temple's base, caves leading to a labyrinth of passages and caverns. Arriving at the Sacred Temple Seana and Kimo stopped. Tian and Ames, a few steps in front of Reed and the two women, looked back when Reed inquired of Seana and Kimo over his shoulder, "Aren't you coming?"

"No," they answered in unison.

Tian explained. "It is not allowed, Reed."

He hesitated; then a tip of his head and, "I understand."

Cached at the mouth of one cave were several torches, and lighting three, Tian and the men entered, soon becoming flickering lights shrinking in the darkness of the passages. Kimo and Seana waited outside as the others went deeper within.

* * *

Shortly...

...Torchlight reflected from the walls of the mammoth cavern of glittering silver metal, the three standing together amidst the vastness of a mysterious library surrounding them. Thousands upon thousands of inscriptions were chiseled into stone, each word inlaid with gold. Everywhere the inscriptions lined the cavern walls depicting every imaginable subject: philosophy, languages, literature, mathematics and sciences. On and on.

"This is only a small cavern," Tian explained. "Within the temple there are too many to count."

Viewing the phenomenal display: "And they are all filled with writings... inscriptions?" Ames inquired, visibly impressed.

"Yes, every cavern. The inscriptions are all throughout the temple."

"K through twelve and right on to a Ph.D.," Reed commented in amazement. "This is un-frickin'-believable..." as leaning forward he began to examine some of the writings.

Tian continued to explain the temple. "There are countless caverns and passages, but I do not know where many of them go. Those," she pointed to other passages, "lead to other parts of the Sacred Temple, and that one," she indicated one in the corner of the cavern, "leads to the Throne of Gold." Ames nodded as he began to read some of the inscriptions.

"There is nothing to fear but fear itself."

"To learn one must think."

"Experience keeps a dear school, but a fool will learn in no other."

"Knowledge is food for the soul..."

"Man may only be a reed in the wind, but he is a thinking reed."

"Conference maketh a ready man, reading a full man, writing an exact man."

"Ask not what your country can do for you..."

"One small step for man, one giant leap for mankind."

Baffled, questions defined in his eyes: "Tian, these are from the past, from our time," Ames told her.

"But, how did they get here, Doc?" Reed knelt, continuing to examine the inscriptions. "For that matter, how did the temple get here? And if all this is just the Sacred Temple, I wonder what the Legends were."

Ames, darting him a glance, "To paraphrase a friend... they must have been un-frickin'-believable."

Reed grinned. "My thoughts exactly."

And turning again to Tian, Ames inquired, "Did you study the inscriptions, then pass the information on to your people?"

"Yes. My mother told me there was more to be learned here than one could ever hope to appreciate, or understand. She also said to remember just one of them always, and the others would be of no greater wealth than it."

"Which one was that?" he asked.

"It is above the passage to the Throne of Gold." They crossed the cavern to the tunnel and Ames read the inscription aloud while Tian listened.

"Blessed are the poor in spirit; for theirs is the kingdom of heaven. Blessed are those who mourn; for they shall be comforted. Blessed are the meek; for they shall inherit the Earth... (Matt. 5:3-5 RSV)." He turned to Tian. "Do you know what these are?"

"They are inscriptions."

"Other than that."

She replied, "No. I do not know."

"They're the Beatitudes, God's blessing for humanity. So this is where you heard about God."

Then Tian recited from memory.*"Blessed are the pure in heart; for they shall see God..."* (Matt. 5:8 RSV)

Ames smiled. "You had a very wise mother, Tian. I would like to have known her."

"She was wise," Tian allowed.

"But why may only the Renoloi leaders enter the Sacred Temple," Reed asked. "There's so much knowledge here, why not let all your people study the inscriptions?"

"It is too dangerous," she explained. "The silver walls burn with white fire and one moment of carelessness could destroy it."

"Silver walls?"

"Yes, Reed. We must always be mindful with our torches; never hold them too near the walls." Both men reflexively drew their torches a bit further from the walls. Reed, with his knife, pried a fragment of rock loose, and after examining it found a sandy spot on the floor. Putting his torch lightly to it the stone burned suddenly with a brilliant white flame and was quickly reduced to white-and-gray cinder. Ames eased closer as Reed lightly fingered the residue, it crumbling to a chalky dust.

"Magnesium oxide," Reed remarked, "pure magnesium oxide ore." Then rising to his feet: "You had good reason for warning us, Tian." The men inspected the cavern walls again as Reed queried, "Are all the tunnels within the temple like this?"

"Yes"

"And the Legends— there were tunnels like this with the Legends?"

"Yes."

"An entire mountain range impregnated with veins of magnesium oxide," Reed surmised, "—lightning, a magma flow or fault shift?" and speculated, "any one could trigger an implosion powerful enough to collapse the mountains."

"Possibly," Ames agreed. Then turning to the woman, "Tian, the Legends lie below the temple?"

"Yes, much deeper."

"What were the Legends?" he asked.

She thought, trying to decide how best to explain them. "The Legends were all that can be known," she finally answered.

"—Inscriptions, Tian. Were the Legends inscriptions?"

"More, John. The Legends were more... things the Renoloi could not understand. Magic."

"The ceremony?" he asked, "The 'White Warrior and Serpent', were they from the Legends?"

"Yes."

"Bingo!" Reed sang, "technology."

Ames beamed, "Gotta be." Then again to Tian, "Has anyone ever tried to find a passageway down to the Legends?"

"Many times, but the passages are all sealed. The Legends are gone forever."

Both men smiling, deliberate eye contact: "There are always possibilities," Reed concluded.

Just then a sudden breeze whisked through the cavern causing the torches to flicker and diminish, and with a glance overhead Tian insisted anxiously, "We cannot continue now. We must leave."

"What about the Throne of Gold?" Ames asked surprised by her unexpected apprehension.

"Our torches are almost spent. If we are trapped in here without light you will never see it. There are too many pitfalls." Urging, "We must leave and return another time."

"She's right," Reed conceded, "some of those crevasses were hundreds of feet deep. In the dark it would be suicide trying to get through these passages."

Reluctantly acquiescing, "Okay, we'd better go." Led by Tian the three moved quickly through the labyrinth of passages and soon again were at the mouth of the cave where Kimo and Seana waited, concerned.

"You were in the temple a long time," Kimo commented. "Your torches must have been burning low."

"They were, but we are well," Tian assured as the five headed across the crater's irregular topography toward the village.

Moving quickly, "I am hungry, are you?" Seana asked Reed.

"Sure am. What's for dinner?"

Surprised he need ask: "Chiqua of course."

"Of course;" then he explained, "I knew that Seana. It was a joke."

Naively, "What is a joke, Reed?"

"Something funny, something that makes you feel good inside."

"I understand," she said innocently, then announced. "Your penis makes me feel good inside. Is that a joke?"

Ames, over a shoulder, dryly, "Pretty much, Seana."

Temporarily distracted but quickly resuming the conversation, "No Seana, it's awesome," ignoring his friend's snickering.

"Yes, Reed. I like Mr. Wrinkle," Seana agreed offering him an inculpable smile.

"Mr. Wrinkle?" Ames burst out laughing. "You named it? — albeit appropriately."

Reed defended humorously, "Well, it was either Mr. Wrinkle or Cyclops the Muffin Monster, and that's too long unless it's a surname."

"Muffin monster?"

"Sure," Reed explained, "if you shave the hair off, they look like muffins."

Tian interjected. "John, it seems that sometimes Reed is quite intelligent, and at other times, he is just strange."

"Really… you think so?" A poker face. "Myself, I hadn't actually noticed." He continued walking.

This time Tian smiled. She was beginning to understand these strangers... these men.

* * *

Along the path...

..."Piggyback, piggyback," a child's voice sang from behind him.

"Hop on," Ames encouraged looking over his shoulder and stooping so Tarin could get on. Tian smiled, content, knowing her people accepted the men, trusted them. They weren't strangers anymore; they had become part of the village. The men were so different, and yet, so like the Renoloi. It made her happy.

"All set?" he asked.

"Ready," Tarin announced from his back.

"Well, let's go then. Hang on." He trotted down the path toward the gathering, Tarin bobbing and giggling all the way.

Walking leisurely Tian followed, and thought, *it is good.*

The evening meal was a leisure affair: a beautiful night, warm, peaceful; crackling campfire, lively, inviting; people together, relating, sharing. Ames and Reed mingled for a while afterward, speaking to the women, learning things from them, and from time to time explaining what life had been like a long time ago. Conversation went on for hours, relaxed, laid back, everyone just having a good time, the way life was supposed to be.

At length Reed, being Reed, couldn't resist and gathered the children around the crackling fire —and he asked, "Do you want to hear the story of Uncle Remus and Br'er Rabbit?"

"Yes!" They shouted all together although not a soul among them had any idea what an Uncle Remus or a Br'er Rabbit even was. Reed smiled, the mischievous smile, the grin the children knew; then he winked, his teasing wink, at a tiny child named Jade. This evening he would finish the whole tale.

"Do any of you guys know what a tar baby is?" he began.

Joyfully: "No!" And Jade climbed onto his lap.

Wrapping his arms around her, "Well then, just let me tell you…" He was a gifted storyteller.

"Come," Tian whispered nudging Ames.

"Where are we going?" he asked, not really caring. By now he would likely follow her anywhere, just as he was doing now.

"To swim."

They left the circle and followed a trail for a short distance through the jungle, to a pool: still, pristine and waiting. On a flat boulder overhanging the water Tian slipped out of her clothes, glanced at the man coyly, then dove in. She was learning. Ames quickly disrobed and there was a second splash as he followed her into the pool leaving two small piles of crumpled clothing on the flat rock —and nothing else.

She tread water, waiting for him in the center of the pool, and as he surfaced rubbing his naked body against her the electrifying, tingling desire filled her. They embraced moving buoyantly in tight circles, the warmth of their bodies encompassed by the cool water exciting them both.

His hands were everywhere upon her, running up and down her back, over her buttocks, her breasts, her sides. It felt so exhilarating and she responded massaging his chest, back and buttocks. They kissed ever so slowly, the taste of growing love and commitment, and the craving returned flooding her with warmth and passion. She spread her legs apart sliding down against him, seizing his erect penis underwater when she squeezed her thighs together again. It felt wonderful, as though it belonged there; rigid, hot, pulsing —and she loved it.

Bubbling with laughter she pushed away, teasing him. The lovemaking game came naturally for her, perhaps part instinct, but certainly because of her feelings deep inside; she loved him, and she knew he loved her.

He followed her leisurely, rolling onto his back, floating alongside her, her beaming smile beguiling, bewitching, having captured him within its trance. If that was love it could keep him forever. There was no one else in the world... only her. She possessed him.

For a time they swam in the pool, touching, separating, leading, following, touching and separating again, almost an aquatic ritual. Their love and their spirits intertwining, closer with each passing moment, two very different people in a primitive, new world... by chance or design, neither knew, neither cared. Eventually they swam to the overhanging rock, lay together, made love... and fell asleep on a flat rock.

Two small piles of crumpled clothing —and nothing else.

CHAPTER NINE

Greylight: just before dawn...

...Tian and Ames ambled into the village, Tian immediately sensing something was wrong. Too many people were awake, too much activity for so early in the day. Ames also detected the restlessness and anxiety.

"Reed," he called with a false smile when he saw the man moving briskly down the path, Seana beside him. As they approached Reed's concern became apparent and Ames asked, "What is it?"

Serious: "Deep shit, Doc. Come on." Quickly, they ran to the cliffs where a small group of Renoloi was assembled looking anxiously over the river to the mountains beyond. Those gathered on the escarpment parted making room for Tian and the others as they arrived.

"What is wrong, Kimo?" Tian immediately asked.

"Trogs." She pointed to the horizon where a procession of giants was crossing the rugged mountains.

Ames studied them. "How many would you estimate, Reed?"

"Hard to say from this distance, best guess, all of 'em, at least four hundred."

Then to Tian: "How long will it take them to get here?"

"Two days. Surely no more than that." She looked back to the procession of Trogs who resembled bugs in a continuous column; then faced Ames, leaned close to him, whispering, "What shall we do?"

In return, discretely, "How many Renoloi are there, all together?"

"Including Tondra's, Lita's, and Denen's villages, almost two thousand."

"At least you've got them outnumbered." Considering, he paused. She already knew what he was going to say. "The decision is yours; unite your villages and fight —or run. If we make a stand a lot of Renoloi will certainly die."

Scanning the horizon, speaking softly, "On the other hand, if we run, they will destroy your homes and your land; and then, in all likelihood follow and hunt your people like a plague." He looked at her, then soberly, "It's up to you. You'd better discuss it with the others."

"The Legends," she surmised, "the prophecy." She turned facing those behind her. "You all know what is to happen. We must decide what we will do."

Kimo glanced over the group and stepped forward as spokesperson, "You have our decision, Tian. We abide by your judgment. You lead, and we follow you." Tian closed her eyes and placed three fingers on Kimo's forehead. Having done this, she turned to Ames and spoke with the hushed, certain voice of conviction.

"This is the land of the Renoloi. We stay."

The man first surveyed the group; then to Tian and Kimo, "We've got to be ready for them. Assemble everyone in the village —and tell them to hurry."

Already moving, "They will be there immediately," Kimo assured.

As she began to leave, "—And Kimo, send your fastest runners to the other villages. Tell them we only have a couple of days."

"They will hurry," her voice trailing back. And Kimo was gone.

Pensive, Tian stood beside him watching the distant mountains. Ames looked at her, proud of her. Turning, realization in her eyes: "There was really only one choice, was there not?" She nibbled her lip, coerced a brief smile and whispered, "The Legends..." then quickly she followed the others down the trail to the village.

Ames turned to his friend. "Any ideas?"

From their vantage point Reed surveyed the area. "I expect they'll cross the river at the lowland," pointing, "down by the beach. We can engage them there."

Ames nodded. "What's the stratagem?"

"Here..." Reed answered as he began diagramming his plan in the dirt, "the river—the Trogs—us. They'll probably cross here and have to come through..."

* * *

Later that morning...

...The two men arrived at the village where the Renoloi were waiting assembled at the meeting circle. Ames addressed the people, Tian and Reed beside him. "The Trogs are advancing in full strength toward your land. If we are to defeat them it will take a cooperative effort. When Tondra, Lita and Denen arrive with their people we should be two thousand strong; but unfortunately we can't defeat them with numbers alone." Pausing, looking over the crowd, then continuing, "Reed has a plan that he and I believe should be our most effective defense against them —and we think it will work. You know where the Sacred Temple is..." Nervous murmur ran through the audience. "Now listen—" he quieted them, then continued, "the mountain is lined with magnesium oxide and we can use that ore against the Trogs. I know it's forbidden for any but your leaders to enter the Sacred Temple, but now your survival may depend on it."

Seana asked for many of them. "Of what use is the stone?"

Having anticipated the question: "When placed in a closed container ore like that becomes explosive." Sensing the crowd's bewilderment he went on, "We'll demonstrate." Reed displayed a wooden casement: both ends tightly packed with clay and a fibrous vine soaked with tar protruding from one end.

"How can that defeat the Trogs?" Seana asked, voicing the village's skepticism.

Quickly Reed assured, "You'll see." Then he inquired, "Does someone have a torch?" A woman removed a burning log from the fire, and bringing it forward offered it to them. The fuse was ignited and both men watched as it burned, bubbling and sizzling. Reed tossed the awkward improvisation onto a pile of rocks near a small tree. A tense moment. The Renoloi waited calmly, unsure of what to expect.

Sudden explosion —blast-pulse flashing through the crowd— the detonation fracturing the rocks and splintering the tree within a column of billowing white smoke that rose thickly from the ground. Stunned by concussion-wind, cringing, the Renoloi were uncertain of what they had just witnessed, the wafting mushroom now dissipating slowly, filtering up through the higher foliage. The men meanwhile exchanged smiles surveying the remains of the shredded tree and crumbled rock.

Reed grinned broadly. "Success."

Ames turned to the people. "Now do you understand what the silver metal can do?" There was an amazed agreement among the Renoloi as he explained, "We can defeat the Trogs, but we'll need a lot of the ore and a great deal of work is involved. We must hurry so we'll be ready when they get here."

* * *

The lowland, bordering the river...

...As the day progressed the Renoloi lines of defense began to take shape. Industriously the children worked together, some grinding points on heavy poles that were more than six feet in length, while others tied magnesium bombs to the makeshift projectiles and carried them into the gnarled branches of the trees just beyond the beach at the river's edge. High in the branches, ten-foot bows were mounted horizontally to receive the stout arrows. Three children were necessary to operate each of the forty, mounted weapons: one to load, two to draw the bowstring. From their positions in the trees the primitive projectiles could almost reach the opposite bank of the river.

Reed explained the weapons to the children who would use them, and they listened intently even absorbing the concepts of trajectory and windage. Children were assigned to the bows because they were agile and their exceptional climbing ability allowed them to reach the topmost branches quickly when danger became imminent.

The second defense was double-triangular spear formations attached to lofty tree branches with thick liana. The Renoloi would release them from above, the spears swinging down in an arc and hopefully impaling the unsuspecting enemy.

Behind the spear sets deep pits remained uncovered for inspection as more children ground points on heavy poles. Once the poles were sharpened and set upright in place in the excavations the traps resembled African pitfalls, and covered over with brush and grass they became almost invisible to the unsuspecting eye.

Next was a wall of spears firmly planted in the ground at a forty-five-degree angle; extremely sharp these were honed to pierce the thick skin of the giants. After being secured in position the spear wall was also concealed with grass and branches.

A wide trench filled with oil and tar was the next defense in the procession and correlated closely with the last, and hopefully most lethal. Magnesium oxide was taken from the Sacred Temple and piled in great mounds a short distance behind the trench. The ore mounds were laced with hundreds of rocks to create a blizzard of shrapnel when the wall of ore would be detonated, exploding in a chain reaction.

With the combined might of the warriors of the other three villages the remaining Renoloi strength lay in the skill and accuracy of Kimo's archers and the bravery of Tian's lances. Their forces would lie in wait for the Trogs on the ridges that bordered the bottomland of the river.

* * *

As they walked…

...Reed and Ames inspected the fortifications, occasionally instructing or assisting the busy Renoloi; moving quickly, seemingly everywhere, a coalesced endeavor. They neared the wall of spears.

Taking hold of the sharpened spears and slipping between two, putting his weight against them, the spears didn't budge and Reed remarked, "Well, they're good and strong." Then seriously, "Doc, what do you think our chances are?"

"Can't answer that. We've never seen these people fight." They crossed a log spanning the trench.

Approaching the piles of ore: "What about us, you and me?"

"Don't know that either," Ames said soberly climbing onto the ore mounds. "Why do you ask?" stopping at the top.

Hesitating Reed scuffed a chunk of ore with his boot and answered, "Just wondering." He turned away watching the Renoloi bustling around them. "They're wonderful people."

"Yeah," Ames agreed overlooking the lowland and those busy working. "Poor in body, great in mind and deed."

"That's been said before."

"It has?" Ames scratched his chin, pretending not to know.

"Uh huh, about thirty-three AD, I believe."

"Really... by whom?"

Pensive, still scanning the length of the lowland, "I think it was Jesus," Reed answered.

Briefly glancing at his friend, then again to the fortifications, Ames smiled. "He said a lot of things like that, didn't he?"

"I guess so."

Ames looked down stabbing a lump of ore with the toe of his boot, his forehead wrinkled with thought, crow's feet traced to his temples. "Reed," he said softly, "do you believe in miracles?"

"Not really."

Chewing his lip: "Then how would you explain Tian being alive today?"

Still looking around, watching the Renoloi, deliberately not facing his friend, Reed responded, "There have been many documented cases of cold-water drownings where the victim was resuscitated after long periods of time with no adverse effects."

"I know, but I asked about Tian. You were there. You don't believe that any more than I do."

"You're right." Reed faced him. "I don't. It makes me wonder."

"Reed," Ames asked carefully, "really... don't you believe in God?"

Solemnly, the young man's eyes fixed on his friend. He answered, "I think every person should be allowed their own conviction—whatever they believe—and no one should have the right to dictate to another. Each person is an individual and each thinks a little differently than every other individual; but their beliefs merit equal respect. What may be good for one is not necessarily good for all."

"I agree, however you evaded my question," Ames told him. Then, direct: "Do you believe in God?"

Reed took a deep breath, let it out slowly. "I suppose you were right; deep down inside even I conceive of Someone more powerful, knowing... whom I call God."

Ames looked at this friend, and for the first time truly saw Reed, the part he'd always kept hidden. Reed smiled, not knowing why really. It just sort of welled up from inside somewhere, and he said, "I like the idea of creation *and* evolution —no beginning, no end— only cycles... going on and on forever."

Ames considered, "God *and* evolution," soft-spoken words. "I like the sound of it too."

* * *

Since beginning preparations for the advancing Trogs...

...There was an atmosphere of urgency, restlessness and anticipation among the people. It lingered, nagging them as they gathered at the meeting circle during the early hours of a darkening night. Tian and Reed held the attention of the villagers while Ames and Kimo scouted the enemy position. Reed summarized the anticipated conflict for those around him.

"We have accomplished more today than I would have believed possible. There is still work to be done, but I am pleased with our progress." He paused scanning the group, all focused, listening to him. Then he continued, "When the Trogs get here there will be a battle, and there will be death on both sides. It will be a difficult struggle and a very decisive one." He paused a second time. "A soldier is taught to remember only what he must do during the battle, nothing more. It will be them or us."

* * *

With all things, there is one constant: change. Be it the passing of one world or the creation of another, it was destined for change, the catalyst, the past... or the present?

A piece of... *The Puzzle.*

* * *

In the Forsaken Land...

...Kimo and Ames were on a high ridge just beyond the valley that lay before the river. Both observed the line of flickering torches as the Trogs marched relentlessly over the distant mountains.

Ames shook his head, concerned. "They're not stopping to rest."

"That is bad," Kimo resolved. "They will arrive at the river sometime tomorrow, likely after midday."

Ames: "We'd better get back." They moved swiftly and silently through the dark: a portent night.

Entering the meeting circle Ames called for the attention of the Renoloi gathered around a blazing fire. "Perhaps everyone should go to their homes and try to rest. We'll be rising before the sun tomorrow." Without conversation the people dispersed, leaving only Tian, Kimo, Seana and the two men within the circle.

After a brief silence Tian moved closer. "What is wrong, John?"

"They're moving faster than we anticipated." He cast a worried glance, first to her, then Reed.

Seana rose. "What does that mean?"

"They'll probably get here sometime tomorrow, early afternoon."

Seana asked, "Would it not have been better to tell them?"

Ames explained. "For some, if not all of us, this will be the last night of rest. They're tired and need the sleep."

Placing his arm around Seana, Reed assured, "It's for their own good."

"Yes, I suppose you are right," she conceded.

Ames: "We'd better get some sleep too."

As they walked along the path that took them through the village Ames hummed the 'Battle Hymn of the Republic'. Still walking, he turned and said, "Reed, do you remember that song?"

"How could anyone ever forget it?" The two fervently sang the song through, then continued on, still humming.

* * *

A little while later in Tian's home...

...Ames sat on the stone couch behind the sepulcher, hands resting in his lap tightly clenching his leather shirt. Dark chest-hair quivering as he breathed heavily and slow, he was lost in thought somewhere distant, worried. Tian, in the opposite corner of the dimly lit room, undressed quietly, watching him. His lips were moving but there were no words, only rhythmical melancholy sounds and breathing. He stared at the flame of the sepulcher, but his glassy expression wasn't focused. Tian, now naked, moved closer straining to hear without disturbing him.

Hushed words: "I wish there were more time, time to know what it's all about, to understand, to know the reasons behind it all, not to just wander randomly from one event to the next, but to understand why. How small we really are. Not enough time; never enough time."

"John..." she finally whispered. He blinked, coming back. She hesitated, wondering; his eyes were so sad. "are you all right?"

"I'm sorry. Yes, I'm all right," he replied quietly. She sat down beside him, wrapped her arms around him and cradled him to her breast. "I'm sorry," he whispered again.

Holding him lovingly, tenderly stroking his face, she asked, "Sorry, for what?" He did not answer, only breathed with rasping irregularity, then would sigh and finally breathe again. She said nothing more, gently caressing him with the soothing touch only a woman possesses.

She waited; held him and waited.

Finally, he spoke. "We thought the government wasn't ready for time travel, would corrupt the past or future with their greed; but now I realize no one ever will be. Time is like an endless library, read forever and there will still be more books, no one could ever read them all. We should not have built the machine and come here. We've changed what might have been. By its very nature mankind was always its own worst enemy, and an entire race who didn't deserve to suffer, now will —because of what we've done."

"John..." She held his face in her hands, looking into his eyes. "you and Reed were sent here. It was not your choice; it was your destiny." He blinked as she smiled lovingly, then told him, "And there was a reason... for everything, there is a reason."

She had learned.

"No, Tian. I have a feeling tomorrow will be my last day here, and I didn't accomplish anything, did I?" Trying to smile, but unable, "Saved Ronto's life, and that one life may cost the lives of all your people."

He paused, remembering a childhood Bible story:

"A long time ago, I was told a story about a shepherd who had a flock of one hundred sheep. *(Matt. 18:12-14 RSV)* One of the sheep got lost in the mountains, so the shepherd left the ninety-nine and went to find the one. It was a lamb. And he found it on a desolate ledge. The shepherd risked the safety of the ninety-nine for that one, lost lamb." Again he paused, then murmured, "I hope we did the right thing."

Tian asked, "You did as the shepherd, did you not?" A nod of *yes,* and softly, she said, "I do not know what a sheep is, but I do understand. There is good in your words and even you can learn from them." There was no reply. "You were not wrong," she comforted.

156

In the dim light the sparkle of tears moistened her eyes. "You were not wrong."

Ames turned back to the fire in the sepulcher. "I would like to have seen the Throne of Gold." A somber lament.

Tian turned his face to hers again and kissed him very tenderly. She loved him with all her heart and soul. "I promise you will see the Throne of Gold, and more, much more," she assured. Then she coerced a smile. "Come. We will go for a swim and you will feel better." As she stood she asked a final question. "John, you also saved my life, did you not?"

Tian had learned.

Ames had never seen the Legends,

But Tian had studied them, over and over... very carefully.

* * *

As the bronze door rose...

...Reed stepped from Seana's hut into the cool mist of early morning air. Renoloi were hurrying, seemingly everywhere. Voices called out from the far end of the path as a large group was entering the village. The locals ran to greet them as Seana approached Reed from behind and tugged on his arm.

"Reed," she said reticently.

He turned, and when he saw her, smiled. "Good morning. Who are they?" indicating the approaching Renoloi.

"Lita and her people. Tondra and Denen have arrived already and there is much talk among many old friends, others we have not seen in a long time."

Reed observed, "Holidays and wars are like that."

Seana, watching the approaching warriors: "That they have come and we are all together again is good, but the reason for their coming causes me sorrow."

"I know what you mean." Reed looked at the visitors again, closer now, nearing Seana's home. He felt this might be his last opportunity to tell her.

"Seana…"

"Yes?" she replied allowing him her undivided attention.

"…Just in case there isn't time to tell you later, or something goes wrong." He stammered a little, "I just want you to know…" a brief pause, "that I love you." —There; he said it.

The warmth of his words cascading within washed the outside world away, emotion bubbling in her heart and flowing to her eyes. For a moment they stood all alone in a cloud, a comforting place where nothing else mattered; and she pressed against him, touching, and murmured, "I love you too, Reed." They kissed.

"I love you, Seana," he repeated after the kiss; then the new arrivals and commotion caught up with them and they weren't alone anymore. Seana had to turn and greet the others. While she did, Reed waited.

"…I will speak with you in a little while," Seana said to one of the women passing her home, bringing the conversation to an end.

"Where are Tian and the doc?" Reed was able to ask after many of the Renoloi had passed on their way to the meeting circle.

"The river."

* * *

When Reed and Seana arrived at the gnarled trees bordering the river…

…They located Tian and Ames, both watching the opposite bank. Shortly, Kimo appeared from the trees —running— bow strung across her back. She splashed into the water and swam, crossing the river diagonally, knowing to use the current not fight it. Met by two warriors on the Renoloi side she continued at a run and upon nearing Tian and Ames reported quickly and breathless, still dripping water.

"They are leaving the mountains now and should be here shortly after midday."

"We'll be ready," Ames assured, and to Reed standing nearby with Seana. "What position do you want, second or fourth?"

"First."

Ames smiled. "I'll take that, your second choice?"

"The first," Reed said again.

Ames conceded, "I'll take the second." He turned. "Kimo, you and your archers wait until the Trogs have gotten through the spear wall, to the trench —if they get that far. Set the trench afire with your first arrow. After that, order your archers to fire at will. You decide when to detonate the ore wall."

Without hesitation: "I understand." Seana left with her as Kimo ran to assemble the archers.

Ames turned to Tian. "You lead the lances."

"I want to stay with you."

Shaking his head in refusal, "No, the Renoloi will need…"

"—John," she interrupted, stepping forward and embracing him. For a moment he held her as Reed stood silently beside them.

Softly, into her ear: "Anyone can fight in a battle. After… your people will need you most. You are a Renoloi leader." She pleaded with her eyes, but his decision was firm. "I love you," he whispered.

"And I love you," sadly, ensuring words as she left for the ridges.

Ames turned to Reed and both scanned the treeline across the river. Reed's voice was moderate, sincere. "Reminds me of an old Sioux adage," he said at last.

"What's that?"

Reed looked at his friend. "It's a good day to die." This time there was no smile.

Serious, Ames whispered, "Today, we could use a miracle."

"There are always possibilities, John." And Reed walked away. Without looking back, he went to a nearby tree and climbed to the bow mounted aloft. Tarin was there, waiting, and he pressed his hand to her cheek causing her to blush.

"No piggyback today," she said.

Fondly, "No, sweetie," gently brushing hair from her face, "no piggyback today."

Ames walked to a tree with a spear set high overhead. He climbed and was met by a young girl above. "Are you ready, little one?" he asked.

"Yes, I am."

From his vantage point Ames surveyed their army: the mounted bows, spear sets, pits, wall of spears, the trench, glittering ore mounds; and beyond, the ridges where Kimo and Tian stood side by side with fifteen hundred warriors alongside them. John Ames drew a deep breath, exhaled. "We're ready." He knelt beside the girl.

Now, they would wait.

* * *

From a barren and forsaken land...

...Trogs marched relentlessly, two continuous columns a mile long raising a murky cloud of gagging gray dust. The force of over four hundred was divided into three factions. The first was the ten mightiest giants who controlled the dinosaurs with massive chains fastened to neck collars. The second comprised the bulk of the army, the trained fighters and backbone of the Trogs' strength, all brandishing a club. The third was the younger fighters and stragglers, unpracticed and unskilled in combat.

The army proceeded ruthlessly, crushing everything in its path.

At length, the mountain dust was behind the Trogs and they arrived at 'Black Water'. The giants plunged forward into the murky swamp frightening several Pterosaurs from their cloistered, brackish surroundings, provoking them to rising majestically on membranous batwings. A Tyrannosaurus craned its enormous head and screamed as dolphin-like Ichthyosauri slipped through the dark water to safety. The Trogs lost a few to the swamp quicksand, but that was inconsequential.

An Apatosaurus emerged near the far shore of the lake and lumbered regally into the cover of nearby trees nearly crushing underfoot a fleeing Edaphosaurus, a four-legged vegetarian. When the army reached the opposite shore an Allosaurus observed but made no hostile overture toward the overwhelming odds. Fifteen or twenty Compsognathuses darted across the path of the contingent and one of the smaller, less agile creatures was unmercifully trampled under the three-toed foot of a monstrous Tyrannosaur. The dinosaurs that followed continued to mangle the poor dead creature until little more than hide, pulverized bone and tissue, and blood-caked dirt remained. Road kill.

The Trog army began to fan out as it moved down the hill overlooking the valley that lay before the river. Ricochet echoes of pounding clubs and splintering wood rang out from the timber. Spanning a mile in width, it smashed a swath through the woods that bordered the river with the factions of army arriving at the space of turf between the beach and trees simultaneously. Then, and only then, did they halt.

A tense moment passed as the Renoloi and Trog forces assessed one another in a silence interrupted only by the frequent, anxious screams of flesh-eating dinosaurs. From the canopy, understory and ridges: scanning, determined eyes. The Renoloi warriors watched in breathless anticipation, tension electrifying their every sense. Ready.

Then, the dominant Trog stepped onto the sand grinding it beneath massive feet and between misshapen calloused toes. He hoisted his club, looked back once, and plunged into the water with his army of malevolent malediction close behind him.

CHAPTER TEN

"—Fire!"

…Sizzling, forty six-foot arrows soared from the ancient trees bordering the river and into the advancing deluge of Trogs in the water. Wounded or killed by explosions in the first strike a number of giants went down.

Piercing its throat and breast the fourth dinosaur was struck twice during the aerial assault, and screaming wildly collapsed into the river after the first explosive ripped a gaping wound in its hide. Then a waterspout tore the river apart erupting with a foaming skyward blast muddying the water.

Struck solidly in the chest, a Trog stopped and staggered back, his skin puckered with vulgar lips of the arrow's puncture wound. The fuse burned as he collapsed and floundered beneath the water and, *whoomph,* the submerged bomb detonated spewing a column of water in a scattering of raw flesh and entrails. Whirling red and rare a slab of falling meat slopped onto the shoulder of the behemoth who had been nearest him, so the simpleminded Trog picked it off, voraciously wolfed a gulp, then proceeded indifferently discarding the rest in the water.

Floating face down or listing buoyantly, a scattering of mutilated Trogs killed in the first wave drifted with the current. Ragged carcasses with missing limbs and opened chests, rolling randomly dispersing a blanket of blood, changed the color of the water.

Another giant was decapitated when an arrow smashed through his face ripping his head from his shoulders, brains spouting from his ruptured skull as the arrow continued striking another behind him. And the second titan's chest erupted with the detonation that flung his arms away like limp boomerangs that didn't come back.

A ragged tear: an arrow struck then went completely through, lodging solidly in one's shoulder. As he tried to pull it out —white-blast and smoke— it exploded tearing him in half, sucking him inside-out with the tremendous ripping force that splattered meat and slop in the river.

"—Fire!"

Three more dinosaurs went down with the second assault, leaving only six pushing waves with each ponderous step. The river blistered reddish brown, the color of death, a corrosive boil of bubbles and froth, and the bodies of giants floating everywhere.

"—Fire!"

Again and again arrows swooshed from the trees with thunderous reports leaving death in their wake. The advancing army's strength was cut by one third and diminishing rapidly as the first of the Trogs set foot on the sand on the Renoloi side of the river. Being ravaged like trees toppling, the repulsive trodding hulks were a forest of mammoth bodies in an artillery barrage: lumbering, hit, then going down.

Another Tyrannosaur was struck, but with a grasping swing of its foreleg snapped the arrow and continued. Stepping over it the Trog holding the carnosaur's chain ignored the arrow and the subsequent explosion directly beneath him blew his legs straight out with such force his body ripped up the middle, both halves cartwheeling in the air as a scattering cloud of twisted red mist. The same dinosaur was struck again. Wounded, its reaction was more lethargic and the bomb detonated ripping its foreleg off and blowing the reptile onto the beach —a sand-crunching crash— crushing a giant alongside it. Rolling, curling its toes and regaining its feet the Tyrannosaur rose slicing through flesh with its gruesome claws, slowly grinding the Trog's broken body into the sand with its enormous hind foot. Pumping blood from its wounds, it continued on.

Three children in one of the knotted trees targeted the dominant Trog. With the command to fire the titan was hit —staggered back— but he tore the arrow from his belly and threw it aside ignoring the injury and blood pulsing from his gut. As he sauntered away the discarded arrow exploded beneath another wounded dinosaur and the beast collapsed onto the sand. With an enormous wood splinter impaled in its neck frothy blood gurgled pink-bubble foam as the terrible lizard heaved momentarily with rasping chest movements, then twisted its cumbersome head and lay still.

The dominant Trog was struck again, forced to his knees, but again wrenched the arrow free, this time hurling it back into the tree. The penetrating sound of a stabbing thud pinned her to the trunk and a cry of pain issued weakly from the canopy as the arrow sliced through the abdomen of a young archer. Then a sudden fiery explosive blast splintered the inner branches instantly killing three children. Swaggering forward the wounded savage cruelly picked up two of the dead children and slammed their bodies together sadistically fracturing and crushing their small frail bones.

From his vantage point Reed caught sight of the leader, swung around and fired —*foomph*. The arrow stuck thickly in the giant's throat hurtling the behemoth onto the sand —eyes bulged, neck swelled— squirming, writhing and pounding violently with clenched fists. The explosion's boil-white flash ended the man-savage's treachery, sucking sand from the beach and shredding him.

Loading an arrow, Reed spied the Tyrannosaur charging the tree. Reflex —he fired. The arrow flew high, skipping off the top of the dinosaur's bulldog-thick head.

"—Climb!" he yelled, and the three children alongside him instantly obeyed scampering upward springing from one branch to the next. Hands shaking, he lit the fuse of another arrow as Tarin and the other two reached the topmost branches, then —ripping shatter of splintering wood— the dinosaur rammed the gnarled tree with such tremendous fury it was partially uprooted and tilted causing Tarin to lose her grip and fall. A shrill, terrified scream. Eyes swept to the sound Reed watched horror-stricken and helpless as she fell past him plummeting toward the ground and Tyrannosaurus below. The dinosaur snatched Tarin's plunging body in mid-air, biting her in half with one vicious chomp: child, life, and blood all splashed away.

Within that instant Reed felt disbelief and shock, and a mounting, sickening, boiling-throb swirling waves of insanity and red-flash of rage. The arrow was in his hands, the fuse sizzling, and he screamed, *"You damned worthless fucker!"*

He attacked, running the length of the ancient's limb, clutching the arrow in his fist, and dove headlong at the Tyrannosaurus. Alerted by his outcry the dinosaur saw him coming and —yellow-slit eyes, a gleam of teeth— its massive jaws opening, leaking drool of saliva and crimson. It lunged at him intending to kill him, but Reed hurtled the arrow into the bloody open mouth —a penetrating tear— and down the throat. With the momentum of his leap Reed seized the dinosaur's nostril with one hand and a six-inch incisor with the other, swinging himself around the reptile's face and onto the back of its head. Still airborne, rolling sideways, he slid recklessly down the dinosaur's neck and back and landed on the ground behind it. Hitting solidly, stunned, Reed slid in the dirt and rolled, then sat up on his butt.

Chicken-stepping, gagging on the arrow jammed deep in the soft tissue of its throat, the Tyrannosaur reeled searching for him. Angry yellow eyes locked on the man and the dinosaur reared back, then lunged to take him. In splashing gray-red winds of brain and blood splattering leaves and limbs with meat and bone, the bomb in its throat exploded blowing the terrible lizard's head to pieces. Pulsing fountainhead blood the decapitated dinosaur's gigantic body teetered momentarily, its monstrous toes curling in the clutch of death, then crashed sideways onto the ground.

"Jab me with a pointed stick," Reed stammered with adrenaline trembles, "blew it to smithereens."

He heard another child scream turning his attention to a second Tyrannosaur devouring a small girl. Indifferent to him, preoccupied with its banquet, a tasty morsel, the dinosaur watched Reed rise to his feet but did not attack as satiating red driveled from its gruesome slicing jaws. The man took a step and stabbing pain shot up his left leg, *sprained ankle*. Picking up an arrow that had fallen from the tree he ignored the pain, forced himself, limping alongside the tree trunk toward the dinosaur.

With crocodile etiquette, savoring two final gulps the Tyrannosaur finished eating the child, raised its head and roared, then watching the man hunkered and charged. At the last possible instant Reed pushed off from the tilted tree trunk on his right foot, and using the leverage to heave himself up he jabbed the arrow deeply into the dinosaur's neck rupturing the jugular vein. Falling back and twisting the shaft he jerked it free opening the wound and letting a pour of blood that rushed from the hole and down the reptile's neck mimicking pulse with each heartbeat.

A rage provoked with pain, the screaming dinosaur backed two steps, then charged a second time. Reed reacted, propping the arrow against the tree, and the Tyrannosaur's momentum impaled the blood-soaked shaft in its gut. Shooting pain to his groin the injured ankle caused him to stumble as the dinosaur crashed down onto the tree trunk and his left leg pinning him beneath its hulking dead weight.

Still advancing, by the time it arrived at the second line of defense the Trog army had been cut in half.

Ames saw Reed straining to free himself, but committed to the Renoloi cause, he waited to help him until one of the lumbering giants crossed the path of his spears. Estimating the giant's stride, untying the restraining rope he watched from above calculating to the point of arrival —timing— and swung down with the mounted spears. Windswept with momentum —focused— the target growing larger in size until —*thud.* The Trog was gutted as four of the six spears sliced through him and he went down with the swing, crashing the wooden framework and snapping the vines. After the impact Ames leapt aside ignoring his twitching victim, immediately running to help his friend.

The Renoloi began swooping down upon their enemies, sometimes successfully, other times failing. A warrior swung from the trees upon a Trog, but he saw her coming and his grotesque club shattered the spears, the intense sudden force throwing her to the moss-covered forest floor. Bleeding badly, she managed to rise to her knees, but as she did he shattered her skull with one mighty swing of his club. A whirling spray of oatmeal red, brains and blood spewed from her nose and mouth as her lifeless body somersaulted onto the ground.

Another fighter launched too late. The Trog stepped aside smashing his club into her spine —snapping— the woman folded in half and toppled forward crumpling under the spears. With its momentum the spear framework swept back to the holding position in the treetops, and as the giant stepped out to strike her a second time his stupidity was equaled only by surprise when the primitive weapon descended again forcefully stabbing him in the back. The Trog grunted a rasping breath of pain and a second victim slumped upon the first.

Downward: the swoop. Near the other end of the lowland spears impaled a screaming Tyrannosaur and it staggered vomiting frothy blood. Then it collapsed onto the crude but effective weapon snapping vines with a tensile bark as it broke the spears with slivering rips. It floundered, retched again, and stayed down.

The Trog who had been controlling the dinosaur bounded from behind the dead beast and buried the knurled wood of his club in the ribcage of the Renoloi assassin splintering bones and hurtling her into the air. Stunned, she landed in a helpless heap and squirmed on the ground, gingerly touching her side, feeling the cornflake-crunch of crepitus where several broken ribs had torn through her skin. Struggling in vain to crawl, feebly she tried to drag herself clear as the ponderous foot of another towering dinosaur crushed the upper half of her body. Undisturbed by the squeezy-soft tissue oozing between its toes the Tyrannosaurus proceeded on its deadly rampage against the Renoloi.

By now Ames had managed to free Reed from beneath the Tyrannosaur, and mindfully helped the man to his feet. Anxiously: "Can you walk?"

Reed eked out a smile: shaken, but not deterred. "Yeah, I think so," but they had only managed a few steps when he detected peripheral motion, and with a jerk saw a Trog closing from their left. "Look out—" shoving Ames out of the way there was a solid, dreadful sound —and he groaned with the impact of the giant's club smashing into his side.

As Reed went down the Trog turned on Ames, and with one powerful swing severed the sapling beside which he had stumbled. Ducking to avoid splintering wood and debris Ames rolled on his buttocks and quickly rose to his feet with a club of his own. Behind the giant Reed crawled aimlessly in the dirt, severely injured.

Ames saw his friend and how badly he'd been hurt, the unconscionable wanton villainy. And within him, staid human qualities vanished. In a voice as cold and hard as frozen sand, staring down the towering Trog primal instinct overpowered him; and Ames growled, "He's my friend..."

His eyes grew dark narrowing with a glare of despise. His jaw clenched gritting clicks in his mind. His muscles flexed with the ache of pure tension and his brain whirled with epinephrine headspins. Rage pounded, burned blood in his ears. Gritting perfect white teeth Ames adjusted the weapon he held in his sweating palm. His heartbeat raced and arteries throbbed pumping adrenaline through him as his face flushed, and the grinding knot twisted inside his stomach.

"Damn you." And as hate and fury exploded inside him, he screamed, *Damn you —I'll kill you!"*

The man leaped swinging viciously, his club smashing the Trog's temple. Grisly —the noise of crunching bone— the giant staggered in astonishment, then another, another, and another fierce blow. Stupefied, vacillating on weak knees, the behemoth's thick skull finally fractured with a squashing sound, then erupted with a massive squirt of brains and blood as it split apart and his face ripped open. The Trog collapsed and the blows continued —arms, chest, neck— too rapidly to tally them all. Soon the giant lay motionless, Ames standing over him, pulverizing him, absorbed with rage and obsessed with revenge.

Sauntering in and without preamble another Trog attacked, the man narrowly fending off the blow as his club shattered in two. The giant's second swing sliced Ames' club in half again so he threw the remaining chunk of wood at the Trog and backed into a clump of trees with the giant pursuing slowly.

* * *

Tenacious...

...The army of Trogs arrived at the concealed pits. A giant stumbled into one of the traps and the spears stabbed through his chest and lungs killing him: first rigid as his body slid down the sharpened poles, going flaccid, pink frothy blood bubbling from the holes torn in his back, then slack. Another man-beast slid feet first —gored— a spear ruptured his groin then cut with squeezing pressure up through his body and finally emerged from his throat. Hanging there he looked like a gruesome totem with a voodoo head, his eyes staring, dead.

Not far away a giant was slaughtered when spears impaled his skull, chest and thigh, his scream captured within a glistening blood bubble that did not burst. Another pit: a dinosaur plunged in dragging its taskmaster, who had tangled the chain around his wrist, behind it.

By now frenzied Renoloi were fighting giants in disarray and were losing badly. One woman ran between a Trog and an exposed pit and was catapulted into the hole with the impact of the giant's club. Curiously the Trog looked into the pit, observed her lifeless body with spears sticking out of her breast and abdomen, casually walked around it, and continued on.

* * *

Avoiding him...

...Ames backed slowly out of the trees, the Trog following, smashing smaller saplings and ripping bark from larger trees with each mighty swing of his club. In the open again and exposed, the man jumped over a boulder ducking only an instant before the brute's club shattered on the granite shredding splinters that pierced his left shoulder with a large shrapnel sliver. Injured and bleeding, Ames staggered to his feet as the Trog seized him by the waist and threw him. Hitting the ground, the man rolled over a fallen sapling and onto his knees discovering he'd landed between the giant and a pit. Thinking, *forget the pain,* he began to grunt imitating and mocking the simian stance of the enraged Trog.

The giant charged ungainly and ugly with outstretched arms as Ames propped one end of the severed sapling in the ground behind himself and hoisted the other end so the attacking giant ran into it, taking him in the gut. With the Trog's forward momentum and the man's strength lifting, the titan was vaulted upward —then over— and as the green sapling whipped and snapped back the Trog was thrown toward the pit. The behemoth slammed down with a fleshy thud and deflated grunt landing at the edge, then rolled, out-of-sight, into the trap. After one coarse scream from below, he was silent.

Ames slumped forward momentarily to catch his breath, then rose and stepped to the edge of the pit. Peering into it, he saw that the giant's head had been run through, the spear entering the back of his neck and exiting his mouth. Spears also protruded from his chest, stomach and thigh. The poles were smeared with blood and bits of raw meat, and remained firmly planted in the bottom of the pit unbent by the giant's massive bulk.

As Ames turned and began walking toward Reed, he gripped the splinter with his right hand and jerked it out of his shoulder, closing his eyes and gritting his teeth until the shiver-wrenching pain subsided. Clutching the wound, he made his way to his friend.

Sitting on the ground, leaning against a tree: "Hurt much, Doc?" Reed asked, forcing a grin.

"Hell-yes, it hurts," Ames grimaced. "Think you can walk?"

Slowly rising to his feet: "He hit me in the side, not the leg." Drawing a guarded breath: "It's breathing that's a pain in the ass, not walking." Standing, wobbly, he spit out some blood.

"But what about…"

"—My ankle?" Reed asked, then coughed. "My side hurts too bad to notice that—and anyway—how can I fight if I can't even walk?"

"You're okay then?" slipping an arm around his friend.

Managing a step and nodding, "Right beside you."

Coaxing a smile, Ames encouraged, "Then let's go kick some ass."

Reed winced, then mumbled, "Gonna need some bigger shoes." And even though it hurt, Ames had to chuckle.

Trying to catch up to the battle but only able to proceed slowly, the two men surveyed the countless injured and dead, Renoloi by far outnumbering the Trogs. To their left, another Tyrannosaur had fallen on a young warrior, her feet protruding from beneath the reptile's massive body. A little farther on, a giant with a spear through his abdomen lay beneath a gnarled tree, his hand still clutching the ankle of a disemboweled woman sprawled nearby. Above them the body of another badly beaten Renoloi was impaled upon the lower, jutting branches of the tree, her distorted expression revealing the agony of her last valiant effort.

Bodies lay everywhere.

* * *

The advancing army arrived at the spear wall...

...Lumbering, the hulks bullied their way through an annoying rampart of mishmash —high tangled grass— and into javelin-sharp points, a number of the remaining Trogs being killed before becoming aware the spears were there. Giants died at the spears hanging by their throats or slumped onto the barrier impaled through the chest all dripping blood —shrike fodder— corpulent rabbits in a briar patch.

Gored a Tyrannosaurus plowed into the spear wall causing a section of it to collapse; and shrieking, it went down with an animalistic scream and the abrasive cracks of splintered wood. Methodically the two remaining carnivores tromped indifferently over the dead animal's body tearing its hide and meat with their toes. And dimwitted giants followed closely behind determined to perpetuate the battle.

As the dinosaurs neared the trench several of the Trogs entered it paying little attention to the viscous petroleum tar. Kimo carefully drew her bow, and —*snap*— sent a feathered missile and the whisper of flame to the feet of a giant. The arrow sank in tar and oil igniting a field of flame with the shadowing echo of a powerful, *whoomph*, as explosion and searing ocher-blast instantly flashed and rolled soaring in a soot-boil of vaporous black smoke.

Burning Trogs scrambled from the trench in a frenzy of horrific coarse screams and licking flames, the fire mercilessly melting their flesh and hair and diaphanous poison scorching their lungs. Fireball giants stumbled aimlessly as terror-stricken infernos, knowing they were burning alive, then collapsing as death and melting fire consumed them.

The archers on the ridge loosed the first barrage of arrows filling the sky with a whistling rain of wooden whisper-death. A giant emerged from the trench —body afire— was struck by four arrows. Staggering dead, he stopped and turned back toward the trench as five more arrows pierced his back, and stumbling two final steps plunged splashing again into the burning froth.

The lead Tyrannosaur was struck numerous times in the first barrage, and attempting to skirt the periphery and avoid the flames lost its footing on the submitting soil sliding then toppling sideways into the infernal roar. A tidal wash of flame splattered burning tar and whorls of smoke as the monstrous creature splashed down and a blistering cauldron of ravaging fire swept over its carcass. Shrill gurgling animalistic screams ceased as the heat and flames consumed it, boiling tar and oil pouring into its mouth and eyes, drawing blood of coagulated broil with the black bubbling fuel. The leathery hide of the Tyrannosaur peeled, rare—welted, medium—and crisped, well done.

A Trog bounded over the trench using the partially cremated dinosaur as a steppingstone. Having crossed successfully and proud of his cunning, the gloating brute stopped to look around when an arrow suddenly penetrated the bridge of his nose, between dead eyes. Dumbfounded, for just an instant the Trog stood motionless with a quizzical stare on his startled face —then backward into the burning trench.

Self-consuming, tense minutes passed until the flames dwindled and the Trogs began leaping over the trench resembling a rush of sewer rats in crude armor plating. The last Tyrannosaurus crossed on the charred remains of the smoldering dinosaur sprawled across the burning ditch as arrows rained from the ridges and giants went down with the incessant fusillade; some managing to get back up, then falling again as the next wave of missiles poured in. Determined, the Trogs moved forward relentlessly, arrived at the huge piles of ore and started climbing over... close now. And the aerial assault continued.

Kimo waited.

Chipped abraded claws digging into rock, the last Tyrannosaur ponderously scaled the ore mounds. Tian ignited the second arrow. Kimo's eyes focused, following her target. Steady. The Renoloi warrior confidently drew the bowstring taut, waiting, until finally the dinosaur crested the ore pile and roared. She released —a powerful, *snap*— the arrow sizzling to its mark between the hulking legs of the terrible lizard.

Magnesium oxide erupted in shatter-white blasts of splintering shards —astonishing pounding rattles and fireball winds— an unbelievable chain reaction of ground shaking, blinding, violent hoarfire explosions. The concussions slammed into the ground vaulting shockwaves back up that pulsed air with ripping lethal force and gargantuan billowing columns of smoke. It was a rising climax-fire of devastation blown skyward.

The Tyrannosaurus was hurtled into the air —ripping apart— shredded by heat, flame and shrapnel cutting it to pieces from underfoot. Landscape trembled and quaked bringing huge trees crashing down upon the giants, balls of wadded dirt spewing up as massive root systems jutted from the ground with the toppling trees. Rocks seeded throughout the piles of ore splattered like bulleting granite hailstorm, a strafing burst of killer fragments spraying trees, giants and Renoloi indiscriminately.

Fracturing and cracking, a section of the ridges broke loose, collapsed and avalanched in a dust-boil rumble crushing the warriors who had been on it and standing underneath. Then sudden whorls and a gagging rush of dust and debris billowed out with loose chunks of stone tumbling and pelting the ground below the stair-step cliff formation. Other warriors dodged the falling rocks, waiting for the Trogs, while across the lowland hundreds of fires broke out dispersing impenetrable ground-clinging haze of asphyxiating smoke over the dark and blood-soaked battleground. The emerald green of jungle now absorbed in tainted gray, the color of dust and congealed blood.

Trogs entered the level terrain abutting the ridges where Tian waited with her lances.

She raised her spear with a sweeping arm and courageously the warriors leaped from the small cliffs charging the ranks of their enemy. Size and might to their advantage, Trogs butchered the fierce Renoloi fighters. For every giant who died ten women fell. Resolute and fearless Kimo led the archers from the ridges to assist the other warriors, hundreds of arrows continuing to pour upon the dwindling ranks of Trogs.

A giant slaughtered four Renoloi with one swipe of his massive club. Nearby two lances fought another man-savage, one stabbing her spear into his stomach as the other went down crushed by his club. Groaning, the giant wrenched the spear from his gut and rammed it through her chest. A heartbeat past —the arrow struck— piercing the giant's lung. Stumbling to his knees, he grabbed it, trying to pull it out, but another splattered his eye —went deep, splintering skull then squeezed into his brain. And he dropped beside the dead women.

A Renoloi lay beneath Tian who single-handedly fought a giant. The Trog swung and missed as she leaped at him driving her spear through his chest with so much force that her weapon split in half. Off balance she stumbled with the impact and tried to back away from the bleeding titan, but tripped on the fallen Renoloi's body.

Realizing Tian's plight Kimo rushed to her aid as the Trog slowly neared them. And now, escape being hopeless, Kimo yelled to her comrades, "—Nitana!"

Instantly understanding, the woman and five others fired at the behemoth and the Trog staggered as he gasped coughing up blood, six arrows ripping holes in him. But closing for the kill, slobbering a wretched drool of crimson, bleeding and mortally injured, he still would not go down. Lumbering one more step he leaned forward to finish the two trapped Renoloi.

Desperate, targeting his head, Kimo let her arrow fly —and an instantaneous, *swack!* He jerked violently from the impact as the arrow bored into his mouth shattering yellow-brown teeth, sliced through his palate, swept death through his brain and ripped out the back of his skull. The sudden jolt to his head caused the Trog to miss Tian and strike Kimo with the last, powerful swing of his club. Then briefly the giant teetered, stupefied, arms drooping, blood gushing from his lower jaw, the arrow sticking out the back of his head; and as he collapsed he caved onto Kimo as Tian barely managed to get out of the way.

Rolling over, Tian turned and saw the giant lying face down beside her, and Kimo wedged beneath him. Struggling desperately, she dragged and rolled the Trog's corpse from her second's beaten body, and gently lifting her, cradled Kimo's head in her arms.

"Tian... you are safe." The woman gasped for breath at last realizing how precious it was. And in spite of the burning pain inside, she smiled. "Perhaps we will meet again..." she paused, managed to swallow, "in a world somewhere beyond." Her words fading, "Please, remember me..." her eyes closing, as she died.

* * *

When Ames and Reed arrived at the ridges...

...The battle was nearly over, both hobbling tediously, Ames helping his friend along. Surveying the carnage Reed located Tian still holding Kimo's lifeless body, and at the same time spied a Trog stalking her from behind, club poised above his head preparing to strike.

Reed clutched his friend's arm, stammered, "Tian—" hoarse with terror.

Before the word was out of Reed's mouth Ames was sprinting over the battleground, absolutely focused, drawing his knife as he ran. Swiftly as resolve his footfalls landed between the broken bodies of fallen Renoloi warriors, then bounding from the back of a dead Trog and hurdling the monstrous trunk of a toppled tree. Over and down, his feet seemed to not even be touching the ground as he raced in blind flight. Fear for Tian consumed him as hate for the looming miscreant seized him. Fiercely leaping —onto the giant's back— he braced his wrist and plunged the blade into the Trog's throat.

Blood-gurgle-pulses splattered from severed carotid arteries as he jabbed and sliced viciously again and again into the giant's throat. Blood was everywhere —the giant's chest and face, on Ames' hands and arms— crazed with fury and driven with hate he couldn't stop himself. Slicing repeatedly —the red, the glistening blade—even after the distinctive, wheezy, crowing sound indicated the larynx and esophagus had been severed. He continued until the ogre's head flopped back, the knife cutting into the spinal column and not able to penetrate deeper, the knurled club slipping from the giant's hands; but he kept slashing until the Trog collapsed to the ground and he fell to his knees.

Sanity recapturing him, Ames looked at the gory blade in his clenched fist, gleaming, still dripping blood; then turning to Tian he opened his hand and let the knife slip from his fingers. With tears in her eyes and overcome with grief she rose and buried her face in his chest muffling her anguished sobs.

"I'm so sorry," he murmured gazing sadly upon Kimo's body.

* * *

Reed felt a wash of relief when the giant went down…

…And he saw Ames tumble to the ground. Clutching the knife in his right hand, left leg stabbing with pain, he hobbled toward his friend and Tian. Then suddenly —from nowhere— a knotted club smashed into his face splashing blue-white fire and searing sparks. The world exploded!

He was thrown backward landing on his side, and he tried to scream but could make no sound. Writhing, rolling to his stomach he slowly began pushing himself from the dirt and shock swept through him. He wanted to vomit and swallowed hard to keep it down, shaking his head, flicking blood away. Swirling white sparks and pain were everywhere, his brain screaming with deafening roars of whirlwind confusion.

A gash across his forehead poured blood down his face; eyes fluttering, he tried to blink it away. Then through smeared vision he could see a mammoth dark being step in front of him. He coughed and tasted the blood, coppery and warm: *difficult to breathe*. Shoulders aching, his chest tightened with the crepitant sensation of crushed ribs, and there was a flash of fire from his armpits through his neck. Then an enormous, callused hand gripped him by the throat, lifting him into the air.

The world was fading... color to gray.

The Trog was barely visible, no more than a smudged silhouette; but that was enough. In a blur of speed and reflex Reed's right hand struck burying the blade of his knife in the left temple of the ogre's skull. Asphyxiating on his own blood he coughed and let go... releasing the knife, delivering its message.

The world was fading... gray to dim.

The chokehold slackened and Reed slipped from the massive hand as the giant slumped to the ground. Falling, Reed crumpled stricken and helpless onto his back, looking up at the sky. And lying there, he smiled momentarily... as though listening to someone. Then earnestly he whispered, "There are always possibilities... aren't there."

Fading... dim... to dark.

The smile melted away...

And he died quietly at the foot of his enemy.

CHAPTER ELEVEN

The battle was over...

...Ames kissed Tian lovingly, then looking around saw Seana kneeling over his friend. "Reed…" he stammered. He ran to him as Seana hoped with pleading eyes. Ames felt for a pulse. None. Her dirty face tracked clean lines where tears ran down her cheeks.

Seana sobbed, "He is gone." And rocking to-and-fro on her knees she cried, wiping away dirt and gently combing Reed's blood-matted hair from his face with her fingers. Trembling involuntarily, she kept shaking her head… and cried. Finally, unable to constrain the anguish any longer, completely breaking down, her body heaved and she lay her head upon Reed's chest as she gasped then sobbed uncontrollably.

"Oh God," Ames muttered, "no," was all he could say. He leaned forward laying a hand on Seana's shoulder trying to console her, but couldn't, he was trembling himself; so wrapping his arms around her, their hearts infolded, Ames and Seana cried together.

Moments later Tian placed a compassionate hand on Ames' shoulder. His eyes were red, wet with loss, and as he looked up at her she tenderly caressed his cheek. Ames expressed his heartfelt sadness. "He was the best man I ever knew." Then, his most profound tribute: "He, was my friend."

Whispered words: "I know, John." She took a deep breath, the pervasive taste of sorrow. "He died with honor, just as many others did today. Reed died for what he believed in, the good that has always been and always shall be; hope for the future... and to save the Renoloi people. For that he will never be forgotten. He has won his battle."

John Ames' memory returned to the October morning when they approached the Complex for the last time. He could clearly see his friend's face: *It could be random chance, one in a billion. It doesn't necessarily mean there's a, God, behind it all... Christmas in ten million years, what have we done to our world. It wasn't God's idea to make war... it was man's. And you know what; it never will end, because there never was a beginning, and never will be an end. I suppose you were right; deep down inside even I conceive of Someone more powerful, knowing. I like the idea of creation and evolution —no beginning, no end— only cycles... going on and on forever.* Ames came back, blinked twice, and looked at Tian. She stood motionless, her hand gently touching his shoulder, silent.

"Mr. Ames, the last of the Trogs went into the Sacred Temple," Nitana said unobtrusively.

He did not look back. His eyes turned sadly to his friend lying before him, and he gently patted Reed's shoulder. "You did your part. Now, it's up to me." A determined sigh: "Time to finish this."

Ames rose to his feet, and turning surveyed the bloody aftermath of the battle. Those who had survived were tending to the wounded or mourning the loss of their friends. Torpid and mutilated, lifeless and still, bodies lay everywhere surrounded by bloody, broken, inert weapons. The ore mounds had cratered the ground and the trench now quietly smoldered; like the tarnished armor of a gallant knight, they served only as reminders of past glory. Wafting smoke clung tenaciously to the ground illuminated by dappled sunlight that penetrated the trees. Destruction and sorrow lay all around.

"Nitana, how many Renoloi survived?" Ames asked.

"Three, four hundred," her hushed reply, "no more than that."

Ames looked at Tian. "You might say we won, but I'm not so sure."

"I am, John."

* * *

At the edge of the crater, on the rimrock...

...Ames, Tian, Nitana, Seana and the remaining Renoloi were gathered, standing quietly, looking across the ragged basin toward the Sacred Temple. Finally, Ames turned to the people.

"I'm going to end this battle so you can live in peace." As he spoke his eyes focused, in turn, on each individual in the group. "Tian is brave and wise. Follow her. Learn from her as I have. She will show you the way to a future with hope and promise, and perhaps your descendants will someday take my place. I don't know."

"There are so many things we don't know, will never understand. And there is no way I can convey my hope and dreams for you; still, I sense you are already aware of them." He paused, then continued, "Today you have fought and died bravely, as valiantly as any people who ever lived before, in all time. You have earned peace, and now it is time for me to go... so you may have peace."

He looked to Tian. "I've grown to love the Renoloi. Take care of them." Tian nodded but could not speak, holding back tears, she had to be strong... a leader again. Ames turned to Nitana who handed him a bow and quiver of arrows. "Good-bye."

"Farewell," she replied softly.

Ames turned, began to leave, and Tian could stand no more. With heaving sobs she flung her arms around his neck and clutched him tightly crying into his chest. Wrapping her in his arms, refusing to cry, he held her. He had to be strong. With tears streaming down her face, she looked up at him, and they kissed... a kiss that must last forever.

Finally, their lips parting, Tian whispered, "I love you with all my heart."

"And I, you." Reluctantly they separated and Ames started across the ragged crater. After a distance he stopped, looked back, and yelled, "I will love you forever." Then he turned and continued on.

Tian whispered, "I know," but he was too far away to hear her, and as she watched him she became very lonely, that bland, hollow of emptiness was returning. The Renoloi stood silently on the rim of the crater while he crossed the vast rocky surface, eventually arrived at the main cavern of the Sacred Temple, and went inside.

At length Tian turned to her people. "Nitana will take Kimo's place now. It will be so." The Renoloi nodded obediently. "It is time to return to the village and care for the wounded. Go now." All began to leave the crater, quietly, pensive, remembering those who were lost.

Nitana said to Tian, "Perhaps it is best it ends this way."

"This is not the end," Tian confided, tears gathering again in the corners of her eyes then stealing down her cheeks. She gripped Seana's arm so she would not leave with the others. "Take care of those in the village, Nitana."

"Of course," Nitana replied amenably. She turned and left, following them.

Tian whispered, "Wait here with me, Seana... please."

"Yes," Seana agreed, wondering why Tian would say please; her leader never had to ask, "as long as you wish." Tian coerced a fleeting smile and sat down indicating Seana should join her, and Seana sat beside the woman without speaking.

Gazing solemnly over the mysterious range of Legend Mountains, soft spoken, Tian said, "We must wait until sunset."

* * *

Within the Sacred Temple...

...Ames continued through the tunnels eventually reaching the cavern of the inscriptions. He stopped there only for a moment to read the words that were carved in stone above the passage that would lead him to his destiny. The words of the Beatitudes murmured echoes in his mind as he proceeded, his torch pushing back the darkness as he went.

The sandy floor of the tunnel gradually transformed to solid magnesium oxide, and at last the passageway opened into a huge and magnificent cavern. Crystalline formations protruded from the shimmering magnesium floor refracting the light from the torch and reflecting thousands of bands of spectral color throughout the expansive subterranean hall. Eons of undisturbed growth had formed stalagmites, stalactites and gigantic columns of beautifully colored minerals nourished by underground springs that bubbled from the floor and crevices in the cavern walls. Floating within vapors of mist air currents flowed in a heavy damp fog, and pushed away as invisible wisps to somewhere unseen and just beyond reach.

The beauty of the cavern paled in comparison to the golden throne, glimmering with the warmth of afterglow as it rose majestically from the pedestal and was absorbed a hundred feet above in the darkness. The throne was made of solid gold, luxuriously padded with ermine and sable, and its rim was studded with precious stones. Its beauty was awesome.

As Ames approached his torchlight was reflected ten-fold casting a shimmering gleam of aureate glow, and quietly he walked up the steps of the pedestal and seated himself. Pensively he delicately stroked the armrests, a final moment of reflection. Then he removed an arrow from the quiver and lit it placing the torch beside the throne. As the torch flickered Ames surveyed the incredible chamber.

"Did You plan all this…" he wondered reverently, "or did things just get a little out of hand?"

For a moment he watched the wadding on the arrow burn and thought he faintly heard music. He tried to see into the far recesses of the cavern but his eyes could not penetrate the surrounding darkness. And then… from somewhere within the capacious cave, or perhaps, only in his mind, he was not certain …voices.

One final, listless gaze and he leaned back in the luxurious seat, drew the bowstring, and let the flaming arrow streak upward…

—Saffron tailflame into the dark

…The arrow struck the cavern ceiling and instantly —everything exploding— deafening, shattering noise and brilliant white light. And he imagined that a choir of angels was descending upon him: alabaster wings on gossamer winds.

They were so beautiful,

    And they sang such a wonderful song.

      They were so beautiful…

PART II

CHAPTER TWELVE

In the collapsed mountain range of the Legends...

...The Sacred Temple exploded with volcanic fury —a pyroclastic cloud. Untold volumes of white-hot rock and searing magnesium ore hurtled outward seething with columns of billowing smoke and flame, a climax-burn that roared into the sky for miles.

The detonation swept throughout Legend Range —rock-shattering, pulsing power— a shearwave surge of thunder slamming through a granite landscape of primitive world. The blinding incendiary blast flashing out over the crater in a boiling wall of fire of superheated dust and matrix debris rushing with such incredible power the crater's ragged face was crumbled to fine pieces and disseminated creating a smooth plain. The blast's melting windstorm filling the crevices with particulate grains that left it resembling a desert surface of sand... a landscape of arid wind and granitic fire.

—At that same instant

The magnificent cavern within the mountain imploded creating a sphere of pressurized air, a bubble of atmosphere with Ames inside it compressing and collapsing so instantly he would never realize it. Shrunken to the size of an atom so quickly it could happen a thousand times in the tick of a second, with time to spare…

—His existence collapsed

...Infinitesimally small, minutiae life, he went through the fabric of time.

Ames shielded his eyes from the blinding light flashing through his black leather shirt and penetrating his arms as though they weren't even there. Nowhere was there escape from the rocket-thrust noise and piercing radiance of blinding-bright exploding magnesium. Incredible wind was sucking him away. And that quickly he felt space whirling around him, snatched away and pushed somewhere... to an endless abyss.

"I'm dying!"

But he made no sound,

And there was no color.

His scream was smothered by the holocaust around him, and blinded, he was lost in the confusion of sensory meld, a depiction of light imprinted in his brain. He saw images of the throne melting and crumbling, crashing to the cavern floor; the floor erupting, stalagmites and crystals toppling, stalactites falling, splintering apart. Incredible wind was sucking him away. All imprinted in his brain.

Then, he heard the angels again.

They sang such a beautiful song. Mellifluous, enchanting, their frail voices rising from the deafening noise and into his mind, the explosions fading away. And he sensed a stirring inside; and Ames realized he had nothing more to fear. He accepted death and waited patiently for the end to come.

* * *

Into a realm of mystery...

...The angels rejoiced and their song grew louder, their voices dulcet and more resonant until the man was no longer conscious of the explosions and the infernal white fire, somewhere far in the past. Now, only their song and the soft arms of space caressed him. He felt as though he were drifting, almost falling, to somewhere unknown, to where reality and the dream world merge: somewhere distant, far removed... to a place beyond.

He felt no fear,

Only wonder.

BEHOLD... I AM THAT I AM.*(Ex. 3:14 KJV)*

The Voice was firm but loving, warm and compassionate; but most of all, it was the Voice of Wisdom. It came from a distant, unknown region, radiating Life. And Ames knew it was the Voice of God.

He bowed his head to his chest and was again afraid. It occurred to him that his time of judgment had come and he knew he was unworthy.

Floating onward... toward infinity.

His hands trembled as his fingers touched one another. In his blindness Ames was lost. Still, no harm came to him, and he drifted ever so slowly through the coolness of eternal time. "Dear God," he cried, "please accept me." Tears in his eyes, and he drifted onward.

Nearer now... where reality and the dream world merge.

JOHN, DO NOT BE AFRAID.

The Voice was reassuring. And deeply humbled, he felt the awesome warmth that accompanies unconditional love. Inside, he sensed the compassion and understanding.

Drifting softly... to somewhere distant.

It gave him renewed strength with which to speak. "Am I dead?" he muttered. "Where am I?" bounding over. "Is this real," drifting sideways, "or is this a dream?"

Far removed... to the realm of Beyond.

THE UNIVERSE HAS OPENED ITS ARMS TO YOU AS I HAVE COMMANDED.

"But I am blind," the man sobbed.

YOU BELIEVED YOU WERE DEAD, THOUGH YOU WERE NOT; NOR ARE YOU BLIND.

And as God's voice touched the man's mind, his vision returned. He was filled with wonder, and attempting to kneel in deference again he bounded in somersaults, suspended... as his body drifted. Trivia of life, gliding along on light breezes... through the eons of time. He searched for the Voice but was unsure where it originated, having seemed not to have heard it so much as he felt it, somewhere deeply inside... An Ember glowing eternally.

All around him were stars... billions upon billions of them scattered throughout vast clouds of cosmic dust, gossamer winds of nebulae reaching forever. And color returned... the purest colors he had ever seen, shimmering and flowing, undulating and spiraling onward through infinite space. He felt insignificant, dwarfed by the majesty of the universe, its serene beauty more than he could have ever imagined.

Then, from beyond the edge of the universe, a Light began to grow... clear, purer than anything he could comprehend. The Light was dazzling with radiance, but did not blind him; more powerful than all the stars of heaven, but did not burn him; more beautiful than all the rainbows ever created, but he could not describe it. And within the Light, the Voice...

I HAVE A TASK FOR YOU, God said warmly.

The man gazed upon the Light as it conveyed peace and tranquility within his soul. Humbled, he inquired respectfully, reverently, "What am I to do?"

His eyes contained the Light of the Universe, and His mind possessed all knowledge, and He answered with love:

WHEN IT IS TIME, YOU SHALL KNOW...   God was gone.

***

In the realm of mystery...

...Slowly, Ames blinked and was enveloped within a gargantuan tunnel that spiraled before him twisting in great coils of ever-changing size and color through the eternal vastness of the universe. Clear cobalt and azure, a corridor of blue gently wrapped itself around him with gradually tightening circles, liquid winds of majesty conveying him with ethereal disguise. Then it vanished and the tunnel was streaked with brilliant scarlet and orange, undulating wave-like, then rippling, flowing backward, then riffles of watery cascade and changing course once again. Transforming, ocher to saffron then ocher to green with pink vapors clinging to the rim of each circular ridge, all a seaswell of motion and a vision of calm.

And so the tunnel continued. Rising, falling, turning gracefully or dropping sharply; then leveling and gently rising again: the flight of a mythical bird crossing the universe, unhurried, enjoying the journey. The glimmering beauty of the pellucid corridor was spellbinding, flecked with countless glittering particles: minutiae of starlight, blinking pulsars, shimmering quasars, burning snowflakes of light.

It was so beautiful.

Ames began to see images in the walls of the spiral tunnel. They were everywhere, millions upon millions of them occurring simultaneously. They appeared and disappeared so quickly that his eyes and brain could not focus upon any single one, only mix them together in an incongruous blur. There were great explosions and raging volumes of fire blinking through the vapors in split second progressions. Amidst gleaming flashes of starfire he believed he was able to recognize volcanoes and the grizzled faces of massive reptiles with intimidating jaws and teeth. Magenta walls of the corridor caused nefarious, narrowed pupils to burn demoniacally evil with each blink of their eyes or turn of their cumbersome heads.

A transcendental metamorphosis, the tunnel swept from purple and dark, burst into yellow and gray. Ames witnessed incredible explosions as stars collided and flung limitless world-sized fragments into space, entire galaxies twisting and folding, everything drawn away to somewhere unknown. Again and again flares of white light zipped through the corridor periphery and disappeared almost before he realized they were there. Gazing upon the spectacle before him, his mind overwhelmed with the sight, his being absorbed within the phenomenon, Ames became dizzy.

He felt himself falling once more and began to roll sideways. The tunnel dropped sharply and the yellow corridor was fading —then instantly gone as darkness swept upon him and a cold breeze washed over him. A green tunnel. He tumbled onward and as he bounded over he caught a glimpse of the tunnel above him. The aperture of the green corridor was quickly diminishing, disappearing, evaporating into waves of blue. He somersaulted again and it was gone.

Light-headed, confused, his stomach tightened twisting in knots and he believed he was retching but couldn't be certain. So much all at once, so bewildering. No longer sure of anything, again he bounded onward through the gentle colors, still trying to focus, telling his eyes to open, and reluctantly they did.

This time the explosions were gone and he thought for just an instant that he could see three crosses on a distant hill surrounded by a great crowd of people. But again, he wasn't sure. Finally, there was an image which he knew very well.

"Reed..." he mumbled. His thoughts and emotions colliding, he lost consciousness.

CHAPTER THIRTEEN

From somewhere else —shaking— and garbled, distorted sounds...

..."Mister, wake up," —a voice— prodding the unconscious man sprawled on the storage room floor. Pushing a mop bucket back under the sink and two cardboard boxes out of the way the Federation sergeant urged shaking him, "Hey, can you hear me? Wake up." The sergeant rolled the man over. Face up on the slate-gray floor, the sergeant studied the stranger's weathered countenance for the slightest movement, the twitch of an eyelid, lip movement beneath the grizzled beard. But other than a weak, thready pulse there was no sign of life.

"Shall I call security?" a second voice inquired.

The sergeant was about to say yes, turned to the soldier, hesitated; then intently looked at the man on the floor again. There was something about the man, something familiar... too familiar.

"Shall I call security?"

"No, call an ambulance."

"But Sergeant, that's a breach of protocol."

"Private, I'm well aware of that. I gave you a direct order —now call an ambulance."

"Right away." He left the room at a brisk military trot, heading for the central control desk.

The sergeant hovered over the unconscious man, again prodding him, trying to arouse him, the ambulance now enroute. "Mister, wake up." Studying him judiciously, "Who are you?"

Stuporous, the man on the floor finally murmured, "Ames... John Ames."

The sergeant's eyes wide with realization, gazed at him. Hushed astonishment: "Oh shit—I knew it!" The sergeant leaned over him, very close. "Mr. Ames, don't say another word until you're out of here." Cautiously, very nervous: "Do you understand? Don't say another word," she whispered.

"This way," the private's voice ordered as he directed the paramedics to the corridor when the elevator doors opened, "corridor two."

Anticipating and hearing the ambulance crew as they approached with their gurney and jump-kits, the sergeant rose and swung wide open the door that had been slightly ajar. "Here," she told them.

The three-attendant crew wheeled in the cot and proceeded with practiced efficiency. Baseball caps, waist-length jackets and pants, all navy blue and letter-perfect, even to the, 'Federation Registry' patches they wore. Crisis and trauma were routine assignment for them: intelligent, well trained and prepared, the emergency responders knew what they were doing.

The lead paramedic, being his talkative self, commented without fanfare, "Bit unusual, Sarge. We don't generally get calls here at the Complex. Don't you guys have your own infirmary?"

"Charlie," she said fixing his attention with a serious stare, "this man is unconscious. He needs to be hospitalized —now." Charlie understood. He didn't know what it was about, but he knew the sergeant well enough to comprehend something was going on, something of consequence.

Without hesitation Charlie ordered, "Forget the vitals, guys. Load and go —right now." Within seconds Ames was loaded on the gurney and being wheeled down the corridor by two paramedics, followed by the private. Charlie hesitated at the storage room door with the woman, his eyes catching hers asking the question.

"Can't explain now," she whispered, "just get him out of here."

Charlie nodded answering discretely, "You got it babe, we're out'a here." As he ran to catch up with his crew he clapped his hands as if coaching them. "Let's boogie guys. Let's boogie."

The elevator doors whisked closed and two minutes later the paramedics, and Ames, were out of the building.

"Sergeant," the private resounded snapping to attention. Academy crisp and still wet behind the ears, the nineteen-year-old wore his uniform straight and his hair so short he bore a striking resemblance to 'Mr. Potato Head' with five o'clock shadow, acne and 'Dumbo' ears. Ass-kisser since way back when, and opportunist to the core, he made his intentions clearly apparent.

"Yes, private?"

"This entire incident violates all procedures of protocol," he stated in military monotone. "I will have to report it even though it may result in a reprimand."

"Whatever, I'll deal with it," she answered, then turned and walked away.

* * *

Out of focus...

...His eyes fluttered, beads of sweat leaking into his eyelashes. Someone had shaved him and cleaned him up; but still he felt hot and uncomfortable, weak. "Where am I?" Ames asked with a dry throat.

"You're in St. James Medical Center, intensive care unit," replied a woman wearing a white, waist-length lab coat examining his chart. Businesslike she added, "I'm Dr. Johnson, Corin Johnson." She was model tall but shapely, her dark brown hair tied back in a bun and the glasses lending an aura of refinement perhaps expected of someone in her position. In her late thirties and never married, rather than husband and children she had chosen a career instead. Seeming younger than her years her appearance conveyed youth tempered with the calm of experience; the texture of her skin, still supple and smooth, unwrinkled. She possessed a beautiful smile, and when she did it drew her chin to a point. "How are you feeling?"

"Thirsty."

"Other than that?"

"Just thirsty," he said.

"You're dehydrated. The saline drip will clear that up. In the meantime, I'll have the nurse bring you some water."

"Thank you, Ma'am."

"Ma'am?" amused, she glanced at his chart again then replied, "You're welcome, John Doe."

"Ames," he said. Doctor Johnson was taken by surprise but didn't comment. "Not John Doe, John Ames." The woman stood motionless, considering. She looked toward the ICU monitoring station where four nurses were working. She didn't speak; nervous, worried, uncertain, deliberating until Ames interrupted her thoughts. "Dr. Johnson?"

"Mr. Ames, I have no idea where you've been or what happened at the Federation Complex today," she whispered, "but there are things going on that are... shall we say, unorthodox."

"What year is this?"

"Calendar's on the wall," she answered without looking at it, still studying him. Ames turned his head, saw the calendar, then looked at the woman, confused.

Eyes focusing: "That can't be right."

"It is," she replied. "It's been twenty-five years since you and Reed disappeared," she apprised, "and things have changed here." Then softly, but clearly: "You have amnesia. Your name is John Doe." Her aspect, not trifling, "Whatever you do Mr. Ames, remember that."

"Is that an oxymoron or epigram?" he quipped.

"Save the wit," she cautioned, "there's more at stake here than you realize. I'll be back later." Dr. Johnson left Ames' curtained cubicle. "Nancy—" she addressed one of the ICU nurses.

"Yes, Doctor."

"I want John Doe in isolation—no visitors—only necessary staff."

"Yes, Doctor."

"Ester," Dr. Johnson continued, addressing a second nurse, a large black woman, "do you have a few minutes? I need to speak with you. There's something we…" her voice faded as they went beyond the nurse's station, crossing the room, down the corridor.

St. James was a model of medical efficiency and technology, expertly staffed, capably organized, well equipped and hospital clean. The corridors were brightly illuminated and rooms were spaciously comfortable, both utilizing bright, cheerful pastels to promote the healing process.

They moved briskly down the corridor, neoprene soles squishing on the tile floor only occasionally. Ester Bloomenthal was a very large, full-figured, buxom, robust sort; her center of gravity lower now than years before, good natured and absolutely loyal if she befriended you, but an intimidating adversary from the other side. She hustled alongside Dr. Johnson without speaking, her arms and shoulders moving to help propel her body, a locomotive-type gait.

Ester never questioned Corin, they had been friends for too many years, and when the elevator doors opened they proceeded again without speaking, toward 'Records'. Pushing through the door and entering the room both were immediately recognized by Sandra, the administrative assistant, a middle-aged woman, the quiet sort. Her desk was abutted by rows of steel shelves containing thousands of hardcopy files, each documenting someone's medical history, an electronic papertrail from cradle to grave: every prescription, allergy, illness, injury, medical procedure and so forth. Every file was color coded and properly cataloged, in its place: from 'A' to 'Z', e-file people, alphabetized and sterilized. The clerk's smile of acknowledgment allowed Corin and Ester passage to the computer terminals at the back of the room where Dr. Johnson sat down while Ester hovered anxiously.

"What is it, Corin?" she finally had to ask.

"John Doe," was all Corin said; then Ames' medical file and photo ID blinked onto the monitor.

"Oh, Lord'a mercy," Ester whispered realizing her friend's urgency, "is it really him?"

"Yes… it sure is."

"But he was in the Federation Complex," Ester began, "who got him out?"

Dr. Johnson looked up at her. "A friend."

"One of ours," the nurse remarked under her breath, fathoming the Doctor's innuendo. "Who else knows he's here?"

"Hopefully, no one," Corin answered, "but we couldn't be that lucky. I'm certain by now Smith has figured it out, and if he hasn't, it won't take him long." Momentarily she studied the records and other background information as she scrolled down the monitor, and after a minute she asked, "Ester, can you access the 'Montana Standard' newspaper's database from one of these terminals?"

Ester grinned enthusiastically seating herself at the next station. "With a bypass and couple of dead ends?"

Dr. Johnson nodded. "You got it."

"No problem." And the nurse woke the machine and went to work. Seconds later she spoke. "Online, Corin. What are we in to?"

"Archives: John Ames. Articles, footnotes, anything that's in there," she answered, "whatever you can find—anything at all. Print it. Everything."

"Let's see what we will see." Ester smiled wryly.

Dr. Johnson picked up a phone, immediately answered by the 'Records' desk. "Sandra, I need to make a call. Can you get me a secure line?"

"Yes, Doctor," the digital voice from the other end, "right away."

* * *

Much later that night...

...Ester Bloomenthal and another nurse busied themselves at the nurse's station of the St. James Hospital intensive care unit. Everything was quiet, all the patients resting under the watchful eye of monitoring equipment. Corin Johnson, having completed her rounds late, slipped in to check on her patient.

"John Doe?" she asked, placing a gentle hand on the station nurse's shoulder.

"In the back, Doctor," the nurse whispered looking up and checking Ames' monitor. Then back to Corin, "Doing fine."

"Thank you, Pat. I'm going to look in on him for a minute." Ester darted Corin a furtive glance but said nothing as the doctor walked to the isolation cubicle pulling the curtain closed.

"Mr. Ames, are you awake?" she asked in the subdued light.

"Yes."

"I suppose Doctor Ames would be more appropriate," drawing a chair alongside his bed and sitting.

"John would be fine."

"Corin," she responded, and smiled.

Ames nodded weakly returning the smile, then asked, "What has happened here? What's going on that's so surreptitious?"

Speaking softly: "Butte isn't the same place you left twenty-five years ago, John. A lot has changed. In fact, the whole world is radically different."

"How?"

"It's a rather complicated story," she began. "I'll give you the 'Reader's Digest' version if that's acceptable?" He nodded and she explained. "Shortly after your disappearance, actually about twenty years ago, the individual European Common Market countries merged forming a trade federation under the pretext of international banking and commerce, giving them more leverage on the world market, so to speak."

"No big deal really, until when overnight the International Trade Federation transformed into the United Military Federation of Nations which is now called the United Federation. That happened when there was a worldwide monetary crisis. Entire countries were collapsing financially and economies were in complete shambles. Consequently, commerce came to a standstill with the entire planet on the brink of disaster. The ultimate crisis. There was no order."

Darting a peek toward the ICU nurses' station, a nervous precaution, before she continued. "Then a nondescript United States general conveniently stationed in Europe at this particularly critical time, magically pulls a rabbit out of the hat—that is to say—in one day arranges to replace all currencies with the ECU, the Euro." She paused. "In a single twenty-four-hour period, this one individual supposedly organizes, reconstructs, reformulates and disperses to every financial institution in the entire world, the ECU —and restores financial stability to a bankrupt world." She paused again. "With me so far, John?" He was listening, intently. "Once the United States embraced the Federation, Canada, Mexico, Australia and the other holdouts had no choice, either go along, or go under."

"Jesus," he whispered, "a global coup?"

She shook her head. "No one knows for sure, and if they do, they're certainly not saying. But you know as well as I do, the logistics alone would take months, or years to accomplish."

"If it ever could be done at all," Ames offered.

Corin continued seriously. "John, do you have any idea who that nondescript general happened to be?" No answer. "Our very own General Smith," she said.

Ames stared at her. "Oh Jesus, the Science Complex."

"Not anymore," she told him. "Now it's the headquarters of the United Federation military."

"Shit." Ames slumped back onto the bed.

"Well put," Corin agreed. "Our average, all-American community of Butte now has the distinction of being the headquarters of the individual who virtually controls the military might of the world, with the exception of China and a few minor allies of theirs."

"No," Ames told her, "it's worse than that."

"What do you mean?"

"The sub-levels..." he said. "That explains sub-levels five and six."

"Sub-levels?" She was puzzled. "What are you talking about?"

He studied her face briefly deciding if he should trust her, then realized he had no other choice. "Corin, my turn to explain now," he began. "The Complex was constructed as a science facility, purportedly, but had numerous design modifications peculiar for scientific research application." He paused, but she didn't question him so he continued. "I was one of the design and format engineers for the Complex. It isn't a circular building two floors high. It's two floors on the surface—and six levels deep—each sub-level separated from the next by two hundred-forty feet. The sixth sub-level rests on the bottom of what used to be the Berkley Pit, sixteen hundred feet underground."

"But why?"

"To withstand a nuclear assault."

"Oh my God, are you sure?"

"Has to be," he said, "and there's more. I thought the specs were inordinately large for ventilation shafts, even back then. Level Six has six vertical ports, one at the outer end of each corridor, with extraordinary stainless-steel armament; and they're sealed with blast covers eighteen inches thick. They've got to be missile silos."

"Missile silos?"

Ames appeared worried. "Yes, consider it, one man, General Smith, with enough nuclear capability to destroy the entire world."

"Oh shit!" Corin said, "that means we're ground zero."

"—'Fraid so."

Corin mulled the situation for a moment, then said, "John... Ester, the black RN, knows your identity. You can trust her, but no one else. The Federation will figure out who you are and try to get to you. They want you very badly. They searched for years after you and Reed disappeared." Stopping briefly, then deciding, "We've got to get you out of here and hidden somewhere, but right now I need to make a phone call." She couldn't use her cell and rose, preparing to leave.

"Corin," he said. She stopped, turning to face him, "why are you helping me?"

Soberly: "Too many people have gone into the Federation Complex and never come out. And not all of us are in favor of a, 'New World Order'." Then she asked, "By the way, where were you for the past twenty-five years?"

He thought briefly, and answered, "Oh, not too far away."

"I understand." Smiling: "I won't be overly curious, but I had to ask." Dr. Johnson left ICU and the hospital. She needed to use a pay phone.

* * *

At 0:400 hours...

...Four commandos moved silently up the stairwell toward the intensive care unit, all dressed in black and heavily armed with military-issue weapons and communications equipment. They proceeded without making a sound, practiced in stealth and precision, obeying orders without question.

On the fourth floor the corridor leading to intensive care was clear, the drowsy inactivity of night lingering throughout the hospital. The commandos advanced cautiously, quickly and absolutely alert, knowing their objective. Assisted by pneumatic openers the heavy doors of the ICU whisked apart and Pat looked up from the desk, startled —*fit, fit, fit*. Three slugs from the silencer-equipped weapon: two center-mass, one to the head shattering her skull, blowing hair and brains out the back of her head.

She slumped forward onto the desk.

Unspeaking, one commando directed the others with a hand movement to secure the area as he slipped to the desk and retrieved an electronic clipboard with the name, 'John Doe'.

"What the—" Ester stepped from a curtained cubicle interrupting the black intruders, but hadn't time to say anything more as bullets ripped into her body and she crumpled onto the floor. An expanding puddle, blood oozed onto the clean tile from beneath her. Without emotion the leader signaled toward the isolated cubicle in the rear of ICU and the four converged, pulled open the curtain and entered just as the patient sat up —eyes wide. He felt a sting in his neck... then everything went black.

"Get his clothes," a voice ordered.

CHAPTER FOURTEEN

Very cold, very empty, all alone...

...The room was sterile, white, brightly lit and very large, typical of others like it within the Military Complex sub-levels. Both ceiling and floors were tiled to avoid the use of acoustic panels which would absorb sound rather than reflect it creating an echo, echoes being useful at times to psychologically instill emptiness and despair in a subject. Everything within the examination room had been carefully planned, orchestrated, to produce the sensation of a void, right down to the faucet that dripped in the stainless-steel sink, unseen, somewhere along one of the walls —*drip, kerplunk, echo*. It was all very useful at times.

Ames was held to the stainless-steel examination table with nylon restraints: ankles, thighs, abdomen, chest, hands and forehead. The straps were tight, pinching and biting into his skin, deliberately so to instill fear; complete restriction of mobility, and naked, to humiliate him. Years of practice had honed the military's psychological warfare as well as its weaponry's destructive capability.

The tactics were all part of the game: overpower, dominate, break the enemy's spirit, then destroy him. Ames knew what it was all about. He was strong, but here in the bowels of the enemy's fortress, all alone, it would be difficult. As soon as he had regained consciousness and become aware of his surroundings he'd resolved to die rather than lose this war. It's what Reed would have done —and he owed him that. They had made a pact: neither would ever give the government the time machine or pulse laser, death would be the better alternative.

Ames couldn't see them but he knew they were watching, recording every movement, monitoring pulse, respirations, heartbeat and brain waves. Inside this fortress 'Big Brother' was omnipresent, knowing everything, constantly invasive; civil rights and privacy having no dominion here. He was well aware the cameras were there even though he couldn't move his head to search them out. He couldn't see them —but he could feel them— cold, calloused Pentax eyes watching him. The air was cold causing goosebumps to rise on his skin, cold like the watchers. But they wouldn't break him. He knew how they played this game. *Goosebumps,* he thought, *pelo erection*. He knew the game too, and the medical terminology made him grin.

"What's so fucking humorous?" The voice startled him from just a few feet away, over his head. He hadn't heard anyone approach, didn't realize anyone was there.

"Nothing."

"What's your name?"

"John Doe."

"Cute, Ames," an officer said stepping into the man's view. "John Doe, that's cute; but I don't have much of a sense of humor so let's be serious, shall we?"

"All right. You know my name; may I ask yours?"

The officer, a medium height and weight individual with brown hair cut military short, hands clasped behind his back, and perfectly tailored in his pressed uniform answered, "Thorne, Captain Rick Thorne, United Federation military." Ames tried to nod an acknowledgment, momentarily forgetting the restraints. "Don't bother to get up. No need for handshakes," Thorne added with a wry smile.

"All right, Captain."

"Mr. Ames," Thorne said flatly, "we have a number of things to discuss. I would appreciate your full cooperation."

"And I would appreciate your untying me," Ames replied, "but that's not likely either, so it would appear that neither of us will get what we want."

"I will," Thorne countered, "you can depend on that." He stepped away from the table and two lab technicians appeared from somewhere behind him, leaned over their prisoner as though examining a specimen. One technician was male, the other female, and each held an instrument similar to a soldering iron. Both wore white lab coats. The man resembled a gap-toothed bug peering through coke-bottle glasses, the woman however, was just plain butt-ugly beneath the mop of frizzed red-orange hair.

"Are you ready to talk, Mr. Ames?" the male tech asked rhetorically. There was no response. "Well then," he said placing the instrument against the prisoner's neck, "where shall we begin?"

"Where I always begin," the female tech replied sardonically pushing her instrument into Ames' scrotum.

An intense, burning, electric pain sizzled from his scrotum to his neck: electricity with fire. He tried not to scream but the pain was unbearable —and he could see her— the pleasure she derived from torture, eyes bright, teeth barred in a twisted smile. For fifteen seconds she held the electric rod against him, languishing in the pleasure of her work. Finally, she quit and the pain stopped.

She examined his penis. "Strange," she observed, "usually makes them squirt."

Ames gasped for breath. "You are one—sick—individual," painfully forcing a swallow.

"Thank you," she responded, quite pleased and genuinely flattered. "I do enjoy my work."

The male tech pushed his rod into the man's armpit, the female tech the sole of his foot, and the pain seared through him again. Next the male technician chose the left ribcage and the female chose the right.

"No, no—" the male tech cautioned quickly removing his instrument from Ames' body, "mustn't cross the heart; that would kill him, and we can't have that." She considered a moment; then the female tech chose a new location, pushed her rod into his anus. When the electricity stopped both technicians stepped away and Captain Thorne reappeared, loomed over him.

"Are you ready to talk?"

No reply. The man simply glared from the table so Captain Thorne stepped back and the technicians went to work again.

The torture continued for several hours, but their prisoner steadfastly refused to speak. Twice the pain pushed him beyond the threshold of consciousness irritating the technicians; but their next jolt of current would startle him back so they could proceed... always careful not to kill him.

After four and one-half hours the male technician finally gave up: no one had ever gone more than two hours before. The female tech was disgusted, thoroughly disappointed that she had been unable to dominate this prisoner. She certainly hated them —men. It was apparent this one was unusual. She hated all men, but this man, withstanding her torture; that could cause her some emotional problems.

"That's enough," Captain Thorne finally ordered the technicians. He would never admit it, but he was impressed.

"Stubborn son-of-a-bitch," the male tech concluded.

"Use the probe," Thorne advised.

"Could kill him, Captain," the technician warned.

"Fuck him. Use it."

* * *

Two weeks later...

...They met at the sixth sub-level, corridor six, in a shadowed quarter of the empty, expansive hall. They were alone, very few ever being allowed at this level.

"Captain Thorne, your progress report."

"Torture was completely ineffective, Sir. However, the probe is producing results, more slowly than we'd hoped, but we are assimilating. In another week or two we should have it all."

"Why so long?"

Captain Thorne chose his words carefully. "The technicians are proceeding in steps, carefully. Both they and I felt it best to limit the duration of each probe to assure full recovery and not risk killing him accidentally, ah... prematurely."

"Very well," General Smith concurred. At six-foot-five he was a large, thick individual, perhaps three hundred pounds, solid hate and muscle. From his head of gray stubble hair to the gleam of his black spit-polished boots, he was thoroughly military. His face was heavily joweled and wrinkled, and his gray eyes were intensely mean: Edward G. Robinson in a gangster movie —only much bigger. "You will keep me apprised, Captain?"

"Yes Sir, of course."

"Good, good. —Oh, one more thing, Captain," the General said thoughtfully, then paused.

"Yes, Sir?"

"Concerning Doctor Johnson," Smith began, "Doctor Corin Johnson, at St. James Hospital..."

"Yes Sir," Thorne said, "I know who you're referring to."

General Smith bit the stub of his cigar with crooked yellow chipped boxer's teeth, puffed lazily, then blew a smoke ring. "Doctor Johnson is becoming a bit of a nuisance since we retrieved Ames — the incident in ICU with those nurses— you recall. We can't have the doctor creating problems at this time, Captain." His gaze drifted away, then back to the man. "She needs to be dealt with. You understand."

"Yes Sir."

"Good, good," General Smith said. He turned and walked toward the end of the corridor.

The answers secreted within Ames' brain would be carefully pried from the crevasses and evaluated by a barrage of scientific and military minds. Then, when the fragments were organized into usable facts and knowledge, the stage would be set... which could alter the course of mankind.

Pieces of: *The Puzzle...* falling into place.

CHAPTER FIFTEEN

Faded, antiquated…

…The city bus slowed, screeching brakes bringing it to a halt at the street corner as shriveled autumn leaves whipped out of the gutter onto dying grass. Dr. Johnson stepped off the aging bus, a part of the mass transit system commemorative of the old days, into the brisk October evening. The engine roared spewing diesel-carbon-soot of hot black exhaust from the tailpipe, and as the bus rolled away from the curb the fumes whooshed between the woman's legs lifting her skirt, reminding her that on the streets she was vulnerable.

Although only a little past six darkness was creeping quickly over the modest suburb and Corin didn't foolishly linger outdoors at night. As with everywhere else in the country, the cancer of serious crime had become insidiously prevalent in Butte. The greed and corruption of the Federation hadn't helped abate the problem, only made it worse; the 'haves' and 'have-nots' were farther apart than ever before. Within five minutes the woman walked the two blocks from the bus stop to her apartment, a brick duplex encompassed by privet hedges and Douglas fir, carefully trimmed and shaped.

The lock clicked as the key rotated in the cylinder. Her finger traced the wall then pushed the mercury switch flooding the previously darkened living room with valance and subdued light accenting the early American, earth-tone furnishings, carpet and drapes. The warmth felt good bringing goose bumps to her arms and the back of her neck as she removed her waist-length nylon jacket throwing it on the couch.

Scratching at one of the windows.

Rubbing down the goose bumps on her arms she walked across the room and drew the drapes. "Well, Samantha," she said sweetly, "what's the matter, are you cold and hungry?" As she spoke she raised the window letting the tabby cat crouched on the sill enter the apartment. The cat jumped from the sill to the couch, twitched its tail, then rubbed the woman as she sat down beside it. Corin scratched the tabby cat behind the ears and petted its belly when it rolled over, inducing a contented, *purr.* "Let me take a shower; then I'll feed you, Sam. I'm about frozen too," she announced pejoratively. As the woman rose and went into her bedroom the cat jumped to the recliner to await dinner.

In the darkened bedroom Corin stepped out of her shoes, pushing them aside with a foot. Unzipping her skirt, it loosened from her slender waist and slid lithely down her shapely legs. She picked the skirt up with her foot, flipped it onto the bed while unbuttoning her blouse and next, casually removed the blouse draping it over a Windsor comb back chair. She removed her bra baring full, rounded breasts, and her nipples firmed becoming erect as the cool air touched them. Putting on her robe, its warmth a comfort, she flipped the light switch and stepped into the adjacent bathroom pulling the door, but not quite closing it. For a moment there was no sound, that interlude of pause, until water began spraying with the rhythmic spasms of the shower massage producing humid warmth of hot water steam.

Thorne, wearing street clothes and gloves, stepped quietly from the closet listening to the water splashing on the shower walls and floor. He tried to imagine the figure of the woman behind the acrylic shower panels only four feet beyond the bathroom door, which was slightly ajar. Furtive, silently, he walked to the queen-sized, 18th century Windsor bed and sat on the pillow at the head. The feminine scents and perfume filled his nostrils: seductive, arousing. With his right hand, from under his jacket he withdrew the sawed-off shotgun loaded with one magnum slug, with the left, a twelve-inch silencer from the other inside pocket. Aligning the threads —a quick spin— as almost effortlessly the silencer rotated onto the threaded barrel of the scattergun, and with one last twist, it was tight.

"Now all there is to do is wait," he said to himself. "Sure seems like a waste though." Then he thought, *orders.*

Several long moments passed as the water continued to run; then suddenly it stopped. Time seemed to stand still, the man waiting in a head-rush of silence. The bathroom door flung open and sultry mist of steam billowed into the cooler bedroom.

"Don't scream," Rick Thorne whispered with icy conviction. She stood petrified in the doorway, backlit from the bathroom, a towel wrapped around her hair like a turban and her robe clinging to the dampness of her skin. "Don't scream," he repeated. "Please don't."

"What's—what's?" but she couldn't speak, terrified.

"Orders, Doctor; you have to be eliminated," he explained as politely as an assassin was capable of being.

The muzzle of the shotgun menaced as intimidating and dark as the bore of a cannon and she felt as though she would vomit. Her legs lost their strength as dizziness swept upon her with a hot gush and she crumpled to the floor. Thorne sat on the bed still brandishing the weapon toward the now-empty doorway.

"Shit," he finally mumbled, "just my fucking luck." He rose and walked to the foot of the bed where Corin lay unconscious, and removing his gloves set aside his weapon lifting her gently to the bed. Her head dropped softly onto the pillow and her arms tumbled slack as he lay her down. Almost musically, "Wake up, Doctor," shaking her by the chin. The woman showed no sign of life, but Thorne persisted until her eyelids finally fluttered and she began to regain consciousness. Suddenly, her eyes wide with realization and fear, she tried to scream but he covered her mouth with a hand.

"Don't scream, Doctor." He looked at her tenderly and explained, "I don't want to kill you; it's orders. You understand that, don't you?" psychotic logic, intending apology.

She shook her head, *no*, eyes still wide, filled with terror.

"Well," Thorne began again, "you've sort of become a nuisance, and you're creating problems. —Oh, by the way, I'm sorry about the incident at the hospital; I was hoping that could be avoided. You do understand?"

Halfheartedly, she nodded pretending to relate on his level.

"Will you scream if I remove my hand?"

She shook her head, *no*. The man hesitated briefly, then slowly removed his hand from her mouth. She didn't scream. "Why do you have to kill me?" she stammered.

"Orders. I already explained that," he answered forthright.

Her desperation, any sliver of a chance: "Isn't there any other way?"

"I don't see how there could be."

"Please," she pleaded, fear in her eyes, "anything —just don't kill me." She entreated, pitifully, "Please don't kill me."

Thorne's eyes wandered from the woman's face, traveling slowly down her parted robe. His hand lay gently on her chest, just below the rounded breasts that heaved with each sob. Her abdomen quivered and the fine body hairs shimmered in the dim light. Eyes traveling still lower, his attention gathered where the robe was tucked snugly between her legs so only the uppermost pubic hair was visible.

"Would you go away?" he asked.

She stared at him. "Where to?"

Looking up from her waist, "Anywhere. Hell, I don't care; just so long as no one ever finds out you're still alive." Suggesting, "You could go to South America—or Australia—or somewhere."

Incredulously, "Would you let me do that?"

"I don't *want* to kill you," he said soberly. His eyes wandered again and became fixed on the robe, just below her waist. Almost imperceptibly, he licked his lips.

A long silence.

"There's only one thing I can give you in return," she said. Her hand moved slowly to the belt of her robe, and pulling at the bow, the belt loosened. She withdrew the robe from between her legs exposing herself, spreading her legs and bending her knees slightly.

Thorne twitched, tense with excitement and anticipation as his hand crept down her quivering body. The hair was matted and still damp from the shower, but resilient like twisted cotton. He leaned forward touching her nipple with his lips, nibbling tenderly. His tongue felt wet and rough as it suckled her breast harder and she trembled with apprehension. Feigning, the woman moaned and he moved his head downward stopping every few inches to kiss tenderly, her delicate, feminine odor becoming more pungent as he neared her thighs; until his tongue slid between the labia, teasing her clitoris. She tasted bitter, but sweet.

Again and again his tongue darted into her, each time deeper than before. Her pretense diminished as her excitement, intensifying, grew. It had been a long time for her. Stimulated, somehow wanting him —the risk, the danger— she perspired, drawn with apprehension and at the same time tense with pleasure, until the warmth of her orgasm overwhelmed her and she cried out through clenched teeth.

She grabbed frantically for his waist seizing him by the hips, pulling him to her and kissing the bulge in his pants. His belt buckle clicked. She pulled them down his legs and his slacks dropped to the floor, as reaching out, her hands clasped his throbbing penis, firm with blood and expectation. It was hot and rigid as she drew it into her mouth. Each time she felt it pump she sucked and stroked harder until finally he climaxed spewing hot semen into her mouth. She swallowed —more came— and she swallowed again.

Next, he turned and slid between her legs; entering, then moving, slowly at first, then faster and wetter, their bodies pressed together. She felt him pushing deeper and deeper, exciting and wanting, more quickly and harder, perspiring and liquid. Every cell became alive with sensation as she climaxed again. His muscles flexed and he squirted again, deep inside.

Then, he lay gently upon her and he kissed her, tenderly, caringly. Both were content and satisfied. They snuggled together for a while, the pool of perspiration in her navel squishing between them with the slightest movement... until she drifted off to sleep.

Eventually, Thorne withdrew from her and sat up. Reaching over he pulled a pack of cigarettes from his shirt pocket and lit one. And as he smoked, he dressed slowly, deliberately. He rose and walked to the foot of the bed, stooping to the floor to pick up his weapon.

"Are you leaving?" Corin asked, still half asleep.

"Yeah," was the only reply.

She drowsily looked at the man silhouetted by the bathroom light; then saw the barrel of the gun. Terrified, she whispered, "But I thought…"

"Couldn't let you go out horny," he condescended. "Nothing personal Doctor… orders."

Twenty-five inches of flame seared through the darkness as the muffled blast resounded, the magnum slug slamming through the woman's sternum, shattering her heart and exploding her chest. Blood and meat splattered the ceiling and walls, her body heaving forward violently as the mattress leapt from the impact of the slug passing through it. Her head hit her knees solidly then bounded back striking the headboard with a, *thud*. Staring eyes —wide with disbelief— glassed over, she lay dead.

Thorne stood silently for a moment then shook his head. "Best fuck I've had in a long time too," he muttered. Breaking the breach, he removed the spend casing and inserted another shell as smoke wafted from both ends of the barrel. He turned and walked into the living room where the cat sat curled patiently awaiting dinner on the easy chair. "Can't have you starving to death, can we, Samantha?" he said whimsically —*whoomph*. Flames and powder burned into the fabric of the chair at point blank range. The deer slug decapitated the tabby cat vaulting its body onto the floor where blood trickled from the animal's neck forming a small crimson pool that soaked into the carpet.

"Helluva' fucked up decadent world we live in, isn't it kitty?" Thorne observed cynically. "Worthless cat. Stupid bitch shoulda' had a watchdog." Then, with a self-satisfied grin he left the apartment.

CHAPTER SIXTEEN

The odor of decay, a dismal place...

...It was like an endless corridor of giant aquariums placed on a dingy gray floor that hadn't been cleaned for an eternity. The cells were constructed of two-inch-thick plastic polycarbonate set in a steel framework that was rusted and pitted from neglect. Black mold thrived in the dark, humid tomb of a prison incarcerating those designated by the Federation as unacceptable. Each cell was a cubicle, ten feet by ten, separated by polycarbonate dividers with a door set into the wall facing the corridor, and the rear walls were concrete supporting the ceiling of the subterranean structure. Each cell had a floor drain for liquid and solid wastes, but no sink or stool, and widely spaced fluorescents in the corridor provided only minimal lighting. There were six inmates per cell in the co-ed facility and all slept on the floor. The plastic walls were scratched and marred from years of use, garnished with dried vomit-crust caked an inch thick in places and congealed puddles of blood-smear elsewhere.

Ames crawled numbly from the floor, and sitting up, braced himself against the rear corner of the cell. He slouched in silence and observed while the corridor guards mouthed words that he couldn't hear through the plastic barrier. One of them took a last puff of the cigarette he held, dropped it onto the floor and crushed it with his boot-heel; then both quit talking and walked down the corridor.

A wiry little man with scraggly gray hair and a bristling beard scurried across the cell and sat by Ames looking at him as though he were something unusual, investigating. Within the ragged old shirt and worn-out jeans the man's frame was emaciated and weathered as old shoe leather, but the green eyes beneath his bushy eyebrows almost twinkled in the darkness. The eyes seemed familiar.

"Good morning," the old man finally said after studying Ames for a considerable length of time.

"Where am I?" Ames asked.

"Right here with me," the old man responded cordially, not sure why the other would ask such a question.

Shaking his head, "That's not what I meant. Where are we?"

"—Oh, Level Five, the Federation Complex, Mister. This is the detention level." He dug in his pants, squinted and sniffled.

"Obviously," Ames granted, then asked, "how long have I been here?"

The little old man fidgeted, picking his nose, then responded, "About a month."

"A month?" Ames was surprised. "Why don't I remember?"

"Drugs, Mister. You been out mostly; 'cept when they came and took you away for a while." He poked a crooked finger into his ear. "But they always brought you back." The old man quit digging in his ear, inspecting his finger; then stuck it in his nose, retrieved a booger, looked it over, and popped it into his mouth. Munching, he awaited Ames' next question.

"Is it morning?"

"Really can't say for sure, Mister. It was only meant to be a prefatory greeting," the old man explained. "Been here for a while."

"Prefatory greeting," Ames reiterated, "where did you learn a word like that?"

But the little man ignored him and said, "Been quite awhile since I was outside." The old man scratched his beard thoughtfully, never removing his gaze from Ames. "Yes indeed, quite a while since I been outside."

"How long?" Ames asked.

"What year is this, Mister?" Then, not waiting for a reply he continued, "—Well, no matter anyhow; not going anywhere soon." The little man puzzled for a minute or more as he counted audibly on his fingers, then his toes. Finally, "Don't know for certain," he stated intently, "but fifteen at least."

Ames looked the little man squarely in the eye. "Fifteen what?"

"Well, years of course," impetuously.

"You've been here for fifteen years?"

"Near as I can figure, 'bout that much, perhaps longer."

"How old are you?" Ames asked slowly, curious.

"Eighty something, but I ain't too sure anymore," the little man answered. "You kind of lose track of time in here, you know." Crouched on his haunches the old man imitated rodent behavior, constantly twitching, jerking, and scratching.

What's your name?"

"You can call me Old Sam; they all do." With that the little man crooked his thumb pointing to the others on the opposite side of the cell. "What do they want from you, Mister?"

"Who?" Ames queried, his eyes focused on the other four figures across the room.

"The Federation."

Ames darted a glance at Old Sam, then across the cell again as he answered. "Information... that I won't give them." Then, indicating the others: "Who are they?"

Old Sam twitched, pointing out each in turn. "That's Donovan in the far corner, Sally's on the floor, Josh leaning on the wall there, and Bernadette on the john."

"What's Bernadette doing?" Ames inquired apprehensively, almost dreading the answer. Squatting over the floor drain she moaned painfully.

"Aborting," Old Sam answered tersely.

"Aborting?"

"Yes, Mister; like when you have a baby you don't want," the little man elaborated.

Disgust was apparent in Ames' expression. "I'm aware of what it means."

"Well, Mister," Old Sam continued, not taking offense, "in here there isn't much to do except..." He paused and squirmed a little.

"Go ahead. I know what you're talking about," Ames encouraged, assisting the little man with an explanation that obviously taunted his morals.

"Well, when the women get pregnant the guards give them a piece of wire so they can abort. Wouldn't make much sense having children in here, would it?"

Ames, having a difficult time believing what he was hearing, spoke again, "Isn't it dangerous?"

"'Spose so," Old Sam answered.

"What about doctors, Sam?"

"Old Sam, please," the little man corrected with a smile that revealed decayed, crooked green teeth. He explained further: "We don't have doctors, just wire. That's how it's been —ever since I've been here anyway."

Ames sat quietly and watched appalled, as Bernadette used the wire to pull the placenta from her uterus. It slid down the drain and clotted blood discharged soiling her legs and dripping onto the floor. Ames felt nauseated.

"What's your name, Mister?" Old Sam asked, shifting his attention back and forth between Ames and Bernadette. No response. "What's your name, Mister?" Old Sam persisted, this time reaching out and gently shaking his wrist.

"Ames," he answered blankly, "Doctor Ames."

"Ames," Old Sam repeated. "Pleasure to meet you, sure enough." Abruptly the little man turned to the others, and succinctly, "This is Doctor Ames," proudly introducing his new friend.

"What if she bleeds to death?" Ames asked, unaware that Old Sam had just made the introduction.

Old Sam turned with a jerk. "Who?"

"Her," motioning, indicating Bernadette.

Old Sam looked at Bernadette, then back at Ames. "Oh... then the guards will take her away and we'll get somebody else." Ames was numbed by Old Sam's cavalier attitude, not realizing the prisoners accepted that matters such as those were beyond their control. He began to say something but Old Sam cut him short. "No more questions for right now. Gotta be quiet; almost time to eat." Without further conversation Old Sam scurried to the front wall, faced the corridor and peered out waiting for the guards to bring the daily meal.

Ames shifted from one buttock to the other trying to make himself more comfortable on the hard, damp floor. Old Sam remained crouched by the front wall, not moving, but unconsciously fidgeting and twitching his fragile frame: nervous habit.

Almost compelled Ames' eyes slowly returned to Bernadette who had crawled to the opposite wall and was now sitting quietly. Her clothes consisted of a tattered blouse that had been white polyester a long time ago, and a green and red plaid skirt ripped up the front. There was an elastic band with fragments of torn cloth around her hips. Her panties had rotted away. With her feet snugged to her buttocks and knees spread apart, he could see blood matted in her pubic hair and dripping mucus forming a gelatinous puddle on the floor beneath her.

Next, he looked at Donovan, huddled in his corner, moaning softly. In the dim light Ames could see the swollen joints of his elbows, hands and ankles, and it was clearly apparent arthritis would soon finish the job the government had begun. Involuntarily trembling his bare torso writhed with each painful breath, his skin sucking through prominent, 'starving dog' ribs.

Sally still lay where she had been when Ames first noticed her. He didn't know it, but cancer was about to carve another footnote in the medical journals. Her hair was white and thin, her body emaciated beyond repair; but to her appearances no longer mattered, she had quit worrying about that years ago.

Josh shuffled slowly across the floor, his bald head momentarily reflecting the dim light as he passed Ames. Josh wore only a gray tee shirt and half-rotted shorts, and when he smiled, seldom as that was, his solitary tooth glimmered lending him the appearance of a cartoon character.

Pushing a large cart with buckets in its lower tray, the guards reappeared in the corridor. "Lunch wagon," Old Sam whispered excitedly. He fidgeted and smacked his lips watching while the guards left buckets in the cells across the corridor.

Through the dirty, scratched, plastic walls Ames could barely make out figures moving about in the other cells and it made him cringe to think the entire prison, however large it might be, was occupied by inmates like his cell mates. He considered the likelihood that the entire fifth sub-level was used for incarceration: that would mean there were thousands of them.

A guard approached their cell and motioning to someone down the corridor —*click*— the electronic locking mechanism retracted, and the heavy Lexan door opened slowly. He placed two buckets inside the cell then removed six tin cups from the top of the cart and threw them onto the floor. They scattered with an offensive metallic clatter when they struck the concrete.

Nimble and compulsive Old Sam gathered up the cups, and with the agility of a youngster aligned them neatly in a row beside the buckets. He dipped each into the closest bucket that contained a thick pudding-slop resembling corn mash. Being careful to fill each cup to the same level, Old Sam measured the portions of food as closely as he could and scraped the bottom of the bucket with his finger so none would be wasted. Despite their dismal circumstances the old man firmly believed in honesty, integrity, and equality.

After a minute of undaunted concentration Old Sam was satisfied the food was fairly divided, and scurrying, delivered a cup to Bernadette who waited patiently from years of familiarity with the old man's custom. Next was Sally, still lying quietly on the floor. Out of old traditions and beliefs, the women were always served first.

"Here, Sally. Got to eat so you can get better," Old Sam whispered leaning close and touching the exposed skin of her shoulders. She felt cold and clammy with the essence of death lingering over her, waiting just a little longer before claiming her. A familiar haunting, Old Sam ignored the feeling he had come to know so well with others he had befriended in the government's hellhole.

Donovan was served next as Old Sam patiently manipulated his arthritic fingers around the tin cup and nodded with satisfaction when Donovan was finally able to grasp it without further assistance. Donovan's painful grimace slowly faded, his discomfort diminishing as his fingers adapted to the shape of the cup. A feeble smile conveyed his gratitude and appreciation of the old man.

Josh ambled toward Old Sam, who had just returned to the food bucket; and as he gave Josh his cup the bald man put forward no recognition, seemed almost mechanical, his vacant stare penetrating Old Sam and going beyond him. Without the insulation of his catatonic state Josh would have succumbed to the Federation's psychological torture years ago.

Old Sam picked up the two remaining cups and started toward Ames, then halted abruptly beside Sally. For a long moment he looked at her, until at length a tear trickled down his cheek. Quietly, respectfully, he placed the cups on the floor and clasped his hands mumbling something, then gently leaned over and kissed her forehead. He knew she would not have to suffer their intolerable conditions any longer. Cancer and the Federation had taken another prisoner.

Ames observed reticently, realizing there was more character in Old Sam than appearances indicated, sensing the compassion, frustration, love, courage, and an obstinate lingering ember of undying hope. The wrinkled old man emanated all the qualities that had made America great, made the people great, a country's ideals that were lost, stolen by a corrupt government. Despite all the system had done to Old Sam, it hadn't defeated him. Within that withered frame was the complex creature of a human being: a man.

Old Sam handed his new friend a cup of mash. "Eat," he said authoritatively.

Ames hesitated, scrutinizing the slop in the tin cup. In spite of all he had been through, he'd never had to tolerate conditions so deplorable as they were here. *So this is what the Federation is all about,* he thought. The resolve was welling up within: *there has to be a way to escape... this hell.* His brain already preoccupied with other considerations, he scooped the mash with his fingers then put them in his mouth. It tasted terrible but he was hungry, and his stomach ached with emptiness; so he ate, slowly. "Why are you in here, Old Sam?" he asked conversationally.

Old Sam peered over his cup, replied flatly, "They called it social nonconformity."

"What?" Ames was surprised. "Diversity is what made America great. Conformity is a concept of Fascism and communism."

Blinking rapidly, "This isn't America anymore," Old Sam told him. "Conformity is a concept of the Federation."

More curious now: "What crime did you commit, Sam?"

"Old Sam, please." He picked chunks of mash from his bristled whiskers, popped them into his mouth savoring them, and began to explain. "Let's just say the government, my ex-wife, and I, had a difference of opinion."

"You were married?" Ames asked.

"For six years or so, I was. I wasn't always cratchety," the old man remarked.

"Don't you mean crotchety?" Ames half-joked.

"I say it like I see it," Old Sam told him. Then he became quiet.

Sequestered memories were creeping back to haunt him: out from woebegone closet, somewhere in the back of his mind. His eyes shifted from Ames to the floor, perhaps watching dark shadows slither from beneath a padlocked door. "But that was a long, long time ago," he continued in a whisper.

Ames asked, more softly, "What happened?"

Old Sam remained silent for a time, then finally began his story. "I had three children, two boys and a girl. They're grown now, but back then they were very young. I returned early with my oldest son from a weekend camping trip one time and my ex-wife was entertaining her boyfriend when we got home. I think my boy was about five then." A sigh, then continuing, "The boyfriend was in government, had connections, that sort of thing."

"What did you do?"

"Oh, I left the house and cried for awhile," the hushed reply. "Then, finally went back to the house. She was sitting there at the kitchen table just like nothing had happened." He looked at Ames with sorrow in his expression. "You know what the first thing she said was?" There was a pause, but no reply. "She said, 'don't expect me to say I'm sorry'." Old Sam shifted, looking back at the floor. "Don't expect me to say I'm sorry," he repeated.

After a pause of silence Ames prodded, "What happened?"

A deep, audible breath of recollection, telling pervasive melancholy, Old Sam went on, "I tried to stay, but things just kept getting worse. She would be out all night with him, then come home like the perfect little wife. Finally, I couldn't take it anymore so I told her to get out —and she did. She never once regretted what she did, destroying the work, the trust, the marriage," shaking his head sadly. "Two weeks after she got an apartment her boyfriend moved in with her; but that was fine, he could have her. I knew from the beginning that I would lose my kids though. That's the part that hurt." Another long pause before he said, "They were my kids."

"Did you get to see them?" Ames asked gently.

"For a while I did," Old Sam answered, tears filling the age lines in his cheeks as remorse for all those precious lost years and memories came back to him. "But she was so full of hate, she couldn't love, couldn't understand love; she was just so angry and hateful. She took my kids too. Wouldn't let me see them, kept raising the child support, that sort of thing."

"What about the courts?"

Disheartened, Old Sam looked at Ames. "We're both here... aren't we?"

"Yes, but..."

Disgusted: "The courts didn't know about justice back then either," the old man scoffed. He thought a moment, then continued. "I tried going to court, but the boyfriend had connections. All the judges cared about was what looked good on paper, and eventually I ran out of money for crooked lawyers to fight a corrupt system. When that happened the new Federation court decided I was guilty of social nonconformity because the books didn't balance anymore." Disquieting, sour words, he almost choked. "They're grown by now. They were just little then."

"When was the last time you saw your kids, Old Sam?"

"Forever ago... when they were still little; a long time before they ever put me in here."

"Do you ever hear from them?" Attempting to encourage him: "Do they write to you?"

"No. They probably don't even know who I am; but somehow, someday they will," he said with conviction. "That's the only reason I'm still kicking, Mr. Ames." He looked at his friend, and with a very peculiar, almost ethereal twinkle in his eyes said, "I'm gonna beat this system. And I *will* see my kids once more before I die."

"But if they're grown now, how will you ever find them?"

"I will." Old Sam blinked confidently. "This time... I will."

Ames, not really understanding what that meant, smiled and wondered, *how can so much courage fit into such a small, old man?* There was something very admirable about that old man... and something very familiar.

He sniffed a runny nose. "Better see to the others now."

For a bit, Old Sam scurried about tending to the others, making sure they were all right, inquiring if they wanted water and filling their cups for them when each, in turn, asked. The ritual took a few minutes less time today than yesterday. Sally didn't need any water.

After that, Old Sam returned and squatted next to Ames again. "How 'bout you, Mr. Ames?" he resumed their conversation. "What information does the Federation want from you?"

"It's a long story," Ames replied, attempting to politely avoid answering Old Sam.

Sagely, Old Sam grinned. "Well, I do have some time to spare."

"I know, but perhaps you're better off not knowing. They would very likely kill you to get the information."

Displaying a pretense of serious consternation Old Sam nodded gravely, twitched and scratched his nose. "That would certainly be terrible, Mr. Ames. They would take me away from *all* this luxury." He swept the cell with a round look and a hand gesture —then he laughed, a high-pitched little cackle. Old Sam was a likable character, and Ames had to laugh too, just a little.

"The Federation wants something that I and another man designed," Ames confided.

"Really? When did you do that?"

Ames considered, then answered, "A while back."

"Don't give 'em anything, Mr. Ames," the little man cautioned sternly. "Don't *ever* give them anything." Picking his nose, then inspecting his finger... "They'll find a way to use it for corrupt purposes." ...and flicking a booger. "The Federation is evil."

"I won't," Ames assured him.

* * *

For the next three weeks...

...Ames and Old Sam discussed many things, each learning more about the other, beginning to understand one another, respect one another; and each grew to trust the other. Sometimes... being imprisoned together can do that.

* * *

The lock mechanism of the cumbersome, filthy Lexan door...
...*Click.*

"Ames, get on your feet," came the demanding voice of the guard silhouetted by corridor lights. The voice startled him from a drifting half-sleep, and in his lethargic stupor he reacted slowly, still not completely aware of what was going on. The guard, irritated that he should have to wait on an inmate, entered the cell, towered over him. "I said get on your feet."

Ames, waking, began to stand. When he got to his knees the guard kicked him, full force in the groin, the steel-toed boot stinging with shock and excruciating pain. He reflexively exhaled a moan with black stomach-sick swirls and sagged to the floor prompting the guard to seize him by an arm and the neck dragging him up onto his feet. Ames wavered flimsily as he was shaken and banged against the wall. "I said get up you worthless bastard," the guard grumbled, still shaking him. "You pass out on me and I'll split your nuts open."

Another guard entered the cell and assisted with the prisoner. They hoisted and dragged him into the corridor, then pulled the heavy door closed behind them.

"Shit, he's heavy," groused the second guard.

"He'll get lighter the longer he's here," the monotone response from the first. "Captain Thorne wants him in, five-five-nine. Can you give me a hand?"

"No problem." The men started down the dingy corridor with Ames draped limply between them.

* * *

Still gaunt from shock when the guards dropped him into the chair...

...Handcuffed and restrained with nylon straps, he sat slumped forward chin against his chest, having difficulty catching his breath. The corridor door opened and Captain Thorne entered without acknowledging Ames' presence. Crossing the room Thorne indicated with a thumb the guards should leave, and without question they returned to the corridor closing the door behind them. With the exception of a small table stacked with bricks, a counter and cabinets running the length of the rear wall, and the chair to which Ames was tied, the room was unfurnished.

Arrogantly Thorne drew a puff rolling the cigarette between his lips with his teeth, and with both hands leaned onto the chair, facing Ames —blew smoke in his face. "Congratulations," he finally said with sarcastic bluntness.

"For what?"

"You and Reed called them frequency pulse lasers."

Ames was surprised. His apprehension showed and he spoke cautiously. "I don't know what you're talking about."

Thorne gloated. "Sure you know what I'm talking about." Ames remained silent. "Are you going to play dumb?" the captain goaded. Then changing the subject: "Where's Reed?"

"He's dead."

"Did you kill him?" Bumping his eyebrows, almost grinning, a display of delight, "huh... did you kill him?"

Ames glared with despise. "No, I didn't kill Reed, but some day..." cutting his words short.

"—Someday what?" Thorne sneered, their faces only inches apart. He paused, then continued, "You gutless motherfuckers make my skin crawl. All talk and bullshit, but that's about it. Not one iota of nerve."

Silence.

The captain's lips parted in a broad smile —then he laughed, confident he'd cowered his adversary. He pushed himself away from the chair and walked toward the counter and cabinets, speaking as he walked. "Whatever happened to Reed doesn't matter a rat's-ass to me; we've got you —and you aren't ever getting out of here." Captain Thorne unlocked one of the cabinets beneath the countertop, opened it, reached inside and withdrew an object, then turned to face the other man.

Ames' face paled with realization. Sickened, his stomach twisted as a canyon whirlwind of near panic swept over him and his mind flashed to the display case of the museum in the year twenty million. Captain Thorne held a replica of the frequency pulse laser. Now he understood how it was possible the weapon was in that museum. He himself, had unwittingly given the world the weapon that could possibly destroy all humanity. Neither he nor Reed ever wanted the weapon in the hands of an unscrupulous military, both aware its simplicity and devastating potential could make nuclear armaments obsolete.

Captain Thorne beamed, a child with a new toy. "One of us will die in this prison, Doctor." And sarcastically, "Can you guess who that will be?"

"How?" Ames muttered, ignoring Thorne's remarks.

"How what?"

"How did you duplicate it?"

"Well shit—you recognize it," facetiously; then he chuckled arrogantly. "You told us how to make it. One might even say, you gave it to us."

"How?" Ames repeated.

"Mind probe, Doctor; surely you've heard of the mind probe."

Ames' stare moved from the weapon to the captain's face. "But that's only speculative research."

"Correction— twenty-five years ago, when you disappeared, the mind probe was only developmental theory. Today it's a reality, perhaps not a well-known reality, but nevertheless..." he smiled, then continued. "The signature encoding was a unique touch, but not very useful for military applications; so we took the liberty of omitting that feature." He held the weapon, admiring it. "Hell Doctor, you should be proud. Twenty-five years ago no one had ever dreamed of laser-focused, amplified sonic pulse, except perhaps yourself and Reed." He grinned, a victory grin. "You should be goddamned proud."

Captain Thorne reexamined the laser continuing his narration, his way of convincing Ames how thoroughly the Federation had beaten him and attempting to psychologically defeat him at the same time. "Strike a tuning fork, assemble thousands of vibrations into one big punch, then push them with a laser beam —all perfectly aligned and all striking the target at the speed of light. Ingenious."

"With a few years of development we'll enhance this weapon to equal the energy released in a nuclear blast, and transmit that power on a beam of light capable of traveling millions of miles without dissipating to—perhaps Pluto—and, minus one Pluto." He paused again allowing his prisoner a moment to think; then he went on, "But the real beauty is that the weapon never has to be loaded, can't jam, and is almost indestructible. The only servicing it requires is to wipe any dirt accumulation from the ruby rods at the muzzle to prevent blockage of the laser beam and periodically change the fuel cell in the gun butt..."

"—I'm aware of its capabilities," Ames finally interrupted.

Ignoring him, "Let me demonstrate," Thorne relished maliciously.

"I'm well aware..." Ames began to repeat, but the captain spun around and fired at the stack of bricks on the table. As he squeezed the trigger there was a whine and blast of light that disintegrated the bricks with the explosion, hurtling fragments of stone that glanced off walls and pinged from the ceiling then showered to the floor before the cloud of dust at the table filtered down.

Ames looked up after the fragments stopped ricocheting. "Smith will destroy the world with that weapon."

Thorne smiled cynically. "Perhaps," he mused, then replied, "but what's left will belong to whomever controls the pulse laser."

"General Smith... and you?" His eyes were as cold as the reality of his predicament.

"Exactly Doctor. I'm going to be on the winning side."

"Jesus!" Ames exclaimed, "you can't be serious. If you go through with this you'll kill us all; is that what you intend to do?"

"Not all of us," Thorne reassured, "only most of us. If all of us were to die, there wouldn't be any point in winning, would there?" For a moment he admired the pulse laser, pondering future possibilities.

"You're insane," Ames stated flatly.

Captain Thorne smiled as he told him, "No Doctor, I just like war."

* * *

Footsteps in the corridor...

...One officer opened the heavy plastic door, the other shoved Ames inside and onto the floor, then stepped back as the cell door closed. Both turned and went down the corridor without speaking. It still smelled the same, and for a minute it was difficult to see in the depressing obscurity of the cell. He lay motionless where he had fallen, thinking and watching for activity in the corridor, his eyes becoming accustomed to the gloomy semidarkness again. Ames detected movement within the cell, a nondescript form scurrying toward him from the opposite wall.

"What happened?" Old Sam whispered laying an emaciated hand on his friend's shoulder. Ames could finally make out the wizen old man's bristly face, but did not respond. Old Sam leaned closer detecting worry in Ames' visage. It concerned him. "What happened this time?" he persisted. "What's wrong that bothers you so much?"

"That obvious, huh?"

"Yes," Old Sam replied shifting and fidgeting nervously. "Tell me what it is, that is, if you want to tell me. If not, I'll understand."

"It's bad this time... real bad."

The little man scampered to the front wall, peeked into the corridor, then returned to Ames; and lowering his voice, finally said, "They're gone. We're in this together, aren't we?"

Ames looked directly at Old Sam fixing his attention on his eyes as they darted back and forth and up and down, constantly in motion, a bristly mouse with green eyes. "I gave them the weapon to destroy the world."

Confounded: "Why did you do that?"

"When I left, mind probes were still decades away," Ames inadvertently admitted, "I wasn't aware they'd been developed to the point they have."

"When you left?" Old Sam repeated, now thoroughly perplexed. "You haven't been gone that long, only an hour or so."

Ames shook his head. "No, you don't understand."

"No matter," the old man replied. "If you were subjected to mind probes they know everything." Then attempting to placate, "But you didn't give them anything —they took it."

"What difference does that make?" Ames asked. "It doesn't matter how they got it; that's academic." His sigh, symptomatic of culpability: "What matters is, they *have* the weapon, and it's my fault."

Old Sam thought a minute, constantly shifting, bouncing from side to side, rocking on the balls of his feet with the agility of a child. It was perplexing, and peculiar, how a man of his years could crouch so effortlessly for such lengths of time without the slightest evidence of arthritic stiffness. At length he asked, "What shall we do?"

"We've got to get out of here." The gravity in Ames' voice was equaled by his resolve.

Old Sam's eyes twinkled at the prospect of freedom, but realizing the probability of that likelihood caused him to shake his head disparagingly. "No one has ever escaped, at least not as far as anyone knows. I don't believe it can be done." Then blinking quickly, his eyebrows raised, "Do you?" he asked gamely.

"I'm not sure," Ames replied, "but I've got to try."

"We—" the old man corrected. He picked his nose.

Ames smiled. "We," he confirmed to his friend.

Old Sam, pleased with the alliance, began by explaining, "In that case, this is a matter to which I've given a great deal of thought, Mr. Ames. There have been hundreds of attempts and none have been successful, but in every case the central elevators were used. By the time the escapees got to the ground-level control hall the guards had already sealed the main hall, elevators and perimeter."

As Old Sam spoke, he indicated the layout of the prison with hand gestures. Ames listened, letting the little man continue. "Think of this whole place as a giant wheel buried underground with the control hall as the hub. Six corridors radiate from the auditorium like the spokes of a wheel," he explained carefully spreading his fingers representing corridors. Noticing a booger stuck on his fingertip, he flicked it away without fanfare, then continued. "The only elevators to the surface are in the control hall, but in the ceiling at the far end of each corridor is a ventilation shaft about three feet in diameter that runs vertically to the surface." He beamed with the excitement of the challenge as his eyes focused on his fingertips imagining one ventilation shaft at each.

"The ventilation shafts don't go all the way to the surface," Ames finally told him.

Sam blinked. "What— how do you know that?"

Grinning, "I helped design this Complex," Ames confessed.

Dubious, studying him, Old Sam thought a moment. "How could you have done that, and if that's so, why did you let me go on like a fool then?" a bit offended.

"The 'how' isn't important, what is important, is you've figured out the way to escape, Sam. The ventilation shafts are the only way," Ames commended him.

Proudly: "And I knew that."

"Yes, you did," Ames agreed, "but we wouldn't need to climb all the way to the surface, only two hundred-forty feet, to sub-level four. Another obstacle is the barrier grate, the reinforcement bars blocking the shafts; but I've figured that out." Determined: "We can do it."

Old Sam voiced concern. "But wouldn't they hear us."

"We would need a diversion so no one would know we were in the ventilation shaft, a helluva' diversion; and I think I know what that could be." Old Sam's excitement grew as he considered the possibility of escape. His first inclination was disbelief, but the more they planned the more confident he became as the prospect of freedom overwhelmed him, until finally Ames said, "We still have one more problem to solve."

"What?" Old Sam asked, settling down.

"To get this cell door open," indicating with a tip of the head; then adding, "if only we had a piece of wire."

Enthusiastic, Old Sam asked, "Will a coat hanger work?" offering the piece of crooked wire.

"Where did you get that?"

"It was Bernadette's, remember?" He wrinkled his nose and crooked his head. "But she's done using it. Doesn't need it anymore."

"That'll work," Ames concluded. "When the guards fall asleep tonight we'll…" He stopped mid-sentence, just realizing there were only five of them in the cell instead of six. "Where's Sally?"

The old man hesitated before he replied. "They came and took her while you were gone."

"I'm sorry, Sam. I know she was a friend of yours."

"Don't be sorry. She's better off now. Her pain is over." Forlorned, Old Sam looked across the cell at Bernadette, Josh and Donovan. "Their pain will continue, maybe a month, maybe for years, or forever. They're too sick to make it to the surface anymore." With an empathetic heart he turned back to Ames. "Do you have any idea what it's like to know you'll never see the sun again, to feel its soothing warmth on your face; or to take a breath and taste that refreshing clean in the air after a spring rain. Can you imagine knowing you'll never again be able to wake before dawn... and hear a robin warble its early morning song?"

CHAPTER SEVENTEEN

The corridor was empty...

...Old Sam peered anxiously through the grimy plastic wall in the direction of the control center. He couldn't see them, but sensed the security guards were dozing at the console. Although day and night within the prison complex merged into an endless continuum of hours the guards on the night shift were more lethargic than the others, and as a result the inmates were able to keep track of time. With less supervision the corridor guards were also more lax than those they relieved, generally not making cell inspections with any regularity. The 'quiet' was also an aspect of the nocturnal atmosphere. Daytime shuffling and noise of the inmates had hushed except for an occasional mournful groan from someone in a dingy cell somewhere.

The time seemed right.

Old Sam turned nervously and nodded. He watched Josh, Donovan and Bernadette where they lay sleeping as Ames moved silently to the cell door and worked the coat hanger into the track of the lock mechanism. Tense moments of anticipation, Old Sam waited while his friend worked the wire deeper into the circuit of the door lock. Then it happened —*ssst, click*—when the wire short-circuited the electronic relay and the bolt withdrew from the strike plate. Old Sam's eyes twinkled in near disbelief as he watched Ames slowly push the door ajar.

"Time to go," Ames whispered easing his way through the door and silently starting down the corridor.

Old Sam looked at the three poor souls sleeping huddled together on the musty concrete floor. Then repeating Ames' words to himself, "Time to go," and following, he stepped into the corridor having made up his mind, succeed or fail, he wouldn't come back.

They sneaked noiselessly along a seemingly endless expanse of hall, the perpetual damp and cold of the concrete floor seeping into the soles of their bare feet; but neither complained. By now, both were accustomed to that incessant chill. Tensely they approached the corridor mid-way security station, anticipation making it difficult to breathe; should the guards be awake, see them, there would be no escape. Now or never, ever so quietly, until they peeked and relief eased through them when they found both guards sleeping: chance or providence, the fugitives would never know.

One man sat slouched in his chair, head back and mouth open, snoring, while the other lay sprawled along the length of a steel, battleship gray bench. The sprawled man snorted and smacked his lips occasionally, but otherwise didn't move.

Crawling silently Ames and Old Sam carefully stole past the sleeping guards, their huddled, creeping forms gradually blending into the gray background of floor and walls. The farther from the guard station they went the quicker their pace until the plastic cell walls ended abruptly being replaced by dingy concrete with evenly spaced steel doors.

In the poor light it was difficult to read the faded paint markings, but Ames managed to finally find door, five-five-nine. It was locked so he bent the coat hanger and began working both ends into the keyway. Waiting impatiently, and nervous, Old Sam twitched and fidgeted then picked his nose, constantly checking behind them, expecting at any moment their presence would be discovered by some evil, omnipotent force. The click of the latch sent an overpowering shudder of relief through him and he pushed Ames through the doorway and into the room where they would be out of sight. With a finger, the ceiling lights came on.

"You've picked locks before," Old Sam commented with a sigh of relief.

Over a shoulder Ames whispered, "No. Saw it on TV"

"What—" Sam exclaimed in a hushed voice, "for pity's sake, TV isn't real, it's make-believe."

Raising an eyebrow Ames grinned, then winked. "I know. Go figure." Without further conversation he crossed the room to the counter and cabinets disregarding entirely the chair and table, as they had been earlier, still covered with debris. He immediately began working the cabinet lock, shimming the coat hanger between the door and jamb. It took three tries and over a minute until the latch lifted, the door opened... the pulse laser lying on the shelf.

"*Yes,*" triumphant whisper, and smiling, he admired the coat hanger wire. "Thank you," addressing the wire rhetorically; then he kissed it.

"—Oh, don't do that," Old Sam insisted squinting distastefully, "remember where that's been," referring to Bernadette.

Ames thought about it agreeing, "You're right." But he really didn't care. Now they had a chance. And carefully, he reached in the cabinet and picked up the weapon.

"What's that?" Old Sam queried.

Beaming, Ames looked at him. "Our ticket out'a here. Let's go." He left the room.

Following, Sam walked to the door; then stopping, looked back and surveyed the room. Scratching his scraggly beard, eyes twinkling with enthusiasm and the excitement of their adventure, "Wonder what he's got in mind," he pondered grinning and licking his lips. "This young fella's a caution," he told himself. "Sure 'nuf, he's a caution." With that, the lights went out and the old man scurried to catch up with Ames.

In the corridor Ames waited quietly. "Sam, the air vent is near the end of the corridor, another thirty yards or so. You wait here, and with luck I'll be back in a little while."

"It's Old Sam," he whispered, then insisted, "and we're in this together. We'll do it all together."

Ames studied Old Sam. "Have you got a death wish?"

"No more than you, but we're in this together." All things considered, Ames could only smile with admiration. "What's so funny?" Old Sam groused in a hushed voice.

Shaking his head and the smile away as he lay a hand on the old man's shoulder, "Nothing's funny. We're in this together."

"You bet— so let's get going."

Wary, they made their way noiselessly toward the control center, each man mentally noting that nothing had really changed in the past several minutes. The corridor was just as dingy as before. The concrete was still chilling and reeked of musty dampness. Both guards at the mid-way security station still slept, and the one still snored and wheezed occasionally.

Nevertheless, something seemed different. Perhaps it had to do with emotions and expectations churning within them, feelings that could scarcely be expressed. To Old Sam the prospect of escaping after so many years of surviving this dungeon was overwhelming. To finally have even the slightest glimmer of a chance was more than he'd dared hope before. More than the challenge of an adventure never before accomplished, it was the opportunity to right the wrongs of a perfidious world. Ames was uncertain of the reason: he only knew there was a reason, and he must escape. For everything... there is a reason.

Both crouched and observed the control center from their position at the inner end of the corridor. Before them lay a circular room of concrete and steel, two hundred feet in diameter with the control room in the center. Closed-circuit monitors flipped images and lights blinked intermittently along the console where four guards were seated inside the metal and glass structure. Secure within the control room and not really paying attention they dozed complacently; but three of the ten guards in the surrounding auditorium moved about randomly. The others slept, or wavered in that stuporous state next to sleep, in chairs and on benches throughout the large hall.

The corridors leading from the control center were arranged like spokes from the hub of a wheel, numbered one through six with barracks of cells along both sides. A cluster of floodlights above the control center illuminated the auditorium, augmented with auxiliary and battery-powered emergency lighting above the entrance to each corridor.

Still peering into the central hall Ames whispered, "Sam, do you know how to use a military weapon?"

"Absolutely."

"Okay, let's see if we can get one for you."

"What have you got in mind?" picking at his eyebrow, then scratching his head.

Looking at the old man: "I have to get to the control center, so you'll have to cover me as best you can."

"You bet— count on me."

Both fugitives moved a few feet back into the corridor and stood erect flattening themselves against the wall. Ames handed the laser to Old Sam advising, "Be careful with it. They're nasty." The old man blinked an eager nod as Ames pulled the folded coat hanger from his back pocket and began tapping on the corridor wall.

Old Sam's eyes batted wide with surprise and criticism, "What are you doing? Somebody's gonna hear you."

"I certainly hope so," Ames confirmed, again watching in the direction of the control center.

Having heard the noise, a guard stepped into view at the mouth of the corridor and Ames swung away from the wall kicking him squarely in the groin. The guard's eyes bulged with pain and amazement, and he faintly puffed a moan and began to fall as Ames, reaching forward, caught him and his weapon before either could hit the floor.

The commotion woke a prisoner in the plastic cubicle behind Old Sam and the woman scurried to the door to have a look. To avoid her alerting others within the cell, Old Sam quickly put an index finger to his lips indicating she should be quiet. Grinning, he winked. The scraggly little woman mimicked the hand gesture and returned the wink, then from within the cell puckered Old Sam a kiss against the plastic, her lips festering grotesquely with chancrous lesions. Politely declining her offer and unable to help himself, Old Sam turned away, his expression conveying, *whew, icky face.*

After laying the guard on the floor against the corridor wall Ames traded the automatic rifle for the pulse laser, and Old Sam was still marveling at the weapon when a voice from the control center called for the unconscious guard. Subsequently, a second voice ordered that someone check to see what the noise had been.

"Are you ready?" Ames asked in a low voice. With a twinkle in his eye, Old Sam grinned. Ames resolved, "Then, let's do it," and he stepped forward from the corridor, into the open, a guard approaching, not twenty feet between them. The man hesitated with incomprehension, began to raise his weapon —but was too late.

—A shrill whine and bright flash

Laser pulse ripped the guard in half: Federation confetti-ribbon and red-splattering meat. Ames didn't have time to see the anguished expression of the guard as his shocked, lifeless body flew backward onto the floor in two pieces. Another whine, another blast —white-flash of force— clustered lights above the control center exploded into countless pieces. For an instant everything was dark, then *snap,* a relay tripped and blinding auxiliary lights came on triggering sirens that blared throughout the Complex, their hollow-echo signals foreboding impending chaos.

Guards stumbled to their feet with disbelief as Ames ran toward the control center. To the right, along the periphery he could see three of them fumbling, then turning and pointing their weapons at him. He squeezed the trigger and the control center glazing splintered — detonating— shattering safety glass in front of him. Still running, again pulling the trigger —bright-fire explosion— the interior of the control room burst into splashing flame, flashing smoke and shrapnel pieces, the men inside being ripped apart, thrown in different directions and going down.

For an instant he wondered how he could still be alive and why the three guards hadn't fired at him —another glimpse— the three falling amidst a hail of bullets and flying stone. The walls seemed to be bursting apart and erupting around them as lead ricocheted lightning bug-sparks, and within that split second came the realization that the peculiar little man had just saved his life.

As his weapon kicked with each flaming report, Old Sam held steady. Dazzling —flickering— barrel flashes lit up the darkened corridor with the shimmering continuity of nine rounds per-second, his slight, seemingly scrawny frame resisting the recoil of the blazing weapon in his hands. Fifteen years of imprisonment may have emaciated his body, but within Sam was still who he had always been. Nothing could destroy that. Between grinning parted lips his green teeth reflected the brilliance of each muzzle flash. His eyes twinkled; his nostrils flared; savoring the sweetness of his long awaited and well-deserved revenge —for all the wretched souls—*he was alive!*

Pins going down, two more guards fell to Ames' left as bullets spit from his small guardian's weapon punching death through their uniforms into flesh and bone. Ames kept running —sprinting. Hot bullets searing past, miraculously missing him by inches, he could see his assailant across the auditorium and reacted —fired.

A shattering noise, the blast cratered the wall six feet behind the guard, ripping it apart and hurtling concrete fragments within a gray-boil dust. The man, slammed from behind by stone and steel shrapnel, lurched and fell forward. Vomiting blood, the guard rose to his knees still clutching his weapon, and before Ames saw the steel rod protruding from his chest he had already triggered the laser again. Torn with the blast, the man's head launched from his shoulders with the splatter of ripened fruit. Teetering, his torso quivered puking blood from the neck then flopped to the floor.

Reaching the control center Ames kicked the remaining doorframe away and stepped inside, over debris, aware of a loud crack and burning pain in his left side, a bullet tearing through his ragged leather shirt creasing a rib. It caused a spasm of involuntary reflex and as his finger jerked the trigger, he barely had time to realize an injured guard lying on the floor had shot him before the laser blast ripped the man apart. Disintegrating, the guard's head and torso vanished as the arm and automatic rifle twirled away —flung across the room— and now, only legs remained. Blood dripped lethargic blobs from the ceiling and console and hung there dangling like crimson teardrops leaking onto the cratered floor, puddling around remaining shreds of uniform and boots with two twitching feet.

Painfully Ames limped to the control panel, typed keystrokes and began pressing buttons and throwing switches as he recited mechanically, "Elevator lockdown, stairwell blast shields, breach detection, motion sensors, perimeter barriers, audio-video," and finally, "override lockout." He heard Old Sam shouting and running toward him.

"Let's go, we have our diversion!"

"Not yet," he yelled back. And he pressed the corridor cellblocks master control opening every cell door in the prison complex — two thousand, *clicks*, in unison. Stepping back from the console he destroyed it with a laser blast and took a breath, satisfied, "Now... we have our diversion."

All six corridors began filling with prisoners, some staggering around unreasoning zombies, others running wildly, haphazardly. Afflicted moans turned to jubilation and the confusion of the past few minutes was multiplied a thousand times over. Sirens still blared and the lights flickered, while above the din of the thousands of released prisoners could be heard gunshots and the screams of terrified guards as their captives overpowered them.

Old Sam entered the control room jubilantly, "Mr. Ames, let's go."

Motionless, Ames stood for a moment surveying. "What a pitiful waste of life," he finally commented sadly. Then turning to the old man, "Look at them, Sam; look at them. What kind of hell has this world come to?" He blinked, and a tear leaked into his eye.

The old man understood and replied, "Radiation poisoning, mind probe overexposure, genetic experimentation, political persecution, and all the rest, Mr. Ames; we didn't do it, but we do have to live with it." He became visibly nervous. "But now, we *must* go," he persisted. "They'll be sending reinforcements."

"The override lockout will buy us some time, but you're right. It'll take them a while, but we'd better get out while we can." When Ames turned the little man saw the blood on his shirt.

Without a breath of hesitation, "You're hurt, let me help you." The old man extended his left hand, still clutching the rifle in his right.

Ames stumbled.

Old Sam looked at the weapon then threw it to the floor so he could help his friend. The gun barrel was discolored from overheating, smoke drift wafting silently from the muzzle. Fire of life on wisps of angelic wings.

As they began pushing their way back to the corridor they had come from —walking away from the rifle— Old Sam asked, "Where are you hurt?"

"My side."

Ames didn't know what, but he knew something must be wrong. He could feel the tepid trickle of blood seeping from the wound and down his leg. And he wondered was it real or imaginary, just like so many other things that had happened since his return.

An entire world in Tribulation —who had done that, men or governments— and how would one define either under circumstances such as these? Then leaning slightly more on Old Sam for support and knowing the little man had saved his life, limping, Ames looked upon Sam, instilled with gratitude he could never express, born of mystery still unrealized.

A piece of... *The Puzzle.*

As they crossed the auditorium tediously threading their way through the throng Ames recalled a different amphitheater where others were dressed in rags. In this arena an expanded-metal platform was replaced with concrete. And now, as then, the seemingly endless sea of disfigured and abused bodies constantly altered, changing around them, new misery with each new wave of faces.

Crowding them, close enough to make it personal, were faces misshapen with the ugly permanence of radiation, knowing the impending, inevitable death that accompanies that horrible scourge; souls searching with eyes begging for mercy and relief. Perhaps this reprieve from captivity, no matter how brief, would make all the pain and suffering somehow worthwhile. Not even able to blink, the victims of mind probe overexposure were less than breathing zombies, in a vegetative state ambling to nowhere in particular, simply destined to wander forever somewhere in their minds.

Scattered through the crowd were casualties of genetic experimentation who had mutated beyond hope or concern from toxic overdoses of chemical and biological warfare, yet refused to die the way they had been expected and intended to. They had become such an inconvenience, but still were useful for study and dissection when it was opportune; so, they were maintained as organ donors.

And last, the majority, the political prisoners who had been condemned to suffer the worst of persecutions, psychological warfare intended to destroy them by every possible means; not only to suffer physically but to be tortured mentally and be entirely aware, then becoming victims of complete hopelessness and despair.

These, and more, were the legacy of the Federation. A sea of misery.

From somewhere above someone shut down the primary and auxiliary lights, and the emergency lights came on then flickered rendering an eerie strobe light effect; but the two pushed on. All around them, crammed shoulder to shoulder and too many to count was a sinuous drift of transient souls, mindless confusion and psychedelic pandemonium of unworldly design. Darkness loomed closer with each passing moment as smoke fed the auditorium a saturating charcoal-black, fires continuing to burn and new ones springing to life. Confusion and dismay became more intense, fueled with pervasive sorrow and reproach.

Forcing their way down the corridor against the steady flood of flesh was no easy task, but Old Sam wouldn't quit. Although constantly pushed back toward the auditorium by the unrelenting surge of bodies he pried his way forward, and determination and adamant tenacity produced slow but steady headway toward the outer end of the corridor that held hope and the faint possibility of freedom.

Gradually the hall became less crowded allowing Old Sam and Ames better progress. Neither could understand why the inmates went toward the auditorium and control center like so many lemmings migrating to the sea. Perhaps it was because of that indefinable aspect of human nature to seek security in numbers, or perhaps the loss of order triggered some psychological drive mechanism, an unexplainable human phenomenon, nevertheless predictable.

Approaching the corridor mid-way guard station, they observed a gathering of inmates crouching, huddled together; and their suspected fears were realized when Donovan looked up with insanity in his expression and a chunk of raw meat in his mouth. Above the dissonance of smacking lips and teeth ripping flesh the two could hear gurgled sounds of labored, suffocating breathing, then saw the traumatized guard in hemorrhagic shock, nearing death but still alive, watching terrified and helpless as the swarm of mouths tore the flesh from his body.

"Oh, God," Ames muttered, "they've gone mad."

"No," Old Sam responded sadly, "they're just desperate... and hungry." He extended an open hand to Bernadette who squatted against the wall opposite the body, but her response was to secrete her chunk of meat beneath her buttocks and snort menacingly. Sensitive to her plight Old Sam withdrew his hand, nodded compassionately, and saying nothing more he and Ames continued down the corridor.

Finally the confusion lay behind them, only a din in the far end of the long tunnel. Ames eyed the air vent overhead, raised the pulse laser, steadied, and fired. The steel grate shattered and concrete disintegrated, with the clearing dust freedom one step closer. Old Sam smiled broadly as Ames stepped under the airshaft aiming directly into the vent and sent another bolt of explosive power up. There was no mistaking the shredding sound of impact when the reinforcing bar and barrier grate were ripped out, and the successive metallic clinks and rattles as small pieces fell through the vertical tube, the noise growing louder until they clattered onto the corridor floor.

Looking into the shaft, "It's clear," Ames confirmed, securing the laser over his shoulder by the sling.

"Can you climb?" Old Sam asked, worried.

"I could climb over hot coals to get out of here," he assured. "Can you give me a boost?"

Cupped hands, a lurch and a heave, and Ames grabbed a piece of the steel grate still bolted to the vent opening. Despite the pain he pulled himself up and into the vent, determination proffering its reward. Once inside the tube he braced himself against the corrugated vent pipe and lowered a leg for the old man. A running head start and stretching his stunted arms full length Old Sam jumped and seized his partner's ankle —left hand first, then the right— and swinging once, Ames lifted Old Sam into the vent shaft, his mind on escape, not his side or the pain still nagging his leg.

The two hundred-forty vertical feet to the fourth sub-level was a task, the ascent difficult and slow. Down there: rifle-fire and explosions. And as both silently climbed they could hear gunshots and grenades echoing the length of the corridor below. Screams of terror and pain sent shivers of remorse through them, both knowing their diversion would cost many human lives. And no matter how miserable, those lives were not theirs to spend.

"Perhaps it's better for them to die quickly now than to suffer anymore," Old Sam whispered.

Ames didn't respond, and didn't look down as the stagnant stench of death ascended the air vent engulfing them with garish, unseen fingers. For those dying below mercy would end the hardships of their memories consigning Ames and Old Sam memories that would linger to haunt them again.

For half an hour they continued to climb and after reaching the fourth sub-level followed a horizontal vent, taking only a minute to rest, not willing to linger longer than was absolutely necessary. Before long Ames cautiously peered from the rim of the vent shaft into a storage room where barrels and boxes were neatly stockpiled according to size, shape and content, and loomed as sinister columns overhead.

Dark with the exception of a few scattered fixtures placed between ceiling braces and metal girders, the warehouse was expansive with endless miles of pipe lining the walls, some inches in diameter, others several feet across, comprising a thoroughfare transporting unidentified substances to unknown destinations. A number of large pipe-clusters controlled by gate valves rose in stately formations from the concrete floor and disappeared in the obscurity of blackness above. And from unseen places within the storehouse, at irregular intervals —unexpected— an occasional click of a pressure switch or check valve was all that disturbed the eerie sounds of silence.

—Noise

Two solid kicks and the grate fell away. The metallic clangs echoing, and finally fading. Then silence again.

After climbing from the air vent Ames helped Old Sam out, replacing the grate; and for a moment they crouched together looking around. Old Sam, grinning with satisfaction, looked directly at his friend, and the twinkling excitement conveyed in his expression caused Ames to smile too.

"Which way now?" Old Sam asked, his eyes scanning, always in motion. Focusing, darting and refocusing, first overhead, then left, then right, then overhead, then behind; constantly moving and blinking, trying to absorb every sight possible.

Ames pointed without speaking and stealthily they crept into the darkness. Progress for Ames was slow but constant, while hopping and jumping Old Sam darted in and around pipes, ductwork and equipment with rodent agility and silence. Disappearing and reappearing from the semidarkness and obstacles, he maintained a constant vigil for whatever danger might be lurking just beyond the next turn. But he always returned to check on his friend who had lost a lot of blood. It was starting to take its toll now.

Ames' coordination was beginning to falter, perspiration beading on his forehead, trickling down his back, saturating his armpits. The bloodstain circling the hole in the left side of his leather shirt had grown larger, more noticeable, and his right pant leg was saturated, telltale droplets now betraying his path along the gray floor. Once he stumbled into an empty chemical drum and the reverberating clang broke the unearthly silence like the toll of 'Big Ben'. With the sound past but the echoes of the peal still bouncing in his head, Ames stopped and looked around uneasily as Old Sam promptly reappeared carrying a roll of cloth, terrified that the noise might alert someone.

"What was that?" the old man asked anxiously. Startled back to caution, Ames apologized. Wasting no time, "Hold this," Old Sam ordered, handing Ames the end of the towel roll and quickly circling him, making a large bandage of several wraps around his chest — shirt and all.

Weary: "Where did you get that?"

Old Sam bit the roll of cloth and ripped it tucking the loose end into Ames' bandaged chest. "Men's room dispenser." Then he winked. Within a minute Ames' leg was also wrapped in the same manner and Old Sam stashed the remaining towel roll under a shelf.

"Sam, aren't the clothes supposed to be on the outside of the bandage?"

Twitching: "No time now. Let's go."

They continued, precious minutes passing, until Ames at last whispered, "Sam, where are you?"

"Not far away," the immediate response, the little man peeking from behind the large pipe his friend leaned against.

Startled: "*Shit*—don't do that." Then quickly, "Help me open this cleanout valve."

"What's it for?" climbing over the pipe. The valve on the side of the tube looked like an air lock hatch commonly used in submarines.

"It's a waste jettison line."

"Why do we want to open it?"

As they turned the handle, unlocking the small hatch: "The jettison lines all lead to the sewer system below the city. Should come out somewhere down on the flats."

Old Sam's eyes twinkled with understanding. "How do you know that?"

Ames smiled. "I helped design this Complex, remember?"

"Jiminy Crickets!" Old Sam's excited whisper; "we really *are* going to get out of here."

When the hatch opened, both men beamed with triumph. "Been a long time since I've heard that, Sam."

"Heard what?"

"Jiminy Crickets."

Old Sam twitched, and raising an eyebrow replied matter-of-fact, "Been a long time since I was free."

Guardedly, "We aren't out yet." Even still, there was a tone of anticipation in Ames' voice.

Unexpected, from a distance:

"You men look over there. You men search that section." The hollow sound of running footsteps drowned out the rest of the orders that originated somewhere in the dark. Beams of light flickered among the shelves, pipe, machinery and other equipment.

Footfalls were everywhere, getting closer.

Fear swept over the fugitives, a spray of cold-water anxiety. "Get in there, Sam," Ames ordered in a desperate whisper. He waited nervously as the little man nimbly climbed into the drain line, not knowing their discovery was only a few paces away.

The beam of the Maglite followed blood spots on the floor as the security officer got closer with each silent step. Ames climbed into the drainline as quickly as he could, slid part way into the tube. Then, reaching for the hatch…

…Too late.

Light blinded him.

Time stood still.

Confusion captured his mind like the rush of wind from a passing train. Tension seized his chest in bass drum heartbeats with rhythm and pulse. Anxiety of expectation distorted his vision with a sickening nausea and a hot rush that burned to his ears. But the order to, *freeze,* he anticipated, never came.

For what seemed an eternity the person holding the flashlight did not move, until finally, the light shifted to the floor, to the officer's feet. Darkness shrouded the identity of the individual, but as the spots in his vision cleared Ames could see the guard wasn't very tall. *What's going on,*he wondered. He dared not move expecting the sting of a bullet if he did. Perspiration lubricating his palm, his hand began to slide from the hatch. He didn't know what he should do, what the guard intended to do. Was he to live or die? Time and again the question flashing through his mind: the uncertainty, apprehension... and a silhouette in the darkness.

Voices in the distance: "Anything yet?"

"No Sir, must have been a mouse, or bat or something," a second voice answered.

"Not unless it weighed forty pounds."

"Maybe a motion detector malfunctioned, Sir," the second voice suggested.

"Bullshit, keep looking," the first voice ordered.

"Yes Sir." More footfalls.

Clicking and slapping sounds of leather soles on cement could be heard as guards hurried about in their search. Ames could barely discern the outline of the face as the guard standing before him turned and looked in the direction of the voices; then back to him. Another minute —that seemed like it would never pass— until the guard finally spoke in soft whispered words. "Take care, Mr. Ames."

And the individual turned,

And slowly walking away...

Faded into the surrounding abyss.

Ames heard and watched with disbelief. Relief overwhelmed him, involuntarily quivering as every muscle relaxed, causing him to lose hold of the hatch and almost fall. His abdomen and chest heaved like an invisible weight had been withdrawn. And still trembling, he crawled into the waste line and carefully, quietly, closed the hatch behind him.

* * *

Death in the air, a lightless trail...

...The hours seemed endless, all flowing continuously in the pitch-black of the drain line. Twisting, turning, always downward, the men crawled on cut hands and bleeding knees, the dirt clinging to the bottom of the metal tube grinding into their skin with each shuffling movement. How far they had come and how far they must go, neither could be certain; they just kept going. The stagnant air they breathed burned fragile bronchi and alveoli as the poisonous methane crept into the delicate tissue of their lungs.

"Are you all right, Mr. Ames?" Old Sam asked, concerned. Although impossible to see, the old man could tell when his friend lay down to rest; he was coughing, and the shuffling sound stopped.

"I'm okay, Sam. Just need to..." he coughed several times, "catch my breath," coughing again, "and rest a minute."

The old man didn't bother to look back; that was pointless in complete darkness. "How far do you think we've come?"

"I don't know," Ames answered, drawing a breath and deciding, "a million miles or so." From the pitch-black ahead the little man's comical snorts of muted laughter prompted him to ask, "What's so funny, Sam?"

"It shouldn't be too much farther then, should it?"

Ames couldn't help smiling despite the jabbing pain in his left side and throbbing ache in his right leg. "Sometimes I wonder about you old man."

"Don't be disrespectful," Old Sam cautioned sarcastically. "And don't you be calling me old man. You should respect your elders."

Ames didn't have time to respond. From behind them —growling and coming— a rumble began to intensify as reverberations traveling through the pipe wall made their thoroughfare seem to vibrate. The echoing noise growing louder, it became apparent to Ames what was going to happen.

"What's that noise, Mr. Ames?"

"Oh damn, I hope it's not what I think."

"Well, what do you think?" Sam persisted with both irritation and uncertainty in his tone. Getting closer —boiling to thunder— the pipe walls quivered.

Ames scrambled forward groping to find his friend, and grabbing the old man's ankles, yelled, "Arms out in front of you —lay flat!"

"Why?" at the top of his lungs, the clamor sweeping upon them. "Because..."

—*Whoompshh!*

As Ames yelled his words were drowned out by the boiling roar of flushed wastewater-wave that overtook them with tsunami force. The rush snatched them from the bottom of the drain line and torpedoed them through the tube riding its crest like shooting whitewater through a straw. The tube banged and trembled as the surge of fluid and debris jetted onward into the darkness.

Time and again the men were bounced from the sides of the waste jettison line snaking their way through its belly, inseparable fugitive submarines. The noise was deafening and air became more than a precious commodity, available only at turns where the pipe forced the rabid water to change directions with foaming resentment. Intense and cold, it was a boiling-liquid roller coaster ride in complete darkness, the inability to anticipate turns causing psychological abuse bordering on panic and terror. Seconds ticked past with unfaltering regularity, constructing minutes that seemed impossibly long. The frigid temperature crawled through their skin and bones, a breathtaking fire hose spray stinging with pressure and bone-chilling cold.

—Banging, pounding, and rushing onward

They rocketed through the pipeline with the swiftness of a submerged waterslide transporting two pieces of driftwood; but driftwood wouldn't drown. Foam in their faces —and a twisting sensation— feeling themselves being lifted by the water, approaching a turn, each would gulp a breath of air at the boil then be swept down as the rushing flow straightened out again.

—Black and water, and deluge speed

Miles of pipe swooshed past at an unbelievable rate. Distances that would have taken hours to crawl on hands and knees were accomplished in seconds.

—Then suddenly into the open

The jettison line ended in mid-air and they were bulleted forward with the gush of outpouring water. In a twinkling they plummeted with the waterfall to the concrete basin below, the impact of hitting the water's surface scooting them more than seventy feet along the channel before they finally glided to a stop, Ames still clinging to Old Sam's shriveled ankles. He let go of the old man and stood in two feet of stagnant water. Wiping his face he searched the shadowy darkness for his friend, and seeing him floating a few feet away, grabbed him.

"Sam, are you all right?" apprehensively standing the little man upright, he shook him. "Sam, are you all right?"

Peeking from squinting eyes: "Is it safe to put my arms down yet?"

Ames burst into laughter, and picking him up, hugged his little friend shaking him like a rag doll. Sam, realizing it was over, began rejoicing with his spontaneous snorting laughter as well. He hung in Ames' arms kicking his feet and waving until Ames dropped him —then popped up like a cork— still laughing, kicking, splashing and jumping.

"We made it old man," Ames reveled.

"Yes, we did," Old Sam shouted. "We did indeed." Suddenly he stopped laughing and sternly confronted his friend. "Now look," he objected with feisty determination, "—for the last time, don't call me old man."

Ames smiled; then under his breath, "Tough old codger."

They were in the storm sewer system under the city, subterranean viaducts of brick and concrete with domed ceilings about ten feet high and walls roughly the same distance apart. A concrete walkway followed each wall and the effluent traveled a channel between them. Dim illumination entered through tile lines descending from grated storm drains at the street curbs twenty feet or more above.

It was a dank world cloaked in perpetual shadows of dingy gray light.

Together they sat on the concrete walkway resting, dangling their feet in the water as it flowed past. Water continued to shoot from the drainline overhead and the pair watched in silence, distracted only occasionally when a drop or two would fall from the sewer ceiling.

"Yup, that's it," Old Sam mumbled, having finally decided.

"What?"

"Why our faces aren't upside down," the little man said. "Because if they were," Sam began grinning, "rain would fill up our noses and we'd all drown."

Straight-faced, "That's older than you are, Sam," Ames bartered stoic. *No sense encouraging him.*

"Your gun," Old Sam inquired changing the subject abruptly, eyeing the weapon slung across Ames' back, "that's what the Federation wanted from you?"

"Yes."

"I thought you were a doctor," and asking, "you don't operate on people?"

"That's only a degree. I'm a design engineer, actually a nuclear science design engineer."

Old Sam considered and blinked. "Well, you're good at it. That's some weapon."

"Thank you," shaking his head, and a grin.

For a while longer they rested on the concrete ledge, Old Sam either digging in his pants or picking his nose, always twitching, shifting and readjusting himself. His eyes peered into the darkness the length of the subterranean corridor; then he would jerk focusing on the ceiling momentarily, then again as far as he could down the sewer tunnel, constantly moving with his peculiar rodent-like demeanor.

"Can't you ever sit still, Sam?" Ames wondered aloud after observing his friend fidgeting.

"Was I moving?" the old man responded suspiciously. Incredulous, he blinked and squinted with the other's accusation, then wrung his hands together, scratched his head, picked his nose, blinked, dug in his pants, sniffled, and squinted again.

Ames smiled. "No, I guess you weren't. Must have been my imagination."

"I figured as much." Old Sam agreed as his eyes skipped here and there for a moment then settled again and narrowed a bit more as he studied the concentration in Ames' expression. "Pondering something?" he finally inquired with marked caution.

"That guard," Ames answered, turning his head slightly in the old man's direction but still focusing his eyes on the shadows of the opposite wall.

"Which guard is that?"

Ames looked at Old Sam. "Before I had time to close the hatch a guard saw me climbing into the jettison line. He didn't try to stop me... just stood there holding a flashlight. Then he said, 'Take care, Mr. Ames'... and turned, and walked away."

There was silence while Old Sam thought. "Why would he do something like that?" he finally asked.

"I don't know, Sam. But it was more than just that... almost as if I knew—I don't know—can't put my finger on it ...something about the voice, the tone of his words."

Spontaneously: "Did you recognize the voice?"

"Not really," Ames admitted, "that's what's bothering me. It seemed as though he knew I would, and tried to disguise his voice by whispering."

"Well, 'parently it worked."

"Apparently it did, Sam," turning it over in his head again he decided, "but eventually it will come to me. There was something familiar about it, and it will come to me." His gaze drifted to the opposite wall again, lost in thought, and they sat quietly for several minutes more until the old man finally tugged at his shirt, bringing him back.

"Your wounds, are they bad?" Old Sam asked. "Can you travel?" Ames nodded. "Don't you think we should be going then?" Ames agreed, painfully rose to his feet, took a couple of steps and faltered as Old Sam watched nervously.

Bracing himself against the wall with a hand and taking a deep breath, Ames asked, "Sam, could I lean on you, just a little?"

Old Sam blinked twice, picked his nose, and said, "That's why I'm here. We're in this together." He helped steady his friend and they began making their way along the wide concrete ledge... one step at a time.

They walked for hours through the storm sewer system, a network composed of hundreds of miles of interconnecting tunnels following the pattern of city streets above. Gradually the bandages began to bleed through, losing blood again, and with the blood its oxygenated strength. Both were aware of it and Old Sam initiated a conversation to distract Ames from the pain wearing him down.

"So, you designed that weapon, Mr. Ames. I am impressed by that."

"My colleague designed it, Sam. We did the actual prototype together, but the concept was his."

"Very adept, was he not?"

Ames glanced at Old Sam, then trodding along looked down the sewer tunnel again. "More than that, Sam. Aside from you, he was the only real friend I've ever known." They continued walking, progress getting slower.

"Was?" Old Sam asked. "What happened to him? Where is he now?"

"That's a difficult question to answer," Ames replied introspectively, contemplating the depth of it.

"Why is that?"

Ames knelt and leaned against the wall to rest. Bloodstains saturated his bandages and he knew he wouldn't be able to go on much longer. He considered telling Old Sam the entire story; so someone would understand what had happened, however unbelievable, someone would know where Reed was and what the future held for this world. For any individual that would be a burden, perhaps too great a burden. Ames wasn't sure of many things anymore, except, for now the burden was his. He must decide. And his decision was to keep the secret, to keep the promise he made with Reed, to tell no one, ever.

Ames could feel his strength ebbing away and knew there wasn't much time left if they didn't find help. He also didn't know where to look anymore. The Federation controlled the world and the struggle to defeat them seemed insurmountable, futile. He and Old Sam could wander for days beneath the city remaining in hiding; but he knew he didn't have days. Time was running out. Dizziness was clouding his head and he needed to sit down, so he did. So many things that seemed important before, really weren't. His thoughts drifted away to Reed and Tian. He missed them, so very much.

"Old Sam, do you believe in God?" Ames asked without preamble.

The old man realized the situation was now desperate; his friend was losing ground. "Of course, but you just rest a few minutes; then we'll figure something out. We're gonna make it, both of us."

"I've seen Him, Sam. At least, I think I've seen Him... inside a mountain, when the world exploded and the angels began to sing. He was standing at the edge of the universe, of all creation... and He spoke to me."

"What did He say?" the old man asked, trying to keep his friend's mind occupied, active. Crouching beside him Old Sam blinked nervously and shuffled his feet; he knew he was losing his friend. "Mr. Ames, stay awake," he ordered tugging at his arm.

His eyelids droopy, turning his head to look at this friend, Ames smiled. "How would you describe the sensation of early morning mist just as the sun's rising on a mountain meadow, Sam?"

Not making much sense, the question surprised the old man; but any question was better than none. Sam thought and finally admitted, "That's a very difficult thing to do. I know what you mean, but I can't explain it."

"Exactly. That's what God said to me, Sam."

Old Sam grinned, his green teeth sparkling between chapped lips. "Wish I could have been there with you."

"Do you believe me, Sam?"

Ames was fading.

"'Course I do. I've spoken with God too," the little man confessed. But Ames didn't comprehend what Sam really meant.

A spark was waning.

The burbling rhythm of water following the sewer channel was harshly interrupted with a splash when a figure sprang to the opposite stone walkway. There were more footsteps and outlines of people materialized from the darkness as Old Sam sprang to his feet assuming his defensive half-crouch. Ames was so weak he couldn't rise, only make a futile attempt for the laser slung over his shoulder.

"—Don't," the voice ordered from the opposite walkway, "unless you want to die today."

"Not really," Ames whispered so softly that it was more breath than words. He looked at Old Sam, weakly laid a hand on his shoulder and said, "There are too many of them. We can't win."

Bristling, the old man gritted his teeth with feisty determination. "I'd rather die than go back."

Figures moved closer to them. "They're not soldiers," a second unknown voice observed. "They've escaped from the Federation dungeon."

"That's impossible," someone else remarked, "no one has ever escaped from there."

Goosebumps swarmed his shriveled stunted body as Old Sam looked at Ames. "They're not the Federation, they're rebels."

"You might call us that," the person on the opposite walkway confirmed. "Outcasts, rebels, whatever— we're with the Alliance."

"The Alliance..." Old Sam repeated, his voice cracking, trembling with squeaks of excitement, "freedom fighters resisting the Federation's control. We're safe, Mr. Ames; we made it!"

Ames tried to smile but his strength was gone, and drifting, he slipped into unconsciousness. Old Sam, fearing the worst, tried to revive him without success. He turned to the strangers.

"Please help me," he entreated, concerned. "Don't let my friend die. He's lost a lot of blood." Again, he tried to revive Ames, shaking him, prodding him. None of the strangers moved, still undecided if this were a ruse. Pleading, Old Sam appealed for their help again, nearing the point of desperation.

At last the man on the opposite walkway lowered his weapon and entered the water motioning to another to help Old Sam as he moved. Two very large men stepped forward and knelt beside Ames and Old Sam.

"I'm David," the first said, his husky voice betraying hidden compassion.

"They call me Goliath," the second behemoth figure added. There was warmth in his expression. "We'll take you and your friend to safety."

Old Sam looked back at Ames. "Will he die?"

"Can't say, Sir," David answered, "but we'll do what we can for him."

With worry in his eyes and gratitude in his heart, "Thank you," was all the old man could manage to say.

CHAPTER EIGHTEEN

Beneath the city...

...The Alliance headquarters was an abandoned subterranean control room connecting the two vertical hoist shafts of the Kelley Mine, a remnant of mining's legacy to Butte, Montana. At the surface stood stark black-steel headframes cloistered within an array of massive empty structures and expansive yards of idle machinery once used to extract ore from a seemingly endless spiderweb of tunnel system underground. The Kelley Mine was ideally suited for its present service, interconnected with the other mines by underground passages and a rail system once used to haul ore. Now a city beneath another used by the freedom fighters.

Located south of the Military Complex, from the Kelley there was access to the Civic Center and the flats, both farther south. West, connections were possible to the high school, Montana College of Technology, the Anselmo Mine, or the uptown area that included the old City Hall, courthouses and numerous commercial buildings. To the north the mine network connected the Kelley to other head frames: the Belmont, Steward, Mountain Con, Lexington, Badger State, Granite Mountain and Bell Diamond. The extensive network of multi-level mine crosscuts and drifts, ventilation shafts known as up-casts, down-casts or working shafts, stopes and other tunnels surrounded the Military Complex on three fronts with only the east inaccessible.

The east face was an expanse of wide-open country abutting the towering mountains of the East Ridge where the statue of 'Our Lady of the Rockies' stood alabaster and dismayed by the empire that had corrupted her valley. In addition to the mine works were hundreds of miles of storm sewers, viaducts and subterranean passages completing the buried system. Down there was a city in and of itself, a dank world cloaked in perpetual shadows of dingy gray light.

Underground:

It was dark and damp, rectangular; with rusted, iron-rung ladders climbing each concrete wall to the manholes overhead, and from somewhere beyond the heavy steel covers myriad sounds of the city above could barely be heard. Shafts of brilliant sunlight peering through the lift holes in the manhole covers were welcome respite to the rebels, perpetual darkness and gloom being far more infectious than the worst disease.

His eyes jerking beneath closed lids, then fluttering, Old Sam slowly began to wake. It had been sixteen hours since he and Ames had arrived, and the time had given the old man rest. The tattered, soiled, military blanket felt warm against his tired body and the mounds of straw beneath it cushioned his aged joints. It was many years since he had slept on such a comfortable bed. He brought a wrinkled hand to his eyes rubbing the matted sleep from them, then stretched full causing several pops along the length of his spine. It felt good to lounge idly without the threat of Federation soldiers looming in his mind, and he languished in the comfort. For several minutes he lay quietly and observed the activity.

In the far corner several people sat near a small campfire. Occasionally one or another would add additional twigs being careful not to let the flame get so large that their presence might be discovered by the city above, the fine traces of smoke wafting gently overhead until whisked away with the air currents following the incessant flow of water along the course of the sewer. Not far from the fire the first stranger sat speaking to others, David and Goliath among them, absorbing his words with intense concentration. People constantly entered and left the room, speaking in whispers, or not at all.

A city of rebels beneath their unwitting noses, Old Sam thought. The irony amused him; so did the Federation's stupidity. Then he noticed Ames, half-submerged in fresh straw and old blankets, still asleep near another wall. There were six others lying in a row next to him. Old Sam watched the methodical expansion and contraction of his chest: slow and shallow, but regular. *You will be all right, my friend.* Ames, quietly sleeping, getting much needed rest, satiated the sense of security flowing through the old man who was now content to simply watch those around him. Then without realizing it, Old Sam's eyes closed, and he fell asleep again.

* * *

Unknown to most of them in the sewers and mines...

...The next morning dawned bright and clear, save the pink cast caused by irreparable atmospheric radiation. The city ground to life with the routine of daily activity, while below her concrete thoroughfares, the other side also awoke.

A warm hand touched Sam's bony shoulder, followed by the feminine words, "Old man... wake up old man."

In a blink Old Sam was fully conscious, his first cranky response a spontaneous, "Don't call me old man, Missy."

"Evening," the woman whispered, "and I apologize, but I don't know your name, Sir."

"Old Sam. I'm called Old Sam."

"That's certainly appropriate enough, mister Old Sam," she said affectionately.

"Not mister Old Sam," he corrected with the compassion of a cantankerous boar grizzly, "just, Old Sam."

"Old Sam."

Then a bit less cranky, "And what's your name?" he asked.

She smiled. "I already told you: Evening." She was young, not more than twenty, absorbing the world through deep brown eyes. Her voice was as soft and gentle as her auburn hair was long, her petite shape and mannerisms creating a sultry blend of femininity. She wore a short sleeve blouse, faded snug Wranglers, and Nike tennis shoes with a hole in the toe.

"Oh, yes, so you did." He studied her tender expression and girlish figure, then blinked and twitched. And his heart melted just a little. "That's pretty. Sure 'nuf, that's a pretty name," he finally admitted, his way of apology, his grin exposing the spaces between green teeth.

"Thank you."

"Yer' welcome, Ma'am." The comical look on his face, combined with his incessant nervous habits and grubby appearance, drew a deep, affectionate smile from Evening. "And how's he?" Old Sam queried directing her attention to the people sleeping near the other wall.

Looking in that direction, "Who?"

"My friend Mr. Ames, Missy."

"Oh, is that his name?" She watched the sleeping man for a minute without answering.

"Well?" Old Sam persisted. Avoiding, she paid him no attention. "Well...?" he pestered irritably tapping her lightly on the cheek.

Quickly: "I'm sorry;" then thoughtfully, "he's lost a lot of blood, an awful lot of blood."

"What's that 'sposed to mean?"

She looked at Sam, the concerned tone of her voice betraying her words. "We're not too sure yet, but he should be all right soon."

"Evening, Mr. Ames and me have been through a lot together. Vinegar doesn't sweeten tea does it?"

"No," she answered, puzzled by the expression.

"Tell me the truth, Missy."

She sighed. "He's got a bullet wound to the left side of his chest that creased a rib and cracked three others. It caused quite a lot of tissue damage. He also had a bone fragment lodged in his right tibia." Then she went on, contemplating aloud, "Strange though, it's not a fragment from his bone. It's from someone else."

"What's a tibia?" Old Sam inquired.

"Shin bone," she answered, then asked, "Old Sam, do you have any idea where the bone fragment could be from?"

He nodded indicating he might know. "We were kind of busy when we escaped."

And finally she told him, "But the most danger will come from infection. The water is a cesspool of infectious bacteria and disease, and any open wound exposed to it will kill you nine times out of ten. The next thirty-six hours will be critical."

"It's that bad?"

"Yes," she admitted, "the chemicals and radiated waste jettisoned from the Complex have even killed some of the sewer rats. He may need a miracle to keep him alive."

Old Sam was quiet for a minute, considering, then told her, "He'll be all right. His friend will take care of him."

But Evening didn't understand; she changed the subject, "Are you hungry?"

"Positively, what's to eat?"

"Porridge. Come, let's have breakfast together," she invited.

"Yes-siree-bob," was Old Sam's reply.

They moved to the small fire, were given bowls of stew, and the little man immediately dug in. Without speaking Old Sam devoured the miscellany voraciously —until he munched into something long and crunchy. He fingered the contents in his mouth, pulled the piece out, and examined it. He finally cautioned a guess, "Looks like the tail of something," and a *very* nervous grin.

"Probably is," Evening confirmed, a bland monotone.

"Probably *is*?"

"Yes," she said unaffected, the others in the group still eating, and listening.

Mustering his courage finally Sam managed to inquire, "Tail of what?"

"Rat."

Old Sam examined his bowl, and spoke very slowly. "Somehow—I just knew—you were gonna say—that."

Mischievously, Evening smiled. "How do you like it?"

Old Sam blinked, twitched, wrinkled his nose, dug at his crotch and completed several other peculiar functions before answering.

"Well," he said frankly, "I've tasted worse. In fact... it ain't really too bad at all." He cautiously munched down another spoonful. "Nope, it ain't that bad." He licked his lips and ate some more, then said, "Evening..."

She stopped eating. "Yes?"

"...Do you 'spose a body could have seconds?"

She smiled. "Sure Sam, I suppose a body could."

"That'd be good." He smiled and blinked. "That's mighty kind of you folks." He offered his bowl to the woman tending the steaming cauldron and she ladled it full of broth, chunks of meat, and vegetables. "A powerful thank you, Ma'am." Still grinning, she nodded a congenial welcome.

"Old Sam, you must tell us, how did you and your friend manage to escape from the Federation detention level?" Older than most of the others, his light brown hair just going gray near the temples and his eyes the color of sky: this man was a natural leader. Years of survival had sculpt him leather tough and honed his mind with an edge of wit and cunning. Resolve was etched in his expression and the warmth of humanity anchored deeply within his soul.

Old Sam recognized the man as the first stranger of those they had met in the sewer. "I reckon I could do that, Mister," he responded. The twinkle returned as he blinked recalling the adventure.

"Forgive me, my name is Alex," the man told him.

"Well, Mister Alex," Sam responded, "it's a pleasure to make your 'quaintance I'm sure." Without further delay, Old Sam began unraveling the details of their escape, not missing anything and perhaps embellishing a few details just a bit. For an hour and the better part of another, he spilled the events of their route to freedom keeping his tiny audience spellbound with the circumstance and color of it. Sam was truly a gifted storyteller, there was no doubt of that, and no one interrupted right to the last. "...And that's when you and the others found us," he finally concluded.

Alex smiled, with possibly just a touch of congenial sarcasm in his words. "You do have a delightful way of making a short story long, Sam."

Old Sam blushed and snickered in his peculiar way. "Perhaps I do at that."

"Now, Old Sam, can you tell me anything about the Complex: where the control bypasses and backup systems are —things of that nature?" Alex inquired.

"No, not really," came the thoughtful response, "but Mr. Ames should be able to when he gets better."

"—If he gets better," David corrected, casting a glance at the sleeping man. David and Goliath sat across from the old man: two behemoths large enough to tromp pro wrestlers without breaking a sweat, then calmly amble to the breakfast table for a bite to eat. Their size was impressive, but neither presented boisterous bravado; they were quiet, possessed depth, and cared about others.

"And you are, Sir?" Sam inquired politely, then explained, "You both look alike."

"David," the man replied; then indicating, "and this is Goliath. We're twin brothers."

Sam grinned. "I figured you might be; you're big rascals." Both men presented friendship with their smiles, and the little man's focus once more returned to their conversation. "He will get better. I can feel it," Sam determined.

"We all hope so," Alex assured, "but he's fevered and it may take some time for him to recover. There's also the possibility he won't get better, Sam. It's time you accepted that. Surely you can appreciate our primitive conditions here, and the fact that we don't have antibiotics to combat infection that comes from the water."

"—I know, I know," Old Sam conceded, "but there must be drugs in the hospital, more than enough."

"Obviously, Sam, but…"

"—But what? Let's go get some," he interrupted. Even as he spoke the solution seemed apparent to the old man.

"It's not that simple," Goliath explained.

Turning: "Why not?" His protest caused his nose to wrinkle defiantly.

"Because..." Alex said, "we have limited resources. Even with our allies among the populace, we are few, and the city is very well guarded. Surely it would be no less than suicide to attempt such a venture." He continued to explain, "We send scouts to the surface nightly, but it's an entirely different matter to burglarize the hospital —and then get out again. It would be impossible, Sam."

The old man was unimpressed. He looked at Evening sitting beside him, then across to David, Goliath, Alex and the others. "Is it impossible to escape the Federation prison?" he challenged. "He is my friend and I am here to help him, and now, even more than before, he needs my help." Then he concluded, "And I will help him, even if I must go alone." Old Sam waited, didn't move a muscle... not even a twitch.

No one spoke, until, "We can get what we need," Evening finally whispered.

"How?" Goliath asked.

Her answer: "I don't know, but I have a feeling... strange, I can't explain it; I just believe we can."

* * *

Night folded her dark wings over the city...

...Like a heron contemplating the activity at her feet in a hunting pond. Three figures slipped from shadowed doorways to alleys, then again into the next protective shadow. Old Sam, Evening and David carefully, covertly proceeded toward the hospital, looming before them like a Federation titan of brick and glass: eight stories of impregnability surrounded by armed guards.

"Where's the pharmacy, Evening?" Sam queried in a whisper.

"Top floor, 'D' wing," her hushed reply.

Old Sam and David exchanged glances while Evening continued to study the hospital grounds. Lightly tapping her on the shoulder, "What room? Just show me which window," Sam clarified.

Pointing: "Top one, on that corner, the one without any lights on."

"Shouldn't be too difficult then," the wiry old man concluded.

"How?" David asked.

Without explaining Old Sam replied, "Give me the rope. I'll go first." To Evening: "You come when I signal." And then David: "Evening will have to go in with me to get the right stuff; then we'll drop it to you."

Evening asked her small friend, "How are you going to get up there?"

"Nothing to it, Missy," draping the rope over his shoulders —and on his way.

He scurried across the grounds and ducked into the professionally pruned shrubbery dodging uniformed guards as they made their rounds with precise consistency. Arriving at the building, the neatly grouted masonry was easy enough to climb for someone of Old Sam's size and arachnid agility. His calloused toes and fingers clung to the mortared gaps between the bricks as he crawled silently toward the roof of the building. And when a guard would appear below, he would freeze, becoming virtually undetectable in the darkness above them. Evening and David watched, nerves taut, concentration fixed on their companion. It was a long five minutes until Sam arrived at the roof.

"Just like a little four-legged fly," David whispered daring to relax again.

"Kind of makes you wonder what's going on inside his head, doesn't it? What he thinks and feels, how complex he really is," Evening mused.

About then, Old Sam signaled from the rooftop and Evening cautiously crossed the hospital grounds evading the patrolling guards. Meanwhile, Old Sam tied the rope off on a large soil stack and waited.

She arrived at the bushes just seconds before the guard appeared on the sidewalk from around the corner of the building, and the junipers rustled when she moved too quickly behind them —but almost as if someone had arranged it, the noise was muted by a propitious gust of wind. The guard methodically paced the length of the building and disappeared around the far corner without noticing anything unusual.

Two and one-half minutes, she thought. The rope dropped alongside her striking the building with a single slap. Quickly she looped the rope under her arms, and making another, smaller loop, recited as she constructed the knot. "The rabbit comes out of the hole, goes around the tree, and goes back down the hole." She pulled the free end and the knot was secure. "Just like downtown."

Pulling herself up while walking on the brick wall, she climbed toward Old Sam, the slack end of the rope tied around her waist forming an increasingly larger loop below her. With each foot she climbed the loop rose half that distance from the ground. "...One thousand twenty-five," she whispered. She stopped and waited. Just as the rope quit swaying a guard appeared on the sidewalk below, his boots clicking with each footfall as he walked the length of the building and disappeared following the sidewalk down the adjacent wall: a battery-operated toy soldier.

"One thousand one, one thousand two..." her counting began again as she continued, Old Sam waiting silently. "Just like clockwork, Sam," she whispered, joining the old man on the roof.

"Don't get cocky, Missy," he cautioned. "We're not done yet." He untied the rope from the soil stack while Evening untied it from her waist, and that completed, he looped it around the pipe without tying a knot and extended an open hand to the young woman. She dug into her back pocket retrieving a roll of masking tape and a glasscutter.

Old Sam clamped his teeth on the tool and tape and lowered himself to the window by holding both strands of rope. Once on the ledge he etched a circle in the window glass, taped an 'X', then tapped it sharply with his knuckles. The circular piece of glass popped away with a, *snap*, and dangled by the taped 'X'. He reached inside releasing the latch, raised the window, and slid into the room on the other side of the glass. He pulled the ropetail in behind him.

The guard made his rounds below.

Evening lowered herself on the doubled rope and disappeared in the darkness of the room. One end of the rope went slack as they pulled the other; it whisked around the soil stack, dropped from the roof and was pulled back up and into the pharmacy window.

A gritty scratch in the dark: match light illuminated a short length of the aisle revealing abundant stores of packaged medical supplies. Evening handed two boxes to Old Sam then blew out the match just before the flame reached her fingers. "This way," she said.

"Oh, that's cute, Missy," came sarcastic words from the darkness. "What, Sam?"

"I can't see..." there resounded the smart thump of a dwarfed body walking into a shelf, "a darn thing."

Evening lit another match and could see the welt rising on Sam's forehead, detailed even to the holes drilled into the shelving to hold bolts, for fastening sections together. Sweetly, "Did you bump your head?" her words tendering a bit of maternal concern.

Fighting back tears Sam blinked a couple of times, raised his eyebrows, twitched, and finally managed a disgusted, "Nevermind. Don't hurt a bit, Missy."

She didn't respond but couldn't contain the mischievous little smile that curled her lips and wrinkled her nose ever so slightly, and promptly she picked up another container stepping to a row of refrigerated lockers located along the rear wall of the room. With systematic methodology born of familiarity she collected numerous drugs and syringes, carefully packing them into boxes as she proceeded. Several minutes and four boxes later she concluded her shopping and they carried their pillage to the window and signaled for David with a match.

Both of them watched silently while the gentle hulk covered the distance between his vantage point and the building. He stepped behind the junipers and waited as the clicking of shoe leather grew louder. Presently, the guard appeared from around the corner of the building and proceeded on his appointed rounds.

"You could set your watch by 'em," Sam whispered with just a trace of arrogance in his voice.

Evening peeked over the windowsill as the guard disappeared around the far corner. "It's a long way down," she observed, ignoring Old Sam's comment. "I hope they don't break."

"Gotta have faith, Missy," the old man replied. "*Pssst—*" he dropped the first package and it swished downward into David's waiting arms.

"Thirty pounds, about eighty feet, the impact would be about..." she calculated.

"You worry too much, Missy; gonna give me ulcers, I swear." The fourth box was plummeting down as he spoke. David caught the container, stooping to break its fall just as a guard appeared from around the corner.

"Freeze or I'll shoot—" the mechanical command. David raised his arms in submission as the guard approached cautiously

"I'm not armed sir; don't shoot."

"Assume the position." David turned compliantly and placed his palms against the building while the soldier surveyed the containers near his feet, then inquired, "Where did these boxes come from?" Sam observed from the window on the eighth floor. David hesitated to answer. "If you don't want a bullet in your back, you'd damn well better tell me where these boxes came from and what you're doing here," the guard demanded.

David replied, "I'm stealing them," risking a cautious glance over his shoulder toward the man.

"Stealing them... from where?" the officer persisted.

"The top floor... the pharmacy," David finally answered, making an overt gesture of looking up.

A reflex response, the guard also looked toward the top of the building, but too late to avoid the box Old Sam dropped to dispatch him. The box struck him —full force on the forehead— shattering its contents and his skull. He crumpled in a heap, his head buried inside the cardboard container to his shoulders.

"Right smack dab, dead center," Sam giggled with a full stomach of satisfaction.

"What's wrong, Sam?" Evening asked, momentarily delaying what she was doing.

"Nothing now. What was in that last box, the one with the green tape?"

"Penicillin, tetracycline, other antibiotics, yeast culture and activating agent."

"Better give me another one of those, Missy."

"Why?" Worried, she looked out the window toward David, who was dragging the guard into the bushes the same time Sam replied.

"Had to use that one."

She, looking again at Old Sam, his green teeth sparkling with his mischievous smile, "What happened?"

"Oh," Sam explained, "stuck his nose in where it didn't belong." He tingled with satisfaction at his wit —and he snickered.

Quickly replacing those drugs, their work complete, Sam looped the rope around one of the shelves and dropped both ends out the window. The wind caught it and set it obliquely into a lower window that twanged on contact, however neither paid much attention to the noise: there wasn't time. They knew within two and one-half minutes the officer would be missed.

As quickly as they could Sam and Evening crawled down the rope, holding both lines so it wouldn't slip, and within a minute were on the ground reunited with an anxious David. Without hesitation the trio gathered the supplies and rope then silently disappeared into the myriad shapes and shadows of the night, following side streets that created checkerboards of out-of-the-way neighborhoods: Jackson to Platinum, Wyoming, Second, Wisconsin, and First.

The alley where they finally stopped to catch their breath was dark and vacant, save an occasional rat scurrying amid the blowing scraps of paper and garbage. In twenty-five years they had become fugitives in their own city; the Federation controlled it. Arriving behind the Civic Center David lifted the manhole cover and the trio went down. Safe again, and out of sight.

* * *

A wiry little man, with scraggly gray hair...

...And a bristling beard to match. Old Sam waited patiently for the antibiotics to help his friend, six days that seemed endless and were precious to him. He knew things the others didn't. On the morning of the seventh day the old man sat opposite his friend, speaking with Evening. Ames' temperature had subsided hours earlier and he finally slept peacefully without the febrile nightmares.

"Your friend will live because of you, Old Sam," Evening commented watching Ames sleep.

Old Sam nodded. "He will be all right now, and it's time for me to go."

"Go where— what is so important?"

Old Sam blinked, trying to remain detached, answering, "I'm going to find my children."

"Your children?"

"Yes," was Old Sam's only reply, and he looked away, down the darkened sewer tunnel so she wouldn't see the tears in his eyes.

"Then I can understand." Evening's words were soft and compassionate. Her heart burned with empathy for what the old man must have endured in prison, a loss that nothing could ever replace. "How many have you?"

"Three."

She offered, "I'll go with you."

"No, Missy. You are my friend, but this I must do alone. It's already too many years overdue." The conviction in his voice caused her to wonder, and it was a long minute before she spoke again, very softly.

"Why must you find them alone, Sam? Surely it would be easier if we did it together."

"No; there isn't enough time left... and I can't tell you why. It's just something I must do alone." The old man, choking on his words, swallowed before he could continue. "I am alone with an emptiness inside; a part of me is gone and I'm the only one who can fix it. It's like having a hole that goes all the way through the world... trying to shovel it full of dirt. No matter what you put into the hole, it keeps falling out the other side, until you put back what was taken away. Nothing else can ever fill it... make it whole again." By now the moist tracks of his tears could no longer be hidden, so he wiped his cheeks and sniffled.

Evening touched his arm tenderly. "It's yours to deal with however you must, Old Sam. I understand."

He looked at her, then wiped his face again. "I'm sorry. I didn't mean to cry."

"A man can cry, Sam," she said. "Being human is nothing to apologize for."

Old Sam rose from his haunches. "I must tell Mr. Ames that I am leaving." Evening also stood, facing the old man who offered her his handshake; but she refused it, instead embracing him with a hug and a kiss on the cheek. "Why are you crying, Missy?" the old man asked when they parted.

"Because I have a wonderful old man as a very dear friend, who still is, what this screwed up world used to be. And I love him."

Sam blinked a couple times, wrinkled his nose and twitched. "Don't call me old man," he said softly: words telling endearment.

"You be careful," she said.

"I surely will."

"Will you be back, Old Sam?"

"Unless I die," he joked. Evening hugged him again. No words were necessary. Turning, she walked to the fire as Old Sam scooted over to Ames.

The continuum of hours composing days and nights had run their course with incessant progression, and once his fever had succumbed to the antibiotics Ames' body had cooled and he had been able to rest. The straw beneath him had compacted into a tight mat from his weight for so long a time. The tell-tale gray of his hair was more noticeable with the new growth, and his face seemed to express what he had been through with its weathered, tired texture.

In half-sleep his eyes opened slowly, then gradually adjusted to the light given by the small fire. The people gathered around him seemed vaguely familiar, but he wasn't quite certain until his eyes fixed upon Old Sam's grinning, green teeth. Ames smiled, clasping the old man's spindly arm with his hand.

"Good to have you back," Sam beamed.

"Good to be back, Sam."

Approaching them, "Mr. Ames, you're better," Alex said; "your fever's gone."

Ames weakly lifted his arm laying the back of his hand against his forehead. It felt cool and clammy. "Just a little shaky." He studied the man a moment. "You seem familiar, have we met?"

"Yes, we've met, but I'm surprised you remember. You've been pretty ill." Alex knelt to help him up "We've got to get some food into you; let me help you to the fire." His legs were unsure and each step was a task, but with Sam and Alex's support they started toward the fire. His attention drawn by the shuffling, David rose and met them part way. He slipped a muscular arm around Ames and lifted him, the man's feet scarcely touching the floor.

"Easy," Alex cautioned.

Ames peered beyond the massive arm that clutched him like a doll, and the shoulders that seemed stout enough to carry an ox, to the face, conveying genuine warmth and heartfelt concern. "Thank you..."

"...David."

"Thank you, David."

"You're welcome, Mr. Ames; don't mention it." David's words were as sincere as his strength was reassuring.

There was a generous bowl of steaming porridge waiting for him as David helped him to be seated near the fire. That accomplished, and noticing his faltering balance, David knelt beside Ames. Prime rib could not have tasted better, but the shock of nourishment pushing its way into a stomach shriveled by days of fasting was, at the least, somewhat painful. Spooning the broth first helped to ease the discomfort until his system accepted the transition.

"Mr. Ames," Old Sam whispered as he squatted beside his friend. Ames turned facing the old man; and he knew it was time.

"Yes, Sam."

"You are in good hands. The rebels will be with you." Old Sam blinked and picked his nose.

Ames smiled as emotions turned inside him, and he and Old Sam clasped hands. Old Sam rose slowly, his eyes focused on Ames, and he smiled as their handshake ended. The others watched silently as Old Sam crossed the room to the storm sewer tunnel entrance, and stopped... his back to Ames.

"I must go now my friend," Old Sam whispered.

"Will we ever see each other again, Sam?"

As he stepped into the darkness of the tunnel Old Sam turned around, facing Ames, shuffling backward; he winked, he grinned...

Then he said, "There are always possibilities."

And he was gone.

Finally, Ames realized, "Of course..."

CHAPTER NINETEEN

A small campfire wafting smoke trails…

…Wisps of mystery and destiny. In subdued conversation hushed voices crossed the illumination of flames. They talked of the condition of things, plans yet to be made and the possibility of the rebels' pending coup, always overshadowed by the hazards and probable futility of such an attempt, yet interspersed with intimations of hope and determination. Ames listened intently while he ate, absorbing every word, trying to piece together the recent history of a world he seemed not to be a part of anymore. Corin had told him some and Old Sam had given a detailed account until the time of his imprisonment, but from that point, the information was only speculation, conjecture and rumors.

He bit into something crunchy, stopped chewing and spit it into the palm of his hand. For a minute or so he scrutinized it, turning it several times, wasn't sure, and curiously leaned toward Evening who was seated beside him. "Is this…?"

"—Rat?" There was a pause. "Yes, it is," she confirmed nonchalantly returning her attention to the council discussion. Her casual response caused his jaw to drop, but he couldn't think of anything further to say. Looking at his bowl again he rocked it, the vortex causing the contents to swish around its confines while Evening watched from the corner of her eye, amused by his reaction but not saying anything.

Probing, Ames dipped another spoonful; then hesitating before he managed to put it in his mouth, raised the spoon, holding it as though he might be able to determine the identity of each piece floating around in the broth. He cast a furtive glance toward Evening, and as her eyes met his, her delicate lips curled in a grin. She didn't say a word as Ames almost carefully put it in his mouth, and swallowed. He looked back at his bowl, then again at her. After earnest deliberation he reluctantly admitted, "Not too bad."

Evening placed a hand on his forearm and squeezed affectionately. "Old Sam said the same thing. Do you want more?" Ames studied her, then the bowl he held. "Do you?" she asked again. He offered the bowl for a refill, and after the second portion of broth lay comfortably within his stomach Ames' attention returned to the discussion of those around him.

Goliath presented the possibility of storming the Military Complex, thus gaining control of the nuclear firepower housed in the depths of its silos. Once in possession of such devastating weapons though, using them may be another matter. Only a fool or madman would destroy an entire world. The purpose of the Alliance was to free their world, not annihilate it.

"That would be nothing less than suicide," Alex replied, his response rehearsed, their conversation almost orchestrated: testing. "There's no way for the Alliance to take a fortress like that with our meager supplies and weapons."

"But if we could get inside the Complex and gain access to the nuclear silos," Ames interjected, joining the discussion, "could the Alliance take the Complex then?"

Alex looked at him. "Mr. Ames," he began, "I appreciate your enthusiasm as much as your conviction, but it's virtually impregnable. Even a nuclear attack would only destroy the surface level —and perhaps the first sub-level. The core of the structure lies below that, invulnerable to a ground assault. Each level and corridor has a steel assault door about a foot thick.

"They're reinforced and eighteen inches thick, stainless-steel."

Alex asked, "How do you know that?"

"I helped design the Complex."

Alex's expression conveyed interest and uncertainty, and something else. He didn't respond.

David asked, "Do you know how we can get into the sub-levels, Mr. Ames?"

Ames looked at the larger man. "No, not yet; but no system has ever been conceived that couldn't be circumvented. Some are more difficult than others, but they can all be defeated given the right materials, means and knowledge."

Alex listened, said nothing.

"But the Military Center?" Goliath queried.

"Not impossible, but probably one of the most difficult," Ames concluded.

A small girl approached him. "Mister," she whispered tugging at his arm. "Mister."

"Yes?" He smiled at her dirty face and innocence.

"What is that word?" Her petite finger pointed to the phrase on a page of the tattered book she held.

"Resurrection," Ames answered amiably perusing the page. He read: *"So is it with the resurrection of the dead. What is sown is perishable what is raised is imperishable." (1 Cor. 15:42 RSV)* His eyes met hers.

"What does it mean, Mister?"

Considering, for a moment he said nothing. Then he answered, "It means someday... the world will be better than it is today." She smiled and rubbed a dirty cheek with her hand. "Where did you get that book, Sweetie?"

"You can't have it," her immediate response, "it's mine. I found it and they said I could keep it," worried, the thought of her sole possession being taken by the strange bearded man.

"No, no—I didn't mean to frighten you," he reassured taking her in his arms and putting her on his knee. As he wiped a smudge from her cheek he listened to Evening.

"It's one of the few books that survived the fires."

"Fires?"

"The blast furnaces," she explained, "about twenty years ago. When the Federation came to power they outlawed home school and seized and burned almost every book in the world —at least those that contradicted their doctrine and policies.

"But it's a Bible."

"All the more reason to destroy it," she said. "Most of us weren't old enough to know what such books meant; and those who were, like Old Sam, were imprisoned or eliminated. The few who are left, who do remember, are afraid to tell or have forgotten much of what they knew of the old days."

"No books, home school outlawed," Ames mused. "Makes sense. If only the state has authority to educate, they can teach whatever they want, brainwash the children. Someone once said, 'Let me control the textbooks and I will control the state… give me your children and I will have the next generation' —or something like that."

"Who?" Evening asked.

He looked at her. "Adolph Hitler."

"Do you know the sacred book, Mr. Ames?" Goliath asked.

"Some," his glance crossed the flames settling on the younger man, "but not nearly enough."

Goliath suggested, "Will you tell us?"

Ames looked at Alex. "What has happened since I've been gone? How did this all come about?"

"The Federation."

"Yes, I know, but how?"

"Black Friday," Evening whispered. She looked at Alex. "I think he means Black Friday."

Ames: "The Friday after Thanksgiving?"

Turning to him: "No one had a very good Christmas that year."

Alex nodded. "Yes, Black Friday was probably the beginning of the real changes, but things were bad for several years before that. Some say that's what caused it."

"What happened?"

Alex picked up a few twigs and carefully placed them on the fire; then he began. "I suppose it started long ago, in small increments that

276

no one noticed—or should I say—no one really wanted to notice. But everything changed dramatically after the turn of the century. There was inflation, crime, corruption, civil unrest; a lot of things going wrong, especially here and in Europe. I believe we could have dealt with the problems as we had for the preceding decades if the weather hadn't gone haywire too."

"There were three or four consecutive years of drought and the crops failed. They weren't bad harvest years, just complete crop failures. No harvest at all. Everything withered or burned in brushfires —thousands of them." Remembering, he paused, then continued, "For the first year or two the world relied on its stockpiles to ward off starvation; but with all those millions of mouths to feed the stored provisions didn't last long."

"Then, when the fires finally burned themselves out, the grasshoppers came. Huge swarms, billions of them —trillions— so many the sky turned dark for days as they made their way from one area to another eating everything that the sun or the fires hadn't already withered or charred. They'd light in a field and strip thousands of acres to bare dirt in a matter of hours. They even ate the bark and needles off the conifers."

"After that the stock had no food. Sheep, cattle, birds, and everything else started dying. It was like a gargantuan plague being carried by the wind, all the way around the world. What had been lush pastureland a few years before looked like the dust bowl littered with thousands of carcasses."

Again he stopped, recalling what once was, and what it became. "Then, inevitably, the people were next. Those who weren't dying of starvation were contracting diseases that no one had even heard of; there was no treatment for them. For every illness medicine and science was able to cure two new ones appeared. People turned to cannibalism to survive, feeding on the rotting carcasses of the dead. It was like living in an endless hell, the same no matter where you went, no way to get away from it."

Remembering sadly, "I was still young then, but I'll never forget the day my father died. When I walked into that shack my mother was devouring him piece by piece, just like a wild dog. That was the last time I ever saw her."

"I didn't think anything could be any worse than that; but then, Black Friday..." He paused a third time, pained with the recollection.

"What I've already told you may seem bad, but the real hell hadn't even arrived yet. That began the day the other countries demanded payment for our country's outstanding debts. Black Friday. On that Friday afternoon the Dow Jones crashed, fell twenty thousand points. NASDAQ was the same —don't remember exactly how much."

"On Sunday, the President, Vice President, Speaker of the House and so on —the entire cabinet— were all assassinated, all within one hour. It was like a horrendous conspiracy, the world's most colossal military giant with no leadership and no structure, just millions of adherents wandering aimlessly. They said it could never happen... but it did."

"With no gold or silver to back our fiat paper currency, by Monday our monetary system was destroyed. There was complete, uncontrollable chaos." Alex stopped, caught up once again in the horror of that time.

"Then what?" Ames prodded.

Alex looked at him. "Tuesday, the International Trade Federation of the European Common Market countries became the United Military Federation of Nations, more commonly known as the Federation, under the pretext of resolving what seemed to be insurmountable problems. Simply put, a trade organization became a world military overnight. To this day, most people believe it was all very carefully planned, contrived if you will."

"The same thing Corin said," Ames murmured.

Alex nodded. "It was just too coincidental that an entirely new system could be established in one day. Hell, it's impossible and we all know it. By Wednesday the European currency unit, or Euro, replaced the dollar as the world trade currency. By Thursday Federation troops were here. Occupation to restore order —so they said. Enter General Smith."

"On Thursday evening Iran and the Soviet Union launched a nuclear attack against Europe. Someone probably double-crossed someone, and they wanted to ensure they'd get their share of the spoils; but that tactical judgment error cost them more than they could have ever imagined." He smiled, a melancholy smile.

"It was termed a limited nuclear engagement, but I doubt there was a single structure still standing in Iran or the entire Russian Empire." Thinking, Alex chewed his lip. "Hell, they almost caused a nuclear winter. It was incredible, unimaginable destruction, millions of people dead. Those not vaporized died terrible, agonizing deaths. Even today, the atmospheric radiation is still lethal in some places, and worldwide, the level is just barely tolerable."

"To me, it's inconceivable any group of nations could have coordinated so complex a plot and orchestrated such an assault without years of preparation." He thought, then admitted, "Hell, three people in the same room usually can't agree for very long, much less governments. Too many minuscule details and fragments converged all at the same time: like someone pouring a jigsaw puzzle on a table and every piece falling exactly into place, interlocking with every other matching piece."

Sitting on the floor, arms propped on his knees, fingers laced together, Ames asked, "Who?"

"No one knows for sure," Alex replied, "but General Smith spent more than six years assigned to the European corridor. Seemed to spend a lot of time there associated with a political activist named Jedediah Jones —that is, until the assassination attempt on Jones. Got shot in the head, but shit, he didn't die. Apparently after that he became very popular politically and amassed quite a following; but none of us really know what happened to him, because by then there was so much going on here."

"Everybody used to joke about it... alias Smith and Jones," Goliath said. "Not very funny though."

Staring into his cupped hands Ames repeated, "General Smith." It all made sense.

"But even with his connections, influence and power that bastard can't eliminate the earthquakes and storms," Alex told him.

Ames puzzled: "Earthquakes and storms?"

"All the time," Goliath confirmed.

"Nearly every day there's a catastrophic natural disaster somewhere," Alex explained. "Seems as though Mother Nature is balancing the scales." And presenting a melancholy analogy, "Fingering the scales would be more accurate, for all the pollutants and garbage we've dumped on her since the industrial revolution. The droughts and grasshoppers were bad enough, but entire cities are being wiped out almost daily now. Volcano, earthquake, flood, firestorm, tornado, tsunami —you name it, it's happening."

Ames murmured, "It's all true."

"What's true?" Alex asked, his curiosity piqued by the man's statement.

"The prophecies."

"What prophecies?" Goliath questioned.

Ames, helping the little girl down from his lap, turned to Goliath. "You asked if I knew what the Bible is about."

"Yes."

"And I said some." He drew a deep breath. "No one really knows what the entire Bible is about, what it all means, but perhaps we're living the conclusion of seven thousand years of recorded civilization and three thousand years of written prophecy. The Bible is the record of the creation and mankind since its beginning with Adam and Eve; then continuing with Noah, Moses, Jesus, and many others. It's a chronology of people, places and events, and its underlying purpose is to teach. The Bible is a textbook, and one of the purposes of life is a learning experience."

"The Bible was written by numerous authors inspired by God," and he quoted: *"because no prophecy ever came by the impulse of man, but men moved by the Holy Spirit spoke from God (2 Peter 1:21 RSV).* Much of it straightforward, but part was written in riddles and parables that must be studied. Certain chapters contained symbolism and prophecies requiring that we decipher the meaning. This format was particularly instrumental in the last chapter, Revelation... predicting the end of the world."

Ames related Bible stories he had learned as a child: included Christmas, Easter and a host of subjects capturing the undivided attention of his listeners until finally he paused and told them. "There's so much more in the Bible it would take a long time to even relate a brief overview; but I think you get the idea. Whether you believe it to be speculation, conjecture, coincidence, fact, or fiction; that single manuscript revealed it all thousands of years ago, with precise accuracy."

"And that's why the Federation banned it, to suppress its most contentious adversary?" Evening asked.

Ames leaned closer, feeling the warmth radiating from her body, "Its only adversary. As Alex said, a poorly equipped army of rebels such as us is no match for today's weaponry. But the Federation can't defeat something intangible: that flame inside every soul, the conviction that affords courage, even against impossible odds."

"Then what is the answer, Mr. Ames?" The voice was tender and compassionate, expressing concern and determination. It traveled across the room from the darkness of one of the tunnels. Ames instantly recognized the hushed voice of the unidentified newcomer. His head jerked, and his searching eyes located the silhouette of the Federation uniform. Confused, he wondered why the others remained calm, not reacting with the intruder's presence. The semidarkness made it impossible for him to identify the soldier, but Ames could see the person wasn't too tall.

"The sub-level."

"You have a good memory," the figure responded. "Impressive," taking a step so the flames illuminated her.

"You've met Kristina," Alex commented.

"She saved my life," he whispered.

"Twice," Alex told him. "She's the officer who summoned the ambulance to the Complex when you first appeared there."

The woman saw confusion in his eyes and said, "We're on the same side."

"But you're…"

"—A Federation sergeant," she completed his statement; then continued, "yes, but just because I was chipped when I was still very young, doesn't mean it's embedded in my heart."

"Chipped?" Ames asked.

She, crossing the room: "A microchip implanted in the back of my neck —all of us. It's been mandatory for a number of years now. Most people believed OnStar and on-board vehicle navigation GPS were good ideas when they were developed; first optional equipment, then standard, then required on every vehicle. But GPS works both ways. You could find where you were going, or your way home… but *they* could also *always* find you."

"And national health care —with that obscure clause far back in those thousands of pages of legislation, in the really fine print, the clause that required the chips. Before anyone could receive medical care or treatment they had to consent to the chip; purportedly to contain each person's complete medical history and have it instantly available in case of emergency. Maybe so—maybe not. But the Federation had their own agenda in mind. The individualized, personal GPS."

"But if you're all 'chipped' can't the Federation track you, even now?" Ames asked.

Arriving at the small fire she smiled. "Our people are better than theirs. Right now, I'm on the other side of town." He understood. "And let me assure you," she said, serious now, "I am still the same person as when I was born, regardless what the Federation, or Smith, want to believe."

"General Smith?" Ames asked.

"It began before Smith," she explained, "but he's the one who brought it to fruition. He is evil —conniving, deceiving, treacherous, deadly— however you choose to describe him, he is the epitome of all that is wrong with this world."

Ames didn't say anything.

"She's one of ours," Alex explained, less suspicious now. "There are others like her inside." Finally, he told him, "It's not exactly us against them."

"Us against him would be closer to the truth," Kristina apprised sitting down next to Alex. "Smith is our enemy, not the Federation troops. Most of them are simply afraid to confront the system. They lack cohesion and organization, following orders like a hoard of lemmings going to the sea, migrating without knowing what it's really all about, this contemptible system we're a part of."

"Then break the cog and the spokes collapse," Ames thought aloud.

"Pardon?" Alex interjected, crooking his head.

Ames teethed his upper lip. "Nothing. It was just a thought."

"One to consider," Evening agreed, taking his arm and pressing her body against him, pensively watching the flames of the fire; a feminine gesture, possessive, letting Kristina be aware. Traces of smoke wafted upward cutting though the dank humidity of the room eventually being lost in the updrafts of the subterranean air channels.

Ignoring Evening, "Mr. Ames," Kristina asked, "how did you come to be inside the Complex?"

"I'm not exactly sure."

She pulled her knees to her chest and pursued her next question. "Perhaps then, you can tell us where you've been for the past twenty-five years."

Offhand: "Not far away."

"Same thing you told Corin Johnson." His expression revealed surprise that she should know. And Kristina went on, "She died helping you, Mr. Ames; are you aware of that?"

This time not really surprised, but saddened: "They killed her?"

"And Ester Bloomenthal, as well as another nurse. This is a serious business; please don't take it lightly."

"I'm not," he assured. "If I told you where I've been you wouldn't believe me —anyway it's a long story and other matters are more pressing."

"That's true." Kristina indicated he should continue.

"How many troops could be persuaded to help us?" Momentarily she studied him, considered, glanced at Alex and quickly back; then answered, "One third—maybe more; I'm not sure."

Ames looked at Alex. "Do you think it can be done?" The rebel leader did not speak, instead, looked at Kristina.

"We have to do it, Mr. Ames," she concluded calmly, yet very seriously.

Ames' attention was redirected by her words. "We will, but any military strategist knows throwing troops helter-skelter into a confrontation is a formula for disaster. We should take time and carefully devise a plan that's most advantageous."

"If we had the time —but we don't," she told him. "You see Mr. Ames, the others don't know where you've been for the last twenty-five years, but Alex and I do."

Ames was nervous. "What do you mean?"

"Because," Kristina replied, "Smith has your machine."

"My machine?" his words sank with his stomach.

"Your geodesic sphere."

Ames' eyes swept to Alex who nodded verifying her disclosure, then again to Kristina. He was worried, aware of the ramifications. "How near completion is it?"

"It's already complete," she told him. "They're going to test it the day after tomorrow."

He was silent, the gravity of their predicament penetrating with reality sinking in. "Jesus... it can't be," he whispered.

"What's wrong?" Evening asked, nudging him. He didn't answer, his concentration fixed on the fire as their dilemma turned in his mind. "What's wrong?" she asked again. "Why is your machine so important?"

"Because," he finally explained, "in the wrong hands, such as Smith's, events could be manipulated rearranging the course of history to suit his whims."

"How?"

"It's a time machine," he finally admitted.

"So?"

Turning, Ames faced her. "I'll give you an example. Lincoln and Kennedy were both assassinated by conspirators; but suppose someone traveled back through time, to the date of their murders, abducted one or the other of them, and returned them the day *after* they had been killed?"

"So they weren't assassinated, served their entire term?"

"Possibly —but even one extra day. What impact would the decisions they made, if even for one extra day, have on the rest of history?" Then changing the example, "What if someone killed Lincoln *before* he became President? Would there have been a Civil War, or not? Even an average person could change millions of future actions and interactions, because everything is relative— connected—to everything else. To change even one incident, no matter how minuscule, could be catastrophic."

"I don't understand," Evening said.

Ames presented another scenario. "What if your great-great grandfather were killed by someone from our time? Instead of him, someone else would have married the woman he did, your great-great grandmother. Consequently, their entire lineage would be altered: sons, daughters, grandchildren… all the way down the line—and zap—you'd be gone. You never would have existed. Someone else, someone entirely different would be in this time, *your space*, instead. And each of his or her actions would be different than what you have done. And not only would *they* be different, but the person who married your great-great grandmother originally would also have otherwise married someone else, so their genealogy would be altered as well. And the alterations would multiply with every subsequent generation affecting more people and events with each succeeding generation. The aberration would mushroom exponentially like a pyramid scheme or chain letter, until hundreds of billions of actions and interactions were altered."

"I understand now."

"We're just beginning," Ames told her. "Suppose, someone from our time —let's call him John Doe— who would be affected by the death of the great-great grandfather just as you would be, was the person who went back in time and was the one who killed him? The instant your great-great grandfather's death occurred John Doe would be gone; but he would otherwise have died a natural death in our time *if* the previous course of history were not disturbed. Instead, John Doe ceased to exist a hundred years before he ever lived. What would happen? How could it happen? How could he even have killed the ancestral grandfather? Could anything related to the incident ever have happened or would all history become a jumble of confusion and scrambled consequences?"

"There might be no world today," Evening proposed.

"Precisely, and *that*, in all probability, would be the least catastrophic consequence," he said. "The worst-case scenario could be beyond our imagination."

A camera lens, winding into focus, created the picture.

Evening asked, "What are we going to do?"

"We can't let Smith use the time machine," Ames told them. "No matter what, that *must* be prevented."

"But the only way to stop him is to destroy it," Kristina said apprehensively.

"True," Ames granted, "or steal it."

"How large is it?" Goliath inquired.

Kristina glanced at Ames, and together they answered, "Too big to steal."

Ames looked at Kristina and asked, "Where is it?"

"On Level Six, but I don't know yet which corridor. And strangely enough, all the techs who worked on it had to fly to Borneo on another project —and their jet didn't arrive." She added, "Went down over the ocean, conveniently."

He didn't respond.

"Could we get a team inside?" Goliath asked.

"Not possible," Kristina concluded almost without hesitation. "As far as I know General Smith and a captain named Thorne are the only two who ever go below Five. I don't know of any way without the entire Federation being aware too soon." Kristina turned to Ames. "Any ideas?"

"No," he said. "Level Six was designed with an extensive layer of special circuitry not incorporated into any other level. I would guess that was intended for security measures, most likely biometric scanners that can't be circumvented. Any unauthorized intrusion would be detected almost immediately and could be defeated in any number of ways once the violation was discovered. A commando team would, without question, be wiped out before they could even present a threat to Smith."

"Could a blackout do it?" Alex inquired. "We could shut down Butte —or the entire northwest grid if necessary. Would that take out the biometrics?"

"No, the Complex is shielded with more alternate routing and failsafe features than the Pacific Power System. Wouldn't work. Unless we could take out an integral link from inside, the Complex wouldn't have a glitch, the lights wouldn't even flicker. It's completely insulated from the outside."

"Sounds impossible," Evening commented.

Ames mused, "Not impossible, but very, very difficult. It's unfortunate we did such a good job with the design. I apologize for that." He scanned their small group with worry in his eyes.

"It's not your fault," Alex reassured, "you didn't know what was going to happen back then. No one knew."

"You're wrong," Ames answered. "Smith knew. This is what it's all been about since the very beginning. We were pawns, expendable pieces in a chess game for the world. Once the pieces were no longer needed each was eliminated without regard, be it an accident, or whatever." He looked at Kristina, and said frankly, "No loose ends."

She knew what he meant.

Each turned to the others, the silence of unspoken words echoing what each knew must be done.

"Then the time has come to conclude this business and hope the outcome is our victory," Alex decided. Ames, absorbed in concentration, said nothing. Goliath, David and Evening nodded. Kristina began to speak, changed her mind, and sighed; then looked into the flames, worried and uncertain. Others whispered mutual agreement.

Alex laced his fingers, made a fist, then spoke. "David, Goliath, pass the word; tomorrow night we attack the Federation Complex. We go for broke. Tell them it's everything or nothing and this battle could decide the fate of the world." The men rose from the circle and stepped away being quickly absorbed within the labyrinth of the subterranean passageways. Alex continued, "Kristina, go back to the Complex and tell those you know you can trust."

"All right." She rose, walked to the mouth of the corridor from which she had first appeared, then stopped, and looking back to the others, "Take care," she whispered. She turned and stepped out of sight.

Evening studied Ames' expression for a moment following his gaze into the darkness where Kristina had stood. She inquired, "What is it that's puzzling you?"

"Is it that obvious?" He blinked as he looked at her. She nodded. "Why is she willing to risk so much? Surely she must know that if even one of the Federation soldiers betrays her she'll be dead before we can lift a finger to help her."

"That's true," Evening agreed, "but she probably has more reason than anyone to want to destroy the Federation."

"Why?"

"It's up to Kristina to answer that," Evening replied. "Perhaps when it's time she'll tell you."

"Fair enough," he said to the petite woman beside him; then changing the subject he addressed Alex. "Why doesn't General Smith attack your forces? Surely he must know you're here."

"He does, but he won't attack us underground. There are hundreds of miles of passages comprising the mine works and sewers and we're too well prepared. We've invested a lot of time and effort modifying and interconnecting the entire system, and with a working familiarity of it one can evade an adversary down here indefinitely."

"The larger mine shafts form a horseshoe around the Complex as well as link us directly to the business district uptown. Some of the more notable historic buildings are used as surface exits, for example the old red-light district with the Dumas Hotel, Stockman's, and the steam tunnels; also the Finlen Hotel with the old stock exchange and the Acoma building over the Smokehouse mine. There are any number of exits: the old city hall and jail, the federal building, Hennessey Building, and the list goes on. It is actually a city beneath a city." He concluded wryly, "We do have running water down here, however electricity would be nice."

Ames smiled. "But haven't they ever tried to rout you out?"

"Yeah," Alex said, "Smith tried once —and he only tried once. For a hundred years Butte was famous for the worst hardrock mining disaster in history. On June 8th in 1917 the Granite Mountain and Speculator mines caught fire killing one hundred sixty-eight miners in that tragedy. There's a monument on the surface at the site. But with less notoriety, I guess we made it more famous. As I said before, we've modified the tunnel system somewhat and one feature we added was closure."

"Closure?"

"That's idiomatic," Alex grinned, "more commonly known as ammonium nitrate. All the tunnels are equipped with collapsing roofs, if requisite."

"The entire tunnel system?" impressed.

"Every linear foot. If necessary, we could blow up the city and everything else half way to Commerce Valley from down here." Alex explained, "A number of years ago Smith decided it was time to exterminate us. He tried gas, fire, and water; but we anticipated that long before they thought of it. The poison gas simply vented upward and a lot of surface dwellers became ill or died. They poured diesel fuel into all the sewer lines once and ignited it, but we simply used alternate routes until it burned itself out. That scheme backfired on him though because the grade runs toward the flats and a couple of exclusive subdivisions with some influential people's homes burned. Created quite a stir of political backlash he hadn't anticipated. And they tried to flood us out, but there isn't enough water in the entire state to overflow the web down here. They plugged the spillway exits and we blew them. They were persistent though, kept it up for two months before finally giving up."

Then, scratching his chin and smiling cynically he brought the narration to a conclusion. "Without a doubt, General Smith's most costly tactical error was when he sent troops down here to eliminate us. We lost sixteen miles of good tunnel system that day, but ten thousand Federation troops died. That, I guess, technically would qualify as the single most disastrous underground incident in history. It took almost three months to clear and rebuild the collapsed tunnels, but it gave us something to do —kept us busy anyway. We returned the deceased to him all in one night, piled the dead bodies in front of the Complex. Now *that*, was a night's work, but well worth the effort. Rumor has it they could hear Smith screaming all the way to Helena." He grinned, a wry grin.

"Since then, the Federation has just tolerated us. I suppose he could rationalize that we're not really enough of a threat to be bothered with anymore." Alex explained, more seriously now, "We literally kicked his ass, and Smith isn't one to forget something like that. He won't ever let it go."

Ames waited as Alex sat quietly without saying anything more. Evening pressed against him and he looked at her offering a smile. Alex finally spoke again, slowly, considering each word. "I meant it when I said it's everything or nothing. This battle will likely decide the fate of the world." And somberly, "We'd better get some sleep." He was tired... the struggle of life has a way of doing that.

* * *

Late that night...

...Ames was unable to rest. His subconscious would not let him go as he slept restlessly, fitfully, everything clouded in turmoil. He turned again in his slumber compressing the bed of straw to a firm mat; and his mind clicked involuntarily in animated images and sounds that manifest...

...*The Dream:*

A pioneer one-room schoolhouse with weathered steps to the front porch and a single window cut into each clapboard wall, painted white and chipped, faded by the ravages of time. It was a beautiful spring day and twelve children played outside at recess, the older children keeping a watchful eye on those younger than themselves as they frolicked laughing with the beauty and youth of spring and life.

Without warning the sun was blotted with ecliptic darkness, and its shadow and a cold wind swept into the valley and over the meadow, coming down from the surrounding mountains, whistling through the lodgepole pines as it moved. The play and laughter stopped, the sun gone now, the children waiting for something unknown.

Then a voice, as pure and loving as any he had ever known, spoke to him, recited for him, narrating, as if revealing the story beginning to unfold. She had studied the Legends very carefully, and with all his heart he loved her.

And Tian said…

And between the throne and the four living creatures and among the elders, I saw a Lamb standing, as though it had been slain, with seven horns and with seven eyes, which are the seven spirits of God sent out into all the earth; and he went and took the scroll from the right hand of him who was seated on the throne. (Rev. 5:6-7 RSV)

"Descended from heaven, a cloud floating lissome across the zenith of the sky… shifting, drifting, forming images. A vision.

In the center, standing alone and gazing down was a Being… disappointed, forlorn, crying for the circumstances of a world below. On His head, piercing His brow and cutting His flesh with pointed barbs was a crown of thorns; His life's blood trickled away. The Perfect Lamb.

And His creatures, the Four Winds positioned at the Corners of Eternity, within the visage cloud… were waiting, listening for a trumpet's note.

First, the Lion: born with the courage to arise with resolve when summoned, and to act without reservation, undertaking the task lying ahead. Second, the Ox: blessed with strength to persevere to its end, unfaltering and determined. The struggle of life interwoven with webs of deception and hardships, and a coalescence of confusion and uncertainty bonded closely within. Third, the Eagle: given freedom of choice, following the footpath of destiny along the solitary way to eternity, the leap to forever. Fourth, the Face of Man: gathered and huddled within cloistered halls, humanity being the recompense, dispersed with Wings or Fire."

Now I saw when the Lamb opened one of the seven seals, and I heard one of the four living creatures say, as with a voice of thunder, "Come!" And I saw, and behold, a white horse, and its rider had a bow; and a crown was given to him, and he went out conquering and to conquer (Rev. 6:1-2 RSV)

"From the peak of a mountain the specter of the white rider thundered down. The hooves of the hundred-foot-tall stallion crushing and uprooting trees as it cut a swath through them —full speed— descending toward the children at the schoolhouse. An unearthly voice heckled whisperings of vicious, deleterious falsehoods; the two faces of deceit, lies and mongering, causing the children to view one another with suspicion and mistrust. They did not understand, too young to comprehend the process of decay; they, being destined to be victimized and absorbed within the treachery and web of life, and trampled before the hooves."

When he opened the second seal, I heard the second living creature say, "Come!" And out came another horse, bright red; its rider was permitted to take peace from the earth, so that men should slay one another; and he was given a great sword. (Rev. 6:3-4 RSV)

"From the peak of a second mountain the specter of the red horse thundered down spewing blood from its nostrils, joining the first rider, descending upon the school and the children. The rider's sword gleamed and was dripping with blood —bound to destroy the world— take captive the small children and lock them away within a maze of darkness. The horse's massive hooves exploding from the Earth with destruction and fire obliterated the lodgepoles, blowing them away as fragmented pieces of a fragile existence. Propelled by greed and power the rider galloped from above, its flame leaving in the wake smoldering ruin and destruction and splintered, burning trees that had been green."

When he opened the third seal, I heard the third living creature say, "Come!" And I saw, and behold, a black horse, and its rider had a balance in his hand; (Rev. 6:5 RSV)

"From a third mountain peak the specter of the black horse and rider, a hundred feet tall, thundered forth joining the others, spreading hunger and famine as lodgepole, barren and dry, crumbled aside when it passed. The land was pummeled to dust —spreading drought with its wake— withered, fruitless and empty so nothing could grow, foreboding starvation. The pounding black steed's nostrils spewed sickness and despair to infest the world with malignant consumption. It dispersed lesions and bleeding sores that would not heal, blindness the scourge of sight, madness and degeneration of the mind gone awry, and invisible, infectious creatures that were absorbed amidst the roots causing disease from within. Three sides of the valley cut off now, only a single path of escape left, the children in the meadow stood terrified as the ghosts of the Apocalypse descended upon them."

When he opened the fourth seal, I heard the voice of the fourth living creature say, "Come!" And I saw, and behold, a pale horse, and its rider's name was Death, and Hades followed him; and they were given power over a fourth of the earth, to kill with sword and with famine and with pestilence and by wild beasts of the earth. (Rev. 6:7-8 RSV)

"From the fourth mountain peak the specter of the pale horse and death thundered forth, the schoolhouse now surrounded on all sides. The rider was devoid of emotion and life —a hollow skull without eyes— shrouded within the stench of pestilence and trailed by a cloak that reeked dismally of hopelessness. The intimidating steed galloped ashen and pale, the bloodless color of a corpse, accompanied with misery and pursued closely by treachery. Devastation and sorrow were ripped out by its hooves and flung through the lodgepole without compassion then scattered forth with rakish abandon. And the pale horse destroyed every living thing it touched on its way down the mountain leaving a path of withered destruction in its wake. Terrified, the children in the schoolyard were paralyzed, not knowing what to do."

When he opened the fifth seal, I saw under the altar the souls of those who had been slain for the word of God and for the witness they had borne; (Rev. 6:9 RSV)

"Inside the weathered clapboard schoolhouse the young teacher stood at the old wooden, pencil-marked desk... at the Juncture of Time and Decision.

Uncertain, the teacher did not comprehend the parable omen and signs manifest in the celestial illusion of tangible truth and born in the matrix of reality and dream...

The vision, a riddle, a piece of... *The Puzzle.*

...And shaking hands reached down picking up a tattered book. With trembling lips and quivering voice, the teacher began to read hoping the innocent children outside would hear... and understand."

When he opened the sixth seal, I looked, and behold, there was a great earthquake; and the sun became black as sackcloth, the full moon became like blood, and the stars of the sky fell to the earth as the fig tree sheds its winter fruit when shaken by a gale; the sky vanished like a scroll that is rolled up, and every mountain and island was removed from its place. (Rev. 6:12-14 RSV)

"The young teacher read and cried, sobbing as the words spilled out, but the children outside could not hear. The thundering hoofbeats of the four horsemen drowned out every other sound —and they swept upon the one-room schoolhouse with a deafening ghostly roar…"

When the Lamb opened the seventh seal, there was silence in heaven… *(Rev. 8:1 RSV)*

Then Tian's voice was gone…

…Another voice:

WHEN IT IS TIME, YOU SHALL KNOW.

Startled awake in a cold dripping sweat Ames lurched upright —gasping, panting— trying to catch his breath. His chest was being crushed by anxiety, an intense vice-like grip that wouldn't let go. Images were trapped in his head. Suffocating with fear and the pain inside, he tossed violently from side to side, then struggled to his feet, anything to escape the vacuum that surrounded him. He couldn't stand and fell back onto his bed of straw. Still trying to get free, but unable, he expelled a painful breath and waited. If it were time to die, so be it.

But death did not creep over him, instead, a long draw of breath filled his chest, and he relaxed with the subsiding pain. He lay still, blinking in the dark, wondering what had just happened. All around him was darkness. Finally, he began to think clearly again, and tears filled his eyes as the constant, nagging emptiness returned when her vision filled his mind… *Tian.*

* * *

In a world of perpetual shadows and dingy gray light…

…And the hope of a possible future. The small fire had burned out hours ago leaving only the full moon to cast light from outside, a diminutive shaft of illumination peering in through the peephole, no more than a faint circular shimmer of moonglow on the floor. Ames sat upright, eyes searching the darkened quarters, his muscles and joints aching with stress. He knew somehow he must get outside for a while, get away from the walls and passages that seemed to close in on him with relentless silence born of the earth around him.

Carefully he stepped to the fire circle, fumbled around and gathered a few sticks, then struck a match tendering it gently as the twigs ignited. The fire felt reassuring as it struggled to life, but not enough; he needed freedom to breathe fresh air again, just for a little while. He picked up one of the kerosene lanterns and lit the wick.

"Where are you going, Mister?" the child asked, still clutching her precious, tattered Bible.

His eyes fixed on her innocence, curled on the floor near the dancing flames and Ames replied, "Just for a walk, Sweetie, not too far. What are you doing awake?"

"I couldn't sleep."

"Me too." The tone of his voice expressed a love not easily put to words, but always understood by the simple comprehension of small children and usually lost on the journey of growing up. "You go back to sleep."

"Okay," her simple reply, and she smiled and rolled over to warm her other side with the fire.

"I'll go with you," Evening volunteered. Ames began to say no, then hesitated and nodded. She accepted his extended hand and they left the room.

Wandering through the tunnels they walked leisurely, the passageway they followed occasionally intersecting with others at junctions near headframes or routes leading to one of the uptown landmark buildings. Even underground there was a marked difference between night and day, less vibration and sound from the city above so early in the predawn hours. The silence of their thoughts kept them company until Ames finally spoke.

"I want to go to the surface."

Obviously concerned, Evening quickly replied, "It's too dangerous."

"Does that really matter anymore?"

They continued walking.

"No," she finally answered, "I suppose not. There's a place along the North Ridge, near the edge of the city, where we can go. It's not too much farther."

"Too much farther?"

Evening smiled, but in the darkness the only indication was a change in the tone of her voice. "I guess I wanted to go too, and get away from these tunnels. We've been walking in that direction almost since we started."

A few minutes later the tunnel ended with a barred entrance and a concrete spillway directing the effluent to a creek below. It would be a while until sunrise and was still dark outside. Just the full moon, and a few waning stars. Evening grasped the rusted iron bar closest to the left wall of the sewer corridor and carefully lifted it from the hole in the concrete structure. The bars were loose and the concrete they were set in was old and deteriorated, weathered with cracks. She moved the bar over and slid outside. Ames snuffed the lantern, put it on the floor, and after he followed, she replaced the bar in its proper position, lowering it back into the hole.

"The Federation guards make periodic inspections of all tunnel openings," she explained. "Don't want them to get suspicious." Leaving the sewage spillway they walked up the steep embankment then a short distance down the other side to a nearby Douglas fir, the chokecherry and fescue grass concealing their silhouettes as they sat down beneath it.

From their position on the high ridge, the Military Complex sprawled directly in front and below them: an evil, circular behemoth of concrete, steel and tinted plate glass. Past the Complex the city spread out onto the flats, thousands of homes with families blissfully unaware, most choosing to remain in that dormant state of denial. Beyond the flats the Continental Divide rose creating a majestic backdrop of rugged timbered mountains cloaked with lodgepole pine, Douglas fir and sprinklings of aspen following the draws as they reached for the mountain peaks.

To their left the East Ridge and Exell Heights blinked with transmission towers and glowed with the pristine, illuminated ninety-foot statue of 'Our Lady of the Rockies.' She quietly waited, watching over her valley, never uttering a sound. To their right lay 'Timber Butte' with more homes etched into the rolling hills, almost to the top: more people not wanting to know. Beyond 'Timber Butte' the valley basin continued on toward Anaconda and Commerce Valley with hundreds of high technology industries and computer related corporations. It reached out as far as the eye could see: southwest Montana's panacea when her mining industry went into decline.

Through clear night air the city lights twinkled with atmospheric distortion like embers of a dying campfire. All the streets were clearly defined by sodium vapor lights ribboned over the landscape and shimmering with deceiving quiet. The tranquility mesmerized them; both knowing it was only superficial, concealing the invisible turmoil churning within its shroud. Yet they wished it were not so.

It did not seem reasonable to Ames and Evening that all the memories might soon be erased forever as her inhabitants destroyed one another in senseless slaughter. Theirs was a world of strange circumstances and impossibly twisted webs wound in a tangled maze like some dormant tentacled monster soon to be aroused to do battle. To them there was no other course to follow, both sides armed with the conviction that their cause was just. And that conviction, now as always, would result in more bloodshed... only this time, neither side could appreciate or predict its magnitude.

"The night air smells so fresh I can almost taste it," Evening commented. Ames acknowledged, but said nothing. Noticing his grin she asked, "What's that for?"

"Nothing really," he answered. "De'ja vu. It just seems as though I've done this before, and your statement is more accurate than you probably realize."

"How?"

"The olfactory lobes and sense of smell controls the sense of taste. Without the sense of smell most things would be bland and tasteless."

"Are you serious?" she replied incredulously.

Scratching his nose: "Completely."

"Well, it becomes you," she said.

"What?"

"The smile, you're always so serious." Tipping her head coyly, "It's nice to know you haven't forgotten how to smile."

Studying the expanse of city beyond their perch, "I haven't forgotten," he replied after a moment, "but perhaps tomorrow night we will all forget. No one left to remember."

"And perhaps not." He seemed to ignore her. "Did you hear me?" she asked somewhat annoyed with his detached attitude.

"Yes," he said gathering his legs and putting his chin on his knees. There was a long period of silence while they gazed down upon the city, its streetlights glittering through the thin atmosphere.

"Do you think I'm pretty?"

Caught by surprise with her candor, he turned, studying her. The innocence he saw made him wonder and she became restless, fidgeting when he didn't answer. The wind wisped her auburn hair across her face catching it on her lips. She pulled it back with delicate fingers and the movement of her arm exposed erect nipples, drawn firm by the cool breeze through her shirt. Everything about her expressed femininity: her beauty, breasts, slim waist, firm buttocks and the smooth contour of her legs.

"Well, do you?"

His concentration interrupted: "What?"

"Think I'm pretty?"

"Yes."

She cautioned, almost in a whisper, "Do you want to sleep with me?"

Calmly, "You're very beautiful, entirely sensuous, and expressly sensitive..." he answered.

"—Please don't be evasive. Answer my question."

"I can't."

"Why don't you want to sleep with me?"

"It's not a question of wanting to," he began to explain.

"But you won't."

"No."

Disappointment traced in her expression and words: "Why—what's wrong with me?"

"Don't think that," he instantly corrected, then explained gently, "there's nothing wrong with you. There's just no point in it, and it would be wrong."

"Why?"

"It would just be a physical act without meaning. Love is something elusive; and even more than that, something very precious. It's wrong to reduce it to a simple animal function like a couple of dogs."

"But what I feel for you isn't dirty or disgusting," she insisted. "You make me feel warm and safe. It could be love if you'd give me the chance. And we could share it together."

Ames gently brushed her hair back with his hand. "I'm very flattered and touched, and what you say may be true, but you're still just a young girl and there isn't time for what you want."

"I'm not a young girl, I'm twenty," she defended. "I'm a woman with a woman's feelings and desires. I'm not ashamed of it."

"And you shouldn't be," he agreed, "but it would still be wrong."

"You love someone else, don't you?"

Surprised by her perception, raising an eyebrow subtly, "Yes," he answered.

"What is her name?"

"Why do you want to know?"

"I just do."

He watched the sparkle in her eyes until she blinked and started to repeat the question. "Tian," he said. He sighed; then told her, "It only happens once in a lifetime."

"Is she older and more mature than I am?"

He couldn't restrain the smile and responded, "Why is it, that somehow I knew you were going to ask that." Evening said nothing, waiting. "I suppose she isn't any older, or any more mature than you. She won't even be born until fifteen billion years."

"That doesn't make any sense."

"I didn't suppose it would," he said. Then he explained, "While I was gone, I was in the future; and Tian is there —or will be some day." His thoughts drifting to a far distant time, he continued, "Time hasn't turned enough of her proverbial pages yet, but she will. And Tian and the Renoloi will have to go through the pain and suffering all over again." He paused. "I wonder if that's what life is really all about, a repetitious sequence of events by trial and error until we finally do things right, if we ever can."

"As you said earlier, it's a learning process," Evening reminded; then added, "a learning process that never ends. And when it's all added together, we each have a collection of memories, and memories are like starlight... they go on forever." She sighed thoughtfully, her gaze drawn to the sky.

Ames smiled. "Eloquently said."

"I didn't make it up; it's from a song, 'Aurora Borealis'," she told him, lying down in the grass, staring at the sky.

Ames looked back over the city, the shimmering lights fading to a soft blur as his thoughts slipped from the Renoloi, to Tian, and finally to Reed, his friend. Everything shuffled together like still frames combined to form a motion picture, all seeming to be a dream, but being only too real.

The images were very clear, his senses acutely alive. The pungent taste of burning flesh of women on three crosses. The hellish, choking heat of the meteor shower. The soothing odor of Tian's body lying next to him. The horrifying screams and cries, the sounds of death during the battle with the Trogs. And the incredible, blinding light of a mountain exploding around him.

So many irreversible, real things had come to pass. Given a second chance, how many would he change; or were all those events part of his learning process, each with its purpose, and a lesson. *How many miracles?* he wondered, and what harm in just one more, *to be with Tian and Reed again.*

As soon as the thought came to him, he dismissed it as ludicrous. The time for miracles had long since passed. The transpiration of leprechauns, dragons, Peter Pan, Bigfoot, the Loch Ness Monster, the

Wizard of Oz and an endless array of comic book superheroes had arrived through the growing pains of adolescence. All were sealed away now, secluded in a reality born from growing older. Reality and fantasy being separate and distinct entities could never again share dormitory. It was time to put fantasy away and focus upon reality, to face it with courage. But despite all that, he could not help wishing... *just one, final, small miracle.*

"Are you all right?" Evening asked, nudging him gently. She brought him back from the solitude of his stupor.

"Yes," he mumbled, "I'm fine." He looked at her, still lying beside him; told her, "I was just thinking."

She nodded. "I was wondering... about Old Sam," she began.

Abruptly, "He must be down there somewhere," Ames commented indicating the city.

"How long were you in the Complex prison together?" she asked.

"I'm not sure, a few months maybe. Long enough to know one another, to trust each other," he answered, "but in days or months, I don't really know." He smiled. "Old Sam probably does though; he was pretty good at keeping track of things like that." Grinding his whiskered chin against his knees Ames turned back toward the city.

Nervously, uncertain, Evening scooted next to him. "Mr. Ames, did Old Sam tell you about his past... about his wife taking his children away and all that?"

"Yes, he told me about it."

"Did he tell you anything more?"

"If you mean about being imprisoned for fifteen years by the Federation —yes, he told me."

"Well, that part wasn't exactly accurate," she said obviously tensed. Raising his head from his knees, attentive, Ames looked at her. "You must understand, the Federation has constantly tried to undermine our security with infiltrators over the years. As a precaution we routinely do thorough background checks and records and data searches on everyone," she explained. "The Alliance isn't as primitive as the Federation is led to believe; and our intelligence has provided adequate protection. It has kept us alive. You can appreciate that, can't you?"

"Of course," waiting for her to continue.

"You and Old Sam both glitched the system. You, because no one knew where you'd been for twenty-five years obviously; but Old Sam was different."

"Different, how?"

Hesitant: "Well, we know where he's been." She paused.

"Just tell me what you have to say, Evening."

She took a deep breath. "Old Sam was perhaps one of the very first freedom fighters. He believed in what this country used to be, in what the Federation has been trying to destroy since its inception. Even before the Alliance came to be, Old Sam was an icon for his compatriots and resisted every effort of the Federation —for over five years— until he was finally captured." She paused again, then disclosed, "Mr. Ames, without either you or Old Sam being aware we verified both your identities: dental, fingerprints, retinal scans, photographic records —thoroughly researched you both— databases and everything." She asked anxiously, "Are you offended by all of this?"

Ames thought before answering, "No. I can understand that it was a necessary precaution." He knew she had something else to tell him and prodded, "What is it, Evening; what haven't you told me?"

She put her hand on his knee. "We positively know Old Sam escaped the prison with you, but there's one thing that creates a problem for us... for me."

"What?"

Carefully, gently, she revealed, "Just to be certain, we also did x-ray and CAT scans of a grave in the Mountain View Cemetery out on Harrison Avenue —for anatomical and dental comparison. Old Sam's real name was Samuel Reed."

"Was?" Ames asked nervously.

"Yes," she hesitated, then told him. "The thing is...

Old Sam was killed by General Smith.

He died twenty years ago."

Ames muttered, "...the eyes."

CHAPTER TWENTY

As the sun rose...

...They sat together on the North Ridge.

"Mr. Ames..." she brought him back from his thoughts.

"Yes?"

"Look at the sky," Evening said, the faint glow of the morning's sun crawling toward the eastern horizon detailing peaks of the Continental Divide.

Preoccupied: "Cloudy, will probably rain today."

"No, there aren't any clouds. It just doesn't look right." Ames looked again and she asked, "What does it mean?"

"I'm not sure," he whispered, his voice trailing off, watching as the sun crawled toward the horizon.

Worry etching her with its razor edge, sensing in his expression something was seriously wrong; again: "What does it mean?" There was no reply.

Ever so slowly, the moon moving in front of the sun…

An eerie sensation,

They waited. They watched.

As the sun inched to the horizon the full moon converged with it… eclipsed it. The moon, darker than the hue of blood, blotted out the sun creating a red corona, a circular specter of eerie flaming light that bathed the world in red-violet ecliptic darkness. Streetlights in the city turned back on. The morning birds remained silent, not welcoming the coming day.

Uneasy, Ames recited: *"When he opened the sixth seal, I looked, and behold, there was a great earthquake; and the sun became black as sackcloth, the full moon became like blood..." (Rev. 6:12 RSV)*

Portending malice, vapid silence hovered closer, all around them now, that unexplainable calm that precedes the storm causing flesh to tingle. The eclipse did not pass. It remained.

"It can't be," he muttered at last, the pain and sadness within him welling forth with his words. "God help us." Evening did not understand, her attention distracted by a sudden distant rumble, the ground beneath them gently trembling with the reverberation.

Then again, everything was quiet. Too quiet.

"Another one," she said, "not more than a three or four, a hundred miles or so to its epicenter —south-south-west." Earthquakes were common and she was familiar with seismic activity, tremors almost routine.

"No," Ames told her. She looked at him but said nothing; she felt it. She couldn't speak. That unexplainable sixth sense... subconscious awareness prevented it.

Then It Began.

Almost imperceptibly at first, but progressively more noticeable, hissing became audible steadily increasing toward the insipid drone of honeybees working a hive. Again the faraway rumblings, intermittently at first, then again, more frequently, and again, as methodical as bass drums. Distant fire accompanied the sound with flashes like heat lightning glowing ocher and saffron skirting the horizon, until suddenly the Military Complex screamed to life beckoning the wail of air raid sirens, an unearthly, ominous keening whine.

Unexpectedly the ground trembled and surged sending ever-increasing shockwaves under them, louder now. And without warning the mountains surrounding the city quavered shifting with an ear-splitting shatter releasing massive rockslides that avalanched toward the valley below crushing everything lying in their path. Splitting apart in vaulting shearwaves of powerful subterranean force, rock fractured and slid crashing with the grumbling roar of destruction, uprooting and splintering timber then pushing it violently down the slopes onto houses on the mountainsides smothering them with obliterating suffocation. Absorbed within the deluge, only fragmented pieces remained of what had once been life and home; and with the cracking detonations of avalanching granite every living thing in the path of the slides was destroyed.

Overhead the hissing increased to festering screeches and an invasive scream, the sickening sound of missiles filling their ears. There were hundreds of them, a black migration of geese saturating the sky, dark formations, each programmed and coursing on toward a chosen, final destination.

The specter of the eclipsed sun and blood-red moon just cleared the horizon…

And it happened.

…Two missiles exploded as gargantuan fireballs above the tense, terrified city —blinding mushroom-flashes in the sky— the hue of pale crimson, amber and glittering death swept in boils of holocaust and fire raining lethal neutron radiation in their winds. The warheads were vaporized in the blasts splashing an overcast of hellish fallout emission like sparkling flames that snowflaked earthbound burning everything organic below the scope of the amber clouds.

Shrubbery and trees withered and died within an instant —then boiled in fire. Vagrant cats, dogs and rats moaned and howled with excruciating pain, burning and dissolving from the inside out. The intense heat melted tires of vehicles and powerline insulation. Asphalt rooftops and lawns burst into flames.

All within seconds.

With disbelief Evening and Ames watched the neutron clouds from the ridge, a deadly pink-orange expanding mist veiling and settling over the city before their eyes. Everywhere trees exploded as withered arms of burning debris, too many to count, detonations of firestorm that swept through city parks and back yards. Brick, steel and concrete structures seemed to glow from the intense heat of the fires while throughout the city electrical transformers short-circuited and street lamps and neon signs popped and sizzled with power lines flaring flashburn and bright arcs of white fire. Overwhelmed by the brilliance of the neutron explosions and fatal radiation, the entire city was swallowed.

Early morning commuters, police, firefighters and newspaper carriers died almost instantly as their bodies cooked, boiled and burst in bubbling masses. All-night gas stations erupted in fireballs when their underground tanks of fossil fuels ruptured sending gas pumps rocketing airborne and terrified attendants into the open to parboil and burn. People nestled snugly in their homes, still asleep in bed would never realize what happened, cooking and exploding under blankets and quilts instantly saturated with blood and steaming with the stench of death.

Thousands of people died in those few brief seconds.

From the distant mountainside they witnessed the carnage and destruction, eyes fixed and minds recording each own's interpretation of the same event. The scream of nuclear missiles in the sky continued, by now an ignoble cacophony —and the formations appeared endless. Swarms of dark locusts in flight.

An unworldly keening howl, air raid sirens continued to wail; and from within the Military Center an unknown hand blacked out the city. A moment more, and through the eerily glowing, death-like darkness came the hollow foreboding echo of silo gates rumbling, opening for the Federation's forthwith retaliation. Finally, six clangs resounded in unison as each gate locked in standby position

Then sudden flames.

Pulsing winds of fire all six silos glowed and fumed with fountainhead plumes of white flame spewing furiously skyward. And slowly, the missiles rose from the launch pads secreted in the depths below. Encompassed in flames, rising from the silos… but the methodical military too late.

As the first missile emerged bound for its target, a pair of whistling nuclear-armed rockets swooped from the surreal twilight-darkness slamming into the Federation Complex. That instant —an incredible splash of white light, melting fire and ground-flattening flash of pyrotechnic eruption— and the structure disintegrated in the explosions.

Ground rattling, the atmosphere shook.

Billions of shredding fragments ripped apart, dissolved, then rose with the climbing fireballs. All six Federation missiles enveloped within the heat and flame detonated in a hellish series of extraordinary explosions that pounded the ground and flashed fire in a wind illuminating the countryside with blinding intensity brighter than the sun.

Ames and Evening instinctively —involuntarily— shielded their eyes from the apocalyptic white-flash of the incredible explosions. With freight train collision of rushing effect, the expanding blast front sprayed through the surrounding city smashing, incinerating, crushing and obliterating everything in its path. Flashing out, the blast front's shockwave rose and poured, towering and growling, melting everything it touched, all of it being incinerated and absorbed in a searing flux of death —roarwinds— a circular firestorm of leaping, boiling flames.

Buildings were torn apart, sucked into the roiling destruction of the shockwave, then were shattered and spewed forth as it enveloped them. Nothing would remain but jutting pieces and debris. Already burning, trees leaned into the explosion as it approached, fiery limbs and leaves instantly snuffed from the lack of oxygen the nuclear vacuum created; and sucked out by the roots they leapt from the ground into the boiling firewall and were disintegrated —vaporized. Vehicles were hurtled helter-skelter as masses of molten fiery plastic and metal —full-sized matchbox cars of liquefied blob— within an instant of fifty thousand-degree-heat. Billboards and highway signs leaned into the boiling conflagration then instantly disappeared. Silver Bow Creek whooshed into the rolling fireball with whitecapped fury, the water instantaneously vaporizing as choking steam — atomizing— broken apart to oxygen and hydrogen. Bridges heaved and crumbled and were swallowed just as everything else had been.

The blast front's destruction was complete.

Spawn of the dark, a mushroom cloud grew from the corpse of the Military Complex while blast pulse seared in winds of fire and death. The rolling shockwave pushed the fireball forward, an ever-expanding circle consuming and dissolving everything standing in its way.

Below, in the valley, the embodiment of Hell had arrived.

When Evening and Ames managed to uncover their eyes, the city was gone, the mushroom cloud still climbed skyward, a molten city burning within its core, and the expanding apocalyptic fireball still speeding across the valley basin rushing toward the surrounding hills. Hot dry wind preceding the shockwave blew in their faces.

"Oh God," Ames stammered.

"It's burning up..." Evening gasped in disbelief "...all gone."

Then realization, and blinking he focused upon the approaching blast front with its boiling wall of flames. "It's not going to stop." Ames grabbed Evening's arm. "Get to the sewer or we'll be incinerated —Run!"

They ran, stumbled, fell, got up and ran again with blind panic. For every ten feet they could move the shockwave streaked a hundred and precious few seconds remained until it would overtake them.

It was coming...

A thundering wind of flashburn and racing firestorm

...An inferno, it roared!

Evening couldn't keep up with Ames' fear-propelled stride and she fell being dragged by the arm until awareness could stop him. Swiftly snatching her to her feet he saw the bruises and cuts spitting blood where brush and rock had sliced her legs, but the amenities of apology would have to wait —there was no time.

The whirling wall of searing fire rushed the mountainside climbing toward them with blinding speed devouring everything it touched. Chokecherry, fescue grass, scrub pine, mountain mahogany and sagebrush were ripped from the ground —into the bowels of tornado flames. Intensifying, a deafening roar and crackling incineration it killed deer and elk as it blotted out cries of gophers, jackrabbits, coyotes, birds and other wildlife consumed by its hellish heat. All living tissue instantly vaporized, granite melted, nothing withstood the awesome fury.

"Run—" he yelled, "we're almost there." Incredible heat was saturating the ground —then a temperature thrust of subterranean shearwave, trembling earth heaving beneath them.

"I can't. Save yourself—" she screamed.

A fleeting glimpse back at the roiling hundred-foot wall of flashover flames, and with adrenaline-surge powering every muscle he yanked her to her feet catching her like a doll. As he ran the brush shredded his worn jeans and cut his legs, rock and cactus slicing into his bare feet —but there wasn't time for pain— run and survive was his brain's solitary, unyielding message. And he kept going —onto the top, a leaping stride, and over— pushing dirt with his heels, sliding and falling down the embankment they scrambled to the barred sewage spillway only seconds before the horrendous flames would arrive.

Liquid fire crested the hill, whirling clouds overhead. Vaporous flame was everywhere, chasing after them, coming for them, down the embankment toward them.

Unaware himself, an involuntary action, Ames seized the rusted bar and with terror-induced strength ripping it from the crumbling concrete structure. In the same motion, his hand opening —let go— hurtling it behind him.

The safety of the protective sewer was his only focus and he managed three frantic steps then one final leap throwing himself and Evening onto the sand-covered floor. Going down —falling— his mind watched as the shutter clicked, seeing the iron bar still airborne outside. Then it was gone —melting— yellow-white flames swallowing it, dissolving iron ice. The image lasted only an instant that seemed like forever, but as he landed on the tunnel floor he was aware that he and Evening were lying face down. *Safe—cover your eyes,* flashed scrambled waves through his head. Wrapping an arm over his face the realization of true human frailty struck home —and he understood what Hell must be like.

The *flash*...

—Yellow-white fire was there

—*Everywhere!*

...Hellfire cascading just above them as a fluid blur of melting inferno with scalding wind for its breath. The cobblestone roof and tunnel walls crumbled and heaved, horrific winds and tongues of roaring flame billowing along the concave ceiling, whisking down its throat.

"Hold your breath!" he screamed.

Windstorm. And with a desiccative burst superheated air flooded over them instantly drying perspiration and singeing their hair. Their clothing smoldered, swept by wild-blow and charred by the tremendous heat. Wind screamed snatching sand and crumbled rock with smelter ferocity, the sandblast-effect of debris gleaning the cobblestone to the luster of polished fire agate. Their skin reddened beneath the fire and fury streaking inches above them in a lemon-white death of liquefied winds.

Then for the briefest instant everything stopped hovering with the still calm of pause. The fire-breathing dragon inhaling a breath.

Outside:

Frothing, hellish flames and blast pulse raged past the sewer spillway and leaped over the other side of the embankment, tongues of instant fiery death racing one another toward the river. Behind the leading edge of the shockwave whirling clouds of blazing fire boiled and rolled with surreal liquid flow and complete silence.

And again, sudden violent wind:

Within the corridor the vacuum created by the holocaust outside inhaled the interior with hurricane force. Hovering debris, flame and smoke instantly roared toward the mouth of the spillway returning to the inferno that spawned it. Sand rained comet trails toward the opening, scraps of burning wood flying overhead skipping spirals of speed, bouncing off walls, knocking cobblestone loose and creating a shower of miniature asteroids. Flames and smoke fumed a vanishing —*whoosh*— leaving in a blue-white, swirling vaporous draft.

Beneath the rushing cloud of debris wind tunnel gale dragged Ames and Evening along the floor, scratching and clawing for their lives, fingers scraping the concrete with a screaming vile suction pulling them toward certain death waiting just outside. Ames' fingers slid over a crack and pried into it, but Evening, still being drawn out by the incredible wind, was helpless, now only a few feet from the inferno anticipating, expecting her.

Desperate, Ames reached for the woman, their fingers barely inches apart, but couldn't reach her, the gap widening as she continued to slide along the floor, her eyes wide with terror and pleading for help. Still clutching the crack in the floor and a rushing storm of noise pounding inside his head, he rolled over and swung his leg upon her back as the blasting sand particles began shredding his tattered Levis, furrowing into his leg. With unrelenting savagery his skin was cut, peeled and whisked away spitting blood from raw wounds of crimson lines that trailed toward his foot then flicked into oblivion.

Rolling over, Evening seized his leg as she slid beneath it, her frantic fingers digging into his raw flesh. Flinching, Ames clenched his teeth to smother the scream and held his breath, resolved, despite the intense pain he would not let her die. Evening, lying on her back, stared helplessly as the cloud of sand streaked past as a glittery blur only inches above her face. Scraped raw and bleeding, her hands were numbed by the abrasive force of ripping sand particles, blood lines trickling toward her elbows designing bright red droplets blown away with the gale. And the roar continued. Too terrified to let go, she closed her eyes, afraid even to breathe.

Outside:

A tremendous explosion —then more crackling explosions.

And finally, the horrifying few moments were over as the wind subsided diminishing to a strong breeze heavy with the pungent odor of burnt hair and blood. The fireball had reached the river at the foot of the ravine beyond the embankment. There, the incredible heat vaporized the water in rattling blasts of shattering steam leaving only the parched riverbed intact. But the explosions of superheated water succeeded in counteracting the wall of flames climaxing in tremendous eruptions of river gravel sucked up with the vapor-detonations and blown with such force the stones punched holes through burnt trees with blistering boils of spewed steam.

The sewer floor:

Verging on hysteria, Evening was too petrified to move and lay trembling and rigid still gripping Ames' leg. "It's past," he muttered. There was no response. "It's over. Please, let go of my leg." The painful awareness of his injuries settled in now that the priority of survival had subsided. Frozen with fear and still shaking she couldn't hear him. "Evening," sitting up, he leaned over her, "it's over; please... let go." Taking hold of her rigid fingers he pried them from his leg and she opened her eyes seeing the blood on her hands.

"I'm sorry," she weakly apologized, "I didn't mean—I'm so sorry."

Carefully lifting his leg: "Doesn't hurt that much." But the pain detailed on his face betrayed him.

Still trembling, Evening quietly stood and helped him up; then realizing the severity of his injury, "Oh, Mr. Ames, you're bleeding badly." She began to kneel but he stopped her placing a raw hand on her shoulder.

"No, there isn't time; it'll be all right. We have to get back."

A loud rumble:

And the ceiling cracked then split pouring black, dumping dirt and loose cobblestone on them as the corridor trembled violently throwing them both to the floor again. Groping helplessly like pebbles in a lapidary tumbler they were bounced and thrown about for a minute or more.

Vibrating across the floor, "Seven or eight," Evening yelled, her words almost drowned out by the noise.

"What?"

"Earthquake—seven or eight."

His expression conveyed fear and, *no kidding*, and as they fumbled about for another moment he chattered, "Let's get out of here." The corridor that saved them from the flames only a moment before now threatened to collapse on them finishing the task itself. Fumbling, Ames crawled toward the spillway opening, but Evening stopped him grabbing his foot. "*Damn*— not the foot!" he screamed, halted instantly by the ripping pain.

"—Oh shit, sorry." She let go. "We can't go that way."

Bouncing and rattled, stones loosening and falling from the ceiling.

Already knowing the radiation outside was most certainly lethal, at the top of his lungs: "Through the sewer?" He looked at the spillway opening only a short distance away —outside— teeming with radiation glow, then peered down the tunnel to smoldering gloom and danger lying in wait in the darkness beyond. Either way would probably kill them. Looking back at the sewer spillway, "Shoulda' known it couldn't be that easy —well fuckit."

The tremors stopped.

"Let's go," she demanded.

They seized the opportunity, running the tunnel toward the rebel headquarters, Ames limping along as quickly as he could. The floor was no longer a comfortable foot trail, now littered with cobblestone debris, bits of wood, dirt and chunks of rock, bruising their feet as they went. Running when possible, scrambling over collapsed earthen mounds on hands and knees or crawling on their bellies when they had to, Evening never slackened her pace, and Ames fighting the pain, tried to keep up.

"What's your hurry?" he gasped pressing an arm against his bandaged ribs when he finally had to stop to catch his breath.

She paused only briefly. "Aftershocks." He already knew what her answer would be and they continued as quickly as possible; but their progress was constantly hindered by obstacles and litter discarded with nature's furious counteraction to the tremors triggered by the nuclear blasts.

At one point an earthen slide formed a dam that stopped the flow of effluent flooding the corridor. They crawled onto the slide squeezing between the debris mound and ceiling, then scrambled into the water ponding on the other side. Despite its pungent odor the stagnant water felt good, washing away blood and dirt and puckering their wounds. They continued doggedly, half-swimming, half-bobbing in the chest-deep channel.

"Just a little farther," Evening encouraged spitting out a mouthful of infectious water, "and the corridor will ascend an incline and level off at the main junction."

Following closely behind her, "If the others are still there."

"Think positive. Where else would they be?" and darting a glance over her shoulder. "Where would they go?"

Ames: "Ain't that the truth."

The corridor suddenly trembled and the walls began collapsing around them churning the water to boil and froth, dumping rock and sheets of collapsing silt. Splitting apart the ceiling partially collapsed as Evening and Ames grabbed one another, sucked in a breath, and dove below the surface.

With tons coming down, the cushion of water buffered the avalanche that buried them pinning both under a viscous mound of sludge on the floor of the tunnel. They were absorbed in silty muck with falling rocks issuing murky trails and turbid clouds of mud-swirl. Darkness. They couldn't see in that distorted world of dark-underwater sounds and the boil of rushing bubbles. Panic. Desperately flailing and kicking in the dark they dug themselves out, and rising amid brown jellyfish bubbles they surfaced again gasping for air, revealing fresh cuts and bruises, but both miraculously still alive.

The aftershock opened a jagged breach to the surface and a blood-red sky that peered in with narrow dragon-like eyes. The water level dropped as it swept past the broken dam flushing mud toward the spillway and dried riverbed, then washed to somewhere farther on. Fighting the rush of water, they pushed their way through the current to the incline then climbed and ran quickly to the Kelley junction.

Alex's voice from the darkness: "Evening, Mr. Ames, we'd given you up for dead." Sobbing for breath Evening couldn't speak and slumped to the floor to rest.

Leaning over and clasping his knees in his hands Ames managed to answer, "Yeah, so did we."

"China has attacked the Federation with an army of two hundred-million," Alex told them.

A side-glance, hands still braced on his knees, Ames looked him in the eye and asked, "On the Plain of Jezreel?"

Alex seemed puzzled. "Yes, how did you know? We only intercepted the transmission two minutes ago."

Eyes trailing back to the floor, "No…" Ames murmured shaking his head as he turned.

Alex began to explain what they knew so far. "The attack was initiated by China, an all-out nuclear assault as near as we can decipher. We believe they've launched more than seven thousand missiles so far —almost their entire arsenal. Most of Europe went down with the first assault. We were next, then the Middle East. At this point it appears entire continents were annihilated. The whole world's on fire. The Federation retaliated with what they had left, but they must have seriously underestimated Asia's capabilities. There apparently wasn't a whole helluva' lot for the counterstrike." No one spoke, so he went on.

"China moved its ground forces west toward the Middle East, two hundred-million strong, not including logistics and support troops. According to intelligence reports they used nuclear weapons as suppression fire, cut a five hundred-mile-swath across India, Pakistan, Afghanistan, Iran, Iraq, Syria, Saudi Arabia and Jordan —to Israel. Rumor has it so much nuclear firepower was expended in Iraq that the Euphrates River was vaporized by the blasts. Imagine, an entire river completely dried up." Alex stopped again.

Whispered words: *"The sixth angel poured his bowl on the great river Euphrates, and its water was dried up, to prepare the way for the kings from the east." (Rev. 16:12 RSV)* Ames faced the man. "And the Federation engaged them at Megiddo."

"Yes," Alex answered, "how did you know?" Ames said nothing, stood silently considering what he had just been told. "What's going on up there?" Alex insisted. Saddened, John Ames muttered under his breath. "What?"

"World War III," Ames answered. Then he looked at each of them, and told them, "Armageddon... the end of the world."

Complete silence, asystole of sound.

No one spoke, until, "We've got to stop Smith," Ames finally said. "No matter what, we can't let him use the geodesic sphere."

Evening asked, "How do we do that?"

Frustrated Ames answered, "I don't know." Worried, still deliberating... "I don't know if we can, but we've got to try," ...and at last, understanding, "I've got to try."

"You've got to try?" Alex repeated.

A deep breath: "That's what this has all been about, only I didn't realize it until now. It's up to me to stop Smith."

"We can't attack, we're not ready," Goliath told him. "We have to wait until tomorrow. It would be a slaughter."

Ames looked at him, the gravity of his words expressed in his eyes, "It doesn't matter anymore. We're all going to die anyway. Whether by bullets, radiation poisoning, nuclear winter—whatever— there isn't going to be a tomorrow."

Silence. Then...

"He's right," Alex agreed. "Break radio silence. Tell the others." With that, Goliath was gone into the darkness of the tunnels. David and three others also left following different corridors and in the distance their voices could be heard conveying the order.

Alex walked to a corner of the room, knelt and opened a weathered, wooden chest. Reaching inside he brought out a communications headset and put it on. Next, he retrieved an automatic rifle, and finally, "You may need this," as he took out a compact weapon that he threw to Ames.

Catching it, then examining it: "Frequency pulse laser." Ames noticed the wooden chest: it seemed familiar.

Soberly Alex asked, "You ready?"

Ames nodded.

Both men understood well the fine line separating courage and recklessness... but the commitment had been made.

* * *

Into a world that had been, and would not be again...

...Climbing the ladder first, Alex pushed the manhole cover aside, followed by Ames, Evening and others. As they ran toward the Military Center what remained of the city lay smoldering in ruin. Crumbling buildings stood gaunt against the blood backdrop of sky teeming with deadly radiation and thick with glowing afterburn of the fallout cloud. The atmosphere undulated and flickered ominously like gargantuan flames encompassing the world, jutting ruins covered with glimmering death and drawn in long blue-black shadows.

Four inches of iridescent gray-orange dust smothered everything, residual ash of a nuclear volcano puffing and crunching beneath their running feet, a gritty snowfall of radiated particulate tracking clearly their footsteps. Moving quickly, constantly alert their minds absorbed the ephemeral reality of what was before an ordinary city enfolded within the weathered Rocky Mountain range and had now become a charnel after a millisecond of mankind's destruction.

Dust devils constantly rose then evaporated in tornado fashion like a ghost army of souls clinging to the ruins of the ravaged city. The structures not completely leveled by the nuclear blasts teetered precariously on the brink of collapse, all charred, burned or melted on the side facing the Military Complex. In and among the jutting chunks of steel and concrete transparent goblins appeared and vanished as radiation afterburn driven and swirled with the hot dry wind. Creaking steel, misshapen and mangled, created screeching moans to interrupt the silence of death; a silence otherwise broken only by the steady crunching sound of rushing footsteps beneath a blood-red sky.

Crossing a landscape of devastation, quietly, rapidly, they continued their approach and Ames witnessed the growth of the rag-tag band of rebels. From the destroyed Civic Center behind them, from below the ruins of the high school and college to the west, from the uptown to the north, the band became an army. The headframes came alive: the Belmont, Original, Mountain Con, Lexington, Anselmo, Steward, Badger State, Granite Mountain and Bell Diamond, with an outpouring of rebels all uniting in a common cause as they surrounded the Military Complex. With the command spreading through the sewer and tunnel system below silhouettes emerged from inspection ports and vertical shafts of the subterranean network, from everywhere, until the few had become hundreds and the hundreds became thousands, all converging on the rubble of the military stronghold.

Ash and crumbled stone beneath their feet, glowing death in the wind.

Running...

Still a thousand yards away, "We designed it well," Ames remarked when he could finally see the outline of the debris mounds encircling the crater. "The assault tubes are still intact."

The surface-level concrete and glass structure of the Complex had been completely destroyed in the nuclear blasts and a crater gouged into the earth two hundred feet deep and a mile wide. Only the military fortifications remained. Previously secreted below ground level the twenty-foot-diameter assault tubes and ports constructed of eighteen inches of stainless steel and reinforced concrete, now stood stark, exposed in the crater caused by the nuclear blasts. Like six shimmering crystal scepters they beckoned defiantly to any force that would try their incredible strength. Glistening evil fingers reaching from the bowels of Hell.

* * *

Moments later...

...Alex, Evening and Ames scrambled behind a heap of rubble and the remains of a concrete wall at the periphery of the crater. Through the eerie darkness they could see others rushing to positions surrounding the fortress.

"How do we get inside?" Alex whispered.

Scanning the crater, evaluating, Ames admitted, "I don't know."

"Can we blast our way in?"

Still studying the dilemma, Ames shook his head. "It just withstood two direct nuclear explosions; our weapons couldn't even scratch it."

"What about your weapon?" Evening inquired hopefully.

Palming the pulse laser, "It wasn't designed to penetrate something like that."

"What then?" Alex asked.

Ames didn't have time to answer. Floodlights built into the circumference of the assault tubes switched on bathing the entire area with light and causing the radiated crater to glow, transforming it to a facsimile of iridescent lunar landscape. Motors whined and a number of portholes opened revealing missile launchers and machine guns installed below the lights. At the top of each structure large doors parted with a mechanical rumble as strange weapons, right out of a 'science fiction novel', rose into position.

"What—the—hell..." Alex stammered, with discouraged disbelief, "what are those?"

For a minute no one said anything, until at length, Ames concluded, "Military lasers: Smith *has* been busy," his words betraying the possible futility of their cause.

"We can't do it," Alex decided. "There's no way in hell we can do it."

"May be close, but we're not in Hell yet," Evening mused defiantly; then quickly, "—look."

Doors in the structures opened near the bottom of the crater and columns of soldiers filed out clad in protective metallic suits and helmets. Resembling hundreds of sparkling bugs armed with automatic weapons they scattered assuming defensive positions until the entire Complex was surrounded.

Alex, not expecting a reply: "What else?"

Ames: "They must know we're here."

His suspicion confirmed, missiles nested in the assault tubes hissed screaming to life, streaking outward in all directions toward the summit of the crater where the rebels lay in wait. Incoming. Missile after missile exploding around them hurled splatter-debris in an incessant downpour of crushing rock and dirt. Pain-filled cries echoed back and forth across the crater as the rebel army took heavy casualties from the explosions, rain of rock, falling clutter and crumbling, collapsing ruins.

Burping machine guns flamed to life conveying death in a lead hailstorm over the Alliance: fifty-caliber slugs marked every fifth round by phosphorus tracers. Far and wide, the darkness was disrupted with brilliant flames of exploding missiles and muzzle flashes that illuminated the sky with white-fire light and shattering sound.

The trio huddled, listening and watching as their comrades were torn apart and killed by the fury spewed from the Military Complex. Wafting clouds of pale blue gunsmoke rising above the assault tubes hovered ominously in evil, ghostly halos as the lasers pivoted on their turrets ejecting tongues of intense red light melting steel and burning through rock with two-second bursts more deadly than dragon's breath.

Commanding the Federation troops outside the Complex Captain Thorne advanced forming an ever-widening circle as they moved across the basin focused on the summit of the crater and rebel army. Muzzle flashes and the drone of machine guns created an unending, expanding ring of fire; a flickering, circular, sparkling flame of death, continuously growing, and killing as it grew.

Screams and death. Unrelenting, the mercenary assault continued, and more valiant rebels went down. Ames saw four bodies shredded and swallowed in flames as a missile exploded, the destructive force ripping them apart —absorbed, vapor— and gone.

Leaping from one pile of rubble to another, the rock beneath a rebel's feet splintered with ricochet-lead shrapnel as a machine gun strafed the rimrock. A round severed his left leg below the knee —falling forward— but before he went down another cut him in half, the tracer sizzling through and out his back. His draining torso flopped onto the ground, flesh still smoldering from the phosphorous round.

Another rebel got up to run, a fifty-caliber slug instantly ripping off his arm, spinning him like a twirling target in a carnival booth. A second took his other arm and spun him the opposite direction. The third hit blew off his head sucking his lungs out through his neck and rammed his flaccid corpse straight down. A dead half-shell slammed to the ground.

Shattering stone, thunderous sound, fireballs in the sky. Dying.

Overcome with the tumult of war three terrified women huddled behind a large slab of concrete. Burning through the stone a beam of red suddenly burst between them searing through the one in the center —and she only half-blinked with immediate death that froze her eyes wide cauterizing a circular two-inch hole through her chest. With the odor of burnt flesh in their throats and realizing what happened when she slumped onto them, her companions sprang up screaming hysterically as blistering, *clickety-pings,* of lead and ricochet barked around them. Both were blown to pieces in the hail of bullets and their maimed bodies collapsed onto the first corpse, still twitching and quivering with convulsions of death.

Pinned down. Ames, Alex, Evening and others hiding among the ruins of a blown-out building could only glance quickly and fire down at the advancing Federation troops then duck again behind the wall of rubble. In a shower of exploding lead and stone machine gun volley strafed the concrete wall concealing them, felling two freedom fighters a short distance away. Peering through a small crack Ames watched a missile lurch from the Complex, only a glimmering flicker at first, but growing to a blistering-sizzle of afterburn as it approached spraying a corona of vanishing flame in its wake.

"Get down—"

Screeching, the missile flew high, a near-miss skimming over the rubble wall close enough to feel the tailflame's heat as it struck the only building still standing behind them. Impact and —*whoom*— slammed in their heads; then hot blast pulse walloped them as shattered concrete dragging clouds of dust hurtled away.

Momentarily blinded by the flash Ames shook his head trying to clear the ringing from his ears, and still rubbing his eyes he turned to inspect the damage from the explosion. Vision gradually clearing, swirling white spots evaporating, he saw a corpse hung by the neck for public display. Suspended from the rigging of a flagpole that was behind the wall that had been destroyed, the small, partially naked body swung lethargically wrapped in 'Old Glory', a tattered, scorched, American flag. Sluggishly the dangling corpse slowly rotated, and Ames realized who it was.

He stammered, "Old Sam..."

The spectral vision swept through him with wrenching anguish and ribbons of cold, and at last Ames understood. Though wizen and slight the soul and the person transcended far beyond his stature, a paragon of humanity in a world that was lost. Old Sam: possessed of integrity and virtue... a true, decent man.

Evening and Alex turned when he screamed, "—Old Sam!" words slicing the darkness with rage and contempt, skipping echoes of profound hatred for the Federation. Focused solely upon his friend Ames scrambled to his feet then ran and climbed onto the huge pile of rubble, driven with anger, almost unaware of what he was doing, scrambling toward the old man.

"Mr. Ames, he's dead," Alex shouted.

"Cut him down," ignoring Alex, "don't leave him like that!" an outcry of fury.

Running, stumbling, and onto his feet again, he kept repeating it oblivious to bullets streaking past with ricochet sparks all around him. Sanity and endurance drawn to its limit, his stability was dangling on the threshold as precariously as the specter of Old Sam's body swaying at the end of the rope.

Evening yelled again; but he ignored her, and compelled, she sprang to her feet running after him. More bullets burned streaks through the air as she stumbled escaping death that splattered a concrete slab only inches above her. She climbed again, jumping from one chunk of rubble to another refusing to stop. A missile exploded fifty yards away —ball of flame— heaving scattering winds of dirt and debris on her and Ames; but he wasn't aware of it and she couldn't take time to duck. She had to reach him.

Still running, Ames raised his weapon, triggered, the blast ripping steel and the pulley from the top of the flagpole severing the rope. And plummeting, Old Sam's body plopped solidly onto the rubble trailing ropetail behind it. Then beside Old Sam. Sliding onto his knees and stunned with pain, for a moment Ames couldn't move. Until finally, carefully scooting closer he sadly looked upon Old Sam's twisted body, one side badly burned and charred from exposure to the nuclear blasts... and unconscionably abused by the corruption of a nefarious, repulsive world.

But in spite of the mutilation and deformity Ames perceived calm in the old man's expression, a peaceful completion, as though he accomplished what he set out to do. And kneeling over his dead friend, Ames noticed a crumpled, burnt photograph in Sam's clenched fist. The splatter of bullets and ricochets around him, the battle went on as he gently pried Sam's fingers apart smoothing the photo enough to see three images: young adults, two men and a woman embracing one another and smiling for the photographer. A family picture.

Ames carefully, respectfully, folded the photo in fours and tucked it in the back pocket of Old Sam's charred, ragged jeans. Then he whispered, "My friend," and smiled, a sad smile, "now... you are free."

Evening finally caught up, now only a few feet behind him, and breathless she stopped for an instant to speak. "Mr. Ames, please..."

—*Thwack!*

The bullet slammed into the back of her head throwing her forward and splattering Ames with blood. Startled by her voice he turned, reflexively caught her as she fell, and tried to help her to her feet; but her rigid body went limp in his arms. Still trying to lift her and not yet realizing Ames jerked her up, the motion causing her head to flop back. Then he saw where the impact of the bullet had torn through her skull ripping most of her face away when it exited her forehead. Blood gurgled bubbles from her throat and pulsed from the gruesome wound as he stood there shocked and horrified, holding her. Staring with disbelief, the wretched pain of death so close, a world of seemingly surreal imagery whirling in dark and confusion. Suffused with sadness...

So gently he lowered her lifeless body to the ground, laying her beside Old Sam.

...Then anger. "Oh, God," he gasped, trembling and clenching his hands until his knuckles turned white. Kneeling, his friends lying in front of him, turning his face to the darkened sky... hands clasped together, the torment of pain twisting inside, anguish and sorrow burning his eyes, confusion and the frustration of desperation impaled in his soul. "Oh, God please..." Tears streamed down his cheeks. *"Oh, God Help Us!"* he cried.

Heaven and Earth paused.

And from somewhere Beyond...

...Viscous and vengeful, the thick twilight-sky churned slowly stirring the layered atmosphere into an immense dark whirlpool with an ominous eye. Radiation crackled. The firmament, mounting and surging, winding and thickening, shuddered with rumbles that deepened like breathing. And retribution congealed. Frightening. Incredible.

Alive with the wrath of thunder, ball lightning screamed and lightning bolts sliced through the amorphous canopy, an amalgam of anger. The heavens were illuminated with blinding flashes of electric flame and ragged fingers of wizard-white fire. And the clouds churned. Thickening, strange... and more dark.

Above the crater the vortex continued growing tighter and deeper toward the black of a hole, a slow-motion maelstrom folding inward like the throat of a tornado, winding and reaching toward the unknown of space. Clouds trembled. Thunder crackled then rolled. Lightning skipped furious streaks of dazzling flare tearing the sky apart, then disappeared a white vanishing power trailing waterfall-sparks of lithe embers that glowed.

And blood-red, the darkness of sky wound itself vengefully black,

Foreboding, apocalyptic... mystical

The Puzzle.

Deep spasms within her breast, the Earth quivered and rumbled a despondent sadness for all the abuse spilled upon her by man. And a final pause of lingering regret... until the crust cracked and the tremors began. Landscape quavering. Beneath them, growing, strengthening, unearthly seismic tremors.

This: a day like no other.

Concrete, boulders, destroyed buildings, the rubble. Everything left on the face of the world shuddered a deep, guttural premonition. Mounting, reverberating, intensifying. The landscape trembled, shaken with the retaliation mankind had brought upon itself.

Then...

...With an extraordinary seismic upthrust shearwaves exploded shattering and vibrating so destructively, so furiously the armies were unable to stand. Staggering, falling, bouncing and tossed, humans from both sides tumbled everywhere. A 10.0, its deafening roar companioned with the destructive force of a full-scale earthquake.

Overwhelmed, paralyzed with fear, freedom fighters watched awestruck and petrified as mercurial and violently huge aberrant jaws opened at their feet splitting the ground into ragged chunks. Singularly, rifts parted as though sliced with unworldly, invisible knife blades that traced a circular path around the periphery of the crater, then suddenly breaking apart in splintering runs that descended converging on the Military Center.

Trembling and growling, the landscape was a blur of confusion. Quaking and splintering, everything shook. Deafening noise of vibration. Thundering, rattling, shivering, the visage of vengeance.

This: a time like no other.

Thorne and the soldiers he led, heavily armed though they were, could not do battle with this prophetical adversary and were swallowed mercilessly as hundreds of crevasses fractured around them, surrounding and capturing them. The ground crumbling beneath their feet, drawing them in and unsparingly sucking them under —then shifting— choking life from each wretched one with more strength than any gristmill ever crushed. Sickening and shrill their horrified screams were muffled by their antiradiation helmets until each was abruptly snuffed by the compressing suffocation only a sacrosanct earthquake can deliver.

Forsaken, a platoon stumbling lost and confused by the upheaval of landscape watched hysterically while splintering crevasses opened the ground around them leaving them marooned on an island of rock.

Two of them tried to jump across the gap, but failed, disappearing into the waiting fissure. With rock breaking apart along the rim, the soldiers stared stranded and helpless. Backing away, terrified they watched as the edge of their sanctuary crumbled apart resembling a huge jutting column. Resounding intense rattling explosions of mind-bending thunder the tower teetered precariously, then fracturing somewhere below, collapsed, delivering inescapable death when the ground shifted again dumping a million tons of rock into the chasm.

Everywhere shaking, roiling ground opened. Crocodile jaws swallowing men: scrambling sparkling bugs squashed and eaten by the crater.

Running frantically, four fleeing soldiers were captured and stopped as the ground vibrated into a semisolid mass creating a dry-quicksand sinkhole. Snatching them by their legs it churned slowly, inexorably sucking them into the drain funnel. And revolving with the rotating twisted ground, screaming horror inside their helmets, they went down. Two others watched the spectacle with panicked amazement until the four disappeared into the whirlpool and the last desperate hand sank out of sight. Quickly both turned to run, but the ground split beneath their feet and grabbed them, then shifting again and dragging them under, it collapsed filling the crevasse.

Ten more: horror-stricken, sprinting— were blown into the air as the surface violently erupted scattering them randomly and injured upon its face in radiation dust and debris. Beneath a charcoal-blood sky the ground churned and twisted and wound with unworldly gathering fingers, collecting their broken, fallen bodies and drawing them in. Then darkness.

Relentless, undeterred, Captain Thorne ordered his troops to advance upon the rebels, but overwhelmed and apprehensive they had covered no more than ten feet when the ground split apart beneath Thorne and he slid waist-deep into a crevasse. With the sound of mighty rock mincing bone, the earthen jaws slammed shut crushing his legs, and in spite of his efforts and horrific screams his flailing could not free him. Horror-stricken, they watched as the crack opened again and he slipped in to his chest. Closing a second time the jaws shifted meting out Thorne's death, his eyeballs popping out onto the faceplate, squeezing brains and blood into his helmet. Finally, the ground parted a third time, and sinking slowly his limp disfigured body disappeared and the gap sealed solidly for the last time squirting plasma spray and tissue out through a narrow seam and onto the surface. A puddling blob. Perhaps Corin Johnson's soul had also watched, avenged.

Without Thorne the Federation troops panicked and fled in disarray as ubiquitously the ground boiled at their feet spewing rock, dust and devastation. In the crater disorder swept as rushing pandemonium amid six shimmering crystal scepters: glistening evil fingers reaching from the bowels of Hell… and dying, pitiful, sparkling bugs.

Retribution and nature prevailed, converging on them,

Laying waste to the last man,

And More.

The fury of Armageddon manifest itself as hundreds of fireflash lightning bolts sizzled across the whirlpool in the sky. Leaping, blinding power. Then, from its opaque texture countless funnel clouds emerged and spiraled down, reaching from the churning amalgam, extending ghostly charcoal fingers to scratch the ravaged ground below. And as though welcoming them, from the ruins dust devils rose as dark twisted winds dancing in waiting anticipation. Explosions within the clouds thundered through Heaven, reverberating, rattling a quaking Earth. Then, as though momentarily gathering strength, there was a strange and mysterious pause, as if an omnipotent being had taken a deep breath, until…

…A nonpareil megavolt-blast screamed from the mouth of the vortex

A magnificent, incredible tongue of white flame

—The Light erupted!

With unworldly fire, lightning seared the gleaming assault tubes of the destroyed Military Center. The sound was deafening, an intense sizzle resonating with extraordinary popping and crackling of static electrified voltage. Jarring, rattling white fire, the sight was blinding. It flashed from the vortex of the revolving funnel in the sky as ragged strafing fingertips of Divine Power. Pure, incredible, white heat, streaked ripping from above, melting and tearing apart and the stainless-steel tubes with unmeasured fury and unequaled electrified-fire. Shattering, violent flames of light skittered and burned leaping from one to another of the towering assault tubes, with intense pulses of pounding, dazzling, unimaginable light scorching the structures below.

Stainless-steel began to glow, then buckled, and melting it liquefied like dripping candlewax in a blast furnace. White-hot flame, blinding beyond belief, dazzling beyond comparison, awesome beyond might, illuminated the crater. Gun barrels and weapons dissolved and missiles exploded absorbed by heat more intense, focused and extreme than any weapon ever devised by the hands of man.

Still the lightning bolt burned —furious and violent, incessant, relentless— reducing the assault tubes to twisted, bubbling masses of molten metal and stone. Once proud and shimmering crystal scepters were now remnant charred and fractured shells.

And Heaven grew darker.

Thunder peeled, then rolled.

Sky-lightning spraying fingers of fire...

...And the earth surged as countless funnel clouds swirled ravaging her barren chest —and the sky spilled torrents of rain. The downpour came so hard and fast billowing clouds of steam couldn't rise, trapped near the ground, clinging tenaciously as gray-soup fog on a Scottish moor. Water streamlets coursed over the jutting, ruptured terrain filling jagged fissures and open crevasses as it accumulated with incredible swiftness, all the water converging on the crippled assault tubes in the center of the crater.

A World on the Brink.

The temperature plummeted fifty degrees and the hot dry gale vanished like the phenomenon of temperature-drop in the shadow of an eclipse. While Ames watched in awe the radiated earth cooled relinquishing its heat to the water.

And a frigid,

Desolate,

Relentless Wind swept over the land.

The cold air sparking the ignition of his senses, he looked from the destruction within the crater, over the wasteland that had once been a city; to Evening's body being washed by the cleansing rain; and then Old Sam, still draped in a tattered American flag...

A World of Lost Dreams

...And in the rain and the darkness, he knew the rest would be up to him.

CHAPTER TWENTY-ONE

"—Attack!"

…Ames' voice echoed. "Attack!"

Alex turned seeing the man with an extended fist, furiously brandishing the pulse laser. "Attack," he joined in. "Attack!"

The rimrock of the crater came alive as the rebels responded courageously to the command. The crater swarmed with freedom fighters appearing from concealment and running —the charge— storming the Federation and all it represented. Fearlessly they leapt into the crater —sliding, running— down the embankment, firing with ardent determination, wiping out the remnant trickle of Federation soldiers still trying to defend the Complex. But true to Kristina's prediction, many turned and joined the rebels, instilled with the hope of their own liberty.

Water and mud, red with radiation and blood, sloshed to rabid foam as the advancing army courageously converged on the Military Center. Steam gushed from its cooling metal and stone interior, the burnt and fractured assault tubes twisted like crippled arthritic fingers of a monstrous disfigured hand reaching up from an earthen grave. Death and villainy filled their nostrils foreboding uncertainty in the final outcome, but the defiant rag-tag army refused to falter.

Moans of weakened metal and crumbling support braces creaked throughout the twenty-foot-wide tubes, each as dark as the lair of a medieval dragon. David and several others whom Ames had seen at the Kelley Junction headquarters joined Alex and himself. Alex

touched the earphone of his com-link and ordered, "Thirty seconds
—now."

David pulled the cord fuse of a satchel charge, dropped the
explosive into the stainless-steel assault tube, and seriously: "Level
Three, going down."

Ames asked, "Plastique?"

"Yeah. We didn't anticipate water in the shafts," Alex explained
watching as overflow poured into the assault tubes, "but it shouldn't
make any difference. In fact, it should amplify the explosions, more
than enough to break the interior air locks." Ames listened as Alex
continued, "Our job is to disable the reactor."

"I've got to stop Smith from using the machine," Ames reminded.

Alex: "I understand."

While the men were speaking the canvas pack had been sinking,
now lying at the bottom of the assault tube. Intense seconds. First, a
muffled, *whoomph*, from below and the subsequent splash of tons of
exploding, frothing water. Next, the resounding crack when the air
lock hatch collapsed sending a metallic ring up from the depths along
the structure wall. And finally, the roar of water-surge, a blasting
force that drained the entire assault tube into the face of the enemy
waiting below.

Rebels poured into the assault tubes reminiscent of an old
schoolhouse fire escape, so many and so quickly they rappelled the
distance to the third sub-level seemed negligible. Alongside one
another Ames and Alex splashed into the water flooding the huge
subterranean arena. Federation soldiers fired blindly as the rebels
attacked simultaneously from six directions precipitating hundreds of
deaths on both sides within the first few minutes. Amid ricocheting
bullets, falling bodies, foaming water and mass confusion, the tide
gradually turned in favor of the rebels and they gained a foothold in
the Federation fortress.

"Where's the reactor?" Ames yelled over his shoulder to Alex.
A string of bullets spit from an automatic weapon flashed between
them ripping the water to scattering spouts. Diving apart —and after
the splash— they reappeared.

"Level Six, Corridor Four," Alex yelled back swiping water from his face. "This way," motioning to their left. Crossing the auditorium the men pushed through chest-deep water, shooting, dodging enemy fire and fighting whipping waves buoying them trying to undo their footing. Within the huge auditorium progress was slow and dangerous, the water four feet deep and rising with six assault tubes still dumping waterfalls —and nowhere to hide.

The stage: resembling a Hollywood movie set for an epic sea disaster, with dead and injured floating everywhere. Except on this set, dead bodies were real.

Around them: flickering emergency lighting, constant ratcheting drone of gunfire, the, *phoomphs,* of exploding grenades ripping through chopping water, a clinging haze of gunsmoke and awful screams of the dying, all wrapped with the tension of war. And still, through the assault tubes, freedom fighters rappelled in with the waterfalls.

A feminine voice yelled, "Alex, Ames—"

"Kristina," Alex hailed. Motioning them toward her she stood at the mouth of a corridor clutching an automatic rifle. Four Federation soldiers opened fire and she ducked back using the corridor wall for cover, their bullets biting loose chunks of concrete and bouncing off the steel plating with metallic pings. Alex fired, the rounds slicing through the closest soldier sending him under. Swiftly leveling his weapon Ames squeezed, the blast pulse slamming through the second man opening his chest in a splattering tear. He sloshed backward forcing a wave as water-spray spewed crimson and shredded meat scattering intestines around him, then floated like a coiling, bulbous dead snake. Their attention shifting to Alex and Ames the two remaining soldiers turned on them as Kristina reappeared, the muzzle of her weapon spraying lead and twenty inches of flame. Both went down amid bullets and shatter-spout water.

"This way," she ordered with the objective indifference of a soldier killing in battle.

Alex asked, "The reactor?"

Pushing water to her shoulders, "We can get to it," Kristina yelled back, "but we'll have to fight our way down. The elevators and stairwells are all sealed and flooded below Level Three so we'll have to rappel through the air locks."

As they waded through the frothing water other rebels followed, the din of explosions, gunfire and ricocheting bullets echoing throughout the hollow structure. Painfilled screams and bedlam pierced their ears sending tangible images of suffering through their brains. Nerves tense as violin catgut they arrived at the air locks to the lower levels of the Military Center.

"We can get to 'Four' from here," Kristina advised, "then we'll have to cross over to the security locks to go lower." She whisked a security pass through the scanner but nothing happened.

"What's wrong?" Alex asked.

"The circuit codes must have failed or were shut down," she told him.

Motioning them aside Ames crossed to the opposite wall and blasted through the metal door, taking out its center. He quickly fired again tearing apart the left door which burst and folded inward creating a water-pour that rolled into the air lock. The third blast ripped the right door in half heaving it into the flooded hall.

A sweeping hand gesture: "After you."

Surprised, Kristina nodded. "Impressive."

Tendering a schoolboy grin of satisfaction, "Lacks the character of its prototype, but it'll do," he replied.

Alex looked into the air lock. From deep below water-splash echoed back. He motioned and a rebel came forward carrying a satchel charge. "Ten seconds." Without speaking the man set the timer and dropped the canvas pack into the air lock. "Smoke." Three others tossed in smoke grenades, half a dozen apiece, before the satchel charge went off.

The explosion below burst the steel doors of the fourth sub-level, heaved a column of water-spray up splashing everyone near the hatch, then flushed into the fourth level dispersing the smoke canisters with the wash. Ames couldn't help but admire the methodical, unquestioning precision of this so-called ragtag army. Each task was accomplished with swift, certain discipline; perhaps due to countless rehearsals unknown to him; perhaps because of the conviction within each individual. For whatever reason, he was impressed.

Ropes were tied off and dropped, uncoiling into the air lock. The three men with the smoke grenades went first, rappelling into billowing grayness, followed seconds later by Alex, Ames, Kristina and others. During the rapid descent Ames could hear the men below throwing more smoke canisters to conceal their advance, followed by the sudden deafening reports of fragmental grenades making the air lock walls vibrate.

Above the whirring sound of karabiner and rope, "Stay low," Alex cautioned just before they touched down. Ames' only reply was a nod.

Invisible bullets zipped and pinged everywhere as Ames leaped from the air lock and splashed onto the flooded concrete floor. He landed hard in a bellyflop that hurt, even in the nearly six inches of water. Seeing anything in the thick gray shroud was almost impossible; occasionally a distant barrel flash would burn its way through the smoke, but not much else. Ames scrambled belly-and-elbows away from the air lock until he crawled on top of a pair of legs.

Startling words: "Slow down —and get off me," Alex's voice whispered.

"—Oh shit!" Ames stammered, his heart leaping to his throat, "that's ten years right out the window."

"Well get off me anyway."

He rolled over ending up less than a foot from Alex's head. Spitting out water, "Sorry," as he looked around, "but I can't see a thing. Can you?"

"Nope." Alex pulled the pin on a grenade and tossed it. "Not except you," he admitted, "and I can't see you very well." For a moment or two they lay side by side trying to distinguish enemy movement as Alex chewed his lip mumbling inaudibly.

"What's wrong?"

"I think we used too much smoke," Alex whispered. For just an instant Alex's humor retrieved a memory: the smoke distorted his image, and Reed smiled —then was gone. "You okay, Ames?"

"What?" he replied abstractly blinking himself back to the present. "Oh, yeah, I'm all right."

Other rebels, moving about, eventually formed lines on either side and behind them. Nodding, "In that case, I think we'd better do something," Alex decided matter-of-fact.

"Fine with me." Eyes scanning, "Which way?"

Alex shrugged. "Not sure."

"We probably couldn't find it anyway," Ames ribbed, "unless we bump into it."

They bellied forward slowly, other rebels following and firing, keeping low, and creeping some more. The fighting continued: no one able to see anyone else, everyone constantly moving about, sloshing and crawling in six inches of water, until eventually Alex found Kristina, lying flat, triggering short bursts, waiting and listening, then shooting again.

"You all right?" he asked.

"Fine, but don't you think you overdid the smoke, just a bit?" emphasizing the last part. Ames' chuckle came from somewhere close behind them. She glanced over her shoulder, a bit annoyed and unable to see him. "What's with him?"

Alex, caustically: "Hell, I don't know."

The sound of sloshing water: "Well," Ames began, scooting beside her, "we've still got a few smoke grenades. Shame to let 'em go to waste."

Kristina grinned as Alex protested, "Don't even start on me you guys. If you don't lower your voices, you'll get us all killed."

"He's got a point," she admitted, "they can still hear us, even if they can't..."

Alex snapped, "—Don't say it."

"Yeah, yeah," Kristina acquiesced.

"—See us." Alex glared in his direction as Ames grinned and whispered, "Couldn't resist."

Changing the subject Alex asked, "Kristina, which way to the security locks?"

"The far wall."

"Where's that?" Ames inquired.

She, raising an eyebrow, "Must be in that direction." They inched forward, staying within arm's reach of one another, firing at shadows that sometimes fell and other times whisked away as flowing chameleonic smoke formed new enemies, imaginary and real.

Footfalls splashed through the water. A Federation soldier running for cover was riddled with bullets as he tried to cross in front of the rebels. More gunfire followed, each side shooting at the enemy's muzzle flashes.

"Ames," Kristina whispered.

"I can hear you, but..."

"—You can't see me. I know." Quickly dismissing his banter she continued, "Fire approximately thirty degrees left, fifteen degrees high."

"What am I trying to hit?"

"You'll know when you hit it."

"Okay," squeezing off a laser blast, "but it might help if I knew..."

"—Quiet. Just keep aiming in that general direction and quit talking —and don't stand up."

Another blast hit the far wall shattering stone and metal. Another whine and explosion followed. Grumbling: "Can't see shit." Another blast and the sound of more shattering stone. Ames fired blindly at the far wall, each time inching forward, half-crawling, half-floating in the water accumulating around them. Alliance rebels continued to advance while all around them invisible gunfire followed: snapping echoes of ricochets and splattering bits of concrete and lead falling to the water flooding the auditorium.

"Left, five degrees more," Kristina advised.

Ames fired and again asked, "What am I trying...?" and as he spoke, the laser acquired the mark —instantaneously— an awful explosion.

"The gas lines—" Kristina yelled.

And that quickly the noise and billowing roll of flames drowned out her words as they were propelled backward sixty feet with the concussion-wind and water rushing toward them. Debris hurtled everywhere and the blast heaved a frothing wave that poured over them. Vaporous flame boiled along the ceiling eating the smoke; then momentarily hovered as a transparent cloud —a bizarre fiery wind— self-consuming, shrinking, and disappeared.

Detonation discharge passed and the shock surge subsided, the wave of water blown across the floor rushed back dragging the rebels and other flotsam along. Ames was splashed against the concrete wall only a few feet from the ruptured eight-inch gas main that furiously spewed tongues of seething, blue-yellow flame. Water rushed past him disappearing into the broken security lock descending to the lower levels, the ragged hole resembling teeth and jaws of an awesome waiting monster.

Alex sloshed against Ames and Kristina hit the wall as a soggy, *thwack,* a few feet behind them. Water draining into the security lock rushed over them until it practically filled the elevator shaft between 'Four' and 'Five', and its draw finally began to subside.

A rebel slid toward them carrying a satchel.

Alex peered into the security lock. "It's almost full." Taking the canvas depth charge he scooped it full of water and set the timer, speculating, "Thirty seconds should be enough time to sink two hundred-forty feet." And to Ames: "What do you think?"

"Worked last time —and if it isn't, we'll know soon enough." Then he asked, "Can I do the smoke?"

Alex grinned, pulled the cord, and dumped the satchel into the shaft. "Level Five, going down."

Thirty seconds later —and the muffled ring of explosion below— spewed tons of water up at them cracking the shaft of the security lock its entire length. The already weakened structure buckled as the doors at the fifth sub-level were blown away and the floor collapsed beneath them dumping them into the shaft and frothing commotion within. Swept up in a whitewater fall of ringing vibration and the distorted wash of bubble-rush, they flushed into the auditorium on the fifth level landing in a pile, a tangled menagerie of arms, legs and scrambling bodies all cushioned by the water that swallowed them.

"Shit," Alex mumbled, sprawled out and trying to catch his breath as water flooded the floor of the dimly lit hall. More rebels were rappelling through the security lock behind them as the dozen people unraveled themselves, and one by one, rose to their feet.

"Mother of God..." Kristina stammered with disbelief when she looked across the prison auditorium.

"Oh—Sweet—Jesus," Alex mused.

Dead bodies were heaped everywhere in wretched, disheveled mounds. Thousands of them.

The water flushed from the shaft spread across the auditorium floor, an expanding shallow pond mixing with the corpses creating a brine of blood as far as the opposite wall. The Federation's extermination of those caged on the prison level had been complete. Not one had survived.

Man, woman, Caucasian, African, Hispanic; it didn't matter. Young, old, healthy, infirm; the Federation hadn't discriminated. Without exception the prisoners had all been stripped naked then slaughtered without compassion or remorse. The stench of urine, feces and death hung like a shroud over the piles of naked, murdered human beings. Piquant, the coppery scent of blood was so strong they could taste it: thick and sultry, sticky sweat on a hot August night in the South.

Beyond stunned, appalled, the rebels stood quietly surveying the horrendous carnage. They were unable to even conceive of any man being capable of doing such things to others: completely vicious, absolutely hateful, and cruel beyond the scope of comprehension. To imprison and persecute so many for so long was inexcusably inhumane, but to be responsible for such an atrocity as this was completely inhuman. For a long moment no one spoke, whether it was shock of the spectacle before them, or intense sorrow within them... they stood absolutely silent.

Finally, Alex began, *"Our Father who art in heaven, Hallowed be thy name..."* *(Matt. 6:9 RSV)* and the rebels bowed their heads and recited the 'Lord's Prayer' for the multitude lying around them.

At length, the prayer finished, Alex turned to Ames... and with a cold voice he said, "Level Six: last stop."

* * *

The place...

...Hushed with silence and an eerie premonition: that inexplicable interlude, and evil lurking nearby; taking a breath then waiting, knowing something was going to happen. Cautiously the rebels scanned the auditorium and corridor openings on Level Six, the depths of the Military Complex.

"...Entering the domain of Hell," a rebel commented almost inaudibly while he peered into the phantasmal red-violet illumination of emergency lights. The huge auditorium and every corridor were completely silent, creating a hollow, empty echo with the slightest sound.

"Something's wrong," Alex whispered. "It's spooky, feels unnatural."

Ames remarked, "They're waiting for us." Then rising to his feet, he corrected, "Rather, he's waiting for me."

"Why do you think that?" Kristina asked.

"That's the way it has to be."

Kristina didn't pursue his conclusion and said, "Your machine is at the far end of corridor Six. It's that way." She pointed indicating the direction.

"First things first," Ames told her, "where's the deuterium fusion reactor?"

Alex said, "I can take care of that."

"We'll do it together."

The rebel leader nodded. "I could use the help."

Softly, Ames said, "We all could."

Cautiously they proceeded down corridor Four. The only sounds disturbing the silence were the hum of turbines, dripping water, and squeaking soggy shoes treading a dry concrete floor. While each step brought them nearer the fusion reactor the turbine drone increased, as did the anxiety of the band of freedom fighters approaching the massive power-generating hall.

At the end of the corridor the immense hall stood before them, monstrous, a lifeless shade of gray, turbines clinging to its perimeter and the deuterium reactor at its core. Without a word the rebels moved into the cavernous facility dwarfed by its enormity and astounded by its engineering complexity. Skirting the perimeter, they spread out, searching.

Apprehension nagged. "I've got a bad feeling..." Alex began.

—Shattering lead

Federation troops opened fire from concealed positions among the maze of conduction lines and machinery within the hall. Flaming muzzle blasts spit lead and death from a hundred directions simultaneously dropping six rebels instantly as the others ran for cover within the twisting, churning spiderweb of steel, concrete, cables and piping. Bullets ripped into steam lines causing pressure explosions that transformed the hall into a humid jungle of stone and steel.

A rebel hurled a grenade into a collection of overhead lines, the detonation shattering and felling the pipes like prodigious broken icicles crashing onto soldiers hiding below. Furiously, more explosions followed as sudden pressure variations in the lines created a chain reaction that flashed both directions simultaneously around the periphery of the auditorium ceiling. Like scraps of meat flung from the salivating jaws of a metal monster, bodies were tossed haphazardly as more people died with each successive blast.

"We've got to get in to the reactor," Alex yelled firing at running Federation soldiers. "Can you blow a hole in it?" Ames fired at the clear plastic shield surrounding the fusion reactor, the blast causing it to tremble and buckle; but it remained intact. He was astonished.

"Polycarbonate," Kristina advised, "eight inches thick. They claim it's impregnable."

"Nothing's impregnable," Ames assured. "I'll have to get closer."

"You can't." Kristina grabbed his arm stopping him. Looking back, he faced her, his eyes asking the question. "You'll be killed. The reactor generates ten thousand rad."

"Doesn't matter," Alex cried, his voice overriding the clamor of battle. Attention diverted Kristina turned. "We've all been exposed to ten times the lethal tolerance already," he explained. She began to speak, then paused.

"We're all going to die, Kristina," Ames told her.

"But…"

"Even if there were a way out, we'll all be dead in a few hours anyway."

She already knew that. "I just hoped that maybe…"

"We are the hope now," Ames said. "This Complex will leave the entire world in ruin. There's no other way; we've got to finish it." Turning, Ames looked at the rebel leader. "Ready?"

"Whenever you are," the confident response.

"Then let's do it."

The two men ran toward the reactor vaulting debris and dodging pieces of machinery raining from explosions above. Kristina, unwilling to let them go it alone, followed, providing cover-fire. As they ran Ames fired a number of times at the polycarbonate sections of the reactor dome, each blast making a giant pucker, but each time the shield absorbed the shock: huge plastic windowpanes vibrating and bowing in a storm.

"The framework—" Alex yelled, "take out the framework."

Ames vaulted a chunk of large pipe and squeezed the trigger, the blast striking the steel framework, twisting it, bending and displacing two of the plastic panels. He fired a second time and the steel shredded tearing the polycarbonate free, throwing it into the hall like a four thousand-pound frisbee. The huge panel hit the concrete floor, skipped fifty feet, and crashed to a halt in a pile of rubble. Another blast tore a second beam loose opening a passageway to the deuterium reactor as the polycarbonate panel spun in giant whirls then crashed aside.

Dripping with sweat and out of breath the trio arrived at the reactor leaping over an enormous block of concrete that had fallen from the ceiling. Just as Alex jumped a bullet punched through his back exiting his chest and almost instantly collapsed his lung. He fell to the floor gasping for breath.

"Oh—shit," Kristina stammered realizing he was hit. She helped him sit up.

"No time—" he inhaled convulsively, ordering, "wad up my shirt and poke it into the wound with your finger." Kristina hesitated.

"So he can breathe," Ames explained. "It will slow the hemothorax." Painfully nodding, Alex agreed. Kristina quickly ripped his shirt and plugged both entrance and exit wounds, pushing cloth deeply into the holes with her fingers.

To Ames, coughing: "You won't have much time..." Alex gasped, "to get to your machine." They helped him to his feet. "Once the deuterium circuit is compromised it's irreversible and critical mass will occur in fifteen minutes."

"That'll be enough," Ames said. "I'll make it."

Kristina corrected, "We'll make it."

A side-glance: "We'll make it."

"God speed," Alex said clasping Ames' hand. "See you on the other side." And drawing a painful breath, "Better get going."

Ames' smile conveyed, *goodbye*. Kristina kissed Alex on the cheek but said nothing. She and Ames turned and within a moment were absorbed in the explosions and confusion within the great hall.

His breathing labored and lungs filling with blood Alex staggered into the reactor chamber, intrepid, unafraid, billions of sparkling radiation particles whirling around him. Staggering, he reset the controls and shut down the override then emptied his rifle into the console, the bullets ripping through circuitry and setting the control panel afire. Alex watched the fire burn for a moment as warning lights blinked disorder within the control room; then confident his mission had been achieved, he stumbled to the wall and slid to the floor. Seated, legs spread apart to keep him upright, rifle lying across his lap, he calmly recited the prayer he had memorized a long time ago: *"Our Father who art in heaven…" (Matt. 6:9 RSV)*

* * *

Nothing moving, very still…

…But It was there.

Once they were beyond the reactor hall Ames and Kristina slowed to a walk, both febrile and nearing exhaustion but still remaining cautious, constantly alert for Federation troops. The din of battle gradually fading, eventually the only sound was the hushed footfalls of Kristina's boots as they proceeded.

"Why did you insist on coming with me, Kristina?"

"Some things are necessary."

"I haven't time to sort riddles," the man remarked.

"General Smith is the epitome of evil," she began, watching ahead, not looking at him. "He's been in power for years and has imprisoned, persecuted, tortured and murdered more innocent people than any man in history." Taking a breath she elaborated, "But there is more to my motive than avenging millions of faceless names in a database concealed on a hard-drive somewhere." Her eyes narrowing: "General Smith killed my mother when I was seven, and dumped me into the sewer to drown, or be eaten by rats, or whatever. To him it really didn't matter as long as we were out of the way."

Kristina thought back in time. "My mother was gentle and quiet, and as a rule, she didn't say much —as far as I can recall anyway. But while I was still very young, she did tell me about two men whom she knew, and worked with, and trusted. It seems they disappeared one day and that drove Smith crazy; not being able to find out where they went or what their disappearance might have to do with his plans, which were apparently by then already underway." She paused a moment.

In the quiet of darkness, still walking, whispering:

"My mother wouldn't ever tell Smith that they allegedly transported themselves into another time —at least that's what she told me." Recalling as she spoke, "I was never sure if the story was truth or fantasy; but it was my fantasy, and I always treasured it, the only thing Mother was able to give me that the Federation couldn't take away. So I kept it for myself and never shared it with anyone, until now." She glanced at him, then down the corridor again. "It remained my fantasy until the day you appeared in the Complex, Mr. Ames... then it became very real." She paused again and he looked at her. She confided, "Mother also said that she knew some day her friends would return."

"What do you mean, 'Her friends would return'?"

"Just that, Mr. Ames," now looking at the man. "She never said how or when, just that someday her friends would return... and change our world." A smile welled from inside as Kristina thought, remembering her mother, and her prediction.

Ames nudged, "What else?"

Kristina's smile was holding back tears... "She told me their names: Ames and Reed —but you already know that." Hesitating, waiting, "Aren't you going to say anything —or don't you believe me?"

Soberly: "I believe you."

She continued, "The very first time I saw you, lying on the floor in the storage room... I thought, I must be wrong. But inside, I knew. You were just as Mother described you, even to the smallest detail."

Softly, sincere: "What was your mother's name?"

"Karen." ...and the tears leaked out.

"Karen," Ames repeated. "I knew there was something about you; your voice, you sound like her..." his words trailing off.

He was not yet aware: a piece of...

The Puzzle...

From the past... and the future.

Attempting to recompose herself, she sniffled. "You remember my mother?"

"Yes."

"Tell me about her, please." Her voice betrayed regret: *if only I could go back, we could be together again... just for a little while.*

"As you've already said, Karen was quiet and gentle," Ames began, "and she was the only real friend Reed and I had; certainly the only person either of us trusted beyond ourselves. She was different, special in more ways than I could ever explain."

"You are everything she said you were too, Mr. Ames," blinking sorrow away, pushing it again to a cloistered soul.

"What do you mean?"

"Didn't you know?" She sighed, then told him, "Mother loved you."

Ames was taken aback. "We were friends, and I knew she liked me just as I liked her. We were close but..."

"No," she broke in. "You were friends. She was in love." Kristina looked at him, realizing, "And you didn't even know." Her voice revealed sadness for her mother, and she went on, "I suppose not; men never seem to see beyond the surface, to be honest, let themselves feel what's inside and not be ashamed of their weaknesses as well as being proud of their strengths." She smiled again, more easily this time. "Were you always too busy to love anyone, Mr. Ames... or were you perhaps afraid to?"

"Neither," he answered. "Wrong place. Wrong time." His candor seemed to surprise her. "Maybe —if things had been different," he explained. "Maybe —if the Federation hadn't gained control of the world. Maybe —a lot of things. But it's late —too late now to wonder what might have been."

"Yes, it is," the woman agreed.

"You said Smith killed your mother and dumped you into the sewer, Kristina. Why?"

"I suppose he couldn't let her interfere with his plan to become the first global dictator in the history of the world."

"You're serious." Not a question.

"Oh yes, I'm serious," she replied. "General Smith wants to rule the world, no matter what it takes or who he has to eliminate. He's determined to let nothing stop him."

"Do you believe he's mad?"

"No, he's definitely not mad." Her eyes narrowed. "He's just incredibly evil... evil for evil's own sake."

"But why should Karen pose such a threat to him?"

"Because she intended to expose him and possibly prevent all this. And Smith couldn't allow that."

"There's another reason too," Ames observed, "isn't there?"

Kristina looked at him. "You know he's my father, don't you?" Ames nodded. Her eyes filled with tears, pent-up with the emotions of a lifetime; and she said, "—That, most of all, is my reason for hating him. He beat her and raped her... and she was too ashamed to tell anyone, even Allan. Can you imagine... *she* was ashamed." Quickly wiping her eyes: "Somehow Allan found out though, and Smith had him killed too, at the Tembale Project."

They stopped. It was Time.

Ames' attention fixed on the solitary, closed door at the end of corridor Six. Determined, he took a deep breath, exhaled. Kristina observed, "Level Six, corridor Six, room Six. The Mark of the Beast... a rather appropriate coincidence."

"More than coincidence," he offered.

There were no Federation troops. The corridor before them lay dark, silent, and evil. Readjusting his grip, Ames palmed the pulse laser, its steel warm and damp with the heat and humidity. Without speaking the two proceeded, every nerve alive.

Ames recounted, retrogressing to that October morning he and Reed triggered the entire unfolding of events by taking their first leap through time. As he thought his body remained taut and wired, but his soul grew calm and reassured. There was a purpose in all this: for everything, there always had been, always would be... a reason.

They arrived at the last door. It opened before them.

Eerie, the chamber glowed an unnatural red-darkness, smoke and dust slithering across the concrete floor, oozing around cabinets, counters and furnishings. Stagnant, repugnant, a choking stench filled his nostrils and Ames softly stepped inside.

Kristina followed. The door closed quietly behind them.

Ames' eyes immediately fixed on the gleaming sphere at the far wall. It appeared exactly as the one he and Reed had constructed so long ago; every detail plucked from his brain, constructed to specifications only he himself could have given the Federation Empire. His only conclusion was of his adversary's complete and contemptuous disregard for humanity: to destroy the body and steal the mind. Knowledge and ideas given willingly are to be shared, thoughts taken, tantamount to the most vulgar and vile rape.

From the dark: *screeeak,* near the back of the room, a creak of wood and the crunching sound of leather as General Smith rose to his feet from a reclining chair somewhere in the obscurity and shadows. Something crushed beneath vibram soles of heavy boots and he stepped into view. A massive man, six feet-five and three hundred pounds, thick and solid as a tree trunk, wearing a tailored Federation uniform and black spit-polished boots: he was intimidating. His gray hair was cut so short he resembled a skinhead —and clean shaven— with a pock-marked face and fat porous nose riding above narrow lips and stained, chipped boxer's teeth, an orthodontist's nightmare. He towered poised, with hands large enough to crush a basketball. But General Smith's most singular feature was his eyes... gray as death, penetrating ...cold and hateful.

"You bring some pitiful fucking bitch to stand for you, Ames," he heckled, speaking past the cigar clenched in his teeth.

"No," Kristina whispered defiantly, "I came to see you die."

"You won't. It will be you who dies, however I expected more than just the two of you. I am disappointed."

"You bastard."

"Oh, I am that, Kristina," Smith replied, "and as you will see, so much more." Methodically he raised a saber, then swung slicing haze and slashing through a cabinet beside him, the blade tip sparking with brilliant fury. Smith shifted his weight swaggering slowly, exhibiting brash confidence. "You are pathetic. Do you really believe you've any chance at all to defeat me?" He laughed, then glared down his nose at them. "Do you know who I am?"

"Yes," Ames replied, the tenor of his voice grave, apprehensive, drawing Kristina's attention as well as his adversary's. "Yes, I know who you are."

Empty silence.

"Indeed," Smith finally responded, firmly now, his gesture of ridicule diminishing to seriousness. He glared at the man through narrowed eyes. "I could snuff your life as easily as this," and demonstrating, grinning with yellow nicotine teeth he pulled the cigar stub from his lips and doused the burning coal with his thumb and index finger, glowing embers and ash drifting to the floor. Unnerved, Kristina seized the laser with both hands breaking Ames' grip and fired cratering the concrete wall behind him as Smith quickly turned sideways avoiding the blast.

"—No, Kristina!" Ames yelled.

She, immediately aiming the weapon at Smith again, puzzled, "Why not?"

"Because you can't kill him."

"Oh, it will be easy," she assured, her words tinged with vengeance, "just as easy as it was for him to kill Mother."

"No," Ames said again, "you don't understand."

Smith glared insidiously.

Her eyes darting back and forth between them, "What makes him any different?"

"You said it yourself: he is 'evil for evil's own sake'. He—is—Evil."

"And you have less than three minutes, Ames," Smith snarled, "before you'll be blown to Hell. And I am looking forward to seeing you there." Then without warning, Smith flung his saber at Ames.

"—No!" Kristina screamed leaping in front of the man. The sword struck her instantly slicing through her chest, severing flesh and bone, not stopping until the hilt struck her sternum with a, *thud.* The sudden impact caused her fist to clench the trigger — slamming blast— knocking Smith back with blinding force. He landed somewhere in the darkness.

Kristina staggered then slumped to her knees in front of Ames as he grabbed her breaking her fall, and holding her, helpless, he watched as blood oozed through her uniform puddling between her breasts. Gasping agonally she tried to speak but couldn't, her eyes glazing, filling with tears. Stricken with despair, "Kristina," was all Ames could say. And as he did, she died in his arms.

Holding her, "Kristina..." Ames murmured. "Oh, God, what's happening?" Desperate, his eyes frantically searching the darkness, "What should I do?"

"There is nothing you can do," Smith's rasping voice returned cynically. The darkness where he had fallen began to glow, aberrant, loathsome, and red, as Ames watched unnerved by the specter before him. Smith appeared to be changing. His face seemed to narrow, gray eyes glowering, chin seemingly drawing to a point, and his hair... just strange.

Slowly rising again, gently Ames lay Kristina down, the sword pushing out of her chest as he did. He withdrew the weapon carefully and turned to face his adversary, blood clinging to the shimmering steel. Sidestepping cautiously, he moved toward the geodesic sphere, trying desperately to conceal his fear, perspiration dripping from his forehead into his eyes, causing him to wipe them with his arm.

"The day of reckoning has come," Smith gloated. "It is time." For a moment he viewed the geodesic sphere; then back to Ames. "You've less than two minutes. Do you really believe you'll prevail?"

"Perhaps," the man whispered.

"You are afraid and that shall be your undoing."

"Yes, I am afraid," Ames admitted facing him. Smith's gray eyes almost glowed, seemed to ooze evil. "But fear is not failure. There is no dishonor in fear, only in duplicity, vanity, and sin."

Widening his stance, "You make a feeble attempt to distract me with petty word games," Smith hissed easily picking up a hundred-pound block of concrete that had been blown from the wall when Kristina fired and missed him.

Moving carefully Ames eased closer to the sphere. But Smith stopped him throwing the broken chunk of stone with incredible strength and precision; and even though he tried to leap from its path —a glancing blow— it struck him in the side tearing his shirt then into his ribs. He was thrown to the floor, his head and leg cut by debris —tried to suck in a breath— reinjured, it hurt much worse now. Without hesitating Smith grabbed another chunk and hurled it at the man narrowly missing as he rolled out of the way, the stone crashing only inches behind him, concrete fragments splattering him in the back.

While Smith bellowed amusement with his game Ames managed to rise to his feet, his forehead and side bleeding and raw, dirt and blood caked on his face. Staggering a moment, he forced himself to breathe despite the grating crepitus of his broken ribs. Resisting the pain, and uncertain, he watched Smith contemptuously; then little by little his fear subsided and calm filled him. It occurred to him that if he should die here, there would be a reason. *For everything... there is a reason.*

Smith lumbered closer seizing a chair, and brandishing it overhead with one hand swung powerfully at the man. Trying to withstand the blows but being forced back, time and again Ames deflected the pummeling with the sword, each metallic collision showering the wine-colored darkness with indigo blue-violet sparks. Enraged, drooling spittle and wrath, Smith finally threw the chair wildly at Ames knocking him to the floor again as the sword, knocked out of his hand by the blow, twirled airborne pirouetting in an arc and stuck in the desktop with a penetrating, *thud.*

In pain and bleeding Ames rolled over bumping into a malleable form and realized he was lying beside Kristina's body, the pulse laser still clutched in her hand. Whether it was instinct or the voice of premonition warning him to move, he wasn't certain; but desperately he yanked the weapon from her fist and rolled out of the way just as another block of stone slammed down behind him rattling vibrations through the floor.

Scrambling away, crawling and stumbling through debris, when he looked back Smith was leaning over to pick up another chunk of concrete that had a thick length of reinforcement bar attached. Then as he rose, he began whirling it above his head like a medieval gladiator using a mace. And he swung, each time stepping forward wielding the chunk of concrete, trying to hit Ames who was pushing with his feet, scuffling back, managing to narrowly evade the rabid blows.

Shards of debris scattered in dusty explosions pounding with reverberations of crushing stone and rage, the floor ripping up with each succeeding impact. And all the while Smith's hideous laughter echoed vile malevolence through the unworldly red-darkness.

Finally regaining his feet Ames staggered then stumbled and rolled over and behind the desk as Smith's menacing strikes crunched it to pieces in a blizzard twisted-wind of pens and flying papers. The desk splintering apart, desperate, intent, eyes locked on the chunk of whirling-gray, squeezing the trigger —a whine, a bright flash— and the concrete exploded into pieces like an asteroid collision in space. Inside his head swept the roar of laughter, flare of detonation, and for that brief instant Ames could see a fist-sized fragment hurtling toward him —then shattering sparks— it creased his head knocking him solidly to the floor and obscurity.

He wasn't sure how long he was unconscious but it seemed like only seconds before the hovering white spots evaporated and he realized Smith was standing over him, towering red and evil, drooling with satisfaction. Heinous gray eyes glaring down, Smith clutched the sword with both hands raised above his head, the blade directed at Ames' heart.

"It is time for harvest."

He bellowed vicious laughter,

And plunged the sword down —into Ames.

The man was helpless except to watch, a vision of surreal slow-motion, the gleaming blade slicing through his tattered shirt and into his chest. His mind racing through a million memories…

…All that had happened. And the whisper: *"There is a reason."*

His face flushed and he wanted to vomit, vision clouding, beginning to blur. He could see the blade but the room was fading, darkness creeping closer as he felt Smith put a heavy boot on his chest, and the sensation of cutting as he withdrew the sword. Looming, leering, Smith seemed amused watching with immense

352

satisfaction as the man's heart pumped blood onto his chest. Ames felt his strength ebbing away, crowding nausea and black confusion swirling waves through his brain. Still grasping the laser in his fisted hand, he tried to bring it up to fire; but his hand wouldn't move, his finger could not obey.

"And now..." Smith anticipated greedily, "now you shall die."

And he plunged the sword at Ames again

—At that precise instant...

...A shattering Flame of Ethereal Power, the roar of four winds and great thunders of Heaven. Incredible, Celestial, and Perfect, a tongue of White Light struck Smith stopping him and...

...The Voice commanded, *JUDGMENT IS AT HAND!*

Suddenly Ames was enveloped within whirling gossamers of transparent light. All around him were winds of starlight: flashes and radiant aftertrails, residual glimmering wisps floating ever so delicately, scintillating minutiae, pinpoint quasars, beautiful shimmering pulsars —then flashes again, whisking away. He watched humbled, awestruck.

The Being was White Flame with Blinding Fury,

All Powerful, All Knowing

And the Light,

Brilliant White Light!

Then I saw heaven opened, and behold, a white horse! He who sat upon it is called Faithful and True, and in righteousness he judges and makes war. His eyes are like a flame of fire, and on his head are many diadems; and he has a name inscribed which no one knows but himself. He is clad in a robe dipped in blood, and the name by which he is called is The Word of God. (Rev. 19:11-14 RSV)

Beyond the Light he thought he saw movement, but it was all so unclear. And Smith seemed to be changing.

Growing larger, his boots split apart, and misshapen his toes emerged. Throwing his arms back violently, still howling, his uniform filled, stretched skin-tight and split apart at the seams. And his chest enlarged popping the buttons of his uniform coat and blouse exposing bruised-looking off-color skin. Then angry, furious, wielding the sword he swung viciously but futilely lashing out at the shimmering Light.

Growing taller, his face contorted and looked like it drew more pointed; and his chipped boxer's teeth became ragged almost… like fangs. Turning pale-green his hair grew long and tangled, and flared wildly. His eyes drew back, sliding wider apart on his abhorrent skull, then narrowed… hateful, and intensely deadly.

Wild with rage, Smith roared and hunched his huge shoulders ripping both coat sleeves up the seams. Then grabbing his chest, he tore the coat and shirt off and flung them away. He swung the sword —again and again.

It all seemed so cloudy, distorted.

Ames lay dying on the floor, his thoughts drifting away. Now it no longer mattered that his life's blood pumped from his tattered body: prepared to die, unafraid, willing to go where life would follow. Security and peace within him washed all apprehension of the unknown away.

Everything just mists of confusion. Was this really happening?

Then, in his mind he thought he could see them arriving, white riders on horseback —and a dark army below. So many there were on both fronts he couldn't count them, but certainly more than millions, the armies going on forever, beyond the horizon. Riding bareback —were they angels?— robed in white with broadswords drawn. And there was blood spraying from wounds and splashing upon the world forming an incredible sea of red littered with endless lost souls from all of history.

The last great battle,

Armageddon…

God's Day of Judgment.

Then, tanks, rockets, missiles, aircraft —as far as forever— thundering from here to eternity, the world set afire for the very last time. Nuclear blasts ripping mankind away in a vaporous heat so intense no one could survive it. And the destruction continued.

Bloodshed of sorrow and retribution swept over the face of the world in the conflict of all conflicts... for all that had been and would not be again.

It was a visage of recompense, the thunder of Heaven. And so the great battle was fought, the war to cleanse the Earth and begin it once more with God's promise of something better and new: a tomorrow.

And he said to me, "Do not seal up the words of the prophecy of this book, for the time is near...Behold, I am coming soon, bringing my recompense, to repay every one for what he has done. I am the Alpha and the Omega, the first and the last, the beginning and the end." (Rev. 22:10-13 RSV)

All the things he imagined... and sounds fading away.

His eyes closing, dying, lost somewhere in the realm where reality and the dream world merge, that place where faith becomes reality... and reality just a single step beyond. He was drifting, lost in the dreams of eternity. And in his mind, serenity was calling, a tunnel of light guiding him, spiraling onward forever and ever, floating into mists of nebulae, being drawn away into the arms of the universe.

So beautiful... the angels sang a mellifluous song.

And gossamer winds of ethereal color: all the beautiful colors, the incredible beauty of Creation. It was there, waiting... the realm of Beyond. Viewing its immeasurable majesty, longing to be a part of it, wanting never to go back. But he felt something more, so very deeply inside, calling his name, someone calling his name.

—Dazzling, spellbinding, light was everywhere

She had studied the Legends and he would love her forever, could not leave her... had to return. Inside his mind, calling his name, wrapping around him, enfolding him, so remarkably beautiful, the Love.

Fluttering, his eyes opened again as a shining hand of sparkling Light lifted him with cradled fingers. Then weightless, floating, moving across the room toward the open portal of the geodesic sphere... then onto the floor inside the machine.

Everything so clouded.

He was numb, and as he looked to his chest where the sword had run him through, the bleeding stopped and the open wound healed —as if a miracle— sealed itself closed. And out there, in the room he could see them. Smith attacked again as white horsemen surrounded him on great, powerful steeds carrying a massive golden chain.

So clouded, so beautiful... the riders, the song.

—Then dazzling, remarkable light all around him

Unable to move he lay still on the floor, tears streaming onto his face and a halo of light clouding his eyes. Through the portal, they were there: the riders, and... was it Smith? And the Light.

Someone was roaring like a beast then screaming and wailing like a woman, then roaring again, the voice constantly changing. Wondering, Ames listened. Then everywhere there were white riders and music again. And he heard Smith scream again —and the roar. And he screamed again and again...

—Brilliant, incredible, sparkling light was everywhere

...Then the riders. Ames was captivated by their wonderful song, one he had heard before, inside a mountain so far, far away. They were so beautiful.

And majestically, the Being of Light turned to the man. And within the incredible, pure Light, Ames imagined he could see God's loving face...

...And God Smiled.

The portal of the geodesic sphere closed as it began to sparkle like fairy dust. Scintillating minutiae, shimmering rainbow colors,

Whisking trails of starlight.

A shrill whine —*pop*— it was gone.

—And at that precise instant...

...Shatter-flash of ripping destruction swept over the face of the world, an incredible wave of exploding landscape —speeding forth, flashing out— ground splintering and blasted away. The Earth quaked in upheaval and volcanic eruption scattering mountains and landscape to shards of oblivion. Thundering, rattling, pounding, a surging pulse-wave swell of blinding, rushing, boiling incineration and nonpareil detonation-burn of vaporous fire-flash white light...

—The world exploded with Cataclysmic Finality!—

CONCLUSION

Then I saw a new heaven and a new earth; for the first heaven and the first earth had passed away, (Rev. 21:1 RSV)

Tian and Seana sat together...

...Side by side, on the edge of the crater, the descending sun inching its way to the horizon beyond the collapsed mountain range and remnants of the Sacred Temple. The haze of smoke and dust remained, clinging to the crater's face, shrouding its surface with an impenetrable fog, still and quiet as the mountains beyond.

Seana did not understand but patiently remained beside her leader because she had asked, 'Wait here with me, Seana... please.' Silently, motionless, Tian watched the lingering sun.

Finally, Seana spoke. "Why must we wait for the sunset?" Not saying a word Tian turned her head, placed a hand on Seana's arm, and Seana knew to be still.

They waited.

The sun sank lower, almost to the horizon...

Footsteps shuffling along the path leading to the crater: "Poke me with a popsicle-stick, Nitana, quit telling me that; you're giving me the willies."

Seana, still sitting and instantly recognizing the voice, spun around as she rose to her feet breathless with excitement and emotion. She immediately saw them emerging from the trees, Reed limping, Nitana walking beside him; she, keeping a bit of distance between them, believing the man might be an apparition. She cautiously brushed with a finger, touching him again, and he protested. "Nitana, you're making me crazy. I *am* here. I'm alive." He placed his opened palms on his chest to prove it; but still, she wasn't convinced.

"Reed!" Seana cried out running headlong to make certain herself, then stopped, unsure, a few feet from him and Nitana. Reed spread his arms to embrace her unable to understand her hesitation.

"I'm *baaack*," he quipped unable to suppress an impish grin.

"Is it really you?" she whispered. "Are you real?"

"Heck yes, I'm real." Touching his forehead, the side of his face still covered with dried blood and coagulated keloid filling the gash, "I was just unconscious, knocked out. Why do you guys keep saying I was dead?"

"But Reed, you were," Seana insisted, wanting desperately to believe him, still, almost afraid to touch him fearing he might disappear. Reed stepped forward taking her hands in his and putting them to his cheeks. He watched as first she delicately touched his face, and waited, as trembling she caressed him. Her fingertips felt exquisite, her palms soft and wonderful. Blue eyes filling with tears of happiness and persuasion she laughed and squealed as he pulled her to him and kissed her.

After the kiss: "I'm real," he assured. "I'm here, and I'm not going to evaporate. Seana, I love you." She was almost giddy with joy. Then out of the blue: "Do we have any Chiqua in camp? I'm hungry enough to eat the butt off a moose. I've got this awful aftertaste like I've been eating swill for a month."

"—Oh Reed..." and again she kissed and hugged him with every ounce of her soul.

From the edge of the crater Tian stood silently observing Seana, Nitana and Reed. Hope welled inside her with the realization: she knew the Legends were true. Always, they had been before, and she believed now, this time, would be no different...

'*Strangers who are different, but not enemies. The strangers would come from Beyond when the black hole spilled out the stars as far as forever, but would not appear for many generations. Finally, they would arrive in a sphere of sparkling light that no one would ever see'.* And the part she had not told the men: '*They must go*

Beyond; then rise up like the Phoenix... and they would change our world'.

Reed and the women approached Tian who stood motionless, waiting on the rimrock, again viewing Legend Range and concentrating on the shrouded crater surface.

Softly, "Hello, Tian," Reed said from behind her.

Turning to face him: "Hello, Reed. It is good to see you are well."

"And you," he offered. The woman coerced a smile but he detected the effort, hesitated, watching her eyes, and asked, "What's wrong?" But Tian didn't respond. Then looking beyond her, he saw the crumbled mountain peak. "Shit, what happened to the Sacred Temple?"

Seana, still clinging to his arm, told him, "Mr. Ames followed the Trogs into the temple and blew it up."

Frowning incredulously Reed looked at her. "Bullshit— if that were true, he'd be dead."

Stepping forward, "He is, Reed," Nitana confirmed.

And at that moment...

...The setting sun touched the horizon bathing the world with the mysteries of sunbeams and a halo of golden light.

"He's dead... really?" Reed remarked.

Saddened, turning her face to the ground, "Yes," Seana whispered.

Reed pointed. "Then who is *that* in the crater?"

A propitious gust of wind swept through her hair, across the expansive crater...

—And Tian reeled

...An invisible zephyr of small miracle clearing away the fog and dust to reveal the entire ruins of the Sacred Temple, a shimmering geodesic sphere with an open portal —and Ames— barefoot, limping toward them, wearing frazzled Levis and a tattered black leather shirt.

—Tian ran

Her heart and soul swept up in the moment bursting with an exhilarating kaleidoscope of emotion. Overflowing with joy her spirit was electric with happiness and her eyes liquid with tears. Golden hair fluid in the wind she rushed to him, met him, falling ecstatically into his open arms and embracing him before realizing the front of his shirt was soaked with blood. Suddenly aware, terrified and not understanding, her eyes asked the question.

"I'm all right," he assured. "Now... I'm all right." His smile beamed from an exhausted face and scruffy beard, and with a sigh of elation and peace of mind, "Oh, God, I missed you so much." They kissed, long and passionately. To taste her lips again, feel her warmth and her body... to feel whole again as the nagging emptiness finally withered, then melted away.

"Hold me, John," and at last, setting free a sequestered tangle of anxiety she folded into his arms. "Hold me forever." For several moments they remained motionless and inseparable, Tian trying not to cry but unable to hold back the tears, she sobbed into his chest. They had each other again.

Together, in the crater. Happiness.

She could see he was weak, wavering, nearing exhaustion, but her love gave him strength, and clinging to one another they slowly and carefully walked the face of the crater. Together again, one step at a time, to the rimrock where Ames climbed onto the rim of the crater... and Reed stepped into view.

Ames stopped, his expression: mingled joy, disbelief, and wonder. With the warmth of true happiness Tian's smile welled from deeply inside; she hadn't told John that his friend was there.

"Reed... you're alive?"

Flushed with pleasure, but still nervous, "Doc, don't look at me like that." Almost hesitant: "I'm not a ghost." Then boldly Reed stepped forward seizing Ames with a heartwarming hug that made them all cry. Finally, taking Reed by the shoulders Ames pushed him back examining him, both blinking and wiping their faces.

"Reed, you look as bad as I feel," as he tried not to cry.

"Yeah, Doc," Reed grinned sheepishly sniffling away his own emotions, "we're both beat to shit, but I'll heal up faster —'cause you're older."

Ames smiled broadly and nodded. "I missed you too."

Reed, now serious: "You know, Doc, I wasn't dead, just unconscious, but…" He waited expecting his friend to comment. Ames only listened, so he continued, "But while I was out, I had the weirdest dream." His brow furrowed slightly. "I dreamed you and I were back at the Complex, in prison together." Ames still listened, not saying a word. Reed twitched scratching his nose with a rodent-like gesture; then decided, "Well, it's a long story and after we've rested up I want to tell you about it."

"All right," Ames replied calmly.

Reed nodded as he reached into the back pocket of his jeans pulling out a piece of paper carefully folded in fours. "But this is strange, spooky. I don't know where it came from." Reed unfolded the paper offering it to his friend. It was a tattered photo with three images: young adults, two men and a woman. And a fourth image only Ames could see… a wiry, bearded, little old man with bright green eyes and green teeth, embracing one another and smiling for the photographer. A family picture. Reed blinked: green eyes. He had no idea how the photo had gotten into his back pocket.

Looking at the photograph Ames smiled warmly. "Yeah, we've got a lot to talk about," and slipping his arm around Tian he pulled her to his side looking into her eyes. "You knew, didn't you?"

"It was in the Legends," she answered. "I hoped, but I was not certain."

For all they had been through, all that had happened,

Still, only pieces…

The Puzzle… and More.

Nitana broke in, pointing across the crater. "Look. It is so beautiful."

In the sky, spanning the crater and collapsed Legend Range appeared a dazzling, brilliant rainbow dissolving and vanishing at each end in shimmering golden light bursting from the rays of a magnificent setting sun. Hope for a New World. The five people stood watching the majestic vision, each with their own thoughts: Tian, Ames, Seana, Reed, and Nitana.

Contemplative, tranquil, Ames pulled Tian tightly to him and she looked up smiling, conveying love and happiness in her eyes. He felt warm and quiet, content inside. The emptiness gone. Peace.

At length, as they watched the rainbow and the sunset Reed finally spoke. "Doc, I can't believe you blew up the Sacred Temple." And as Seana snuggled more securely within his arm, he mused, "The Legends are still down there somewhere; now, how will we ever find them?"

Ames held the woman he loved close to him, turned to his friend and smiled; then he said, "Reed,

When You Believe…There Are Always Possibilities."

ENDNOTES

1   'Big Brother' ref. George Orwell's novel "1984" written in 1949, depicts life and conditions when citizens are under constant surveillance of an intrusive government.

2   Grey or Greylight... denotes mood, or misty, predawn effect, as opposed to gray the color, or metallic, bland, harsh and unfeeling.

3   Wind or Relentless Wind... certain words are capitalized for emphasis or symbolism. The Relentless Wind is God's sorrow and curse on the battleland of Armageddon.

4   Time Shear...a fictional phenomenon of transitional flux. Passing through time at such an incredible speed that it manifests the illusion of punching holes through eons, resembling a space capsule's reentry into the atmosphere. A sparkling, burning meteoric fireball dragging a rainbow flametrail of spiraling atomic cloud trailing through portals or windows of time.

5   Tian... pronounced TI-an

6   Renoloi... pronounced RE-NO-loy

7   Tarin... pronounced Tar-in

8   Seana... pronounced Shaw-na

9   Kimo... pronounced KE-mO

10 Nitana... pronounced Ni-ta-na

11 Nemuk... pronounced NE-mook

12 Lita... pronounced LE-ta

www.ingramcontent.com/pod-product-compliance
Lightning Source LLC
Chambersburg PA
CBHW050615110726
47899CB00001B/122